THE GIRLS IN BLUE

ALSO BY FENELLA J. MILLER

The Spitfire Girl Series
The Spitfire Girl
The Spitfire Girl in the Skies
A Wedding for the Spitfire Girl
The Spitfire Girl: Over & Out

THE GIRLS IN BLUE

Fenella J. Miller

An Aria Book

This edition first published in the United Kingdom in 2020 by Aria,
an imprint of Head of Zeus Ltd

A CIP catalogue record for this book is available from the
British Library.

E ISBN: 9781838933470

PB ISBN: 9781800245976

Typeset by Siliconchips Services Ltd UK

Printed and bound by CPI Group (UK) Ltd, Croydon, CR0 4YY

Aria
c/o Head of Zeus
First Floor East
5–8 Hardwick Street
London EC1R 4RG

www.ariafiction.com

For Charlie Harrison Miller

1

September 1939

The church was packed and the vicar was in the middle of his interminable sermon when the verger appeared from the vestry and hurried to the base of the pulpit.

Jane guessed what the interruption might be. Talking was strictly forbidden but she risked the wrath of her father to touch her mother's arm and whisper to her. 'It's war, isn't it, Mum?'

'I believe so.'

'Be silent. You are in God's house.'

Mum squeezed her hand and muttered a quick apology. Jane shivered and immediately looked down, not daring to meet his eyes. She was the one who had spoken first so it would be her that would be punished.

'Ladies and gentlemen,' the vicar said quietly. His knuckles were white where he gripped the edge of the lectern. 'We are at war with Germany. Hitler has refused to leave Poland.'

There was a moment of silence and then the congregation forgot the rules and began to talk amongst themselves. The service was abandoned. A quick blessing was said by the vicar and then everyone poured out, eager to get home and discover for themselves what was going to happen next.

'Mr Hadley, will there be a run on the bank, do you think?' A flustered woman forgot herself and grabbed her father's arm as he walked past.

'There will not, madam. Kindly excuse me – I have urgent business to attend to at home.'

Jane knew what this comment meant. The business he referred to was beating her for her disobedience. The crowd surged forward, separating her from her parents. Some instinct of self-preservation made her slip backwards through them until she was inside the church again.

She would have to go home as she had nowhere else to go. But not now – she would postpone the inevitable as long as possible. However much she tried, she could not prevent the shivering.

'My dear girl, this cannot go on,' the Reverend Jackson spoke quietly from behind her. 'You must come with me. I'll not have you return to more abuse.'

The vicar and his wife were the only people in the village who knew what took place behind the smartly painted front door with its immaculate brass knocker. They had found her sobbing at the back of the church after a particularly brutal beating earlier that year. Things had been better when she'd been at school – she only had to get through the school holidays – she was safe when away from him.

'I'm eighteen tomorrow. I'm going to volunteer to join the WAAF. I've just been waiting for Mr Chamberlain to make that announcement. I want to leave in the morning and my bag's packed. I have to go back to collect it.'

'You'll do no such thing, Jane. I know you told me not to interfere but I'm not going to stand aside a second time. Does he abuse your mother as well?'

'She's terrified of him, but I've never seen him hit her – but I don't know what happens when I'm not there.'

'My wife and I have always thought Mr Hadley over-strict with you – an occasional spanking for a small child is all very well but you're an adult. You're a lovely young woman and what he does to you is unacceptable.'

Mrs Jackson bustled down the aisle. 'Come along, my dear, we'll leave by the back door. Tomorrow you can go to London and offer your services to the Women's Auxiliary Air Force. You'll never have to go back to that dreadful man again.'

Jane's heart was thudding as she followed the vicar's wife through the churchyard and into the vicarage garden through the small wicket gate. The voices of the departing congregation carried quite clearly across the grass and tombstones and at any moment she expected to hear that dreaded voice demanding that she return at once if she knew what was good for her.

Not until she was safely inside the vicarage did her hands unclench. That man could hardly barge in here and drag her out.

'Why don't you sit down at the table and I'll make you a nice cup of tea. We all had a bit of a shock in church today and it must be even harder for you.' As Mrs Jackson busied herself at the old-fashioned range Jane was able to steady her breathing, regain her composure and begin to take stock of the situation.

'Arthur and I have talked about *that man* more than

once. How he could sit in the pew every Sunday as if butter wouldn't melt when he was so wicked, I don't know.'

'I'm sure that he's not the only parent who thinks a good hiding is an acceptable form of punishment when any of their offspring disobey or misbehave. Children are regularly caned, get the strap or some such thing whilst in school.'

'My two boys got the occasional slapped leg, but no more than that.'

'I had a brother you know, a twin, but he died at birth. My father's never forgiven me for that.'

A mug of tea was placed in front of her and she cradled her hands around it. She shook her head when she was offered a piece of fruit cake.

'You are far too thin, my dear, if you'll forgive me for saying so. Were you not fed either?'

'I'm naturally slender, Mrs Jackson, but have lost weight since I left school in July. I just can't swallow food when sitting at the same table as him.'

'Arthur said you were looking for a secretarial job. Did you learn to be a shorthand typist at your grand school?'

'I did – the headmistress suggested it might be a useful skill even for the daughters of the very rich who intend to marry well and do nothing at all with their lives.'

'Well, that's going to change and no mistake. This war's been coming for a long time and everyone will have to do their bit. Both my boys signed up last year and both are pilot officers – James is a fighter pilot and David will be training the new boys.'

'Then at least one of your sons won't be in constant danger once the fighting starts.'

Her tea remained undrunk. She jumped every time she

heard a noise, dreading who might appear in the door. Mrs Jackson stopped trying to engage her in conversation and continued with the preparation for Sunday lunch. The wireless crackled and hummed, almost drowning out the suitably serious music that was being played.

Then the back door opened and the vicar called out cheerfully, 'I have your belongings, Jane, and your mother had already written a letter, which she slipped into my hand as I left.'

The wave of relief almost crushed her and for a few seconds she was unable to move or respond. Then her world righted and she sprung to her feet just catching the back of the chair in time to prevent it crashing to the floor.

'Thank you so much, Mr Jackson.'

He handed her an envelope and her small suitcase. 'I got the impression that your mother was aware of your plans. She certainly didn't have time to write such a thick letter so quickly.'

'She knew I intended to volunteer as soon as war was declared but I never discussed the specifics with her.'

'Arthur, can you show Jane where she'll be sleeping tonight?'

She was familiar with the downstairs layout of the vicarage as over the years she had attended afternoon tea, Bible classes and Sunday school there. However, she'd never been upstairs.

'Here you are, my dear, you might as well sleep in James's room as the bed is made up with clean linen. The bathroom is at the end of the passage, the WC adjacent. Come down when you're ready.'

He vanished, leaving her to examine her temporary

surroundings. James was four years older than her and she'd always admired him from afar. He looked exactly like his father – medium build, mouse-brown hair and blue eyes similar to her own. David was a couple of years older and she'd had very little to do with him.

She dropped her suitcase on the floor – no point in unpacking as she was only going to be there for one night. Thank goodness she was wearing her Sunday best and could travel to London knowing she looked like an adult as for once she was wearing silk stockings, smart navy court shoes and a pretty, floral printed frock with a nipped-in waist and matching belt. Her cardigan was navy as was her hat. This was more a fancy beret than an actual hat, but it served its purpose.

Her everyday clothes consisted of skirts and blouses with Peter Pan collars worn with white ankle socks and her school shoes. All she had in her suitcase were changes of underwear, nightclothes, her stationery folder and her toiletries. Inside this leather folder was her precious post office savings book, her identity card and her ration book. She was hoping that she would be issued with a uniform once she was enrolled in the WAAF and therefore her civilian clothes would be redundant.

The bedroom had a masculine air, no sign of boyhood toys or books anywhere. Sitting on one's bed was forbidden so she perched on the chair. Then her lips curved; from now on she could sit anywhere she pleased. She was free of rules, of physical punishment, and could please herself, and she was going to make the most of it. Once she was a WAAF there would, of course, be structure but this would be no worse than being at boarding school and she'd always enjoyed that.

For some girls the thought of sharing a dormitory with possibly dozens of others might be daunting but for her it would be nothing new. Until she was in the sixth form she'd had no privacy at all. The last two years of her school life she had shared with her best friend. What was Victoria doing now? Probably preparing for the Season and beginning her hunt for a suitable husband.

She was still clutching the thick envelope from her mother. She carefully peeled it open. Her eyes widened. There was only one sheet of paper, the rest looked like folded five-pound notes. With shaking hands she pulled the money out. Fifteen pounds was a fortune – how had Mum managed to put this aside without *that man* knowing?

The large, white, flimsy paper notes would be enough for her to buy anything she needed for the foreseeable future. When combined with the eight pounds in her savings book, and the handful of silver and coppers she had in her purse, she considered herself a wealthy young woman.

My dearest Jane,

You have done the right thing. If I could run away like you I would do so. Take care, my darling, and I shall think of you every day.

Please don't write to me at this address. Perhaps you could send an occasional letter to Mr and Mrs Jackson and I will pick it up from them.

I love you and think you are a brave and courageous girl. Whatever you decide to do, I know that you will do it well.

Your loving mother

Jane rubbed her cheeks dry with her sleeve. Would she ever see her mother again? Unless it became possible for them to meet in London one day, she doubted she would. She couldn't return to the house. She wasn't brave; she was a coward and too terrified to stand up to *that man*.

She carefully hid the precious notes behind the new Basildon Bond writing pad with its matching envelopes. This would have to go into her savings book once she got to London. She certainly wouldn't risk venturing into the local post office in order to do it.

Until she was on the train tomorrow morning, she wouldn't feel safe. *That man* had frequently told her she was his property until she reached her majority and that was still three years away. He'd told her he had the law on his side. He was a respected figure in the neighbourhood and no one would have believed her. Mum did her best but would never speak out against her husband.

She remained where she was, unsure if she should go downstairs or wait until she was called. She had no watch, there was no clock in the room and neither was there one on the church tower.

'Jane, lunch is on the table. Are you coming down?' Mrs Jackson called from the bottom of the stairs.

She was at the door in seconds and had to restrain herself from hurrying – making any sort of noise was always a bad thing.

'I'm sorry, Mrs Jackson, I didn't want to intrude.'

'We thought you might have gone to sleep and didn't like to disturb you. We eat in the kitchen. It's cosier and easier for me.'

'It smells absolutely splendid. I'm starving. I haven't eaten since yesterday teatime.'

'Good heavens, no breakfast today?'

'Not on Sundays, no.'

Jane sat down eagerly. The only times she'd been able to eat normally was when she'd been at school. At home she was in constant fear of inadvertently offending *that man*.

She had second helpings of everything and couldn't remember ever enjoying a meal so much. 'Thank you, that was delicious. I don't suppose the food in the WAAF will be very good, but I expect it will be plentiful.'

'You're far too thin, my dear; I'm sure that once you're away from here, you'll thrive,' the vicar said with a benevolent smile.

'My mother has asked me to write to her but to send my letters here. Would that be permissible?' There was no need to say why.

'Of course, we'll be happy to help. Mrs Hadley can write a reply when she collects your letters and we can post them for her.'

Jane blinked away tears; if only she'd had the courage to come to them sooner maybe her life would have been less miserable.

'May I be excused?'

Mrs Jackson looked startled by this request. 'Goodness, you don't have to ask. You're an adult, you can make your own decisions.'

'I'll help you with the washing-up. Do you have a daily, like my mother does? *That man* didn't like her to do anything he considered menial.'

'That would be kind and most appreciated. I do all my own housework but Violet from the pub comes in to do my laundry.'

The sun was shining, making the garden look inviting but Jane couldn't bring herself to go outside just in case *that man* came to snatch her away. She was safe indoors – even he wouldn't come into the vicarage uninvited.

When Mr and Mrs Jackson went to church for Evensong, she had the house to herself. The moment they stepped outside she raced around locking all the doors. Not until she was certain all of them were firmly bolted did her heart stop pounding.

She would be safer upstairs. The vicar had a fondness for detective stories and she selected one of Agatha Christie's novels and took it with her. She was about to sit on the hard, upright wooden chair but then forced herself to stretch out on the bed.

Something had been bothering her since her arrival and she couldn't think what it was. What had she forgotten? She looked at her suitcase. Something she should have wasn't there. She jack-knifed in horror. Her gas mask – it was on the hall table.

Everyone had to carry a respirator in case there was a gas attack. These had been issued weeks ago. Would she be arrested for travelling to London tomorrow without one?

Then common sense returned. It would probably be weeks before Germany sent bombers of any sort to England. Plenty of time to obtain another one even if she had to pay for the replacement. She couldn't be the only person to have mislaid theirs.

Mrs Jackson had told her she could have a bath if she wanted, wash her hair ready for her big adventure. Such luxury to be able to have unrestricted use of hot water and the bathroom. No doubt the facilities for a WAAF would be basic, similar to those she'd endured at school.

With the bath brimming with hot water, far more than she'd ever had in her life, she removed her clothes, carefully folding each item and placing it neatly on the chair as she'd been brought up to do. Hopefully, this ingrained neatness would come in useful in her new life.

There was a mirror over the sink but fortunately this was steamed over so she couldn't see herself. The marks and bruises from her last beating hadn't quite faded. She could count her ribs, her breasts were non-existent, and her arms and legs looked too thin to support her.

She ran her fingers through her long hair to remove the tangles that always appeared after it had been washed. The brother of one of her school friends had attempted to flirt with her when she'd been staying at his house last Easter holidays. What was that he'd said? Yes – that her hair was the colour of corn and her eyes reminded him of the summer sky. Vanity was a sin but secretly she'd always been rather pleased with her crowning glory.

She wallowed in the water until it was tepid and then stepped out. She barely had time to dress and brush her hair before someone knocked loudly. For a moment she panicked. Then she remembered she'd locked the doors.

'I'm so sorry,' she said as she unbolted the back door to allow Mr and Mrs Jackson to come in. 'I forgot that...'

'No need to explain, my dear, we know exactly why the doors were locked. Did you have a lovely bath?'

'I did, thank you, Mrs Jackson. I feel tickety-boo now. Is there anything I can do to help you prepare tea?'

'We just have sandwiches, tea and cake.'

'Then please let me do it whilst you read the paper.'

'That would be lovely, thank you.'

Jane had expected to toss and turn all night but was asleep the moment her head touched the pillow and didn't wake until she heard someone going down the stairs. Today was the start of a new life. Other young women and young men would be flocking to volunteer because they wanted to do their bit for their King and Country. Her motives were purely selfish – she just wanted to get away from *that man*.

2

Mr and Mrs Jackson accompanied her to the station. She'd avoided the early morning train as *that man* caught it to his bank in the nearby market town.

'Good luck, my dear girl, you deserve it. I don't know when we'll see you again, but you have our good wishes to take with you.' The vicar patted her on the shoulder but his wife embraced her.

'I'll keep an eye on your mother – don't worry about her. You have our telephone number and can always ring and tell us your news and I can guarantee it will be passed on to her.'

'I'll do that. Thank you for your help. I couldn't have done this without you. I expect you'll be busy with evacuees any day now. Your house will be overflowing with children by the end of the week.'

'Poor little mites, I expect there'll be a lot of wet sheets to wash until they settle. Take care of yourself, Jane, and keep in touch if you can.'

The train steamed in and Jane clambered into a ladies' only carriage. Everything seemed absolutely normal – one wouldn't have known the country was at war from the way people were going about their business.

There were two other ladies in the compartment who turned to look at her with disapproval. Was her hat not on straight? Were her stocking seams crooked? She straightened her shoulders and ignored them. Whatever they didn't like about her appearance it was nothing to do with them. Then she shrunk into her seat regretting her behaviour. If she offended these women they might remember her and tell *that man*.

It would have been more interesting to have had a window seat but they were both taken. From what she'd seen on her brief glance in their direction they were about mum's age, but there the resemblance ended. Whereas Mum was tall, almost as thin as she was herself, with faded blonde hair and watery blue eyes, both of these matrons were stout, wearing tweed suits despite the weather, and sat as if they had an unpleasant smell under their noses.

They must think they were somehow superior to her – if that was so then surely they'd be travelling in first class? The vicar had kindly given her the book she'd started and she revelled in the opportunity to read without interruption.

An hour and a half later she was standing outside the station not entirely sure in what direction she should go to find Victory House in Westminster. A helpful policeman told her she could walk along the embankment or take an underground line called the District and Hammersmith.

It would be better to travel on the underground as her lack of an essential piece of equipment was less likely to be noticed. She joined a long queue to purchase a ticket and then got hopelessly lost looking for the correct platform. Eventually she arrived where she should be just as a train was due. The whoosh of air as it approached, the ominous rumbling noise, was almost too much. If she hadn't been pressed forward by those eager to get on, she would have reversed and walked along the embankment instead.

There were no seats and people were packed in like sardines in a can. She'd never liked crowds and being crushed against complete strangers in this intimate fashion made her stomach roil. By the time she arrived her pulse was racing, her palms wet and her head was about to explode.

She threw herself out of the doors and pushed her way through the exiting crowd in a desperate rush to reach the surface and fresh air. Did her panic mean that she was claustrophobic? Most air raid shelters were underground. She would just have to pull herself together if she was going to fit into her new life.

When she arrived at the WAAF recruiting office she was horrified to see there was already a queue almost to Whitehall. Seeing so many eager to join was good for the country but not for her. They couldn't possibly see everybody today.

Two girls a bit older than her stood behind her. 'Cor blimey, I ain't standing around here for hours, Nancy. I got better things to do with me time,' one of them said loudly.

'Stay with us for a bit, Ruby. I ain't keen to do this on me own,' the one called Nancy said.

'I'll stop for an hour, then I'm off.' The speaker, with peroxide blonde hair, bright red lips and enormous thrusting breasts, saw Jane looking at her and Jane shrunk back, expecting to be snarled at.

'All right, ducks? You look a bit lost. Ain't you got no one with yer?' The girl was smiling.

'I haven't got anyone. Do you think they'll get to us before the office closes?'

'What's yer name, love?'

'Jane Hadley – today's my birthday.' Why had she blurted this out? Would they think she was asking them to sing happy birthday to her or buy her a cup of tea to celebrate?

'Well I never!' Nancy said. 'It's mine too. I'm nineteen – I reckon you're younger than what I am.'

'I'm eighteen. What a coincidence for us both to have the same birthday. But you didn't answer my question, either of you: do you think we'll have to come back tomorrow?'

The queue shuffled forward a few feet and stopped again. 'It closes at ten o'clock tonight so there's eight hours to go. Depends how many they've got looking after things in the office,' Ruby replied.

'I can't possibly stand in this queue for so long,' she replied. 'There were no facilities on the train and I couldn't find them on the station.'

The two Londoners exchanged a puzzled look. 'Facilities? Oh, you mean the privy. There's a caf we passed down a side street, not as posh as what you'd expect to get round here,' Nancy said. 'I'll take you. Ruby can keep our places. You'll do that won't you?'

'As long as you bring me back a bun or somethink. Me belly thinks me throat's been cut.'

'Can I leave my suitcase with you?'

'Go on then, luv, I'll see no bugger takes it.'

Nancy grabbed her arm and before she knew it, she was running along the pavement – something she'd never done before. Neither of her new friends carried a gas mask so maybe she would get away with it until she could purchase another one.

Despite her skinny build she was fit and not at all out of breath when they skidded to a halt outside the café. Nancy was pink and perspiring but was unbothered by this.

'It ain't up to much, but I reckon we'll get permission to use the bog if we buy somethink. I ain't got a lot on me…'

'I'll treat you and Ruby this time. I don't suppose they'll let us take a mug of tea away but hopefully we can get her something to eat.'

The door was propped open with a brick and the smell of frying bacon, sausages and chips wafted out onto the pavement. Her stomach rumbled loudly and her companion giggled.

A lady, her grubby wraparound pinny barely meeting at the back, beamed when they stepped in. There was one table free; the others were occupied, mostly by smart businessmen in pinstriped suits and one or two by secretaries. 'What can I get you? Tea, egg and chips? Only one and six including bread and butter.'

'Thank you, that would be lovely. Our friend is holding our place in the queue at Victory House. Would it be possible to take a sandwich and a cake for her when we go?'

'I've got a nice bit of greaseproof paper I can wrap it in, dearie. I've got a bottle of pop you can buy if you want.' Jane nodded vigorously and the woman returned behind the counter and yelled their order to somebody the other side of the bead curtain.

'Ruby will be pleased with what yer getting for her.' When the fat lady returned Nancy called across the café. 'My friend needs the bog. Can she use yours?'

Jane's face was scarlet and she tried to shrink into her chair. How could Nancy have shouted something so personal across the room? There were men in here. Now everyone knew she needed to pee.

'Course she can. Come along with me, ducks, it's out the back. It ain't up to much but it's clean.'

When she returned the food had arrived. Egg and chips weren't something she'd had before – *that man* didn't allow such common food to be eaten under his roof.

'It looks scrumptious. I'm absolutely starving.'

They cleared the plates in record time and then she paid the bill. With the greaseproof paper parcel in one hand and Nancy holding the other they raced back, dodging around startled pedestrians, laughing at their shock at such unseemly behaviour.

There were now another thirty or so hopeful young ladies behind Ruby and the queue had shuffled forward quicker than she'd expected so that the recruiting office was now in sight.

'Here you are, Ruby, I hope it's all right.' She handed over the parcel and Nancy gave her friend the bottle of ginger beer.

Inevitably when the marble was prised from the top the contents sprayed all three of them. Shaking a fizzy drink wasn't a sensible thing to do.

Eventually they stepped into the building and in turn they gave their particulars and were told to wait on the benches that had been set out down either side of the room. There was barely room for the three of them to squeeze into the space along with the dozens of other eager recruits.

'I wonder how long we have to wait here and what will happen next,' Jane whispered to her companions.

'I need the bog. I'm going to look for one. Save me place, Nancy.' Ruby was directed through a door at the far end of the huge room and although she was gone for some time no one on the benches had been called up.

'There's another room down there what's full of girls filling in forms. I reckon that's where we go next.'

Eventually Jane was called over to see a recruiting officer. She was smartly dressed in her Air Force blue uniform. She explained about discipline, and said that they were looking for girls with good secretarial skills at Hendon. She then handed Jane a form and sent her into the room at the back to fill it in.

Ruby and Nancy joined her and were frowning at their papers. 'Would you like me to help you fill yours in? I can write neatly and very fast.'

They spread out the three forms side-by-side and she wrote down their details using her precious fountain pen. She would have to try and buy herself a bottle of ink as it was bound to run out if there was much more form filling to do. It took far longer to complete the section about her own education than it did for them.

Everything went swimmingly until it came to the question requiring her to put her home address. Her new friends came from Poplar, they lived next door to each other.

'Why ain't you writing down your own gaff, Jane?' Nancy asked.

Ruby answered for her. 'You running away?'

'I am. I can't risk them contacting that address. I don't know what to do. I can't leave it blank.'

'Put down my address,' Nancy said. 'You can stop over with us – bit of a squeeze, mind, but beggars can't be choosers.'

'You'd better keep your trap shut when we hand them in,' Ruby said. 'Someone posh like what you are wouldn't live where we do.'

'That's very kind of you to offer, Nancy, but won't we be taken on today?'

'Gawd love us, I don't reckon so. It might be weeks before them bleeders are ready for us.'

Jane flinched every time Ruby used bad language but wouldn't dream of saying that it offended her. 'I'll have to find a B&B, or a cheap hotel. I couldn't possibly put your family out for more than a night.' She had still not filled in the space that required a forwarding address. She came to a decision.

'I'm going to tell them that I've yet to find myself accommodation in London and ask them if they can recommend somewhere respectable I can stay whilst I wait.'

'Suit yourself then; we ain't good enough for you obviously,' Ruby said with a sneer. 'Come along, Nancy, I know when we ain't wanted.'

The two of them marched off with their completed forms before she could explain that she hadn't meant to infer their home wasn't respectable. By the time she was on her feet there were three other people in the queue ahead of her. Nancy turned and waved but Ruby had a firm hold of her arm and almost dragged her from the building. She could either follow the two girls and lose her place, or stay where she was and be entirely on her own.

She straightened her spine, pushed her shoulders back and remained in her place. When it was her turn, she handed in the form with an explanation.

The WAAF officer nodded. 'You are the third volunteer

in the same position, Miss Hadley. I have sent them to the Sanctuary House Hotel in Tothill Street. I shall put that as your address. It might be some time before we send you your papers. Are you able to remain in London until they arrive?'

'I am, ma'am. I have sufficient funds until the New Year.'

'Excellent, I'm sure you will hear before that. We need your sort of girl – someone with a good education.'

'Yes, ma'am. Thank you for your assistance.'

'You will report here tomorrow morning for the medical examination.'

This is the first Jane had heard about this. If she had to remove her clothes the doctor would see the bruises and want to know how she'd got them. No point in worrying about it now. Her first priority was to check into the hotel.

She had no idea where this hotel was situated. There was an attractive dark-haired girl, holding a battered suitcase, looking up and down the street as if unsure in which direction to travel.

'Excuse me, are you by any chance on your way to the Sanctuary Hotel?'

'I am indeed. Charlotte Fenimore at your service.'

'Jane Hadley, and I'm delighted to meet you. Do you know where this Tothill Street is situated?'

'Haven't the foggiest, but I'm certain a policeman or news vendor will be able to direct us.'

This proved to be the case and half an hour later they had secured themselves a shared room in this establishment. The fact that it was on the third floor meant it was inexpensive, which suited both of them.

'The only good thing about this room is the view,' Charlotte said as she threw up the window, letting in some welcome fresh air and large amounts of pigeon droppings. The criss-crossed brown tape put on the window had made the room dark.

'I can't imagine why they think it necessary to put that on windows on the third floor.'

Charlotte laughed. 'If a bomb drops on this hotel broken glass will be the least of our worries. I suppose that we should find out how to get to the cellar.'

'Do you really think Hitler will be dropping bombs on us before Christmas?'

'From what I've read his air force is much larger and better prepared than ours. I suppose we'd better unpack our meagre belongings. You don't have a gas mask.'

'I left it behind. I'm hoping I can buy another one somewhere.'

'I'm sure you can. We'll make it our priority tomorrow morning. Have you been to London before?'

'Never. There's so much I'd like to see whilst I have the opportunity. I just hope my funds last until I become a WAAF. That reminds me, I need to find a post office too and pay in my spare cash.'

It didn't take long for either of them to empty their cases and arrange their toiletries. There was a sink in the room so they could wash and clean their teeth but she needed to know where the loo was.

'The nearest bathroom is on the next floor – did you notice where the WC was?'

'I didn't, but the fact that there are chamber pots under the beds isn't a good sign. I wonder if we have to empty them ourselves or if the maids do it for us.'

Jane looked under the edge of the shiny satin bedspread and shuddered. 'I'm not using that. However clean it looks I hate to think how many bottoms have sat on it before me. I'm going in search of the lavatory just in case I need to find it in the dark. I don't have a dressing gown or slippers. I'll have to get dressed if I need to find it. What about you?'

'As you've seen, I've just got the minimum. We can't keep any civilian clothes once we're enlisted, everything's provided.'

They spent the remainder of the day exploring the neighbourhood. The Houses of Parliament were admired from the outside and Westminster Cathedral from the inside. When they emerged, blinking in the sunlight, Charlotte suggested that they go in search of some tea.

'I know where there's a decent café. I had lunch there earlier today. Nothing fancy, only egg and bacon and that sort of thing.'

'Sounds fine to me. I don't suppose there'll be either egg or bacon once rationing kicks in. Better make the most of it whilst we can.'

The city was quieter now shops and businesses were closed. Belatedly it occurred to her that the café might also be closed as it was there to serve the people who worked in London. She was right – the door was locked.

'Pity, but it won't do either of us any harm to go without tonight. Maybe we can get a meal and drink of some sort at the hotel,' Charlotte said.

This proved to be the case and although double the price they would have paid at the café, just this once it was worth it.

As Jane scraped the last of the gravy from her plate she smiled. 'I still can't quite believe that I'm here. It doesn't seem real yet.'

'We don't know much about each other. Shall I start with my potted biography?'

Jane nodded as she was unwilling to reveal the real reason she was here.

'My father was killed in France in the last war. My mother never recovered and my two older brothers and I had to look after each other. They are both officers in the army but I didn't want to join the ATS – think we'll be more useful helping the RAF. What about you?'

She swallowed the lump in her throat. 'I must have been the only person in the country praying for war to start. It gave me the opportunity to escape.' She paused not sure if she could continue but for some reason she trusted Charlotte to keep her secret. 'My father is a brutal man. I think one day he might actually have killed me.' She had revealed more than she'd ever thought but would never tell anyone the full truth.

'How absolutely dreadful. You did the right thing, Jane. You'll be safe now and can forget about him. We can be chums. The officer that I spoke to said they particularly want girls with a good education. With any luck we'll be posted together.'

'I met a nice girl called Nancy. I don't think I told you about her, did I?'

The following morning, they reported for their medical. She joined a queue of girls waiting to be ushered into the room.

They seemed to be in and out quickly so it couldn't be a very thorough examination.

There were screens behind which she had to remove her clothes. Jane was going to have to join the line wearing only her brassiere and knickers.

'Don't worry about it, Jane. I don't suppose anyone will notice.' Charlotte spoke softly from behind her.

'I hope you're right.' There was no time to continue the conversation as she was called through. The doctor barely looked at her. He listened to her chest, took a pulse and then she was asked to lower her knickers.

'Quickly, I haven't got all day,' he snapped.

She was scarlet from head to toe but managed to do as he said. 'Fine, you've passed.'

She'd never dressed so fast in her life and dashed outside to lean panting against the wall whilst she waited for Charlotte. She'd hoped to see Nancy amongst the crowd but either she'd come earlier or hadn't arrived yet.

'Golly, that was fun. I told you he wouldn't even notice your bruises and scars. First time any man has seen my nether regions.'

Jane giggled. 'What on earth was that all about? What could they possibly expect to find in our knickers?'

'Don't know, and not going to ask. I bet those two from the East End you told me about would be able to tell us. It's a pity they weren't here as I'd like to meet Nancy.'

'We'll get two shillings and sixpence a day, plus our food, clothing, accommodation and medical treatment for nothing. Sounds like a good arrangement, don't you think?'

'The recruiting officer mentioned Hendon to me, but I said I didn't want to be a secretary; I wanted to be a radio or wireless operator. I learnt the Morse code when I was a Girl Guide,' Charlotte said.

'The woman suggested I was suitable for special duties but didn't specify what she meant. All we have to do now is wait until we get the letter to tell us to report.'

3

October 1939

Spending time in London despite the inconvenience of the blackout was most enjoyable and Jane got to know and like Charlotte. She had been there for a month when she came up with a suggestion that she wasn't sure her friend would agree to.

'I want to go and see Nancy and Ruby, the two girls I told you about. They live in Poplar – I kept their address. They were so kind to me when I arrived and I don't want to start my new life with bad feeling between us.'

'I should think it highly unlikely that you'll ever see either of them again. However, I've never been to the East End so it will be an experience for both of us.'

'It's a Saturday so hopefully they won't be at work. I seem to remember that Nancy's a seamstress. I think Ruby's a barmaid.'

*

They caught the underground to Liverpool Street and mistakenly thought they could walk the remainder of the distance. On enquiring at the ticket office, they were told it was too far and they should catch another underground train and get off at Mile End. From there they had to walk down the Burdett Road until they reached East India Dock Road. After that they would have to find their way to Cottage Street, which was one of the many narrow streets that ran between East India Dock Road and Poplar High Street.

On emerging into Mile End they were staggered at the difference between this part of London and the one in which they were temporarily living. It was louder, livelier and far more interesting. Jane exchanged a happy smile with Charlotte.

'It's like stepping back in time. This could be a scene from one of Charles Dickens' books – street vendors, rag-and-bone men with their horses and carts, and everywhere you look there's something that catches the eye.'

'We're attracting rather a lot of attention. I think we should have dressed down – we look rather too smart for this area. I'm not sure this is a good idea. We don't even know if we'll find them and if we do, if they'll want to speak to us.'

'We've come this far, Charlotte, and it's an adventure. We don't have much money on us and you left your expensive jewellery and wristwatch in the hotel safe. Even if somebody did try to pick our pockets, they wouldn't get a great deal.'

Eventually they found the street they were looking for. It was narrow, strings of washing stretched across from the upstairs windows, children were playing hopscotch and football in the road. The houses were jammed together, but every doorstep was spotless and the windows shone. A group of housewives in their wraparound aprons, their hair hidden by headscarves tied like turbans, turned to look at them curiously.

'What you two doing down 'ere? You looking for someone, lovey?' The nearest woman spoke without removing a cigarette from her lips.

'Actually, we were hoping to find Nancy or Ruby. I'm afraid we don't know their second names. I have their address here – but there don't seem to be any numbers on your doors.'

'Cor blimey, you must be the posh bird what they told us about. Fancy you coming all this way to find them. Nancy Evans lives across the street, right opposite 'ere, with her parents. I don't reckon Nancy's in – she's probably down the chippy fetching dinner.'

'Thank you. Do you think Mrs Evans will mind if we visit now?'

'No, she'll be tickled pink.'

As they were crossing the road the door to Nancy's house opened and an older woman the image of her daughter beckoned them over.

'I saw you talking to Ada. My Nancy won't be a tick. Come along in; it's a bit of a squeeze but you're welcome.'

Jane wasn't sure if she should remove her shoes as the linoleum inside the door was polished to a dangerous shine. She leaned down to slip them off but Mrs Evans stopped her.

'No, you're all right. Leave them shoes on, lovey. I ain't worried about a few marks on me lino.'

They were ushered into the back room, which was already occupied. Mr Evans, a burly man with a bald head and missing front tooth, didn't get up from his comfortable seat in front of the fire. He gestured with his cigarette to the only empty chairs on the far side of the scrubbed wooden table that took up half the space.

'Sit yerselves down. Our Nancy won't be long. She's told us she'd met up with a nice girl, but we ain't heard about there being two of you.'

'Thank you, Mrs Evans, we're sorry to intrude at a mealtime,' Jane said as she edged past two silent youths who were so alike they must be twins. 'This is Charlotte. She signed on the same day as Nancy, Ruby and I did.'

Mrs Evans chimed in. 'Ruby ain't going now. She's got herself a job in a factory making good money and she can stop at home.'

'I'm so glad that Nancy's still going to join. We got on so well when we met last month.'

'Always pleased to see a friend of our Nancy, 'specially someone like you. She ain't heard nothing from them WAAF lot. Don't see why it takes so bleedin' long to sort things out,' Mr Evans said as he lit another cigarette from the end of the one he was smoking before stubbing that out in an overflowing ashtray.

'Language, Stan, not in front of the ladies.'

He grinned, unrepentant. 'I reckon they'll 'ear far worse once they join up so might as well get used to it now. Won't be such a shock then, will it?'

'Bertie, Joe, move your arses, don't sit there like a couple of puddings,' Mrs Evans said to her sons. They ignored her and continued to play a silent card game. 'Them two ain't so clever as my Nancy, but they're good boys and already working down the docks with their Pa.'

Jane had been surprised that the menfolk were home on a Saturday as ships had to be unloaded every day of the week.

Mr Evans answered as if he'd read her mind. 'On the late shift today – we ain't starting work until after dinner.'

So far Charlotte hadn't spoken and Jane was worried she'd made a mistake bringing her there. Perhaps she was like *that man* and thought working people were somehow inferior to her.

Then her friend surprised her by talking to the boys about the card game they were playing. 'I used to play that when I was your age. I know another one that's a bit more exciting – would you like me to show you?'

They nodded but neither of them looked up. Soon Charlotte, Bertie and Joe were engrossed in a different game and after a few minutes both boys were more animated. She'd underestimated her friend.

Nancy rushed in with a large newspaper parcel under her arm. 'I never expected you to come and see me. Ada told me you was here. I'm so glad you've come, Jane – I wouldn't have gone off like that but Ruby insisted.'

The fish and chips were distributed – eaten from the paper and were even more delicious with the addition of vinegar and salt. There was ample for everyone but when Jane offered to contribute towards the cost she was shouted down.

'I reckon we've got to be going, lads. It doesn't do to be late as that bastard Frank's foreman today.'

Nancy and her mother deftly rolled up the newspaper. It

wasn't put in the rubbish but in a cardboard box under the sink, presumably to be used for lighting the fire.

She scrambled to her feet, as did Charlotte. 'Thank you for allowing us to share your lunch. That was very kind of you, Mr Evans.'

'My pleasure – not often we get visitors like what you are. You take care of my Nancy, both of you; she ain't as worldly as you. Not like that Ruby, any road.'

Mrs Evans handed her sons their thick jackets, mufflers and caps whilst they laced up their heavy work boots. The three of them trooped out and in the entire time they'd been there neither of the boys had spoken or looked at either Charlotte or her directly.

'I'll make us all a nice pot of tea. You'll need to get off before the blackout; don't do to be wandering around this area in the dark.'

'Thank you, Mrs Evans, we intend to do that. It doesn't get dark until seven o'clock so we've plenty of time.'

She was pleased that Charlotte and Nancy seemed to be getting on well despite the difference in their backgrounds.

'I bin looking into things, seeing what's what in the WAAF. I don't reckon I'll get offered what you two will be. I'm going to ask to go into catering or equipment – don't need to 'ave much book learning to do that.'

'With any luck we'll get our papers at the same time, as we handed in our applications so close together. I don't know what sort of training we get, but hopefully we'll be together initially at least,' Jane said.

'Remember that article in the *News Chronicle* we saw the other day, Jane? It said that the first WAAF arrivals didn't even have uniforms. All they were given was a blue cardigan to go over whatever they already had.'

'Goodness! We're both relying on them supplying everything we need in the way of clothing and so on. It's been almost two months since war was declared so let's hope that's long enough for them to get organised.'

Mrs Evans, who had finished her chores, joined them at the table. 'Do you think you girls will 'ave to do square-bashing and all that?'

'I hope so,' Charlotte said with a smile. 'I'm actually looking forward to learning how to march, to salute properly and all that sort of thing.'

'I ain't no good at dancing – I've got two left feet. I reckon I'll be 'opeless at keeping in time.'

Jane quickly reassured her. 'It's much easier than dancing. It's just walking up and down in time and following the instructions of the person in charge. I'm sure you'll be able to do it.'

'I expect you two will be made up into officers before long. You talk proper, just like them blokes on the wireless, not like my Nancy who's a bit common like.'

'I don't want to be commissioned; I want to stay in the ranks. My brothers are officers and they are both obnoxious – my father was even worse,' Charlotte said firmly.

'What do you mean?'

'They bark orders and expect to be obeyed. I'd rather follow them, than give them. What about you, Jane?'

'It's not something I've even thought about. I just want to fit in, do my job and not get into any trouble.'

Mrs Evans was having none of it. 'It ain't about what you

want, ducks, you'll be told what to do and have to follow orders like what everyone else does. Better for girls like my Nancy to have someone like you bossing her around and not some stuck-up bitch what looks down her nose at anyone what don't talk proper.'

'That was a very persuasive argument, Mrs Evans, and I will now reconsider my decision. Mind you, I might be so hopeless at whatever trade I go into that I'm not considered for promotion,' Charlotte said. Jane was still determined not to do anything that got her noticed even if it meant promotion.

They left soon afterwards and she found herself unable to respond to Charlotte's remarks as they walked briskly back to Mile End. Jane had been dismayed by Mrs Evans' vehemence and her language. She supposed she must get used to hearing such things if she was going to survive the WAAF.

Her stomach turned over when she remembered the one and only time *she'd* used inappropriate words. She'd been about seven or eight and had heard two workmen talking. Innocently she'd asked her mother what *a silly sod* was. *That man* had overheard and before she could explain she was face down across his knee being soundly spanked.

From that day on she'd been careful not to say anything that would offend him. However hard she tried, no more than a few weeks would go past before she was punished again. As she grew older the discipline became more severe and the last few beatings had been administered with a cane. She feared she would have the scars across her back and buttocks for the rest of her life, a constant reminder of the abuse she'd received.

She doubted that she would ever trust a man and had no intention of ever getting married and putting herself under the control of one. Everyone who knew *that man*, apart from the vicar and his wife, believed what they saw. They thought *that man* was a kind and charming person – appearances were always deceiving.

'Jane, what's wrong? You've not said a word since we left Nancy's house.'

'I'm sorry, unpleasant memories. Now, you have my full attention. What were you saying?'

They were eating breakfast in the hotel the following week when a waiter came across and said that Jane was wanted on the telephone. She dropped her napkin and hurried after him.

It was Nancy on the other end of the line with the news that she'd been told to report to the Air Ministry the following day. 'I was 'oping you'd got a letter too.'

'Just a minute, I'll ask at the desk.' She turned to the concierge and without her having to ask he handed over two buff envelopes. 'We've got ours as well. See you tomorrow.'

She replaced the receiver and dashed back to join Charlotte. 'The letters have arrived. That was Nancy saying she'd got hers.'

They tore open the envelopes and saw they were to report at the Air Ministry at nine o'clock, 0900 hours, the following day.

'Our last day of freedom. What shall we do?' Charlotte asked.

'Before we go out I need to write to my mother. She won't

have time to reply, but I promised to let her know as soon as I had any news. I wonder where we're going to be posted and if we'll even be allowed to write and receive letters.'

'I can't see there being a problem with that. Remember, we might only be at our first posting, the one where we'll be trained et cetera, for two or three weeks – no point in sending that address wherever it's going to be. Might as well wait, Jane, until you get a permanent posting after you've been allocated a trade.'

'Where is Kingsway, Charlotte? Do you have the foggiest?'

'I'm pretty sure it's somewhere along the Embankment. We've settled our bill so shall we be extravagant and use a taxi just this once?'

She checked her purse. 'I've got thirty shillings and a few coppers. What about you?'

'Almost as much. It won't be more than two and six including the tip.'

'Then let's do it. Leave here in style.'

The concierge hailed the cab. It rolled to a halt beside them. It was massive, had a hood at the back similar to the one on a perambulator. The space for the cases was beside the driver and they shoved them in.

'Where to, ladies?'

'The Air Ministry, on Kingsway, please,' Charlotte said.

'Righty ho. Hop in then. Give the door a good slam.'

The cab driver squeezed his horn, waved his arm out of the window, and the vehicle lurched off.

'I hope our luggage doesn't fly out as the space hasn't

got a door,' Jane said as she slid across the shiny seat and cannoned into her friend.

They were giggling as they untangled themselves. 'You need to hang on to the strap by the door, Jane.'

They rattled and banged the short distance and jumped out outside the Air Ministry. After grabbing their cases, they joined the flow of other girls heading the same way.

'Golly, it's busy out here,' she said as she dodged a couple of RAF lorries. 'Look, that's piled up with suitcases. Shall we go in?'

The building seemed to be full of efficient RAF and WAAF people rushing about giving orders. 'Look, over there, it's Nancy waving at us,' Charlotte said.

They hurried across to join the huddle of apprehensive-looking recruits. At least the three of them were happy to be there even though a lot of others looked as if they already regretted their decision.

'Goodness, it's packed in here. We seem to be in the way,' she said as she reached Nancy.

Charlotte looked around. 'Some of them are actually in tears. Why on earth did they volunteer if they're so worried about leaving home?'

'I expect that they want to do their bit, like us really,' she said. 'I think that sergeant's looking in our direction.'

The man beckoned her over. 'Name?'

'Miss Jane Hadley.'

He ticked her off the list. She was about to return to her friends when he glared at her. 'When you address me, miss, you answer "yes, Sergeant". Is that clear?'

'Yes, Sergeant, perfectly clear.' She was proud her voice didn't betray her nervousness.

'Right, onto the lorry.'

Helplessly she looked behind in the hope that her two friends were called next but they were still in the huddle. She daren't refuse or argue with this formidable sergeant so she meekly clambered into the waiting vehicle.

There wasn't room for anyone else – the canvas flaps at the back were dropped and the vehicle lurched away. Only then did she remember her suitcase remained in the dispersal area. With any luck Charlotte or Nancy would bring it with them.

In the gloom she couldn't see the other girls perched on the benches that ran down either side of the lorry. She was on the very end so in the event of an accident would be pitched headfirst through the canvas door.

Someone with an extremely loud voice spoke from the driver's end. 'Anyone know where we're going?'

'King's Cross station, I thought everybody knew that.'

Someone answered. 'Thank you for telling us, whoever that is up there.'

The aggressive speaker continued. 'We're going to Harrogate for our initial training. I don't expect everyone in here will survive that.'

Jane kept silent. There was always somebody, a bossy boots, who wanted to dominate a group. She wasn't going to get involved so pressed herself against the side and prayed she wouldn't fall off the bench.

They arrived at King's Cross, which looked grey and unfriendly. She really wanted to travel with Nancy and Charlotte so whilst everyone else was headed towards the platform she slipped away and into the ladies' waiting room. She couldn't have done this if she was in uniform, but she was pretty sure no one would know she was supposed to be getting on the train.

She just had to hope the rest of the girls would also be sent to King's Cross otherwise she was going to be in trouble. Less than fifteen minutes later a second wave of would-be WAAF recruits arrived. Thank goodness – Charlotte and Nancy were amongst them. Nancy was carrying two suitcases so had obviously remembered to bring hers along.

She raced across the concourse and slid in behind them. 'We're going to Harrogate on that train – did you know that?'

'Jane, we was right worried about you. Glad you waited for us,' Nancy said as she handed over the case.

'Jolly good show. Harrogate is miles away – it's going to be a long day. We didn't have the foggiest,' Charlotte said.

'Thank you for bringing my case, Nancy. None of that first lot of girls had anything with them so their cases must have gone in the luggage van or something.'

They trooped onto the train and had barely time to find a seat before the guard waved his flag, blew his whistle and the train steamed out of the station.

4

Eventually they disembarked at Harrogate. It had been dark for an hour and the blackout was in full force. As they'd got on the train last, the three of them were obliged to join the end of the shuffling queue of girls.

There was no chatter, just silence, as they stumbled through the darkness with only the occasional flicker of torchlight to stop them tumbling onto the railway track. This wasn't how she'd expected things to be. Jane felt miserable.

'This way, ladies, your chariots await,' a cheerful soldier could be heard yelling.

There were three lorries similar to the ones that had delivered them to King's Cross earlier in the day. Nancy was too short to get over the tailgate and Jane and Charlotte had to lift her in. This broke the ice a little and those nearest, who'd watched the struggle, were giggling too.

'Love a duck, I ain't doing that again, I reckon them soldiers got a good view of me knickers.' Nancy's indignant comment caused a further wave of giggling. Maybe the others were just tired and not really miserable at all.

Despite Jane pressing her feet firmly into the floor of the lorry, twice her bottom slipped and she ended on the floor.

Several others found themselves in a similar predicament and it was hard to be anxious when one was laughing so much.

After half an hour the lorry turned sharply to the right and this time everyone was tossed into the middle. By the time they'd untangled themselves and found another place on the narrow benches they were all laughing and talking as if old friends.

They tumbled out of the lorries and were directed into a massive Victorian building. The strident tones of the bossy boots echoed down the line. 'This is the Majestic Hotel; we're going to be billeted here whilst we train.'

How on earth did this girl know these things? It was hard to see anything apart from its size in the dark but once they were safely in the main foyer Jane had time to look around.

'This must have been a very grand place before the RAF took it over. There are no carpets, pictures or elegant furniture – just what looks like standard service fittings.' Charlotte pointed at the carved woodwork and fine ceilings. 'At least we can admire this and imagine what it must have been like to be a guest here before the war.'

Nancy, the least confident of the three of them, was standing between her and Charlotte looking around nervously. 'I ain't sure I'll fit in here. I ain't used to all these goings-on and that.'

'You'll be fine – you've got us,' Charlotte said reassuringly.

The three lorry loads of recruits had divided into dispirited groups waiting to be told what to do. Everywhere Jane looked there were people in RAF and WAAF uniforms looking frighteningly efficient. Would the three of them ever walk about with such confidence?

'Look, there's some non-commissioned officers heading this way and they look friendly – at least they're smiling.' Jane automatically straightened and the other two did the same.

One of the smartly dressed young women headed in their direction. 'You must be exhausted, chilled to the bone and starving. I'll take you to the mess hall. I'm sure you'll feel much better when you've had something to eat and a nice cup of tea.' She gestured towards the benches that ran alongside the walls. 'Put your coats and things on there and you can collect them on the way back.'

There was already a queue of eager young women in front of them and they joined the end of it. She was asked if she wanted tea with or without and she said no sugar, but when she took a sip it was sickeningly sweet.

Clutching her mug, she moved along and was handed the biggest plate of food she'd ever seen in her life. Charlotte tried to stop the eager server from giving her so much but Nancy was happy with the mountain of food. They found a table with enough seats for the three of them and sat down hastily before they could be occupied by someone else.

'I'll never get through all this. There's enough potatoes and mushy peas to feed half a dozen.' Then she spotted two sausages under the mound. 'Good grief – the poor things look as if they're drowning in all that green liquid.'

Her friends laughed and tucked in with gusto. To her astonishment despite the unappetising appearance of the food it was perfectly edible and a jolly sight better than the food she'd had at boarding school.

Halfway through she abandoned the meal. 'I can't eat any more. I don't have a big appetite.'

'You're too skinny by 'alf, my girl. I reckon you'd be a bit of all right with some meat on yer bones.'

'We haven't eaten since breakfast and that was hours ago – heaven knows when we'll be fed again. Try and eat some more. There's a war on so we shouldn't waste food.'

'You sound like Matron, Charlotte. I'm going to upset you even more as I can't drink this tea either because it's got sugar in it. It'll make me sick if I do.'

Nancy immediately swapped the mugs. 'You 'ave mine – there 'ain't none in this.' She stood up and nodded towards the servery. 'There's afters. I'm going to get some.'

To her surprise Charlotte also stood up. 'I'll get you some as well; if you don't want it then I'm sure someone else will be glad to have it. I'll take your plate with mine and with any luck no one will notice how much you didn't eat.'

Her dessert was happily passed down the table – it looked like spotted dick and custard – not something she was fond of so she was happy to give it away. The friendly NCO who'd brought them to the dining room – she supposed she must get used to calling it the mess hall from now on – was waiting expectantly at the far side of the room.

'We better go – she'll 'ave our guts for garters if we ain't sharpish.'

Nancy was right. It didn't do to keep those in authority waiting. She was on her feet, empty mug in her hand, before anyone else was up. She walked fast to the box into which they had to put their used items and dropped hers in.

The others weren't far behind her and once the waiting NCO had all five from the table in a neat line, they were led to the second floor and into a room with five iron bedsteads. 'Good night, ladies, lights out in fifteen minutes. The bathroom and WC are at the end of the passage.'

There was a pile of bedding in the centre and none of it looked very comfy. The sheets were stiff and unpleasant and the grey blankets little better. The worst of the items was the pillow, which had no give in it at all. She wasn't going to sleep a wink in such an uncomfortable bed.

Jane was woken by a deafening clatter and all but fell out of bed.

'Bloody 'ell, what the devil's that?'

'I think it's telling us to get up, Nancy. If we want to use the bathroom we'd better get a move on as we have to share it with at least five other dormitories,' Charlotte said as she snatched up her toilet bag and ran for the door in her nightie.

Jane was close behind her but Nancy and the other two girls, Joan and Nora, remained in bed. Presumably an extra few minutes was preferable to first use of the facilities.

It was definitely a lick and a promise – there were others clamouring behind her. Her bare feet were icy and she was shivering when she dashed back. She skidded to a halt so suddenly Charlotte cannoned into her sending her sprawling.

'Good morning, that was a spectacular entrance.' The NCO laughed and offered her hand to help her up. Nora was in her knickers and vest; Joan was just rolling up her stockings but miraculously Nancy was fully clothed and looking rather smug about it.

'Right, now I have your attention, I want you to watch me very carefully whilst I show you how to make a bed in the correct WAAF fashion.'

Jane watched in amazement as the complicated procedure

was revealed to her. It wasn't called 'stacking a bed' in the RAF for nothing. It had to be carried out perfectly, everything in the right place including the mattress, which Jane now found out were called 'biscuits'.

Small wonder she'd been so uncomfortable as, like the others, she just pulled the pile apart in a random fashion and then tried to find herself a comfortable spot.

'I give you due warning, an improperly stacked bed will not be tolerated. You will have to do it again and could be put on a charge if it happens a second time. Now, as you're the only one dressed, would you like to demonstrate how it's done with your own bedding?' The NCO pointed at Nancy.

Her friend might not be able to read and write fluently but she'd obviously had no difficulty following the complicated arrangement as within a few minutes her bed was perfectly stacked.

'Well done. After breakfast you will be taken for "kitting out".' The NCO nodded, told them they were expected downstairs for breakfast in fifteen minutes, and then marched out.

Jane was at a loss as to how to fold the sheets and blankets in the correct manner but Nancy demonstrated again and they all followed her instructions and in the allotted time were ready to go down.

There was lumpy porridge for breakfast, which she ignored, but as much toast, margarine and marmalade as she wanted. This time they poured out their own tea, which was preferable. They had been almost last to eat yesterday and today they were amongst the first. Heaven knows what the porridge would be like by the time the stragglers arrived.

'That NCO's hovering by the door; I think we'd better hurry up. I'm not sure what being put on a charge actually means, but I certainly don't want to find out,' Jane said with a nervous smile.

Her fingers were sticky and what she really wanted was to find a washroom but didn't dare to be late. Obedience was ingrained in her and she thought she was going to find it somewhat easier following orders than some of the others. Communal living might also prove problematic to those girls not used to it, but as Nancy had lived in cramped surroundings, and she and Charlotte had been at boarding school most of their lives, they wouldn't have the same difficulty adjusting.

So far all that Nora had told her was that she'd been a secretary and was going to ask to be in admin. Joan hadn't spoken at all and was constantly dabbing her eyes.

There were half a dozen other girls already waiting in line. A jolly, middle-aged RAF flight sergeant was in charge of handing out the uniforms. He didn't ask for their measurements, weight or height, but ran his expert eye up and down before calling to his minions what size they should be given.

'Thirty-six for you, miss.' He handed her over a large pile of clothing and she carried it to the far side of the room where it seemed they were to change behind a row of screens. Although she'd been warned that everything, including underwear, was supplied she was shocked to think they had to strip in so public a place.

'What a palaver. I ain't never 'ad so much of me own in me life,' Nancy said as she dumped her pile on the bench next to Jane.

Charlotte arrived next. She held up the bra, which was made of thick, coarse, pink cotton with straps the width of a man's belt. 'Good heavens, this is the most unglamorous article of clothing I've ever seen. Look at the hooks at the back – I can't see them giving way.'

Jane held up the enormous navy blue, knee-length knickers. 'At least we won't be cold in our nether regions wearing these.' No sooner had she spoken than her stomach clenched. She wasn't allowed to say such risqué things – *that man* would punish her.

'Are you all right, Jane? You've gone white as a sheet,' Charlotte asked anxiously.

'Sorry, bad memories. We'd better get a move on before there's no room behind the screens.'

Despite the lack of privacy, she and Charlotte stripped off without a second thought – it was Nancy who kept her back turned and fiddled about under her skirt to remove and replace her knickers.

'These grey lisle stockings are hardly glamorous either, but the black Oxfords are really comfortable.' She laced these up and then stood up to admire herself in the full-length mirror thoughtfully provided.

'Not a bad fit considering, but the skirt's a bit short and so are the sleeves of the jacket.'

Charlotte smiled. 'I think we both look absolutely splendid. I prefer your hair in a roll at the back of your head.'

Nancy arrived beside them. 'Oh my Gawd – I look like a bleedin' orphan in this rig.'

'We can turn the hem and the sleeves up so it fits properly. It's not baggy, just far too long,' Jane said with a smile.

'I'm a bleedin' seamstress – I were panicking – I can do it meself.'

'Let's go back to our room and do it now. It's going to take an hour or more for everybody to get kitted out so I don't suppose we'll be missed.'

Not only did they have their spare uniform and their civvy clothes to carry, they also had an overcoat, a groundsheet with a hole in it, which was for wearing in the wet, and a tin hat.

'Do they expect us to get all this in that kitbag?'

'That's what everyone else is doing, Charlotte, so we'd better do the same.'

Once it was full it was too heavy to carry so, with some difficulty, they dragged the bag with one hand and carried their old clothes and tin hat with the other. Bumping them up the stairs was hilarious and Jane was surprised no NCO appeared to reprimand them.

Joan and Nora arrived looking equally smart in their new uniforms.

'We've got to polish all the buttons, and the belt buckle and make them shine, before we go back downstairs,' Nora said.

An hour later they rejoined the other recruits in the recreation hall and Jane was pleased to see that the five of them had the shiniest buttons. Nancy had shown them all how to apply both spit and polish and a great deal of elbow grease to the task and they'd all achieved a magnificent result.

An announcement blared out over the tannoy, telling them to report to the desk to receive their numbers.

Yet another RAF sergeant, again in his middle years, was waiting for them.

'There's something you need to know,' he said loudly and his voice carried wonderfully down the line of expectant girls. 'From now on you answer to your number. You eat by number, get paid by number, go on leave by number, get put on a charge by number; if you don't know your number inside out, you're in big trouble. You need to learn it immediately.'

He handed her a slip of paper and she hastily moved aside whilst opening it. She was now Aircraft Woman Second Class number 472374. It was as if a weight had lifted from her shoulders. There was no chance *that man* would ever find her as she was now anonymous.

Over tea and a couple of ginger nuts they recited their numbers to each other and she was confident none of them would ever forget them. The evening was spent sewing on name tapes.

'Tomorrow we can go into Harrogate to shop,' Charlotte said as she bit the thread on the last tape.

'We are supposed to be sending postcards saying that we've arrived safely but I don't think I'll bother. I'm going to wait until we're posted,' Jane said.

'I don't expect to get any letters from my horrible family so I'm not going to do it either. What about you, Nancy?'

'I ain't too clever with writing and such but I'll send a card anyway. We've got to bundle up our civvy clothes and send them back as well.'

'I certainly can't send my things to the vicarage. I'm not sure what I'll do with them.' She hesitated and then continued. 'Do you think I could send them to your address,

Nancy? Maybe there's someone your ma could give them to.'

'She'll get a few bob for them and it'll make all the difference. I ain't proud and neither is she.'

'In which case, I'll do the same,' Charlotte said.

The following morning everything was different. The room was immaculate, every bed stacked as it should be, four of them ready for inspection. Joan still hadn't spoken and she was the only one not smartly turned out.

Before they were allowed to leave, they were to have their first drill instruction and were going to learn how to salute. This didn't seem too complicated and she was actually looking forward to spending a morning becoming a proper WAAF.

The unfortunate sergeant given the task of teaching them was practically tearing out his hair after an hour. Half the girls didn't appear to know their right from their left and they kept colliding with each other or walking in the wrong direction. She was weak with laughter and he was practically apoplectic with rage.

Eventually he abandoned the drill. Now came the lesson on how to salute. 'This shouldn't be so difficult,' Charlotte whispered to her. 'I can't believe that any of us will have trouble grasping this.'

How wrong she was. The palm of the right hand had to face forwards, straight fingers and thumb held tightly together so that no light could be seen between them. The longest finger had to be placed exactly one inch behind the side of the right eye on the temple.

She was paired with Nancy and Charlotte with Nora. Joan hadn't been seen since breakfast.

'Righto, you go first, Jane. I ain't too sure exactly what we got to do.'

On her first attempt she poked herself in the eye. Nancy's first go pushed her cap off the back of her head. Eventually they mastered the technique and were dismissed.

Some of the girls were meeting up at the YMCA as their passes were until 21:45, nine forty-five, but Nancy advised against it.

'There'll be blokes up to no good, looking for a bit of the other; better we stay away.'

Jane wasn't entirely sure what this meant but was happy to comply. Mrs Evans had said Nancy would need protection but the reverse was true.

'Then shall we go to the pictures? Might be months before we get another opportunity,' Charlotte suggested.

'I've not seen *Wizard of Oz*,' Nancy said eagerly. 'What about you, Jane?'

'I've never been to the pictures. I'd be happy to see anything at all.'

They returned to the Majestic in good time and after cocoa and a bun retired to their room. Joan's locker was clear, the two hooks provided for her spare uniform empty.

'I thought she'd leave. As we volunteered we can change our minds anytime. Do you think Nora has gone as well?'

Nancy checked and the locker was full. 'No, she ain't left. Wonder when we get to hand in them parcels of clothes?'

She pointed to the lumpy brown paper and string bundles waiting on the floor by the door.

'The tannoy said after breakfast. Then we've got drill and then some sort of medical thing,' Charlotte said as she looked at the notes she'd made in her diary. 'Think we're going to be inoculated – hope you don't mind being a pincushion.'

5

The ever-present and noisy loudspeaker informed them they were to take their parcels to the mailroom immediately after breakfast.

'Does anyone have any idea where the mailroom's situated?' Jane asked.

'Haven't the foggiest, but I expect someone will know. Let's hope it's not outside as its tipping down out there,' Charlotte answered.

Unfortunately, they had to cross a large expanse of concrete to take the parcel of no-longer-needed clothes. As drill was to start in half an hour, they couldn't hang about waiting for the rain to stop.

'We've got these cape things, so we shouldn't get disastrously wet. I'm game if you two are.' Charlotte had got her parcel beneath the voluminous wet weather garment and she and Nancy did the same. They set off at a run.

She was halfway across when she stepped into a large puddle, lost her balance and dropped her parcel in the water. She recovered it immediately but the damage was done. The paper was sodden, the clothes not much better. It couldn't possibly be posted in this condition.

Either she could return and try and find some more paper

and risk being late for drill or see if the person in charge in the mailroom would accept it as it was. She decided on the latter. She'd been dithering long enough to be drenched to the skin – this wouldn't go down well with her superiors either.

Her explanation was received with indifference. 'Get it done properly and bring it back. Dismissed.'

It took her far too long to find another piece of brown paper and rewrap her parcel. Perhaps it would have been better not to change out of her wet clothes, which took up a further fifteen minutes but she was prone to bronchitis and didn't want to risk getting ill.

Eventually she was able to hand it in but was then disastrously late for drill. At least it wasn't raining now so she wouldn't get wet a second time.

She approached the area at the back of the hotel where drill took place with some trepidation. No point in procrastinating. If she was going to be put on a charge she might as well get it over with.

This time the manoeuvring and marching was slightly better than yesterday. She joined the end of the line and completed the session without putting a foot wrong. Should she go and apologise to the sergeant or wait until he summoned her?

The group was dismissed; he disappeared and she was left to wonder if her absence had been noted at all.

'Jane, they did a roll call. I'm afraid you're in for the high jump,' Charlotte told her as they headed for the medical room for their various inoculations.

'I guessed as much. I suppose I just wait for someone to summon me. I dropped my parcel and it took ages to get it sorted out.'

Nancy appeared to have bonded with Nora who came from Stratford so, although not quite an East Ender, she had a similar background to hers.

There was no time to dwell on this as immediately after lunch she followed her friends to the medical rooms where the doctor proceeded to stick several needles in her left arm. This was done so quickly she had no time to ask for it to be done in her right as she was in fact left-handed.

By the evening her arm was throbbing, twice the size it should be and red-hot.

'That doesn't look good, Jane. Mine's just a bit pink and sore,' Charlotte said. 'Is it very painful?'

'What do you think? I've got some aspirin in my toilet bag – I think they might help a bit. It's a good thing we haven't got anything else official to do as I doubt that I could do it.'

She'd forgotten about her misdemeanour until an NCO stalked in. 'ACW 472374, on your feet.'

She jumped to attention and then her head spun and everything went black. When she came around she was in bed – someone had made it up for her – and Charlotte was sitting beside her reading a book.

'The doctor said you'd had an extreme reaction but would be fine in a day or two. It's a good thing really.'

Blearily Jane opened her eyes. She didn't take in what her friend had said as she had other more urgent matters in her mind. Her arm was agony, and she needed the WC immediately.

'Can you help me to stand up? I must go for a pee.'

When she returned and flopped into bed she recalled

what Charlotte had said. 'Why do you think it's a good thing that I'm so unwell?'

'The NCO said she hadn't decided whether to put you on a charge as the drill sergeant said you were the best of the bunch when you did arrive. The fact that you're so ill from the injections made her feel sorry for you.'

'I won't be able to go downstairs for dinner – I don't suppose you could find me a drink of some sort?'

'Voilà! Nancy and Nora managed to find a thermos flask and get the canteen to fill it with tea – no sugar. It's eight o'clock – I suppose I should say 20:00 – and we had our tea ages ago. There's a plate of half-decent sandwiches and a sticky bun if you fancy them.'

'Tea would be wonderful but I don't want anything to eat. They mustn't go to waste so why don't you eat them? You seem to be able to devour everything on your plate and yet remain lovely and slender.'

'My family are tall and thin and we all eat like horses – not eat horses, I hasten to add, although I'm quite certain that they do that in France.'

Over the next two weeks they became a homogenous whole and were no longer raw recruits who didn't know the left foot from the right. Jane enjoyed the camaraderie and knew that she'd made lifelong friends with Charlotte, Nancy and Nora.

'It would appear that we're being split into two groups and posted to either Pannal Ash or Ash Vale,' Charlotte told her as they sat reading in the recreation hall.

'Where's that?'

'Both places are in Harrogate somewhere. I just hope we

don't have to march there lugging that great kitbag full of stuff.'

'It won't be much of a march as most of us will have to drag it behind us. The bag's almost as big as Nancy.'

'I'm not going to worry about it now. Everything's tickety-boo as far as I'm concerned. I can't believe how well we've adjusted to all the rules and regulations. I'm rather enjoying being a WAAF, aren't you, Jane?'

'It's like being in boarding school only better, as we get paid.'

'I do hope we get posted together, but I doubt it. We'll stay in touch, won't we?'

'I think there's a good chance you and I will remain together but that Nancy and Nora will go in the other group. Haven't you noticed that the NCOs are segregating us for the different activities? The groups we tend to be in consist of the ones more likely to get the complicated trades,' Jane said.

'Have you decided what you want to do? I think I'd like to be a wireless or radio operator but I'm not entirely sure what the difference is between them.'

'I think one is to do with listening and using Morse code and the other speaking directly to pilots and so on. However, I'm not really sure.'

Nora and Nancy had gone to fetch them all some cocoa and overheard the conversation. 'Me and Nora are going to ask to be in equipment or catering. I reckon that way we'll be mixing with all sorts.'

'Now we've completed our basic training we should get given our trades and then be sent somewhere else for specialised training,' Jane said.

'I don't reckon we'll need much training for what we want to do. It'll be different for you two.'

'I was saying to Charlotte that we must keep in touch. I've got your home address, Nancy, so even if we don't write to each other after we're posted, I'll send the occasional letter there so your mum can let you know where I am.'

'I ain't too clever at reading, but me ma reads all right. There's another lot arriving tomorrow so we've got to be downstairs ready to leave right after breakfast and that ain't at the usual time but six o'clock. That's the middle of the bleedin' night.'

'Then we'd better get packed as soon as we've finished our cocoa.'

Charlotte was right. It wouldn't do to be late on their last day here. The NCO had already told them they had to put their dirty sheets in the laundry box and then collect fresh linen and restack the bed ready for the incomers before they departed. This would mean getting up even earlier.

The lists were up when Jane staggered downstairs bumping her kitbag behind her. She was wearing her greatcoat, groundsheet-cape and tin hat and her gas mask was dangling round her neck. She propped her things against the wall before going in search of the others. Her three friends, who'd got there before her, were studying the lists of names on the noticeboard. They turned and from their expressions it wasn't good news.

'Not as I thought, Jane – the three of us are going to Ash Vale but you're going to Pannal Ash.'

She swallowed the lump in her throat. 'At least you can

stay together. Hopefully, we'll meet up in town as both places are still in Harrogate.'

'That's the spirit, Jane. You have to take your kit out and put it in the correct lorry. We march to our new home but those wretched bags will travel in style.'

Only then she noticed there were only one or two drunken kitbags in the entrance hall. She grabbed hers and dragged it behind her. Two cheerful airmen were waiting outside.

'Pannal Ash or Ash Vale, love?'

'Pannal Ash, please.'

'Give us your cape and tin hat – you don't want to be wearing those. It's a three-mile march.'

All her kit was clearly labelled with her number, as was her kitbag, so she was happy to hand them over.

They slung her belongings into the designated vehicle. The sky was leaden, the wind bitter, and she shivered. It was only the beginning of November, scarcely winter at all, but it was cold enough for snow today.

She'd been glad of the distraction as by the time she returned to join her friends she'd regained her composure and was certain they couldn't possibly see how upset she was about being sent for further training on her own.

Her appetite had deserted her but the others devoured everything put in front of them with enthusiasm. She settled for a slice of toast and a mug of tea. There was a tub of hot water and a couple of cloths for them to rinse and dry off their irons – this was what their personal set of cutlery and mug was called – they never had to put them away dirty.

Far too soon the tannoy told them to muster outside. Her friends embraced her, which she found difficult, but she managed to respond with a brief hug for each. After a final flurry of farewells, she fell into the column of girls who were marching to Pannal Ash.

Despite the biting wind and small flurries of snow they marched with gusto, three across, arms swinging in unison and not a single person out of step. If it hadn't been for the constant thump of her gas mask against her side she would have enjoyed being part of the group. She exchanged a raised eyebrow with the girls on either side of her.

It would have been fun to have marched through the centre of the town but the place they were going was in the opposite direction. There were a few pedestrians who waved and clapped when they went past but most of them kept their heads down and went about their business.

Three times they were tooted at by passing motorists as they were occupying half the road, but the sergeants leading the cavalcade ignored the cars. Eventually, the cars overtook, their drivers scowling sideways at them.

There was a war on, surely being a few minutes late for work was less important than allowing them to walk safely to their new posting?

RAF Catterick

Flying Officer Oscar Stanton had been a flyer for over a year when war was declared so had been told he was likely to be promoted fairly rapidly as more volunteers joined the ranks. It had taken him a less than the usual year to get his wings – he doubted the new bods would get as long.

The Luftwaffe had practised their skills on the poor sods in Spain so the RAF were already at a disadvantage.

His reverie was interrupted by his closest friend, Roy Cross, also a pilot officer. 'Just been told we've got a twelve-hour pass. We're going into Harrogate.' Roy looked expectantly at him.

'What you're trying to tell me is that you want to go into Harrogate as long as I can drive you. I might as well use the car as long as I can. Petrol will be non-existent for us by the New Year.'

The Austin Seven was his pride and joy and he would be sorry to put it in mothballs for the duration. Next time he got sufficient leave he would drive it home and leave it in his father's garage. It should be safe enough there as they were in the wilds of Suffolk and unlikely to be bombed.

The car could safely seat four but there were six inside when he set out. 'None of you blighters smoke whilst you're in my car. Can't bear the smell.'

Roy was in the passenger seat and swung round to speak to the blokes squashed on the back seat. 'It's not the smell I'm bothered about, it's being set fire to.'

The drive from Catterick to Harrogate was about thirty miles but it was worth the effort as there were plenty of decent pubs, a couple of cinemas, Harrogate Theatre, and even a rather seedy nightclub. There was also the YMCA if you were looking for a bit of feminine company. The main hotels had been commandeered by the government for use as relocated London offices and training bases.

As they approached the outskirts of the city they had to pass Pannal Ash where WAAF recruits were now being trained. They already had a handful of girls at Catterick and there were likely to be many more as soon as the very basic accommodation was completed. He didn't envy the girls who would be unlucky enough to spend the winter in a Nissen hut, which was all they were going to get.

When he turned onto the main road a body of smartly turned out WAAF were marching towards him on the other side of the road. His companions immediately wound down the windows and wolf-whistled and cheered.

Not a head turned – every girl kept in step, eyes front. He decelerated as the road was wet and he didn't want to splash the girls marching closest to the oncoming traffic. Then a huge brown and white dog jumped out of a garden the column was passing and launched itself into the girls.

The ranks disintegrated. The well-ordered group were in chaos. Several girls were on the ground and others were screaming and pushing those closest to them in order to get away. Thank God he'd already slammed on the brakes and was almost stationary when one of the girls fell beneath his wheels.

He was out of the car in seconds, heart thudding, expecting the worst as he dropped to his knees by the girl spreadeagled on the tarmac. Her eyes were closed; blood trickled from a gash on the side of her head.

The wheels were touching but hadn't actually run over her. He closed his eyes for a second, sending up a brief prayer of thanks to anyone who might be listening.

Roy knelt on the other side. 'I'll see if she's broken anything. You check her vitals.'

Oscar put two fingers at the junction of her chin and her jaw. A definite steady pulse, but a bit weaker than it should be. 'We need to stop the bleeding. Make a pad with your handkerchief and I'll use my tie to keep it in place.'

Both of them had taken the St John Ambulance course and knew enough to deal with the situation until a medic arrived. His fingers were red by the time the temporary bandage was in place.

One of the other blokes was crouching beside him, his face pale. 'There's so much blood. Is she going to die?'

'Head wounds often look worse than they are because of the bleeding. Her pulse is steady – she's concussed but hopefully no worse than that.'

The others were out of the car and four greatcoats were handed down to him. The racket from the column of WAAF had subsided. He couldn't hear the dog snarling. Bloody animal should be put down.

He and Roy carefully tucked the coats under and over the unconscious girl. Where the hell was the woman in charge? Had someone found a house with a telephone to call the ambulance? Probably the base was where the closest telephone was.

'Freddie, stay with her.'

Satisfied he'd done as much as he could for the patient he stood up and turned to see if he and Roy could be any help to anyone else. Even limited medical knowledge was better than none in the circumstances.

'Jesus wept – this is worse than I thought.'

There were two seriously injured girls; these must be the ones the dog had mauled first, and they too were cocooned in greatcoats waiting for the ambulances to arrive. There were also half a dozen walking wounded being comforted as they sat on the kerb or leaned against the wall in tears, nursing their cuts and bruises.

He looked ahead and saw those who were unharmed marching briskly through the gates of the base. 'I've got first-aid training,' he said to the sergeant kneeling by one of the injured girls. 'Is there anything I can do?'

'No, sir, I carried a first-aid kit in my pack and we've done what we can. What about the girl under your car?'

'Concussion and a head wound but not critical. What happened to the dog?'

'One of the girls found a large stick and beat it off. It ran away, thank God.'

He leaned down and patted her on the shoulder and then returned to the patient he considered his concern.

6

From a distance Jane heard voices. She was cold. Her head hurt. Why was she lying in the road? With some difficulty she opened her eyes to see a face peering down at her.

'I'm Oscar Stanton. I almost ran over you. Keep still, help is on the way.'

Initially her vision had been blurred but slowly it cleared. She blinked a few times. The young man was a pilot, had strange blue-grey eyes and a mop of almost white curls.

'You look like an angel. I hope that's not a sign.' She managed a lopsided smile.

'Absolutely not. You're concussed, will need a few stitches in your cut, but nothing worse as far as we can see.'

His use of the plural made her move her eyes – moving her head wasn't feasible – it hurt too much. Not one, but six RAF airmen were surrounding her. She couldn't quite remember how she'd come to fall underneath the car but no doubt her memory would return when she didn't have such a shocking headache.

Had she told him her name? For some reason this seemed important. She couldn't remember it – but she did know her number. '472... 374.' Speaking was becoming more difficult. The light was hurting her eyes. She closed them and blackness swirled over her for a second time.

When she awoke, she was in an unfamiliar bed. It was far more comfortable than the one she'd used for the past two weeks. Where was she? She was about to open her eyes when a wave of nausea overwhelmed her. Unseen hands held a cold receptacle for her.

Eventually she came around without vomiting and her head, although painful, was no longer such agony. She desperately needed a pee. She daren't risk opening her eyes.

'Here you are. I'm going to slip a bedpan under your bottom.'

It arrived just in time to avoid an embarrassing accident.

'There, you'll feel better now. Lie still and then someone will come and give you a bed bath. You'll perk up no end after that.'

Jane would much rather have a cup of tea and some toast but didn't like to say so. At least she now knew she was in hospital. How long had she been there? More importantly, why couldn't she remember what had happened to cause her accident?

What she did know was that she was ACW 472374 – Jane Hadley. She thought she'd only been a WAAF for two weeks and already had required medical attention twice. First, she'd reacted badly to the inoculations and then had been run over. Why couldn't she remember how this second incident had occurred?

She opened her eyes and slowly turned her head, pleased it didn't send a shaft of agony through her any more. She was on her own in a small room. The curtains were drawn but she wasn't sure if this was to stop the light or because it was night-time.

As she dozed she recalled the face of a handsome young man – she couldn't remember his name but she was almost sure he'd told her what it was – he had wonderful, almost white curls and lovely blue-grey eyes. She thought she might have told him that he looked like an angel.

Then the image changed and *that man* glowered at her, his lips thin and his expression cruel. The stranger's face had metamorphosed into *that man's*. She jerked awake, forcing the unpleasant thoughts aside. Most men were the same and whatever her rescuer had looked like, he wasn't to be trusted.

A far too jolly nursing assistant rushed in carrying an enamel basin and plonked it down noisily beside her. 'I've come to give you your bed bath.'

'No thank you, I don't want one. I'm perfectly clean as I had a bath yesterday.'

The nurse shook her head. 'You didn't – it's not on your notes. If someone had given you a bed bath it would be written down here on the chart at the end of your bed.'

'How long have I been in hospital?'

'Three days. The accident was Monday and today's Thursday.'

'I'd no idea I'd been here so long. I suppose you'd better get on with it then.'

The flannel was hot in the middle and cold around the edges – quite horrid. The nurse was enthusiastic but inefficient and by the time she'd finished Jane was shivering and fearful she would get the dreaded bronchitis.

The nurse who'd arranged this torture bustled in, crisp white apron crackling as she walked. She didn't need to ask if Jane felt better for the experience. 'Good Lord, what did the wretched girl do this time? I'll fetch hot water bottles and extra blankets.'

Through chattering teeth Jane managed to speak. 'I'd love a cup of tea as well.'

It took an hour, three hot water bottles and two cups of tea for her to recover and feel warm again. She was just enjoying a slice of hot buttered toast when two porters came in.

'You carry on, love, we've come to move you to the ward. You'll be better in there, more cheerful like,' one of them said as he grabbed the end of the bed.

Still munching her toast – she wasn't giving that up for anyone – she was wheeled from the isolation room into the main ward. There were eight beds down each side of the long room, and a nurses' table at the far end and the sister's room behind that.

Her bed was pushed into an empty space halfway down the left-hand side. Immediately a nurse arrived at her side. 'I'm sorry, Miss Hadley, I have to confiscate your toast. The consultant will be making his round at any moment and wouldn't be impressed to find you eating toast at this time of the day.' She reached out to take the plate but Jane hastily moved it under the covers.

'I've not eaten for three days and I'm jolly well going to finish my toast. If the doctors don't like it then that's just too bad.' As soon as she'd spoken, she regretted it. What was happening to her? Her heart pounded but she didn't give up her precious toast.

Oscar couldn't get Aircraft Woman 472374, previously known as Miss Jane Hadley, out of his mind. There was something about her that appealed to him but he couldn't put his finger on it. Was it her vulnerability? She had an unloved air, too thin, and a haunted expression in her eyes. She was a girl who needed taking care of and he'd always been a sucker for a lame duck.

By the time the ambulance had arrived the six of them had decided to abandon their trip and return to base. Since then he'd enquired at the hospital and had been told that the patient was unconscious but stable.

He was determined to visit as soon as he was allowed to. He'd suffered from merciless teasing all his life for his ridiculous curls but she'd thought he'd looked like an angel. No one had ever compared him to a heavenly messenger and he was intrigued by her comment and wished to get to know her better.

Chamberlain had declared war on Germany weeks ago but so far nothing had changed – no marauding Luftwaffe had come to bomb Britain and people were carrying on pretty much as usual. The only action so far had been in the Atlantic and the *Royal Oak* had been sunk in Scapa Flow by U-boats a couple of weeks ago. There had also been an air attack, the first of the war, in Scotland but nobody had been hurt.

The only sorties his squadron had undertaken had been rehearsals for the real thing. They were all experienced flyers so would be ready when needed. His Hurricane wasn't as fast as a Spitfire but he loved it. He'd flown both and like everyone else preferred the Spit but was happy with his lot. The Hurricanes would be the workhorses when it came to a fight and the Spitfires would be the racehorses. Fast, but not as dependable.

Four days after the accident he had a free day as his kite was in for maintenance – landing gear wasn't working as it should – so he decided to drive over and visit the girl he couldn't stop thinking about. He'd not seen her at her best and wasn't even sure she was particularly attractive, more a 'plain Jane', but he was definitely intrigued.

The drive took him an hour as he'd got caught behind a convoy of army lorries. He enquired at reception for the ward Jane was in.

'It's not visiting time, sir, so you'll have to come back at two o'clock. Sister Reynolds won't countenance visitors outside of the designated times.'

'Thank you. I'll come back then.' He walked out but doubled back as soon as the woman was answering the telephone. He wasn't hanging about until then. He needed to be back before dark as driving in the blackout would be impossible. He'd not yet covered his headlights so the required pinprick of light was all that would be seen.

As he approached the ward he heard raised voices and increased his pace. He stopped in the entrance and his mouth curved. There were two nurses attempting to remove something from Jane's bed but she wasn't cooperating.

He moved swiftly to her side trying not to laugh. 'Can I be of assistance, Miss Hadley?'

'They want my toast but they're not having it. I've not eaten for days and I'm starving.'

The nurse in blue, obviously the woman in charge,

released her grip on the blue bedspread and turned to glare at him. 'This isn't visiting time. What are you doing in my ward?'

'I've come to see Miss Hadley. I heard the racket down the corridor. I don't think your consultant will be impressed.'

The sister's nostrils flared but she understood. 'Nurse Bennett, return to your duties.'

The other nurse reluctantly let go of the opposite side of the bedspread and slunk off, glaring over her shoulder at Jane, who was unrepentant.

'Thank you, whoever you are. I'll get on with my toast now.' Then without apparent embarrassment to be the centre of attention she pulled out a plate and tucked into the toast with enjoyment. There were no chairs – presumably visitors had to fetch their own and he wasn't going to push his luck by asking for one.

He was already *persona non grata* so might as well sit on the bed, which even he knew was frowned upon. 'I'm Oscar Stanton. I almost ran you over a few days ago.'

She looked up and smiled. Even with a bandage around her head, and bruising down the side of her face, that smile changed everything. How could he have thought her plain? She was quite beautiful when she smiled. Her hair, a deep chestnut, was loose around her shoulders and despite being too thin and knocked about, she looked like a film star from a Hollywood poster.

'I'm sorry, I did know who you were. I'm not comfortable talking to… to men of any sort. You shouldn't be in here – they already hate me and now my life will be even worse.'

'As you rightly say the damage is already done so there's no point in me leaving immediately.'

She looked down at her empty plate and frowned. 'If you really want to be useful, Mr Stanton, you would go and find me something else to eat and a cup of tea. There must be a canteen or café somewhere close by.'

'It's Flying Officer Stanton – didn't you notice my stripes?' He grinned and she nodded.

'Of course I did. In which case, I'll rephrase that. Would you be kind enough, sir, to fetch me some more toast and some tea.' She then sat bolt upright and saluted smartly.

He got to his feet and smiled down at her. 'ACW 472374, I should be delighted to go in search of your requirements.'

As he was strolling out of the ward he almost collided with a phalanx of white-coated doctors. 'Good God, is that you, young Oscar? I didn't know you were posted to Catterick.'

The speaker was his uncle, his mother's brother, whom he'd not seen for several years. 'Uncle Edward, I didn't know you were working here. Last time my mother spoke about you, you were at St Thomas's in London.'

They shook hands enthusiastically. 'Quite so, my boy, but this place is expanding rapidly to accommodate military personnel when necessary. I transferred here under duress, I can assure you. Now, explain yourself. What are you doing in my hospital?'

Jane's bravado had evaporated. It was quite unlike her to make a fuss as doing so always brought severe punishment from *that man*. She wished she'd not refused to give up her breakfast and that she hadn't antagonised the nursing staff as they could make her life a misery.

Maybe she could discharge herself and get away from any unpleasantness? The nurse had rushed to her bed and quickly straightened the counterpane and taken away her empty plate. There were voices outside. The consultant must be coming in.

She was tempted to pretend to be asleep but decided against it. She wanted to know when she could leave and rejoin her unit. A consultant was God around here and if she hoped to escape then she had to convince him she was well enough to go.

A small army of doctors as well the woman in charge of the ward, and an even more formidable lady who was probably the matron, approached the first bed. Curtains were drawn around the patient. If she hadn't been so terrified she would have laughed. There were so many in the small space that the curtains around the bed bulged alarmingly.

The same process was repeated twice more before the group arrived at her side. She braced herself.

'Ah, Miss Hadley, I must say that you look a lot better than you did last time I saw you. My nephew has told me what happened and the nurse is making you some tea and toast. I can't have my patients fading away from lack of sustenance.'

The consultant didn't look anything like Flying Officer Stanton but she assumed he was referring to him. Why didn't doctors introduce themselves? They had an unfair advantage knowing everything about the patient and the patient knowing nothing about them.

'I'm feeling much better, thank you. I want to get back to my unit. I've only been in the WAAF for two weeks and am missing out on crucial training by being in here.'

'My dear young lady, you sustained a serious head injury. You only regained consciousness this morning. You will be here under my auspices for another week at least. It doesn't do to take chances with head injuries.'

'I see. Thank you for taking care of me.'

'My job, my dear, and my pleasure.' He turned to the sister who was taking notes. 'Miss Hadley can be assisted to the lavatory when required but mustn't attempt the journey on her own.'

Jane's cheeks burned. It was humiliating being talked about as if she wasn't there. The consultant and his entourage of junior doctors moved on. A tray arrived with the promised toast and tea whilst the ward round was still in progress.

Half an hour later they left the ward and the RAF officer returned. He strode in as if he had every right to be there and to her astonishment the sister smiled and a student nurse rushed off to fetch him a chair.

'I managed to find you two sticky buns and a cheese sandwich. However, I can see that you've already had something else to eat.'

'I have, but I would really like whatever you've managed to find. What a bit of luck that the consultant was your uncle – I shudder to think what might have happened to me if he hadn't been a relative of yours.'

'As a matter of fact, I think even without my intervention he would have been on your side. He thought you fighting over your toast was funny.'

'I'm not usually so assertive – in fact the opposite. I'm sure if you smile nicely at the nurse, she will fetch you a cup of tea too and then we can share the buns.'

He swivelled on his chair to catch the eye of the girl and this gave her a few moments to study him without being observed. His eyes were almost exactly the same colour as his uniform. It was his hair that made him so memorable. Ash blond curls should have looked strange on a man but they just enhanced his good looks.

'Do you still think I'm an angel?' He'd turned back so suddenly that he'd caught her staring.

'I'm quite certain I didn't tell you that I thought you were an angel. If I remember rightly, I said that you looked like an angel, which is quite different.'

'My oldest sister, Olivia, has straight brown hair and has never forgiven me for having what she always refers to as "her curls".'

The tea arrived and there was another cup for her as well. She received several baleful glances from the women on either side of her who weren't getting such treats.

The sticky bun was scrumptious and she couldn't remember eating anything with such enjoyment before. Maybe being deprived of food for three days had restored her missing appetite.

'I'm surprised you haven't been turfed out of here. I think it will be lunchtime soon and now I'm so full of bun and toast I won't be able to eat it.'

The woman in the bed next to her overheard this comment – in fact had probably overheard every comment as the beds were so close together.

'You won't be missing much, love – you're better off eating toast and buns.'

Jane smiled at her. 'There's a cheese sandwich left over. Would you like it?'

The woman beamed and held out her hand. Oscar handed it over. 'Thanks, love, just what the doctor ordered.'

'Thank you for coming to see me and fetching me the food. I'm sorry that I fell under your car wheels in so dramatic a fashion. Do you know how the two girls are, the ones who were so savagely attacked? I saw this before I got knocked down.'

'I don't, but I'll find out for you when I leave and will inform you when I come and visit again.'

She was about to tell him not to bother but said something else entirely. 'I look forward to that. I don't suppose you're very busy at the moment as nothing's happening. Do you have any of us on your base?'

'A few girls arrived last month but we're expecting a lot more. They will release the airmen for more urgent duties and the WAAF will be a godsend once things get going.'

There was a rattle of a trolley approaching and the unmistakable whiff of overcooked cabbage. 'That's your lunch arriving, Jane. I'd better go. Don't want to push my luck. I've got permission from Uncle Edward to visit in the mornings if I can get away. Hopefully, my kite won't be functional tomorrow and I can come again.'

He picked up the chair, smiled and nodded, and then was gone. He was a charming young man, handsome and an officer, so why on earth did he want to visit *her* again?

7

Oscar, as promised, went in search of information about the two girls who were bitten by the dog. He was relieved to discover they had been discharged already.

On the drive back he scarcely noticed the passing scenery as his head was full of images of Jane. Even after spending so short a time in her company he wanted to get to know her better. He wasn't sure how tall she was but he thought she would come up to his shoulder. Not many girls did as he was over six feet tall.

He'd worried that he'd be too large to fit into the confined cockpit of a fighter plane but, as his height was in his legs and not his body, he'd been considered an acceptable size. A pilot had to be able to eject safely and get in and out of the cockpit at speed – and a couple of his friends were now bomber pilots because not only were they as tall as him, but they were also much broader in the shoulder.

Fortunately, his kite was still unavailable the following day so he was given permission to leave the base for the morning. Twice his car skidded on the icy road and he considered himself lucky to arrive at the hospital in one piece.

He parked and then went in search of a bakery so he had something to give her. If the hospital food was as bad as the other patient had said, buns and cakes would be more popular than flowers. It took all his charm and powers of persuasion to be able to purchase three sausage rolls, two sticky buns and another cheese sandwich. Jane would have ample to share with her neighbours.

Uncle Edward had told him he wasn't discharging her for at least a week. This meant he had a captive audience as once she was at Pannal Ash he might not have the opportunity to meet with her. He'd asked one of the girls stationed at Catterick how long basic training lasted and had been told Jane might well only be there for a couple of weeks before being sent to her permanent posting. It was highly unlikely he would be lucky enough to have her on his base.

He walked into the ward and nodded at the sister busy scribbling at her desk. This time she smiled, albeit a little frostily. He looked across at the bed where Jane should be and it was empty, neatly made. For a second his heart plummeted to his boots.

Then common sense returned. If anything had happened the nurse wouldn't be smiling at him. The empty bed was the one next to hers. However, this too was empty but not made up for a new patient. She must have gone to the bog.

There was a chair beside the bed, so he was expected. He glanced at the large wall clock at the end of the ward and saw there was another hour before Uncle Edward would make his rounds. He moved the chair so he could watch the doors.

He stood up as she came in escorted by not one, but two nurses. From her expression she wasn't too happy about this. She smiled at him. 'Good morning, Flying Officer

Stanton, I didn't really expect you so early but I'm glad you're here.'

'Good show, I've brought you rations. Thought you would prefer this to flowers or chocolate.'

'Absolutely spiffing. The only thing edible in here is the toast as the nurses make it in a little kitchen just outside the ward themselves.'

Only then did he notice she wasn't wearing her own nightwear, was barefoot, and two hospital gowns did the duty of a dressing gown. Why the devil hadn't someone brought in what she needed?

She hopped into bed, nodded her thanks to the nurses, and pulled the covers up. 'I'm tickety-boo and going to insist that they let me go. Someone from my new posting visited yesterday and said the medic is happy to remove my sutures so that's no obstacle to my leaving.'

The tea trolley trundled in and once it had moved on, he handed over the bag of goodies. 'This should keep you going.' She peered inside the brown paper bag and beamed.

'Perfect. There's enough here for me and Irene, the lady on the other side of me.' Her cheeks turned a becoming shade of pink as she nodded at her hospital gowns. 'Dreadful, aren't they? I don't own either slippers or a dressing gown.' Something flashed in her eyes and he thought it might be disappointment. 'The three girls I got friendly with were posted to Ash Vale and I don't know anyone else well enough to ask them to go through my kit and find what I want. The hospital has supplied me with a toothbrush and comb. That'll have to do until I leave.'

'You look much better than you did yesterday. I know

my uncle said you had to stay here for another week but I think he might change his mind when he sees you today.'

They talked like old friends. She asked intelligent questions about his duties as a pilot and he asked her what trade she intended to apply for.

'I don't know, but by the time I get out I expect decisions will have been made. I haven't been able to tell my friends at Ash Vale what happened, but it's probably better they aren't worried about me.'

This time he decided to leave before Uncle Edward appeared – didn't want to push his luck. 'I'll come tomorrow if I can...'

'No, please don't. I've already been asked twice if you're my young man. We only met by accident and we hardly know each other.'

'I thought we were getting on really well. Do you have someone special?'

'Absolutely not. I don't want to get involved with anyone; I want to concentrate on doing my bit for the war effort.'

'I see. I was just hoping I could take you to the pictures, for a drink or a meal somewhere – nothing serious – just friends.'

She shook her head. 'That's very kind of you, but I'm going to be far too busy for anything like that.' She offered her hand. 'Goodbye, Flying Officer Stanton, I do appreciate how kind you've been. Take care of yourself.'

He had no option but to shake the extended hand. 'If you change your mind, Jane, you know where to find me. Good luck, and I hope you're out of here soon.'

He walked away wishing things could be different.

Probably for the best as she'd be posted away in a week or two and there'd be no opportunity to meet again.

He turned at the door to wave but she was reading and not looking his way.

Jane counted to a hundred before putting her book down. She couldn't have been reading it even if she'd wanted to as it was upside down. When he'd taken her hand for a few seconds she'd allowed herself to imagine what things could have been like if it hadn't been for *that man*. The touch of his skin against hers had made her heart beat faster. It didn't matter, as it was unlikely they could meet again even if they'd wanted to.

The consultant duly arrived and pronounced her recovery remarkable and agreed that she could rejoin her fellow recruits as long as she avoided doing anything strenuous until her stitches were removed. The bandage was replaced by a more discreet dressing and she was ready to go.

Two hours later she was standing outside the hospital in her uniform waiting for the taxi. Her arrival several days later than the others wasn't ideal. She was directed to her new dormitory and spent an age looking in all the lockers until she discovered an empty one, so knew that this neatly stacked bed would be hers for the next week or two.

Her kitbag was already there and she quickly unpacked. She'd been told that she could spend the day getting familiar with her surroundings and didn't have to report for duty until the following morning. As she wasn't to do anything remotely interesting she expected to be given office duties of some sort.

This dormitory was on the ground floor of the three-floored building. The room held thirty beds and was even colder than the previous one she'd shared with only six others. The ablutions, as they were known in the services, were in a separate block. She just hoped she didn't need to use the loo at night as it would require getting dressed in order to do so. There were spiral staircases linking the billets but she didn't go up them to investigate.

The recreation room had to be warmer than here so she went in search of it, her stationery folder and cloth bag of irons clutched in one hand and her bag of edibles in the other. She was going to write to Charlotte and tell her what had happened. Flying Officer Stanton would be omitted from her story.

The mess hall was vast and deserted. The appetising smell of beef stew lingered and her stomach rumbled. Thank goodness she had her bag of buns and sandwiches.

There were dozens of uniformed women criss-crossing the central hall but none of them spoke to her. Why should they? She was a stranger to them and no doubt they thought she was equally busy.

She followed the sound of chattering and laughter to the recreation room which was, thankfully, half full of women of all shapes and sizes, the only common denominator the fact that they were in the same grey-blue uniform.

Immediately someone called out to her. 'Over here – you must be the other walking wounded.' The girl who'd spoken had an arm in a sling and several sticking plasters on her face and neck. Beside her was another girl similarly covered but with both arms free.

'Hello, I'm Jane Hadley. I can't tell you how pleased I am to escape from hospital and join you here.'

'I'm Daphne Smith, this is Jenny Read. You came off worst and it wasn't even the dog that hurt you.'

She sat down next to them, eager to discover exactly what she would have to do once she was cleared for duty.

'I think we're only here for them to break our spirits completely,' Jenny said with a rueful smile. 'Fiona, she's in our dormitory, spent the past five days cleaning the toilets. There are eighty of them and they all have to be shiny bright. She said she even has to put her arm round the U-bend. The wooden seats have to shine.'

Daphne joined in gleefully. 'She also has to scrub the floors and wash down the doors – every day!'

'Good grief! What else are they doing?'

'Peeling potatoes, working in the laundry, sweeping floors and polishing furniture – in fact they're nothing better than skivvies.'

'No drill? I rather enjoyed that.'

'Oh yes, rain, snow or shine they do an hour every morning after breakfast and before they start their menial tasks.' Daphne laughed. 'I never thought I'd be glad to be bitten by a dog, but I'd much rather be sitting here in the warm than doing what the others are.'

'Haven't you been given light duties?'

They both shook their heads. 'No, just told to remain in here,' Jenny said.

'I wonder how long this will go on. I can't see that we're helping the war effort at the moment,' Jane replied.

'One of the other girls said next week we get allocated to

a particular branch of the service and then the specialised, intensive training begins.'

'Do we get a choice?'

'We're interviewed and the bigwigs decide what they think we're suited for. Didn't you fill in a form saying what you wanted when you signed up?' Daphne joined in the conversation.

'I did. I asked for radio or wireless operator. Our stitches come out before then so I expect we're not going to escape entirely from having to do the horrible jobs.' She held up her paper bag. 'I'm absolutely starving and have missed my lunch. Can I share these with you?' She carefully tore open the bag so they could see the contents.

'Golly, what a treat. I'll see if I can rustle up some tea to go with them. Give me your mugs, ladies.' Jenny rushed off and returned triumphantly bearing a tray with three steaming mugs.

After sharing the goodies with her new friends Jane began to relax. She eventually found the time to write a quick letter and put her last stamp on the envelope.

'I think I saw a post box in the hall. I'll just pop this in. I want to let the girls I shared with before know what happened.'

This time she wasn't going to offer any personal details, become too friendly, as this would make it easier when they were separated at the end of next week.

Three days later she reported before breakfast to the medical officer to have her stitches taken out and was declared fit for duty. She dreaded what she might be given to do and was right to be apprehensive. Her assignment was to clean the billet, including the linoleum that covered the spiral staircase.

A particularly nasty WAAF officer hauled her into the office after she'd finished. 'It just will not do, young woman. If you don't want to be put on a charge you must perform better than this. You've been lazing about for a week and there's no excuse for such poor work. The stairs are a disgrace. You will be kept on fatigue duty indefinitely if you don't buck up your ideas.'

Jane saluted smartly and marched out feeling sick. She didn't want to get into any more trouble; she'd worked incredibly hard and was confident no one could have done any better.

The next day she applied double the amount of polish to the linoleum and was satisfied that even this fussy officer couldn't find fault with the shine. She was just finishing the bottom step when she heard voices and footsteps approaching along the corridor above her.

Her work was being inspected by the officer and her NCOs. Hastily she jumped to her feet and gathered up her rags and so on, not wishing to be seen on her knees when they appeared above her. Suddenly there was a shriek, followed by crashes and thumps.

She dodged into the nearby broom cupboard and watched through a slit in the door as the officer appeared at speed on her backside, the NCOs skidding down behind their superior. As Jane watched in horror, expecting to be discovered and put on a charge at any moment, the officer stood up, put her cap back on, adjusted her tunic and marched off.

Revenge was sweet – but she was relieved no one had been seriously hurt by her over-industrious application of polish.

The next ten days were spent performing similar, numbingly boring activities. Eventually the morning arrived when they would be interviewed and then allocated their trade.

Oscar was involved with his squadron leader planning mock sorties. As dogfights would often be conducted when flying upside down, pilots had to learn to handle their kites under all circumstances. The G-force when climbing steeply at full throttle or diving when upside down made one's head spin and one could lose consciousness for a few seconds.

He tried to push Jane from his thoughts but she constantly intruded at the most inconvenient moments. He couldn't understand why he'd become so obsessed with a girl he scarcely knew. He must try harder to forget her as he was unlikely to see her again.

The more they practised the less likely they were to be shot down on their first real sortie. They'd all had to undergo parachute training before getting their wings – he hoped to God that he'd never have to use this knowledge.

Two weeks after meeting Jane he heard that the NAAFI were putting on a dance to welcome the new WAAF who'd just arrived at the base.

'Roy, do you know if invites have been sent to Ash Vale and Pannal Ash? There're hundreds of men here and only about thirty girls – we could do with more if this dance is going to be enjoyable.'

'Good thinking, old boy. I think we could arrange

to collect a couple of coachloads and then return them afterwards. Of course, it all depends if they can get leave of absence.'

'I shouldn't think any of them are needed at night – there's damn all happening on the home front.'

The two of them headed to the admin office and spoke to the adjutant. He assured them that invitations had been extended to both places and that the COs had agreed that any girl who wished to attend could do so.

'You hoping Jane will come? You were rather taken with her, weren't you?'

'I was – in fact I still am. I hope she comes, but somehow I doubt she will.'

'Surely, all girls like to dance?'

'Not this one. I think she's very young, inexperienced and innocent. Probably just left a select girls' boarding school and is finding real life a bit of a challenge.'

'Bloody hell! You think she might be only eighteen years old? That would make you a cradle snatcher, old boy.'

'A bit of an exaggeration, Roy. I'm twenty-three not thirty-three. Anyway, whether she comes or not I'm looking forward to a bit of female company. Sodding about doing very little whilst waiting for the things to start is getting on my nerves.'

'Crikey, old boy, enjoy a quiet life whilst you can. Once it begins, we might have no life at all.'

'That's a depressing thought. You're right, Roy; I'll appreciate today and not anticipate tomorrow.' He'd not been entirely honest with his friend as the only female company he wanted was that of the lovely girl who'd somehow embedded herself in his heart.

*

On the evening of the event all the bods were in their best bib and tucker – buttons polished to a high shine and immaculate shirts and ties. The NAAFI girls had managed to find a few dozen balloons, which were festooned around the walls making it look quite jolly.

Catterick was fortunate as they had their own band. Once things got going on the military front it was highly likely the members would be separated as they were posted elsewhere. But tonight, and hopefully for the next few weeks, they had their own live music.

The resident WAAF were already in the room, clumped together in giggling groups, waiting to be asked to dance once the music started. This shindig wasn't restricted to officers only but open to everyone. He expected there to be a lot of beer consumed and several lower ranks appearing on charges of being drunk and disorderly tomorrow.

There must be over a hundred boys in blue milling about, glancing expectantly at the double doors, waiting to see if the promised influx of extra females turned up. There was a ripple of excitement and he couldn't stop himself turning to look along with everyone else.

The room was invaded by sixty or more girls of all shapes and sizes. He scanned the throng and picked Jane out immediately. She was hovering towards the back of the group, looking nervous and uncomfortable. Being half a head taller than most of them, she'd been easy to spot.

He shouldered his way through the eager press of airmen trying to grab themselves a partner for the first dance, which was going to be a Glenn Miller number from the sound of it. He reached her side as three others were about to pounce.

Her face was white, her eyes wide as she looked from side to side for a way of escaping. 'Excuse me, gentlemen, Miss Hadley is with me.' He moved swiftly putting himself between the would-be partners and herself.

'Oscar, that's the third time you've rescued me. Thank you. I can't tell you how pleased I am to see you.'

8

Jane had been reluctant to accompany the others to Catterick, not just because she didn't want to see Oscar again but because the thought of being surrounded by eager young airmen filled her with horror.

When the coach had arrived she'd wanted to remain on it but had no option but to follow the other chattering, excited girls into the building. Immediately she was overwhelmed by the noise, the brightness, the press of unfamiliar people.

She was panicking, her head pounding, when Oscar barged through the group of hopeful young men trying to claim her hand for a dance and, with his bulk, protected her from further pestering. She'd never been so glad to see anyone in her life, despite her earlier reluctance to meet him.

'Jane, let's get out of here until things have calmed down a bit. I'll take you to the mess – it's likely to be empty at the moment.'

He put his arm lightly around her shoulders and guided her out of the mass. The further she got from the crowd the better she felt.

'I'm not an officer. I can't go in there and I don't want to get you into trouble.'

He chuckled. He was walking beside her, not touching

her; he seemed to understand she didn't like physical contact. 'Tonight's different, Jane, no one will complain. I should think you won't be the only WAAF invited to have a gin and it or a sweet sherry.'

'I don't drink alcohol.' This sounded very abrupt so she qualified her statement. 'I should say that I've never drunk alcohol, which is different I suppose.'

'I expect they have ginger beer or lemonade. You could always try a shandy – a gentle introduction to the world of drink.'

He'd whisked her so quickly through the building that she scarcely had time to look around her. It smelled different to her base – a definite masculine odour made up of tobacco, beer, and something else she couldn't identify. She sniffed and then smiled.

'Engine oil.'

'Excuse me?'

'That's what I can smell.' She turned her head and breathed in next to his shoulder. 'Yes, you definitely have the aroma of engine oil but not tobacco. Don't you smoke like everyone else?'

'I tried cigarettes, pipe and cigars but didn't like the taste. It's supposed to be good for you, open your lungs, calm you down or something – but I'd rather have a pint of beer if I want to relax.'

The Officers' Mess had a bar at one end, a dartboard, half a dozen leather armchairs and several tables with battered wooden chairs around them. Hardly luxurious, but she didn't suppose the young men cared about such things.

There were three other occupants leaning on the bar deep in conversation. All had gold braid and many stripes – they must be very senior officers. She froze and was prepared to back out before they saw her intruding.

'Don't worry about them. The one with dark hair and grey temples is our wing commander, Jack Sugden – he's a good bloke and won't mind you being in here. One of the other two is the adjutant, Bill Jones, and I've no idea who the third one is – he must be a visitor.'

He ignored his superiors and guided her to the comfortable chairs, which fortunately were at the opposite end to the bar. 'Take a pew, Jane. I'll get the drinks.'

He strode away, full of confidence, and she envied him. It must be so much easier being a man – being in charge – being able to... She pushed the unwelcome thoughts aside. That part of her life was over and she was never going to put herself in danger of being abused again.

She settled into the chair, pleased that the deep seat and high sides almost concealed her. With luck no one would know she was there. Oscar was talking to the three men at the bar and he hadn't saluted; in fact was addressing them as if they were friends. Hadn't he said that tonight everyone was mixing together at the dance?'

She closed her eyes and forced her fingers to unclench. The faint sound of lively music drifted down the corridor. There must be a band and she'd never heard one of those. Maybe she could go back if she had him beside her and he promised not to let strangers drag her onto the dance floor.

'Here you are, Sleeping Beauty, a very weak shandy. I've also brought you neat lemonade in case you don't like it.'

'Thank you, I wasn't asleep I was just listening to the music. I panicked rather at all the people, at the men trying to grab my arm. I'm not used to crowds and I've never been to a dance.'

'I thought as much.' He was looking at her in a peculiar fashion, his amazing eyes narrowed, with a very intense expression. 'I know you said you didn't want to get to know me better but if I give you my word that I'll not be anything but a friend, do you think you could bring yourself to come out with me occasionally?'

The tight band around her chest vanished. 'I'd like that. But sadly, we're going to be sent to our next posting for training the day after tomorrow. So I doubt that we'll get the opportunity before I go.'

'Then we'll make the most of tonight. After that, could I persuade you to write to me?'

'I'm not sure how that will work. Isn't your squadron likely to be moved at some point?'

'I'm certain that we will be, but not for the next few weeks. I'd hoped you would come tonight and so have written down my number and details. All you need to put on the envelope is my name, number and Catterick RAF base and it will find me.'

She took it and slipped it into one of the many pockets on her uniform jacket. The shandy was quite palatable and she took a second sip. 'I like this, thank you. This is what I'll ask for if I ever go into a bar again.'

'You didn't answer my question. Are you going to keep in contact?'

She hesitated, not sure if she was ready to be closer to anyone. Then her confidence returned. It would be perfectly safe writing to him as long as they didn't meet too often. Being with him in person was far too unsettling. 'I certainly will write. I've never been alone with a gentleman and only left my boarding school in July. I must seem like a silly little girl to you.'

His smile was warm and not at all threatening. 'I worked that out for myself, Jane.' He paused and raised an eyebrow in a comical fashion. 'I'm assuming I have your permission to use your first name.'

She nodded. 'I don't suppose you'd take any notice if I did say no. It's very disconcerting being on first-name terms with a man I didn't know two weeks ago.'

'If you don't mind me asking, what made you join up?'

'I wasn't happy at home and this gave me the opportunity to leave.' Even telling him so little made her feel sick. Nobody else must ever know exactly what had happened to her – it was too humiliating.

'Okay, I won't press you for more details. Do you have any siblings?'

'Only child. What about you?'

'I have two sisters, both older than me, both married with nippers of their own. My dad's a vicar – he was horrified when I chose to join the RAF after Oxford. He doesn't approve of violence of any sort, however justified it might appear.'

'Is he a pacifist? There was a girl at school who was a Quaker and she was anti-war. I understand how they feel but sometimes you just have to fight back. Good versus evil – or something like that.'

Oscar nodded. 'The Nazis have given us no option. Appeasement didn't work – Hitler wants to conquer the world and we just can't let him do that. My brothers-in-law will get called up eventually – they are in their thirties so not too old to do their bit.'

'I was wondering, what made you choose to be a pilot?'

'I was always fascinated by flight. I was left a hundred pounds by a great-aunt and used it to pay for flying lessons. I already had my licence when I joined so my training was shorter than it might have been. That's why I've been promoted already.'

'Did you know that they don't have officer training in the WAAF? I suppose you had to go away somewhere to become one.'

'All pilots are officers – at least they were before the outbreak of war. I think they'll have to take other ranks eventually as there just won't be enough flyers otherwise.' The mortality rate for aircrew was likely to be high but best not to dwell on that.

He noticed that her foot was tapping in time to the distant music. 'Do you know how to dance?'

'I do, we had lessons at school. But as I was tall, I always had to be the man so I've no idea of the steps for a woman.'

'No problem.' He was about to *tell* her to accompany him but then reconsidered. 'Would you like to dance with me? If, when we get there, you don't feel comfortable then we'll come back here.'

'Can I take my drink? What exactly is a shandy? It's really quite delicious.'

'Lemonade and bitter – that's beer – not too strong.' He stood up and offered his hand and to his surprise she took it. It seemed small and delicate in his. 'Probably better to finish our drinks as we can't dance with them in our hands and if we put them down some blighter will take them.'

He drained his pint and she did the same with her shandy. He'd released his hold as soon as she'd been on her feet. For some reason she was wary of being touched and he didn't want to scare her away.

The noise from the temporary dance floor washed over them as they approached and he expected her to shrink back but the reverse was true. She looked up at him, her eyes bright, her cheeks flushed with excitement. 'I hope you don't regret this, Oscar – I think I'm very likely to tread all over your toes.'

'I'm looking forward to the experience, crushed toes or not.' He was about to pay her a compliment but reconsidered. Telling her she was the most beautiful girl in the room might put her off. It was going to be bloody difficult keeping her at arm's length when the more time he spent with her the more he wanted to kiss her.

They arrived at an opportune moment as the band began to play a waltz. She came willingly into his arms and he moved them smoothly onto the floor. For the first few moments she was stiff and unresponsive then gradually softened and began to follow his lead.

Soon they were twirling around the floor like professionals. He'd always been an expert dancer but had never enjoyed the experience as much as he was now. He risked drawing her closer and she looked up and smiled at him.

'I think you must be an expert to be able to make it seem so easy.'

Was she a mind reader? 'It helps that we're the perfect

height for each other. Don't look now, but we're gathering a lot of attention.'

To his astonishment she laughed, turning even more heads in their direction. He tightened his hold so every inch of her was pressed against his body. They dipped and swayed in perfect harmony and he was disappointed when the dance finished.

There was a spontaneous round of applause and she hid her face against his shoulder as he walked her to the edge of the room. 'They're going to play something different from the sound of it. I don't suppose you know how to do the Charleston?'

'Actually, I do. It might have been an all-girls establishment but our dance teacher wasn't at all stuffy.'

'Then, shall we give it a go?'

She glanced down at her uniform and pulled a face. 'I think my skirt's too tight to do it justice, but I'll do my best.'

The band struck up a lively number. He'd no idea of the title, but it had an American flavour suitable for dancing the Charleston. He'd spent a few months in the States after leaving university and before joining the RAF and had learnt the moves when he was there.

The floor was only half full now as those who didn't know this modern dance moved to the edges to watch those who did. It was energetic, great fun; it didn't really matter if you didn't get the steps right as long as you were in time to the music.

One thing he did remember was that swivelling the feet was essential. Jane knew exactly what to do and was better than he was. After a few minutes, others joined in copying the basic moves and there was a lot of handwaving, feet swivelling and laughing.

He'd never seen her really laugh – he didn't think she did a great deal of it. Maybe one day she'd tell him why she was so wary.

Red-faced and sweating, they staggered from the floor in search of a drink. 'Let's go back to the Mess. It'll take too long to get a drink in here. I'm shattered – I'd forgotten how exhausting that dance was.'

She mopped her face with her handkerchief and then wriggled her hips in an attempt to get her skirt to return to the place it should be. During their performance she'd pulled it up above her knees so she could move more freely.

'I hope I don't get put on a charge for interfering with my uniform.' The wriggling had failed to achieve her objective but it was doing nothing for his self-control. She reached down and grabbed the offending hem and pulled it back in place. 'There, that's better. Come on, Flying Officer Stanton, don't dither about here. I need my shandy.'

He grabbed her hand and they ran through the building, dodging past those who were travelling at a more sensible speed, and burst into the bar. Fortunately, his superior officers were no longer there and the place was now much busier.

'There are a couple of seats over there at that table. Why don't you grab them whilst I get the drinks?'

Jane flopped into a chair, her pulse still racing from all that jumping about. She couldn't remember ever having had such a wonderful time or being so happy. She straightened and all desire to smile vanished. She'd never been happy – not once in her entire life – even before the mistreatment began.

She'd deliberately chosen a chair that left her with her back to him but now she swivelled. He was waiting patiently to be served behind several other like-minded officers. Somehow, he sensed that she was looking in his direction and smiled. She couldn't stop herself reciprocating.

He really was a handsome man, but more importantly he was kind, funny and for some miraculous reason appeared to be interested in her. Would it be such a bad thing to get close to him? What would he expect her to do? She knew nothing about what went on between a man and a woman in the privacy of their bedroom and didn't want to know.

She'd seen courting couples walking along holding hands, seen a young man with his arm around his girlfriend, had even seen the shadowy shapes of two figures kissing in the doorway of a shop – but there was more to it than that.

She fiddled with her buttons, flustered by her thoughts, and decided however much she liked Oscar she wouldn't allow him to get any closer. She would be safer keeping her distance. Most men couldn't be trusted – she'd learnt that very early on in her life.

When he returned with the promised drinks, she'd recovered her composure but her short-lived happiness had gone, to be replaced by her usual feeling of unease when in company.

'Sorry I took so long, but I got us each a pint – then I won't have to queue up a second time.'

She nodded her thanks and buried her face in the glass. She drank several large mouthfuls with enjoyment.

'This is quite delicious. Thank you so much for getting it for me. I could really do with a sandwich – I was too nervous to eat my tea and haven't had anything since lunchtime.'

'There's no food available at this shindig but I'm certain I've got something edible in my room.'

She couldn't prevent her look of horror. Instead of being surprised he laughed out loud.

'Good God, I'm not suggesting you come with me. Wait here, you'll be perfectly safe as there are already at least a dozen girls in here. I can promise you no one will bother you whilst I'm gone.' He pointed to his beer. 'Guard that with your life. Thieving blighters in here will take it if they get half a chance.'

He didn't wait for her response but dashed off, threading his way through the crowd, and then he disappeared from sight. No one had ever done anything just for her. All she'd said was that she was hungry and he'd rushed off to find her something to eat. The music had stopped so the band must be taking a break too.

Two inebriated young officers were eyeing the beer. She drew it close to her shandy and glared at them. They laughed and wandered off. The babble of conversation washed over her head. She didn't feel isolated, but part of the group. Her uniform was the same as theirs. Her lips curved. She was now part of a family, a group of strangers, but they were all linked by the blue-grey that they wore.

'Wake up, sleepyhead, I've brought you sustenance,' Oscar said as he dropped into the seat adjacent to hers.

She didn't open her eyes. 'I'm not asleep. I'll have you know I'm thinking deep and meaningful thoughts. Not something you do very often, I assume.'

His rich, baritone chuckle made her look at him. 'Excellent. I have two cheese sandwiches, two apples and two – I'm not sure exactly what they are – but I think they were once sausage rolls.'

Her eyes widened. 'Where did you find all that? I don't believe for one minute that you had this in your billet. Who have you stolen it from?'

His eyes were dancing and he leaned over and put his finger on his lips in an exaggerated fashion. 'Loose lips lose lives – or something daft like that. I nipped round to the NAAFI and called in a favour from one of the girls in the kitchen.'

The impromptu meal was perfect and so was the shandy. 'Thank you so much for that. Much better than being poked in the eye with a burnt stick.'

'I've not heard that one before. Can I persuade you to dance with me again or have you had enough for tonight? I'm quite happy to sit here and talk to you if that's what you prefer.'

'Actually, I need the ladies' room before I do anything else. I suppose I've got to go outside to find the ablutions.'

'I'll take you to the one the girls in the office use. I doubt anyone else will know about it.'

He gave her directions and said he would wait for her in the passageway. The adjutant's offices where the admin WAAF worked had been in darkness and she'd been given strict instructions to turn the lights off when she left.

As she was plunged into darkness, she heard footsteps approaching. Her hair stood on end and she was paralysed with fear.

9

Oscar had been hanging about for some time waiting for Jane to appear from the offices when his CO called him over.

'Just heard I've been told to form another flight. This will bring the squadron up to full strength. The new chaps arrive tomorrow. You're being promoted to Flight Lieutenant and will take it over. Roy will be your second in command. These chaps are recently qualified and need knocking into fighting shape.'

'That's good news, Skip. I didn't expect to be promoted quite so soon. I won't let you down – I'm ready for this.'

'Good show. I knew I could count on you. Piece of cake for someone with your experience. Unfortunately, they won't all have their own kites initially but will have to share what we have. Let's hope the balloon doesn't go up before we're ready.'

'The Luftwaffe have far more trained pilots than us and actual battle experience. If Hitler started bombing Britain now, we'd not be ready.'

'None of that negative talk, Stanton. We'll be ready and will defeat the Huns when it comes to a fight.'

'Yes, sir, I'm sure you're correct. Excuse me, but I should

be meeting a young lady outside the office. Can't think why she's been gone so long.'

As he approached the corridor where the offices were located he saw someone ahead of him. He recognised the figure. It was Humphrey – a blighter he didn't like. Had a rotten reputation with the ladies. Had he seen Jane go down there unescorted?

He increased his pace and was running as he hurtled around the corner. This end of the passage was in darkness. Where the hell was Humphrey? Jane screamed.

He was at her side in seconds and grabbed her attacker by the shoulder, swung him around and punched him in the face. The blow sent him crashing to the floor.

'Are you okay, Jane? Did he hurt you?'

She ran past him without answering, her head lowered. He could hear her crying. He was about to go after her when he was struck a glancing blow on his jaw. The blighter had got up. A right hook finished the job. He'd been boxing champion for his school.

The racket had attracted unwanted attention and there were people coming to investigate. Officers fighting was a court martial offence. Too late to avoid the inevitable. Humphrey was out cold.

The CO and adjutant rushed around the corner. 'Good God, Stanton, have you killed the bastard?'

'No, sir, just knocked him out. I'll face the music later. I need to find Miss Hadley.'

'Someone's taking care of her. Poor girl. Disgraceful behaviour from one of my men. Not the first time either. I'll have his stripes for this and get him posted elsewhere.'

'Am I not to go on a charge?'

The CO shook his head. 'Absolutely not. Just glad you got there in time. Would have done the same myself. Go and find your young lady, and offer my sincere apologies for her unfortunate experience.'

Oscar hurried off to search for Jane but couldn't find her. After an hour he abandoned the attempt and decided he'd had enough jollity for one night. He would get leave of absence and drive to Pannal Ash tomorrow and speak to her. She wouldn't be posted out until late afternoon at the earliest. His orderly was waiting to speak to him.

'I've put your stripes on your jackets, sir. If you'll give me that one, I'll do it too.' He pointed to an envelope on the chest of drawers. 'This came for you a while ago.'

He shrugged out of his jacket and handed it over before picking up the note. When Brown had gone, he perched on the bed and opened it.

Dear Flying Officer Stanton,

A taxi has been called for me. Thank you for coming to my rescue again. I am unhurt thanks to your timely arrival.

I have changed my mind and do not wish to stay in touch.

Yours sincerely,

Miss Jane Hadley

No point in going to see her now. She'd made it very clear their brief acquaintance was over. Things had been going so well until Humphrey had attacked her. He'd really liked this quiet, intelligent girl with glorious hair and a wonderful smile. No doubt he'd get over it. There was a war on and he had a new flight to knock into shape.

Jane sat in the taxi clutching her greatcoat around her as if it could protect her from harm. All men were beasts and she wasn't going to put herself in danger of being hurt ever again. Oscar had stopped the horrid officer from doing her any serious damage but the stranger had pressed his mouth on hers, his teeth had cut her lips, and then he had touched her bottom.

She shuddered. Being touched and kissed was almost as bad as being beaten. It was a good thing she had her interview tomorrow. She prayed she'd get allocated to special duties – this would mean she would be sent away immediately for training. She'd no idea exactly what these special duties were – just that only the girls with a good education were selected. With any luck they would be billeted away from any RAF base and be segregated from the airmen.

She felt hot all over just thinking about having to explain what had happened to the senior officers who had seen her sobbing and trying to stem the blood from her mouth. They had been very kind, understood at once she didn't want to go into details, and arranged for her coat to be fetched, and a taxi to take her home.

Pannal Ash was eerily deserted when she hurried inside. Either everyone was at the dance or they had already retired. As she headed for her billet she noticed there was a new notice on the board. She paused to read it. It was the order in which they would be interviewed tomorrow and her name was a third of the way down. Someone called Amy Williams would be going last and Mary Adams would be first. The interviews started at eight o'clock so hers was scheduled for ten.

Arriving in an empty room was strange but tonight she was glad to be free of questions and chatter. By the time she scrambled into bed, her teeth were clicking. Her breath had condensed in front of her and she thought it was probably the same temperature inside as out.

Despite the cold and her agitation, she drifted off to sleep and only roused briefly when the others trooped in a couple of hours later. She was up first and pulled on her greatcoat over her nightwear, rammed her feet into her shoes and then gathered up the rest of her uniform. If she arrived at the ablutions block first then hot water would still be available. Getting dressed in here was preferable to the freezing dormitory but was only possible if you got up really early.

As she was fastening the last button on her jacket dozens of girls began to flood in. The early birds like her exchanged smug smiles. She sailed past, lovely and warm, whilst the later arrivals were still shivering in their flannelette pyjamas.

'Blimey, you must have been up quick, Jane,' one of them said.

'I was. Worth it though.'

Nobody seemed clear about whether they would be leaving immediately they knew what their trade would be or if they would depart the following day.

Daphne and Jenny were waiting to go into breakfast and she joined the line behind them. 'Do either of you know if we've got to get ready to go immediately after our interview?'

'I asked an NCO and she said the interviews might well go on all day. But as we're the first lot through here she doesn't know much more than we do,' Daphne said as she held her plate out for food.

'You've both got your interviews towards the end of the proceedings – mine's likely to be in a couple of hours.'

'I wonder if we get what we put down on our applications,' Jenny said.

'I wanted to be a wireless or radio operator although I don't know exactly what either job entails. To be honest, I'll just be glad to get away from here. I can't see that this past two weeks has done anything for any of us.'

'I don't think they knew what to do with us so just got us doing cleaning and so on. I enjoyed working in the kitchen and peeling the potatoes.' Jenny had a healthy appetite and now had two slices of bacon, two fried eggs, fried bread and was collecting toast as well. 'I put down catering so hope that's what I get. What about you, Daph?'

'As long as I don't get made an orderly – I've done more than enough domestic work these past two weeks. I wouldn't mind working in the office – I was a telephonist…'

'Then that's what they'll get you to do,' Jane said. 'An RAF officer told me that they're desperately short of girls to work in the office.'

'I'll keep everything crossed that they want me. Talking about RAF officers, what happened to you last night? One minute you were dancing madly with one and then you both vanished.' Jenny giggled and waggled her eyebrows.

'I didn't feel well and he got a taxi for me. I came home early, which is why I was up before you. Didn't you bother with the ablutions block today?' Jane had hastily changed the subject as the last thing she wanted to do was talk about what had happened last night.

The smell and look of the fried food was making her nauseous. She grabbed some toast, held out her mug to be filled, and then headed for an empty table hoping the other two didn't follow her and continue to ask awkward questions.

Daphne put her breakfast down on the table. 'No wonder you're like a scraped matchstick, Jane – you don't eat enough to keep a fly alive.'

'I'm still not fully recovered from last night – it's probably something I ate at lunchtime yesterday. Toast and tea are exactly what I want.'

Why didn't she eat more? Had living with *that man* ruined her appetite? He'd dictated what she ate. She'd never dared to leave a morsel, and the slightest transgression even if it didn't lead to a beating meant she was deprived of a meal.

The tannoy crackled and she turned to listen. It announced that fresh bedlinen was to be collected and the dormitory cleaned and left ready for the next intake. Once they had been interviewed, they were to muster with their kit in the entrance hall.

'Blimey, that means we'll be off today. I don't see how they know who's going where until all the interviews are completed,' Daphne said.

'I expect those are just a formality,' Jane said. 'They've probably already made up their minds where we're going. I'd better hurry up and finish this or I won't be ready by ten o'clock.'

As she was stacking her bed she regretted not saying

goodbye to Daphne and Jenny. She'd only known them for two weeks but they might very well be hurt by her rudeness. There was nothing she could do about it as she only had another quarter of an hour to complete her packing and take her kit downstairs.

Two of the beds were already stacked, the lockers cleared and the linoleum polished to a high shine around them. She collected her belongings and stood back to check that her temporary bed space was equally pristine. Satisfied it would pass any inspection she plonked her helmet on her head, her gas mask around her neck, her greatcoat over her shoulders and then dragged her heavy bag behind her.

From the bumping and swearing coming from the stairs above her other girls were similarly occupied. She carefully propped the kitbag against the wall and then draped coat, gas mask and helmet over the top. Her lips curved as she looked. There were several of these shapes and they all looked like rather small, but smart, scarecrows.

She headed for the room where the interviews were taking place. She knocked and a brusque voice told her to enter.

'Aircraft Woman Second Class 374.' Having had to shorten her number in order to be handed her meagre pay each week she was now confident she'd got it right. She saluted and then marched smartly to stand to attention in front of the three interviewers. One was an RAF officer, a squadron leader from his stripes, the other two WAAF officers. None of them looked particularly pleased to see her.

There was no chair. Either this interview was going to be very short or they wished to see how long she could remain at attention.

'ACW 374, you have been designated Special Duties. Dismissed.'

Stunned by the brevity but delighted by the result she saluted again, turned about-face and marched out.

When she reached the entrance hall an NCO was waiting for her. 'Good, they said you'd be out quickly. Transport will be leaving at one o'clock. Put your kit by the door with the other three. Underneath the yellow marker.'

'Yes, ma'am.' She would have liked to ask how many people were in her group, where they were going and what exactly special duties were but the NCO strode away and she'd missed the opportunity.

It seemed strange that all the girls in her group had their names in the first half of the alphabet. Surely there must be several others with the same educational qualifications as her with names ending in T or a W?

The sooner she learnt to follow orders without questioning them the better. They might have volunteered but until she resigned, she was theirs to command.

Oscar had been sharing a room with Roy but his new promotion meant he was now entitled to a single room. He would prefer to remain where he was. He valued the time he spent with his friend as it gave him less time to dwell on what might have been if Jane had agreed to carry on seeing him.

'I'm not moving out, unless you want me to, Roy.'

'I'd rather have you than some bugger I don't know.'

'Good, because I've informed the adjutant I'm staying

put.' They were in the mess and he had a file of papers in front of him.

'Have you learned anything about the new bods?'

'A bit of a mixed bunch – see for yourself.' He pushed the information across the table and waited to see his friend's reaction.

'Jesus Christ... Sorry. Slipped out and I know you don't like me to blaspheme. But, bloody hell, Oscar, one of these blokes is five years older than us – seems a bit ancient to have just decided he wants a career in the RAF.'

'I'm not too worried about him. If you look you can see he's been a flyer for the past ten years – an instructor no less. Keep looking.'

Apart from this previous flying instructor, the other three had only a few months' training and scarcely any time in their logbooks as solo flyers. What were the RAF thinking? Things must be desperate indeed if such inexperienced pilots were considered ready for battle.

Roy completed his perusal and shook his head. 'They're all regulars and had signed on before war was declared in September. That must be what has persuaded the bigwigs they have enough flying time to be safe.'

'It's not helpful that we don't have sufficient kites. We've only one spare functioning Hurricane between six of us. I need to see just how good they are at acrobatics. As far as I can see they only had a couple of hours of the essential training needed for flying in a sortie.'

'Then why don't we show them ourselves? Take them up one at a time and demonstrate. Then let them have a go. Have we any idea when the rest of the Hurries are arriving?' Roy pushed the file back to him.

'Haven't the foggiest. I expect they'll have to go and fetch them themselves when they're released from the factory.' He thought for a few moments. 'We'll start with manoeuvres in daylight and then progress to flying in the dark. They'll have had to pass a night flying test, but it will only have been circuits and bumps. I need to see them do more than that to know they're safe.'

'You're right; better to get experience without having a dozen bloody Messerschmitt on your tail.'

After a gruelling day involved in mock dogfights with Roy and then watching the new bods have a go, Oscar was confident his flight wasn't as green as he'd feared. He arranged for them to meet the following morning at first light to continue the training.

Johnny Wright, the older, more experienced pilot, had proved to be the least confident. He took him to one side after the others had gone off to get something to eat.

'Johnny, what's the problem?'

'I don't know. I just can't seem to get the hang of it. Maybe I'd be better as an instructor. After all, it's what I've been doing for the past few years. Would you recommend me for transfer?'

'Don't decide today. We're desperately short of experienced flyers – I don't think the CO will part with you so easily. Give it another couple of days. It might fall into place tomorrow.'

'Okay, but I doubt it. It was too bloody real up there. The thought of shooting to kill fills me with horror. I know Hitler has to be stopped but I don't think I'm going to be much use as a fighter pilot. I know I'll hesitate to pull the trigger and by then it'll be too late.'

'Why the hell did you sign up? You must have known you felt like this? We will have to kill people – that's what happens in a war.'

Johnny nodded and patted his shoulder. 'I didn't think it through. I want to do my bit and because I'm an expert pilot it seemed obvious that I should join the RAF. I'm not a pacifist or conscientious objector; I suppose you could say that I'm a coward.'

'No, I certainly couldn't. I would have the same difficulty with being a bomber pilot. Somehow it seems fairer to be shooting down German bombers and fighter planes than dropping bombs and probably killing innocent civilians. If you're certain, then there's no need to continue with the training.'

'I want to do it – if I'm going to instruct then I have to be clear in my own head what the lads need to know. Let's get a beer. Everything makes more sense after a jar or two.'

10

Jane said no farewells, just grabbed her kit and heaved it into the lorry alongside the belongings of the other twenty or so girls. Having travelled on the slippery benches before, she fully expected to be tipped on top of the bags more than once during the journey.

She recognised quite a few of the girls, but none had been in her dormitory. It was no good – she would have to ask if they all had surnames that fell in the first half of the alphabet.

The lorry trundled along and as her ears adjusted to the racket it was possible to hear oneself speak. 'Excuse me,' she said to the two girls closest to her. 'Do you mind terribly telling me your surnames?'

'Thomas – Ivy Thomas. Why do you ask?' The fair girl sitting on her left looked puzzled by the question.

The one on her right also answered. 'Valerie Welham. Go on, what's yours?'

'Jane Hadley. It's just that the interviews were alphabetical so I don't understand how either of you can be in here when your interviews wouldn't be happening until later this afternoon.'

'Oh, that's easily explained. We were told yesterday that

we were going to be allocated to special duties. I think they'd already decided so the interviews weren't really necessary.'

'I just marched in and was told I was special duties and then marched out. They didn't ask me anything. I hate a mystery and like to have everything clear.'

'Not sure you're in the right place, Jane. Everything's a mystery in the WAAF. *Ours not to reason why* and all that,' Ivy said as she tumbled from the bench with a despairing cry as the lorry took a sharp left-hand turn.

All those sitting on the bench on that side of the lorry ended up on the floor. Once they were back in place, roughly where they'd been sitting before, it was as if they were old friends and not recent acquaintances.

'Does anyone know where we're going?' someone on the other side of the lorry called out.

'Would be grand if we were going to London. Absolutely no nightlife available anywhere else,' Valerie said with a sigh.

The very last place Jane wanted to be was London. She'd seen quite enough of that city in the few weeks she'd spent there with Charlotte. In fact, the further away it was from anywhere she might be forced to socialise the happier she'd be.

They stopped briefly for a comfort break and managed to find an indifferent cup of tea and an even worse teacake. Several uncomfortable, cold hours later the lorry eventually stopped. It was completely dark.

It took them a while to collect their own kit and by that time someone had discovered they were in Leighton Buzzard – wherever that was. It was certainly much colder so it must be further north.

'Good grief, this place looks grim,' Ivy said.

She was equally dismayed by what she could see in the darkness. 'I think they're Victorian buildings. Golly, it's starting to snow. That's all we need – it's like something out of a Dickens novel.'

They were herded, dragging their belongings behind them, through an archway and into a quadrangle. On either side were two blocks – hopefully one of these would be the accommodation. They were ushered into a guard room where a jolly WAAF Flight Sergeant was waiting to speak to them.

'Welcome, ladies. I expect you're cold, hungry and tired. Dump your kitbags here and come with me. There's a hot meal and a hot drink waiting for you.'

There had been so many girls at Harrogate that although they had all been posted from there, nobody knew each other. The food was much better than she'd had so far and she took this to be a good sign.

By the time dinner was over the atmosphere was happy and the room full of noisy chatter. The Flight Sergeant got to her feet and slowly the room became silent so she could speak to them.

'You must be wondering where you are. This place was once a workhouse. You will be billeted here but your training will take place elsewhere. It's a two-mile march in each direction.'

Jane exchanged a glance with her new friends. Walking two miles in all weathers and probably in the dark didn't appeal to her.

'Not ideal, but there's a war on and you have to adapt to circumstances. Your training will be intensive and secret.

You have to be in your billet by eight thirty every night except Friday and Saturday when you will be given a late pass until eleven o'clock.'

Briefing over they returned to collect their kitbags and be escorted to the dormitory blocks. The upper floors of these were accessible only by an iron staircase on the outside of the building. Each one had an exterior gallery and there were rows of doors opening into individual rooms.

Valerie whispered to her as they bumped their belongings up the iron staircase. Although the snow was light it was already slippery underfoot. 'This is extremely dangerous. I hope nobody breaks her neck.'

'I just hope none of us have to go to the ablutions block in the middle of the night. It doesn't bear thinking of.'

The room she was to share with five others was small and bare but had one thing that made it acceptable. 'Look at that. We've got our own little heater. It's lovely and warm in here. Makes up for everything else as far as I'm concerned.'

This small, upright coke fire had a metal stack that presumably went into a central chimney. It made up for the lack of comfort everywhere else. They sat around the strange heater holding their hands out to the warmth and getting to know each other.

She slept surprisingly soundly and didn't wake until someone opened the door wide and a gust of icy snow blew in.

'It's absolutely perishing out there. I was so desperate I didn't stop to get dressed but I suggest the rest of you do so. I think it's going to take me all day to thaw out.' Prunella – whose father was a lord or some such thing – said as she struggled to close the door behind her.

'I wish you hadn't mentioned going for a pee – now I'm desperate,' Jane said as she scrambled out of bed and began to throw on her uniform. The only good thing about this new posting was that the dormitory was warm. They'd filled up the stove with coke last thing and it had stayed hot all night.

She grabbed her wash bag, buttoned up her greatcoat, tied her scarf around her head and then was ready to brave the elements. Valerie and Ivy were still half asleep and nowhere near ready. The other two girls – she'd already forgotten their names – had remained firmly asleep despite the chaos in the small room.

No point in procrastinating. She would have to go if she didn't want to wet her knickers. She opened the door just wide enough for her to slip through and closed it easily behind her. Prunella's dramatic entrance had been quite unnecessary in her opinion.

By gripping on to the icy metal railing, she was able to negotiate the treacherous steps and arrive in the quadrangle without breaking her neck. She hadn't stopped to check the time but thought it must be very early as there was no sign of life in the main block as far as she could tell with the blackouts down. She certainly couldn't hear anything.

The WCs were spotless and she smiled wryly. No doubt some unfortunate girl had been put on fatigues and spent the time with her arm around the U-bend as she had last week. She had no intention of undressing again in order to have a bath especially as the water was stone cold. She settled for a lick and a promise, cleaned her teeth, brushed her hair and was ready to return to her lovely warm dormitory.

The wristwatch she'd been given by her mother when she'd matriculated was in her pocket. This had remained in her toilet bag as *that man* knew nothing about it. She'd forgotten she had it until the other day. She now got it out and strapped it on her wrist, pleased to see it was in fact already a quarter past six. The Flight Sergeant last night had told them breakfast would be served at six thirty and they had to be ready to depart to the secret destination at eight o'clock. Before then they had to stack their beds, clean the dormitory as well as eat their breakfast.

She now had three letters to post. The first was for Mrs Jackson into which she'd put a second letter for her mother. There'd been no opportunity for either of them to reply as she'd given them no forwarding address. Hopefully, once her training was finished and she had a permanent posting, things would be different. The other two were for Nancy and Charlotte, which she was sending to the address in Poplar.

She just had time to put her space in order before breakfast. Marching two miles in the dark in this appalling weather was going to be beastly.

Oscar continued to push his new recruits until by the end of the second day he was satisfied all of them, including Johnny, had mastered the climbing and diving that would be necessary in a real dogfight. Tonight, he would see how they flew in the dark.

He'd arranged for a flare path to be lit and his flight would have the sky to themselves. This might well be the last time any of them could practise night manoeuvres. When things kicked off it would be different and such practice jaunts wouldn't be allowed.

'Roy, I think we'd better do a dummy run before they go up this evening.'

'Okay. A couple of circuits and bumps with the blokes watching and then they can have a go?'

'That's what I was thinking. Hang on, Chalky's coming over.' Pilot Officer White, better known as Chalky, was a member of the flight that he and Roy had just left.

'What ho, how can we help?'

'Skip wants us to take advantage of the flare path being put out for your bods tonight. He thinks we should all hone our night flying skills.'

'Tickety-boo with me, Chalky. We'll go first. It's dark by five o'clock so we'll start then. An hour should be enough. After that it's all yours.'

'Good show. Your new lot seem a decent bunch. I think I heard that you'll be getting your full complement of Hurries tomorrow. You won't have to fetch them yourself after all.'

'That's good news. Thanks for the gen.'

Chalky wandered off. Roy looked as happy as he felt about the news. 'We'll take two of the new kites – has to be some perks for those in command.'

'Damn right. We'll be the envy of the squadron. Each new batch is an improvement on the last.'

'We've got an hour to get a wad and a cuppa. It feels colder. The last thing we want is snow,' Roy said as he rubbed his gloved hands together.

'At least if it's snowing the Germans won't be able to fly either.'

'I wasn't thinking of us, I was imagining how grim it

must be for our soldiers in France. No way to spend the festive season, being up to your armpits in white stuff.'

Whilst he was drinking his tea his mind wandered, as it often did, to the girl he'd met and lost. Why was it that when he'd met someone he thought he could really like, things had gone pear-shaped? No time to dwell on what might have been – duty called.

He and Roy clambered into the cockpits of their kites watched by the other four. He ran through his preflight checks and it brought back to him the first time he'd flown at night when he was training. It now seemed a long time ago. He'd been terrified he'd make a hash of it but, like everything else he'd done so far in his career, his worries had been unfounded.

He took off smoothly, did his circuits of the airfield and then for the second time lined up with the flares and landed. A few minutes later Roy taxied in behind him.

His flight mechanic was there to open the cockpit and assist him out. He hopped down and walked over to the assembled pilots waiting for their turn.

'It's a piece of cake. Remember to concentrate on the instruments – ignore what's outside the cockpit until you've done your circuits and come in to land. Do only two circuits and bumps as the temperature's dropping.' He couldn't see their expressions but they all murmured a response. 'Good. Remember your training and you've got nothing to worry about.'

Johnny had drawn the short straw and was going last. Oscar wasn't going to risk having two of them up at the same time so there would only be one Hurry circling the base at a time.

The first three bods did a first-class job and Johnny was eager to get his turn. 'Actually, I enjoyed night flying. There's something about being up there in the dark, all alone, that appealed to me.'

Oscar and Roy had sent the three that had completed their circuits back to the mess. No point in standing around freezing if you didn't have to. The other chaps who were going to make use of the flare path after Johnny landed were already clambering into their kites, waiting for the runway to be clear.

The lights from Johnny's kite got further and further away until he was airborne. 'Christ, Oscar, he's climbing too steeply and looks as if he's drifting to starboard as well.'

It wasn't Roy's imagination. Johnny was definitely off to the right and going up too fast. He held his breath and then let it out with a hiss as the rate of climb slowed. 'He's still too far to the right. What's the matter with him? He's the most experienced flyer we've got. He said he likes night flying.'

'He needs to turn to the left and watch his height.' Oscar watched in horror as Johnny over corrected and began to lose altitude. There was nothing he could do. His stomach tied into knots.

The scream of the engine filled the night and they were no longer alone watching the tragedy unfold. Why didn't Johnny pull up? Had he lost consciousness? Had a heart attack? *Come on – pull up before it's too late.*

Oscar sent up a fervent prayer to the Almighty. The lights of the Hurry continued their downward spiral and disappeared from view. In the darkness there was a dull thud. The screaming engine was silenced. Then another noise, a hideous, ghastly sound and the sky behind the trees was lit by a red glow.

He was running towards the crash site without being aware he'd started to do so. The pounding boots of his friend were beside him. Then two fire engines and an ambulance raced past in the vain hope that Johnny could be saved.

The Hurricane was in flames. The fire engine was already dousing them whilst the ambulance crew stood by. They were no longer needed. No one could have survived such a crash. Oscar prayed that Johnny had died on impact and not been burnt alive.

He turned aside and vomited. When he'd finished retching, he straightened and stepped away from the mess. His cheeks were wet. This was his fault. If he'd listened to Johnny, he would still be alive.

'Bloody awful way to go. Does he have a family?' Roy was standing beside him staring at the flames.

The heat from the conflagration made the night warm. At least the snow had stopped. He dragged his mind back to the question his friend had asked.

'He wasn't married, if that's what you mean. There must be next-of-kin I have to inform, but their names weren't on his file.'

'There's nothing we can do here, mate – let's leave them to it. There'll be an inquiry of some sort and hopefully we'll find out what happened then.'

They trudged back to base. The flares were out – no further flying would be done tonight. He'd never forget the sound of the screaming engine, the thud as the plane crashed and the noise of the exploding fuel tanks.

The CO was waiting for him. 'Bad business, old boy.

Spare me a few minutes in my office before you go to the mess.'

Oscar was still in his Sidcot suit. By rights this should be removed after flying and hung in readiness for the next flight along with his parachute, the rest of his gear and his Mae West.

'I'm going to get out of this and then I'll join you. I won't be long.' He turned and hurried away before he could be called back.

Squadron Leader Riley was about the same age as Johnny had been, but he was a happily married man with two children. He wondered why Johnny had been a bachelor. None of his business – the man was dead and he wasn't going to have any unpleasant speculation about his private life.

Roy was ahead of him and already shrugging on his greatcoat and pulling his scarf tightly around his neck. 'I'll come with you, Oscar – makes sense as we both saw the same thing.'

'No, thank you. This isn't about what happened but why I let him fly at all. I think he must have told Riley he didn't want to be a fighter pilot but an instructor. I shouldn't have allowed him to continue with his orientation knowing how he felt.'

'You didn't order him to do it. It was his choice, wasn't it?'

'I suppose it was but I'm his commanding officer – I was his commanding officer – and should have made the decision for him. I'll see you in the bar – get me a pint and a chaser. I'm going to get disgustingly drunk tonight.'

He marched into Riley's untidy office and was waved to a pew but he ignored the gesture.

'I don't understand how such an experienced flyer made such a balls-up of something so simple.'

'I blame myself...'

'Stuff and nonsense, Stanton. It was nobody's fault. Just a bloody stupid accident. Good thing he's no family to bother us with demands for an inquiry. That isn't why I wanted to speak to you. I just wanted to tell you that you've got to toughen up. You can't fall to pieces every time someone goes for a Burton.'

'What sort of man would I be if I wasn't upset by the death of a fellow officer? I'm not stupid or naïve, sir, I know what's going to happen. However, I don't want to "toughen up" as you suggest. I'll handle it in my own way and I can assure you my ability to do my job won't suffer.'

He stood to attention and saluted smartly, then about-turned and marched out parade-ground stiff. Tonight he'd learned some valuable lessons. One of them was that he really didn't like Riley and didn't want to serve under him any longer. He decided to put in for a transfer even if it meant demotion.

II

Jane lined up with Ivy on one side of her and Prunella on the other, ready to march to their secret destination. Despite the fact that it was still totally dark there was enough light from the glimmer of the torches to see that they were marching through Leighton Buzzard. This wasn't a big town as they were in and out quickly.

Half an hour later a shouted command of right turn was issued. She saw ahead of them a pair of enormous gates guarded by armed RAF men. For a moment she couldn't understand what she was seeing. Where had the sky gone?

'Good heavens, everything's covered with green camouflage netting,' Prunella said as they continued their brisk progress up the drive.

'It must be very top-secret,' Ivy chimed in.

'There's miles of it. I rather like the idea of being involved in something top-secret. I wonder what we're going to learn to do.'

They were scarcely given time to remove their greatcoats and straighten their skirts before being herded into a large room in the centre of which was a massive table covered with a green baize cloth. It looked like a card table for giants. There was an RAF officer waiting to speak to them and they were told to sit down.

'You girls are going to be trained as plotters to work with Fighter Command. At this point none of you will know what the word plotter means, so I am now going to enlighten you.'

She exchanged a nervous glance with her new friends. Plotter sounded like someone nasty, someone who hatched schemes behind your back. She didn't think this could be what they were going to do.

The officer continued. 'Before you begin your training you will be required to take an oath of secrecy. I cannot stress too strongly the secretive nature of this work. Once you have sworn this oath you will not be able to mention what you're doing to any member of your family. In fact, not to another human being.' He paused and glared around the table to see that his words were being heeded. 'If you break your oath for any reason you will be dishonourably discharged. Do you fully understand what I've just told you?'

She nodded vigorously as did every other girl. The entire group looked like marionettes having their strings pulled from above.

'There will be two days of lectures explaining how the RDF chain works. Those initials stand for range and direction finding. The air defence of Britain depends on this warning system. The information that you handle is what will allow air raid sirens to be sounded, for the fighter squadrons to be directed towards the incoming bombers, assist rescue operations and instruct any gun crews for gun-laying and firing.'

This was a really important trade to be in. Jane's pulse raced at the thought that she would be doing something valuable for the first time in her short life. Then two WAAF NCOs handed out sheets of paper – some sort of official secrets document – and they all signed their names. These were collected and then they were dismissed and told to reassemble for the first lecture in half an hour.

Plenty of time to find the ablutions and the mess for a quick coffee and biscuit. Prunella and Ivy were good sorts and she thought they would become chums.

'I don't like the sound of having lectures. I'm not good at taking notes,' Ivy said.

'I don't think we have to know all the technical stuff off by heart,' she replied. 'We just have to be able to do whatever it is we're being trained for. Do either of you know what our particular special duties are going to be?'

'We're going to be plotters – not that I really know what that entails. I expect we'll understand once we start the actual training.'

Prunella joined in the conversation. 'Ivy's right, Jane, no point worrying about it. Look, the others are starting to move so we'd better go with them. Being last wouldn't look good.'

There was a scientist in mufti to deliver the first lecture. He explained that they should think of the way that a stone dropped into a pond and made ripples travel out from it. The radio waves worked in the same way and the ripples spread outwards until they came in contact with something metal – an incoming or outgoing aircraft – and then a signal would appear on a cathode-ray tube (whatever that was) and whoever was watching the screen would know there was a possible enemy raid.

The next day was taken up with similar technical lectures and at the end of it, Jane thought she had grasped the essentials. The main thing, it seemed to her, was being able to work quickly. She'd been impressed by the films of radar stations where she saw the radar operators sitting in front of the screen.

Her head was spinning and her eyes sore and she actually welcomed the march back to their billet as the crisp winter air cleared her head wonderfully.

'It will be Christmas in a couple of weeks. Do you think we'll have finished our training by then?' Ivy asked as they sat down for tea.

'I don't think they'll post us until the New Year as one of the others told me the training lasts for four weeks. We have to take a series of tests and if we don't pass then we get sent back and have to take up normal duties.' Prunella always seemed to know what was going on.

'I think this whole thing sounds fascinating and I'm so glad I'm part of this team. I really don't want to be one of those who fails the tests.' Jane was determined to concentrate and make sure she didn't get the dreaded tap on the shoulder.

The work was so engrossing that she had little time for anything else and ignored the invitations to go out when they had their late passes and remained in the snug little billet to study on her own. The only drawback to this privacy was that she had far too much time to think about Oscar. At odd times of the day or night she would see his face with his angelic curls and mesmerising blue-grey eyes and wish things could be different, that she was different and could allow someone into her life.

Christmas Day was like any other apart from their meal being served to them by a couple of officers and NCOs. What a strange tradition that was – she didn't enjoy having her superiors watching her eat but it didn't seem to bother anyone else.

No one got any leave and the following day it was training as usual. Learning the RAF code names for each letter had been a doddle for her as she had an excellent memory.

The filter room was huge and dominated by an enormous strangely shaped table. On closer study she realised it was actually the coastline of England. The table was divided into large squares each bearing capital letters to identify its position. She was given a box of counters of different colours each representing a different station. To add to the confusion there were different shapes amongst the counters. Triangles were for the estimated number of aircraft, circles were used to show position and squares the estimated height of the incoming aircraft.

Once she had the headset on and had plugged in the lead they had been connected to the mock station. A man's voice announced the tracks and it was her job to plot what he said. Anyone doing the job of teller or plotter had to speak clearly and have no regional accent so they could be easily understood.

The first few days she'd been slow but then it had fallen into place. She was now confident she understood her role and could plot the information about incoming and outgoing aircraft smoothly. She had no difficulty passing the various tests and was delighted to pass out top of the group.

Ivy and Valerie had vanished from the billet halfway through but Prunella was still there. She wondered if the two of them would be posted together. Only half the group were going to Fighter Command headquarters and her new friend, unfortunately, wasn't in the group. In fact, no one from her billet would be going with her.

She was glad she hadn't made close friends as having to say so many goodbyes would have been more difficult. She was now an Aircraft Woman Second Class, was no longer a recruit but a fully qualified member of the WAAF. Writing to Nancy and Charlotte was her only comfort as for some reason she no longer received any letters from the vicarage. Perhaps the reply to her last letter had yet to catch up with her. She often wished she'd not turned down the opportunity to exchange letters with Oscar.

By the middle of January Oscar's flight was fully equipped with both men and kites. Johnny's death had knocked them all sideways but life moved on and no one even spoke about him now. The funeral had been small and attended only by his squadron. Johnny was buried in a churchyard where space had been reserved for RAF fatalities who had no family to insist that they were buried closer to home. A miserable place to end up.

After talking to Roy he'd decided not to put in for a transfer. Better the devil you know, and all that. He was certain his squadron would be moved once things kicked off. They were too far north to intercept any Huns that came in over the channel. That's where the action would be. His speculation proved correct as when he and his flight returned from a practice sortie there was a message for him to report to Squadron Leader Riley.

Things were still a bit sticky between them but they got on as well as they needed to. 'Sorry, took longer than I thought, sir.'

'Well, Stanton, you're here now. The squadron's transferring to Debden. We're being replaced by Spits. The weather's excellent – no ice or snow forecast this week. The Met thinks there's some foul stuff coming in next week so that's why we're going now.'

'Right, sir. What's the gen? Do we go when ready or fly down as a squadron?'

'As long as you get off today.'

This meant he had an hour at best to get the rest of the flight organised. Sometimes it could take half an hour to get all the kites fuelled and checked. Roy was hanging about outside the office knowing there must be something important going on.

'Good, we're moving to Debden. We've got to get there today and I really don't want the new bods to land at a strange base in the dark.'

'I think they're still getting changed. Do you want me to round them up or speak to the erks? Get the kites refuelled?'

'I'll speak to the mechanics. You gather the chaps.'

In just over the hour he was back in his cockpit doing his preflight check. It was a bit cramped with all his gear jammed in behind him as well as his chute. He was wearing his sheepskin flying jacket under his Sidcot suit – these weren't official issue but anyone who could afford to have one made would have one on. Having to wear full uniform plus a tie was madness – hopefully things would relax a little once they were actually doing the job they were trained for.

They were going to fly in loose formation but everyone had the coordinates and none of them should get lost on such a short hop.

He raised his thumb and Roy on his left responded as did Donald on the right. He took off smoothly and climbed steadily to 10,000 feet. It was just over two hundred miles and a Hurry's max speed was 340 mph. They would cruise at around two-thirds max and complete the journey in under an hour.

Engine noise meant a flyer never really got to experience the silence of the sky. His headset, which he wore over his helmet, cut out the worst of the roar and the rattle of the fuselage. He'd told his men to maintain radio silence – good practice for when they were flying in battle and had to concentrate on what was being relayed from the ground.

When he was ten minutes from Debden he connected with the base and was told they could land as they arrived.

'I'm going in first. Roy next and then the rest of you come in when the runway's clear.' The green light flashed below, his flaps were down, the undercarriage lowered and his touchdown was immaculate. Always a bonus to do it well when you had an audience.

He was guided towards an empty space on the apron. There was more than enough room for all twenty-four of the squadron to park safely. He'd visited Debden a couple of times and was pleased to be posted there. It only had grass runways and like most of the RAF bases was still frantically trying to build extra hangars, accommodation and so on in order to be ready when the fighting started. From here he could catch a bus to his home in Suffolk easily enough if he got a twenty-four-hour pass.

The only downside about this move was the fact that he'd had to hastily sell his beloved car to one of the blokes who was remaining in situ.

The last letter he'd had from Mum had been more encouraging about the attitude of his pacifist father. He rather thought he was no longer considered the black sheep of the family for making the RAF his career. Like most young men he'd known this war was coming and wanted to be ready to protect his country.

He unclipped his harness, released the Perspex cover to his cockpit and reached behind him for his kitbag before standing up.

'Welcome to Debden, sir. I'm in charge of the ground crew for your flight. Bobby Mullins is me name.'

Oscar chucked his belongings to the ground and scrambled out after them before answering. 'Good to meet you, Bobby. Flight Lieutenant Oscar Stanton – call me Oscar unless the CO's around.'

With his kitbag over one shoulder and his chute over the other he headed for the main admin building where, if he remembered rightly, there was a locker room to stow his gear. God knows where he would be billeted as he doubted there would be accommodation on the base for all of them. It would have been nice to have had some sort of transport provided as the hike across the airfield was almost half a mile.

'Good afternoon, sir, welcome to Debden,' an NCO saluted him as he stepped into the building.

'Thank you.' He pointed down the corridor. 'Do I put my gear in the same place as last year?'

'Yes, sir.' The man looked at his clipboard. 'Could I have your name, please?'

Oscar gave it and was about to wander off when the NCO called him back. 'I have the address of your temporary billet, sir. Unfortunately, things aren't quite ready to accommodate your squadron here.'

He held out his hand and was given a piece of paper. He would be living in the village of Debden, which was about two miles from the base. Fat lot of good that would be when action started. At least there were a couple of decent pubs where he could spend his free time.

As he made his way to the locker room the corridor filled up with the remainder of the squadron as they arrived. He increased his pace. It would be a scrum in there if all of them were trying to undress and sort themselves out at the same time. Roy was right behind him.

He found himself an empty locker and hung up his flying kit, removed his boots and rummaged about in his bag for his shoes. It was marginally warmer but he still needed his heavy coat. He'd had a gas mask but he hadn't seen it for weeks. He supposed he'd have to scrounge another one if he went off base. Nobody bothered to carry one otherwise.

His friend nabbed the locker next to his. 'They'll have to move this lot nearer to our kites. Bloody shambles, if you ask me.'

'We're living in the village – I hope bicycles are available.'

'That means when we're on duty we'll have to kip somewhere here. As I said before – bloody shambles.'

By the time they were ready to leave the room was jampacked. He shouldered his way out of the crush.

'I think a drink is called for, Roy, don't you? Something to eat would be good too but I expect we'll have to wait until we find our billet for that.'

They made their way to the Officers' Mess, which was strangely empty. In fact, the whole place was like the *Marie Celeste*. Plenty of admin blokes but no sign of any flyers. 'Where on earth are the other bods? Surely, we can't be the only active squadron here? Debden is part of Fighter Group 11. It's going to be our job to protect London and the south-east from the Luftwaffe when they come.'

Riley overheard his last remark as he came in, closely followed by the rest of the squadron. 'We're the first but there are two others already based here. God knows where they are today. Bloody bad show having to put up in the village. They'd better get their fingers out and get our accommodation finished.'

After a few jars no one was binding about having to travel to the village. The NCO who'd greeted them poked his head through the door and yelled above the noise.

'Transport's outside, gentlemen.'

He and Roy were billeted in an ancient house three doors down from a pub. Their landlady was an elderly lady who greeted them with a marked lack of enthusiasm.

'Meals will be served in the dining room. You will also use this as your sitting room. You will use the WC and wash room downstairs. You will not use any other rooms.'

'Right. Please direct us to our bedroom so we can get settled. Then we'll eat.' He didn't introduce himself and didn't ask for her name. Keeping it formal and accepting her rules would work best for all of them.

'It's the room at the end of the passageway. The door is open. There are towels provided.'

Roy muttered something rude under his breath and Oscar smiled. Why had the irascible old lady offered to accommodate them when she so obviously didn't want them there? To his surprise the room was large, well appointed, and had a decent fire burning in the grate.

'Which bed do you want? The one on the right or the left?' Roy asked.

'They're identical. We've also got our own wardrobe and chest of drawers.' He dropped his bag on the bed on the left. 'She might be a grumpy old lady but we can't complain about this.'

There were also a pair of old-fashioned washstands with hot water in a china jug and a matching floral basin to tip it into.

Roy pulled open the cupboard underneath the marble top on his. 'We've got a matching po.'

'Let's hope we don't need to use it. I'm not going to unpack now. I'm ravenous. If the food's as good as the accommodation then we've landed on our feet.'

The dining room had obviously been rearranged to accommodate them. The table was now under the window and two comfortable armchairs had been put in front of the fireplace. To his delight, and astonishment, there was a wireless in pride of place on the sideboard. The food was equally impressive and served by a giggling young girl dressed in a maid's uniform. She, unlike her employer, was delighted they were there.

'That one's trouble, Oscar. She's already got her eye on you. Transport's going to collect us at eight o'clock. Do you fancy another beer or two before we turn in?'

'Not for me. I've had my quota for today. You go ahead.' He grinned. 'Better check there's not a curfew before you go. I'm going to listen to the wireless.'

'Then I'll join you. I don't want to miss the nine o'clock news. Shall I put it on for the news later?'

They had carefully stacked the used crockery and left the table to be cleared – hopefully when they'd retired. The less they saw of their landlady the better.

12

Bentley Priory was more like a small town than a RAF station. Jane, and the others, scrambled out of the lorry bumping their kit behind them and looked around with interest. They were directed to their new billet, which was referred to as a hut. This was an accurate description as it was a low, wooden building.

There were around thirty beds, all neatly stacked, and they were directed to the ones at the far end. Unpacking and stowing her small items of kit in the locker and hanging up her uniform on the three pegs provided took only a few minutes.

A helpful NCO was waiting to give them a quick tour of the base. 'WAAFs are stationed at this end in these huts; our ablutions are over there.' The woman pointed at an identical hut but didn't give them time to visit. They marched briskly behind their leader and Jane was pleased when they went into a larger building in which was housed the mess, the recreation room and the various offices.

'Get yourself something to eat and report to this room in half an hour.'

The food was palatable but she was too excited to eat much. There were dozens of WAAF eating but she made no attempt to make eye contact. Time enough to make friends once she was certain she was staying here. It was quite possible some of them would be relocated to other bases at some point.

An RAF officer with a bristling grey moustache waited until they crammed themselves into every nook and cranny before clearing his throat noisily. 'You girls will be divided into watches. You will work one week on nights and one week on days. The night watches run from one a.m. to five a.m. and five a.m. to nine a.m.

'Daytime they run from nine a.m. to one p.m., one p.m. to five p.m. and then five p.m. to nine p.m. You will now be informed into which watch you've been put.' He nodded and then the NCO who had been their guide took his place.

'It's a ten-minute coach ride to the Operations Room. You must be waiting to embark a quarter of an hour before your shift starts.'

She then told them when they would be starting work and with whom they would be sharing with. Jane and her three cohorts were to work nights but not start until one a.m. the day after tomorrow. They had been given a thirty-six-hour pass and as the other three girls were heading for London first thing next morning, she decided to go with them.

It was snowing heavily by the time they reached the city and she was grateful to be wearing her warm greatcoat over her thick blue uniform. She parted company with the others and they agreed to meet up at the hotel in Tothill Street, the Sanctuary, at midday and go in search of some lunch together. They would then make a trip to the cinema. It would be dark when they came out of the cinema. Wandering around in the blackout wasn't something she was looking forward to but she would be with the others so it shouldn't be a problem.

It was just possible there might be some correspondence from either Nancy or Charlotte in Poplar as they had arranged to send their letters there until they had a permanent address. The last time she'd braved the East End she'd been in civilian clothes and accompanied by Charlotte. Now she was in uniform and quite happy to complete the journey on her own.

Apart from the brown sticky paper criss-crossing all the windows and an abundance of men and women in uniform, things seemed very much the same in the city. The sandbags were still there, signs pointing to communal air raid shelters prominent on street corners, and despite the horrible weather people seemed quite cheerful.

She'd managed to buy a bag of pastries and she hoped this gift would make her unexpected visit a welcome one.

This time there were no women gossiping on their doorsteps when she turned into the street in which Nancy lived – or had once lived – to be more accurate. She knocked on the door and it was opened by Mrs Evans, wraparound pinny firmly tied and her hair in curlers under a headscarf.

'Well I never did! Come in, miss, my Nancy said you might call in one day. She ain't here – she's been posted to Catterick where she's doing ever so well.'

Jane handed over the bag of cakes. 'I thought you might like these to go in the lunchboxes.'

'Ta, ever so. We'll have one between us now.'

The kitchen was warm and the kettle hissing gently over the range. There was no sign of Mr Evans or the two youths.

They must be on a different shift to the one they'd been on last time.

'Sit down, I'll make you a nice cuppa.' She took a currant bun from the bag and carefully cut it in half before putting the rest in a metal bread bin. 'I've got a pile of letters for you. I reckon some of them are from your folks but there's one from my Nancy and two from that posh girl what came with you for a visit.' Mrs Evans rummaged about behind the assorted china dogs and other ornaments on the mantelpiece and pulled out a satisfyingly thick pile of envelopes.

'How exciting. I've been writing here to both my friends in the hope that they will call in like I have to collect them one day. If Nancy is now settled at Catterick I can send my letters there in future.'

'I ain't too clever with writing and such, none of us are, but I'd be ever so grateful if you'd put my Nancy's new address on them three letters.'

One of the envelopes she recognised as having come from her, the other two had Charlotte's handwriting. She quickly crossed out the London address and replaced it with the one for Catterick. These could be popped back into the postal system without having to put another stamp on them.

She sorted out her correspondence and put the ones from Mrs Jackson to one side to be read in privacy. She didn't want Nancy's mother to see two letters fall out of the envelope and have to explain the reason.

The ones from Charlotte she opened immediately and looked at the dates. One had been written in November and the other only last week. She would read them in order.

Dear Jane,

As promised I'm writing to Nancy's home address in the hope that you are able to get there and collect my letters.

I can't tell you exactly what I'm doing now but it's special duties. I'm certain that you are doing the same – signing the Official Secrets Act was a bit of a bind but necessary. I should complete my training by the end of this month and then hopefully be posted somewhere where you can write.

I was told that just sending letters with my name and number on to Victory House in London should be sufficient for them to be forwarded on to me. I think I shall do the same for you in the New Year.

Nancy is going to be an equipment assistant – the person who hands out the spare parts to aeroplanes and clothes to airwomen. She and Nora are hoping to be posted to the same place as they've both been accepted for this trade.

I've been too busy to socialise – I expect it's the same for you. Also, like you I have no contact with my family. I can't say that I'm bothered by this.

Maybe we'll eventually both be posted near enough to London to meet. I really do want to stay in touch.

My very best wishes,

Charlotte

Dear Jane,

Unfortunately, my posting is too far away from the city to even contemplate coming up to see you. Therefore, letters will be the only way we can stay connected for the moment.

There's no telephone available for us and the nearest one is three miles away in the village. I'm billeted with a delightful family, delicious food and a very comfortable room. However, because I work shifts, I'm rarely there.

I look forward to hearing from you when you get one of these letters.

Very best wishes,
Charlotte

Was it possible that her friend was doing the same work that she was? Was she somewhere in the RDF chain, possibly a plotter too? It was confusing that their job was referred to as being a plotter or a filterer – neither of which sounded anything like the actual work involved. She supposed that they were actually filtering information from the radar stations positioned around the coast and then plotting it on the big table with the map engraved on it.

Mrs Evans plonked a mug of tea and half a bun on a chipped floral plate, in front of her and then sat down opposite. 'Do you have an address for your other friend now?'

'I do, thank you. I'll write to Nancy when I get back to my base and give her the instructions for writing to me. I do want to stay in touch with her. I think it's doubtful that we'll be able to meet in person, at least for a while, as our postings are so far apart.'

'Never mind, love, it'll all come out in the wash. They're ever so busy down at the docks and I don't reckon my boys will be called up as long as they work there. That's what Ruby's ma said, any road.'

Jane picked up the grubby envelope with the almost illegible writing. 'I'll read the one from Nancy now. It's good news about your boys. It must be a dreadful worry for those with sons not in reserved occupations.'

'Half the little buggers what were evacuated last year have come home. They ain't too keen on the country life, that's for sure. It didn't seem natural having no kiddies playing in the streets.'

She looked up from the letter, which was more a note than anything else.

Dear Jane

I hope that you are doing okay. Me and Nora are happy. I got a letter from Charlotte but I ain't had one from you. Write me soon.

Luv,

Nancy

'It won't be safe in the East End when the bombing starts. But I can see why the children wanted to be with their families and not living with strangers miles away.'

'There's a shelter down the end of the road and one of me mates says as she's going to use the underground, not so cramped and dark as one of them blooming things.' She pointed proudly to a battered pram parked by the door. 'I got me things ready in there. Pillows, blankets and such what we'll need. All I got to do is shove in a thermos of tea and we're tickety-boo.'

'I just hope things aren't going to be as bad as everyone says.' Jane drained her tea and ate the last few mouthfuls of bun. 'Thank you so much for keeping these letters for me. The tea and cake were delicious but I'm afraid I have to go as I don't want to be late back and be put on a charge.'

This wasn't strictly true as she didn't have to be back at Bentley Priory until tomorrow evening. Wearing uniform gave her the courage to do things she wouldn't have dreamt of a few months ago.

Elizabeth was the only one of her group waiting for her when she arrived at the hotel. 'The other two are still wandering about Oxford Street. I'm afraid it's only the two of us.'

The weather deteriorated and the heavy snow and freezing conditions meant no flying was possible. Not much had been going on even when it was safe to go up. Oscar's flight was given a forty-eight-hour pass and he thought he might go and see his family.

'Bloody horrible weather – I doubt the buses will be running. These narrow roads will be blocked with snow,' Roy said gloomily.

'In which case there's no point in trying to get to the vicarage. I should think the trains will be running, albeit slowly. What about heading for London? We could catch a show, go to the pictures. What do you say?'

'I'll speak to the rest of the blokes. If we're all going maybe we can borrow some transport that could negotiate the road to Saffron Walden.'

'Good show. Going in that direction might be better than trying to cut across country into Suffolk to see my folks.'

Since his arrival two weeks ago he'd settled into his billet and managed to buy a battered bicycle from a villager who no longer used it. Roy hadn't been so lucky so had to travel on the crossbar. So far they'd managed to avoid going headfirst into a ditch but it was only a matter of time, especially with the weather so dire.

An hour later he was squashed in the front of an army lorry with Roy and the others were rattling about in the back. The driver had arrived at an opportune moment to deliver ammunition to the ack-ack guns that protected the base and had been happy to drop them off at the station.

Again fortune favoured them and as they tumbled onto the icy cobbles the sound of a train whistle meant they didn't have to wait. The ticket collector waved them through and they skidded onto the platform and dived into the end carriage just as the train pulled out.

Eventually they disembarked at Liverpool Street. 'If it's going to take so bloody long to get back, we need to be here lunchtime tomorrow,' Roy said.

Oscar made sure the others were aware that being late would get them put on a charge. Satisfied they understood he parted company with the others who already had plans to carouse the night away at a seedy nightclub they knew somewhere in Soho.

'Shall we find ourselves a hotel before we do anything else?'

'Where we stay depends what you want to do tonight. I fancy a film and a slap-up meal.'

'Exactly what I was going to suggest. We need to head for Piccadilly – there are half a dozen cinemas around there. I'm sure we can find a guesthouse in our price range somewhere in one of the back streets close by.'

They caught the underground and emerged into flurries of snow. The pavements were, as one would expect, quieter than usual. The pedestrians tramping, heads down, presumably eager to get out of the nasty weather as soon as possible.

'We should have worn our gas masks – everyone else has one dangling round their neck,' he said.

'As you still don't have one, that would have been a bit tricky. We should have worn our flying boots – my feet are already frozen.'

Roy had a tendency to moan but always did it with a smile. They found somewhere to stay, dumped their overnight bags on the candlewick-covered beds and then went in search of some lunch.

'Over there, that looks promising. I just saw a group of WAAF go in so we won't be the only ones in blue.' Roy had a keen eye for the ladies.

Oscar smiled. 'I didn't notice. However, as long as we get out of this filthy weather and find something hot to eat, I don't really care where it is.'

The entrance to the restaurant was narrow but it opened up into a substantial space with two dozen tables. He stumbled and both he and Roy went crashing forward into the lectern where the head waiter was standing checking the reservations book before sending people to unoccupied tables.

The lectern, the waiter and the two of them tumbled

inelegantly to the carpet in a tangle of arms and legs and a great deal of bad language – from the waiter.

The resulting chaos caused every head to turn in his direction. From his position flat on his back with Roy trapped underneath him he watched as the reason for the accident, Jane Hadley, recognised him. Her eyes widened. Then she was on her feet and hurrying towards him.

'My goodness, Oscar, are you injured? What on earth happened?' Her friend arrived and appeared to enjoy helping two RAF officers regain their feet – their dignity was long gone.

'Jane, I can't tell you how surprised I was to see you.'

She laughed – a wonderful, joyous sound – and in that moment he knew he was lost. She was the one for him and he intended to persuade her to become his girlfriend.

'You don't have to tell me. Everyone in here is well aware how surprised you were.' Jane seemed different somehow, more confident, more grown up than when they'd met last time.

Roy was laughing too. 'Very pleased to see you again, Miss Hadley, and this time you're not unconscious on the ground. Not sure anyone else is pleased at our somewhat unconventional arrival.'

Oscar couldn't stop smiling and to his delight she was smiling back at him. He turned to the unfortunate chap he'd flattened. 'I do beg your pardon. Incredibly clumsy of me. I hope this will help improve the situation.' He handed over a pound note and the waiter seemed somewhat mollified.

'Do you have a reservation, sir?'

'I'm sorry, I don't. I'm hoping that you can squeeze us in somewhere.'

The waiter smiled and nodded at the table Jane had left. 'Perhaps the young ladies, as they are friends of yours, would allow you to join them?'

'That would be splendid. What about it, Jane? Will you take pity on two freezing officers?'

Jane looked at her friend who nodded. 'It's true, we do have a table already laid up for four.'

'Then we'll join you. This will be our treat as we've foisted ourselves on you uninvited.'

A young girl in a maid's uniform took their greatcoats. As every uniform was labelled with the owner's number it should be no problem reclaiming them when they left.

Jane looked pleased to see him, which surprised him almost as much as the fact that she was by some miracle in the same restaurant as him. There was no time to say anything personal before they arrived at the table.

'This is Elizabeth. Elizabeth, meet my special friend, Oscar, and his friend Roy.'

There was a mutual greeting and shaking of hands and then he took the seat next to Jane, and Roy the one remaining next to Elizabeth.

'We've only just arrived,' Jane said. There were only two menus on the table so he shared with her.

'I'm surprised they still have any choices now rationing has started. This will probably be the last time we can eat like this so shall we push the boat out?'

Roy had picked up the wine list, which was equally extensive. 'Blimey! A bottle of wine is the same as a week's wages. They don't appear to have beer.'

The girls exchanged glances. 'Actually,' Jane said, 'neither of us drink much and certainly not in the middle of the day.

We thought we would order coffee – that's soon going to be a luxury item too.'

'A large jug of coffee would be perfect. Remember this is our treat as we've gate-crashed your luncheon. Are we having three courses?'

'We'll pay for the drinks. We can hardly expect you to foot the bill when you didn't actually invite us out,' Elizabeth said with a smile at Roy.

'Fair enough. If we fill up now, we won't want more than a sandwich tonight.' He waited for either of the girls to tell them that they had other plans but they both nodded. 'Roy and I intend to go to the pictures – is there anything you two particularly want to see?'

'We rather wanted to see *The Four Feathers* with John Clements and June Duprez, as both Elizabeth and I have read the book. It's based on the novel with the same name by someone called Mason.'

'Never heard of the author or the film. What's it about?'

Jane giggled. 'To be honest, I thought the book deadly dull. I do remember it's full of action and romance.'

He raised an eyebrow and she pulled a face. She really was the most adorable young lady.

'Sounds fine to me. As long as the cinema's close by, I don't really mind what we see. There's a cartoon and a newsreel as well if we don't like the film.' Roy put down the menu he'd been perusing.

'I'm having potato and leek soup, steak and kidney pie and any sort of cake that's available.'

A waiter appeared with his pad and to keep things simple they all selected the same meal. They also asked for a jug of coffee immediately and another one with dessert.

Elizabeth, who was half a head shorter than Jane, had abundant platinum blonde curls and startling blue eyes, and seemed taken with Roy, which gave him the ideal opportunity to talk quietly to the girl he had just fallen head over heels in love with.

'My squadron has moved to Debden and I've been promoted to Flight Lieutenant. I've got until tomorrow afternoon. Now – your turn.' He'd deliberately kept the information brief and hoped he'd given no indication of his feelings.

'I've just been posted to Bentley Priory, and as we don't start our shift until tomorrow night, I'm also free until lunchtime tomorrow. I'm now an ACW2.' She didn't tell him what she was doing and he didn't ask. There was no need for him to get the specifics as any WAAF working at Fighter Command headquarters must be doing something hush-hush.'

'Special duties?'

'Yes.' Her cheeks coloured slightly and she looked down. Then straightened her shoulders and turned to look at him directly. 'I'm sorry I ran away from you. I expect you know what happened. I've only been a WAAF for just over three months but I've changed a lot. I was a shy, silly schoolgirl when I joined up but am now finding my feet.'

13

Jane's heart was thudding uncomfortably and her palms were clammy. Whatever had made her say something so outrageous? Would he get the wrong idea and expect her to kiss him and possibly other things that she couldn't bear to think of? His expression didn't change; he merely nodded and gave her one of his charming smiles. She was actually enjoying his company and really pleased they'd bumped into each other again, which surprised her.

'Excellent. I can see the change in you. I hope that means you're prepared to write to me and meet up whenever we get leave that coincides.'

'I would like that.' Should she tell him why she was prepared to be his long-distance girlfriend or would he be offended? If only she wasn't so scared of getting close to anyone, wasn't so damaged, she would love to be his girlfriend. There was something about him that made him very special and his smile made her feel warm inside.

'I do like you, Oscar. I'm not ready for anything serious, but I'm surrounded by hundreds, possibly thousands, of airmen and it will make things so much easier for me if I can say with some degree of honesty that I have a boyfriend.'

'That arrangement will suit me too. Things are going

to get busy soon and neither of us will have time for socialising. Knowing that I can write to you and that we can occasionally meet in London will be perfect.'

'It might not be safe to come to London once the bombing starts. Maybe we can meet somewhere safer when that happens.'

'Let's not worry about that now – let's enjoy today.' He was about to compliment her new hairstyle when he overheard something Roy was saying to Elizabeth.

'Things are already hotting up at sea – did you hear that a tanker was sunk in the Thames estuary this morning?'

She really didn't want to think about the war but enjoy the moment, pretend that she didn't have a dark secret, that she wasn't really terrified of getting close to any man in case he hurt her.

Oscar picked up on her disquiet and put his hand over hers. Her instinct was to snatch it back but somehow the warm weight of it was comforting.

'Keep it light, old bean, no shop talk today. Good, the soup's coming.'

The first few mouthfuls were hard to swallow but gradually her throat relaxed and she began to enjoy her meal. Elizabeth was chatting to Roy as if they were old friends and she envied her new friend's confidence.

By the time they were ready to leave she and Oscar were getting on equally well. Like the charming, gallant gentleman he obviously was he assisted her with her heavy coat before putting on his own. When he offered his gloved hand, she didn't hesitate. After all, she too was wearing gloves so there would be no skin contact to set alarm bells ringing.

The snow was crisp underfoot but no longer falling. Every icy breath was invigorating and she couldn't stop smiling. This was what being a normal girl felt like and she wished it would go on forever.

Oscar bought her ticket to see *The Four Feathers* and presumably Roy did the same for Elizabeth. Unfortunately, the film was as tedious as the book but she enjoyed the cartoon and the newsreel made everything seem positive. Even the fact that the British Expeditionary Force were having a horrible time in the snow in France was made to seem jolly good fun. How the soldiers must have hated being forced to throw snowballs and smile as if they weren't freezing cold and missing their families dreadfully.

They stood in the foyer putting on their outdoor things whilst they discussed what they were going to do for the remainder of the evening.

'Shall we find a convivial hostelry or would you ladies prefer something grander?' Roy asked the question but from his expression he was rather hoping they would choose a pub over a hotel.

Elizabeth shook her head. 'I don't want to do either. The hotel we're staying in tonight has a bar and a small restaurant. Why don't we go there?'

'We can't expect Oscar and Roy to find their way back to their own hotel in the blackout. Wouldn't it be better to find somewhere halfway between Piccadilly and Westminster?'

His smile made her feel warm all over. 'We're big boys, walking a mile or two in the snow in the dark is nothing to a brave fighter pilot.' He struck a ridiculous pose and she snorted with laughter.

'In which case, I think Elizabeth's idea is a splendid one.

If we hurry, we might get there before we are falling over our feet in the dark.'

The doorman ushered them through the blackout curtain and, once they were safely in the small space between that and the outside, he opened the doors for them.

'If we hurry you won't need to use up the precious batteries in your torches.' She turned too quickly and with a despairing wail her feet slid from beneath her. She braced herself for an embarrassing and painful fall onto her bottom but Oscar got to her first.

'Not so fast, young lady. No broken bones allowed tonight.' He put his arm firmly around her waist and drew her close. He was only being a gentleman and keeping her safe so there was nothing for her to panic about.

The pavement was so treacherous they had to pick their way through the snow and on several hysterical occasions they almost lost their footing. She was sorry when they reached the hotel. She couldn't remember ever having enjoyed herself so much. Being with him made her feel different, made her forget her miserable past.

After negotiating the complicated blackout curtain arrangement, they emerged into the foyer. There was buzz of conversation coming from the bar, but an unpleasant fug of cigarette and cigar smoke caught the back of her throat.

'If you don't mind, I'd much prefer not to go in there with all the smoke. I'm afraid I don't like the smell of cigarettes and so on.'

'Neither do I, Jane. Maybe there's a table free in the dining room and we can get something light to eat.'

'If you don't mind, you two, Elizabeth and I are going to have a beverage or two. Are you sure you won't join us?'

'No, Roy, thank you. We'll be more comfortable away from the blue haze in there.'

'Elizabeth, give me your things and I'll run them upstairs to our room.'

With her arms full of coats, hats, scarves and gloves she'd raced up the two flights of stairs before remembering she'd not asked for the room key. She was about to stagger back downstairs when Oscar appeared waving it in front of him.

'I think you're going to need this, sweetheart. The concierge asked me to bring it up.'

'Good heavens – I'm surprised he allowed you anywhere near our bedroom.'

He laughed as he deftly turned the key and pushed open the door. 'Only on the strict understanding both of us would be back downstairs within five minutes. I expect he's timing us so we'd better get a move on.'

She tossed the items on the nearest bed and they were running downstairs together moments later.

'There's no space in the dining room but there's a small coffee lounge we can use. Smoking isn't allowed in there.'

There was a dainty plate of sandwiches and a large silver coffee jug waiting for them. There were two other couples and two elegant matrons enjoying the relative peace of this reception room. They all looked up and smiled and nodded and then, apart from the ladies, returned to their own conversations.

'Good evening, my dears. Forgive me for intruding

on your evening,' the older of the two said quietly, 'but seeing you two so happy together has made my evening. Bless you both, and I hope, when this dreadful war is over, you will have come through it safely and can be together for the rest of your lives.'

Oscar saw Jane's expression change and quickly stepped in to disabuse the speaker. 'Just good friends, ma'am, enjoying an evening out.'

The old lady smiled knowingly, unabashed by his denial. 'That's what you think now, young man, but if you both survive this dreadful war, I'll eat my best hat if you're not together.'

Her remark was so outrageous he laughed and luckily Jane saw the funny side too. He turned his back on the two women and winked at Jane. She blushed and hastily helped herself to sandwiches, keeping her head lowered, and left him to pour out the coffee.

'I'm not sure which you thought was the worst option, not surviving or finding yourself saddled with me.' His remark was meant to make her laugh but it did the reverse.

'Don't say that – don't even joke about not making it through. I can't bear to think of you or Roy being killed.'

'Sorry, you looked so horrified at the thought of us being a couple...'

'To be honest, I don't see myself with anyone. However, if I was to become serious about anybody, I'm sure it would be you.'

A somewhat contradictory view but he'd take what he could get. He had a feeling that something had happened to her that had made her reluctant to become close to anyone. Hopefully, when he got to know her better, she would trust him and tell him what it was.

As she couldn't discuss her duties in the WAAF and obviously didn't want to talk about anything personal, it was down to him to talk about himself and his life in the RAF.

'I'm not surprised you wanted to be a fighter pilot rather than a bomber. I know it's going to be incredibly dangerous but, to be honest, flying a Spitfire or Hurricane seems exciting and somewhat romantic.'

He choked on his coffee, spraying the immaculate white tablecloth with brown drops. She jumped to her feet and began to thump him on the back. When he'd recovered his breath, he grabbed her hand and held it for a moment.

'Enough, for heaven's sake, your help is worse than the complaint.'

'Look at the tablecloth – I hope we don't have to pay for the laundry,' she said as she resumed her seat next to him. She sounded genuinely worried.

'Absolutely no chance of that. Don't you want to know what made me splutter all over the table?'

She nodded.

'It was your description of my work as being romantic. Is that really how you girls see us?'

'Not me, I don't find any man romantic. But it will certainly do no harm to my reputation to have my name linked to a flight lieutenant who is a fighter pilot. I don't suppose going out with a lowly ACW2 will improve your standing?'

'Going out with an intelligent, stunningly beautiful WAAF will certainly make me the envy of my squadron.'

He loved the way her cheeks coloured at his compliment. Her smile was quite enchanting and it took all his self-control not to lean over and kiss her.

'Thank you, Oscar. I'm glad that you put my brainpower before my looks in your assessment. The fact that you're not only a fighter pilot – a flight lieutenant – but also very attractive will make every girl who knows I'm your girlfriend incredibly jealous.' She was laughing as she counted off his good points on her fingers and he joined in.

His strict church upbringing had kept him on the straight and narrow whilst at school but since he'd left home he'd had a couple of brief liaisons so wasn't entirely inexperienced in the bedroom department. One thing he was certain of – he would remain celibate until he could make love to her. That wasn't going to happen without benefit of clergy. There were girls you slept with and didn't marry but she wasn't one of them.

Roy and Elizabeth joined them, both a bit tiddly, but he really enjoyed the remainder of the evening and both he and Jane were just as silly as them despite the fact they'd consumed no alcohol.

'That's the third time the waiter has come in, Oscar. I really think you and Roy must go now. It's been such a lovely day. I do hope we can do it again sometime.'

Jane was right. It was time to end the evening. Roy and Elizabeth were on their feet instantly and vanished, no doubt somewhere private where they could exchange a kiss or two. He wished he could do the same with her but knew this wasn't the right time.

'If things don't kick off then I'm sure I'll get leave again next month. Do you have any idea what your schedule will be once you start?'

'I think we do get a thirty-six-hour pass, but I'm not sure exactly how many shifts we have to do first. As soon as I know I'll send you a postcard.'

'It would be easier if you rang.' He'd already written the number of the telephone that was available for aircrew to use. 'There's always someone in the vicinity to answer it and you can just leave a message.'

She took the slip of paper and pushed it into her pocket without looking at it. 'Actually, I'm not sure there's a public telephone available for us. Mind you, I've only been there a few hours and haven't really had time to look around. I'll definitely give you a call if I can, otherwise it will have to be the postcard.'

'It might be easier if you just let me know when you're free as I think it will be simpler for me to get a pass than it will be for you as, at the moment, we're just hanging about.'

'I've really enjoyed spending the day with you and to be honest I didn't expect to. If you'd asked me to meet you I would have said no, but you turning up without warning prevented that.'

'We'd better go as the cleaners are about to move in. I've overstayed my welcome as far as the hotel is concerned.'

The lurking waiter shoved his coat and things into his hands. 'Good night, sir, the other gentleman is outside already.'

'Thank you. I apologise for keeping you waiting. Good night, Jane, take care of yourself.'

She smiled and waved and then was already on her

way upstairs before he reached the exit. He was positively bundled out with his coat only half on and he didn't blame them. It was now after midnight and the poor devils probably had to be back on duty in a few hours.

Roy was waiting for him looking equally dishevelled. 'What a bit of luck, meeting up with those two like that. I really liked Elizabeth and it's quite obvious you and Jane are meant for each other.'

The streets were deserted, the snow underfoot treacherous, and he had to concentrate on staying upright, which gave him no time to continue the conversation.

Jane was almost on the third floor when she realised for the second time that night she'd forgotten to bring the key. Then Elizabeth peered over the banisters and dangled it in front of her. She waved back but didn't call out as she'd no wish to annoy the other guests. Once safely inside their own room she laughed and found herself dancing around the room like a five-year-old.

'I had such fun. What a wonderful day – I hope you enjoyed it as much as I did.'

'I did, Jane, but obviously not as much as you. Roy's very nice but I don't see it coming to anything. Although, I have to admit he's very attractive and certainly an excellent kisser.'

Jane stopped mid-spin and stared open-mouthed at her friend. 'Golly, you kissed him after only knowing him for a day.'

'No harm in a little light flirtation. Are you telling me you've not kissed your gorgeous Oscar yet?'

Her elation vanished like air from a deflating balloon. She collapsed on her bed, ignoring the coats and bags that were already there. 'Are you saying that he would have been expecting me to kiss him?'

'Don't worry about it – not everyone's as liberated as I am. Your Oscar is the son of a vicar so probably doesn't have the same expectations as his friend. Don't look so horrified, Jane. I'm sure he won't take advantage of you. He's a true gentleman. I could tell that immediately I met him. You're lucky to have snagged him for yourself.'

'I've only agreed to write to him occasionally and said that we'll all meet up together if we can get leave at the same time. Like you, I'm really not interested in anything serious. I want to concentrate on my career. My aim is to become an officer eventually.'

'Mine too – I don't think they have anything in place for officer training so far. Hopefully, in a few months things will be different and if we work really hard then we might be put forward for a commission.'

Jane was pleased the subject had turned away from romance. She did enjoy being with Oscar but becoming more involved, being obliged to kiss him and possibly more made her feel unwell. To hide her distress she jumped up and began to hang up the discarded coats in the wardrobe.

'Don't bother, Jane, we're only here one night. We won't get put on a charge for leaving things draped over a chair.'

'I like things to be tidy.' If she'd ever dared to leave the smallest thing out of place when she was at home *that man* would use it as an excuse to beat her. A wave of misery engulfed her. Her mother obviously knew, so why hadn't she done more to prevent the abuse? Was Mum being treated as badly as she had been?

'I say, are you all right? I didn't want to upset you. Let me help you put things away.'

Jane gulped. 'I need the bathroom,' she managed to say before she broke down completely. When she returned she was composed and sure her new friend didn't suspect anything was amiss.

It was a relief when they both scrambled into bed and turned off the light. 'I asked for tea to be brought to us at eight o'clock – that will give us time to eat a leisurely breakfast before we have to head back to Bentley Priory.'

'Thank you, Elizabeth, that sounds perfect. Good night.'

Somehow the rhythmic breathing coming from the other side of the room was soothing and, instead of crying into her pillow as she'd expected, Jane fell asleep almost immediately and didn't wake until the chambermaid knocked on the door the following morning.

14

The freezing weather remained until the end of January and Oscar and his squadron was unable to fly. The base was quickly coming into shape and when this phoney war was over he was sure they would be ready to fight.

It had been two weeks since his unexpected but delightful meeting with Jane and he'd yet to hear from her. He was sitting, staring morosely into his pint in the Officers' Mess with Roy, equally despondent, sitting beside him.

'I know, bloody boring all this hanging about doing bugger all.'

'What? Sorry, I wasn't thinking about the lack of action but the lack of a letter or phone call from Jane. Have you heard from Elizabeth?'

'Now you come to mention it, I haven't. But unlike you, I'm not pining for her. You've really fallen for Jane haven't you?'

"Fraid so. As soon as the roads are clear again I'm going to ask for another forty-eight-hour pass. Riley seems happy for us to shove off whenever we like at the moment. If there was a flap on only half the blokes would be here.'

'Have you written to her?'

'No, I didn't want to frighten her away by seeming too eager. I was waiting for her to make the first move.'

'For God's sake, no wonder you haven't heard from her. She's a shy young thing; she wouldn't dream of writing to you first. You've got her name, number and base, write to her today and it'll be there tomorrow.'

He drained his beer, slapped Roy on the back and headed for the admin offices. There were already more WAAF working there, which was allowing the RAF bods to be released for active duties. One of them was bound to let him have a sheet of paper and an envelope.

There was only one girl in the office and she beamed at him. 'Flight Lieutenant Stanton, what can I do for you?'

'I'd like some paper, an envelope and a stamp so I can write to my girlfriend.'

Her smile slipped and her mouth pursed. 'I'm sorry, sir, I'm not allowed to give out valuable items to anyone who drops in and asks.'

For a moment he was bemused by her comment but then understood. 'That's fine, I'll just help myself then. I don't want to get you into grief.'

She stalked off, pretending to have something to do at the far end of the room, leaving him to collect the items he wanted. The adjutant wandered in as he was writing.

'If you finish that quickly, Stanton, it can go in the post now. Some poor blighter is about to try and take the bag to the post office in Debden.'

'Actually, you're just the man I want. Any chance of being able to nip to London the day after tomorrow?'

'Absolutely, old boy. Nothing much doing here. The

snow's not expected to clear for another week at least and it's too damn cold to fly.'

'Excellent, thank you. Righto, sir, just done.' He signed his name with a flourish, blotted the paper, stuffed it in the envelope and wrote Jane's name, number and whereabouts. He knew those by heart. The note was brief, friendly, just asking her to meet him at the same restaurant at midday in two days' time.

Roy erupted into the office. 'Hang on, I'm going to write to Elizabeth.'

They returned to prop up the bar in better moods. Regardless of the outcome to their letters, they were going to London and would reserve a room at the Sanctuary rather than the guesthouse they'd used before. That way if the girls turned up they couldn't fail to see them at some point.

Unfortunately, none of the other chaps wanted to accompany them so they would have to find their own way to the station. With his overnight bag slung over his shoulder, his flying boots on as they were warmer and more weatherproof than his shoes, he and Roy headed for the gate.

'It's bloody cold, but at least there's been no more snow recently. Maybe the roads will be clear and the buses running as usual.'

'I checked the bus timetable. There should be one in the next ten minutes if they are running. It's worth waiting that long before we start walking. We can hitch a ride if anything goes past. Might be better to go to Saffron Walden, bigger station, bigger town and more chance of getting a lift there and the train to London.'

As they were approaching the gate the guard yelled to

them. 'It's coming. So you'd better run if you want to catch it, sirs.'

He and Roy set off at the double, which wasn't as simple as it sounded wearing flying boots. They skidded past the guards and were just in time to flag down the bus. They scrambled on and were unsurprised to find the vehicle packed.

'Up here, young man, there's a free seat beside me,' a stout matron called out cheerfully. Roy, who was in front of him, was up the bus like a rat out of a drainpipe leaving him to wedge himself between the two rows and hope he didn't go headfirst when the bus next stopped.

On this excursion he'd put on his precious sheepskin flying jacket underneath his greatcoat, so after running a hundred yards he was unpleasantly hot. The bus lurched off and he almost lost his balance. This wasn't going to be as enjoyable for him as it obviously was for Roy who was already chatting away to the lady beside him.

The conductor couldn't get past to collect Roy's money. 'You can't stand here; you're in the way. You'll have to move up and down the bus so's I can do my job. I don't hold with standing passengers, but there you are. There's a war on – could hardly leave two blooming heroes standing in the snow, now could I?'

Oscar smiled at the garrulous old man who looked as if he should be sitting by his fire in his slippers, not collecting the fares on a country bus. 'Thank you, I'm glad you did stop as it's a long walk to Saffron Walden.'

The passengers were mostly housewives bundled up in a variety of outdoor coats, some with headscarves, some with smart hats, but all with shopping bags of some sort in their laps. Maybe it was market day today. Now rationing had kicked in basic foodstuffs were in short supply and being able to buy from a market stall, which as far as he knew weren't restricted in the same way, would be the incentive for coming out in such filthy weather.

He decided to remain next to Roy and not shuffle back down the bus. It was unlikely any of the ladies would disembark at an earlier stop so he was resigned to standing all the way.

Twice the bus drove past people waiting at a stop and he felt sorry for them. The buses only ran every hour so it would be a long cold wait if they decided to remain.

'Don't look so despondent, young man; anyone with any sense would know this bus would be full. The next one will have plenty of seats – they should have stayed in the warm until then.'

'Yes, ma'am, I'm sure you're right. We much appreciate the fact that the driver has broken the rules by picking us up.'

Roy offered to change places with him but he refused. 'No point, we'll be there in fifteen minutes, barring accidents, of course.'

From his vantage point he could see they were approaching a sharp left-hand bend – surely they were going too fast to negotiate it safely? Instinctively he braced his knees against Roy's seat. The driver, realising his error, slammed on the brakes. Never brake hard on icy roads – any bloke should know that.

The bus lost traction. The wheels skidded. The vehicle slewed sideways. The passengers were screaming. Then the front end slid into a ditch and he was flung sideways as the bus tipped half onto its side.

He was trapped with Roy above him and someone ominously silent below. People were floundering about; there was moaning, shouting, hysterical crying and general chaos. Someone had to take charge. The bus was full of vulnerable women, some elderly, and the only other two men were the ancient conductor and the equally old driver.

'Roy, if you're not hurt can you move? Then we can try and help. No one else seems to be doing anything.'

'I'm fine. Bruised but functioning.'

The weight shifted and he was able to breathe more easily. Too much movement might be catastrophic. At the moment the vehicle was listing heavily to the right but the floor was more or less in the right place, but as the front of the bus was in a ditch the usual exit wouldn't be accessible.

He scanned the passengers and was relieved to see that most of them were now sitting up and taking notice. Now he was off the floor, the unfortunate woman who'd been trapped under them could be tended to. Before that he had to get their attention.

'Right, ladies, please remain still. Please stop shouting.' He used his parade-ground voice and it did the trick. The noise subsided into quiet sobs and gulps but there were still a few worrying moans from women who were obviously more seriously injured.

'My friend is going to kick out the rear window and then we'll start getting those of you who are relatively unharmed out that way.'

Roy helped the ladies nearest to them to sit up whilst he searched for a pulse in the comatose lady who'd been crushed beneath both him and Roy. She was alive – but her pulse was weak and irregular. Someone would need to find a house, not only with a telephone, but able to accommodate the thirty or so passengers. They couldn't possibly stand around in the sub-zero temperatures after they'd been through an experience like this.

'Here, let me help, young man. I worked as a nurse in the last war.'

'Thank you, she's barely breathing. I'm going to have to move her or no one else will be able to get out as she's blocking the way.'

He was unable to continue as Roy kicked out the window and the hideous sound of breaking glass drowned out everything else.

'If you can give me room, I'll give her a quick examination. Hopefully she's not damaged her neck or back.'

With the rear window removed, the temperature in the bus plummeted. The sooner those that were mobile were out the happier he'd be.

'I'm ready, Oscar. I'll get these ladies out first and then you work down the bus. One of them has broken her wrist, cuts and bruises on the others but they're all capable of scrambling out.'

'Do that. If there's anyone fit enough, send them for help.'

The bus rocked alarmingly each time someone climbed out but so far had remained in situ.

'Young man, you can move this patient. There's no need to delay things any further.'

He understood immediately. The poor woman had died. Carefully he put his arms under her shoulders and gently moved her so she was slumped against the windows. Only then did he see the dent in her forehead.

He was about to strip off his greatcoat and cover her but

his helper got there first. 'My shawl will do the trick. You're going to need your coat – this poor soul is beyond our help.' She deftly draped the cloth across the dead woman's face making it obvious to anyone who crawled past there was at least one fatality.

He was concerned that he'd heard nothing from the conductor or the driver and feared they too might have met an untimely end. The exodus continued smoothly but the bus was still half full when he heard the welcome sound of wheels crunching to a halt on the road.

Roy was in a better position to see who it was. 'Army trucks – just the ticket.'

It took another hour to get everyone else out and as he'd feared both the driver and conductor had perished in the accident. It was a miracle that there were only three fatalities considering the seriousness of the crash.

Those who needed hospital attention had been taken in one of the trucks and warmly wrapped in army greatcoats. The remainder of the passengers had now been reunited with their possessions and escorted to the nearest houses where they were being plied with tea and biscuits.

The police were in charge of the scene and then two ambulances belatedly appeared. The drivers now had the unpleasant task of removing the corpses and taking them to the morgue.

'Jane, there's a letter for each of us,' Elizabeth said as she looked through the pigeonholes in the main foyer. These were set out in alphabetical order and each one was stuffed full, making it difficult to find anything for oneself.

They moved aside to allow others to find their mail. Jane tore hers open. 'It's from Oscar saying that he and Roy are going to be staying in London for two nights and they would like to meet up at the restaurant we used last time if possible.'

'Golly, mine says exactly the same thing. What's the date today?'

'January the twenty-fifth.' She smiled and continued. 'It's a Thursday in case you hadn't noticed.'

'They're going to be there tomorrow and Saturday – I can't believe that we've got a thirty-six-hour pass starting after our shift tomorrow afternoon. This means we can also stay both nights as long as we're back really early on Sunday morning. Shall we go?'

'Absolutely spiffing idea,' Jane said with a smile. 'It's very intense here and I think it will do us good to get away for a bit.'

'One of us had better ring the hotel and check they have accommodation available. I don't want to turn up and find there's no room.'

'I think I've still got the receipt for the last time somewhere in my locker. There's no time to find it now as the coach will be here in a minute to take us to work.'

Jane was competent at her job and, although eager to be involved with plotting the passage of actual enemy aircraft, she was dreading the day when her skills would be tested for real. Elizabeth was equally expert – in fact they were expecting to be moved to the Dover section of the large map, which would be the busiest and most crucial, and only the very best worked there.

There were often periods of time when there was nothing

to plot and they could stand and talk to each other and were sometimes allowed to take a short break away from the table. This was the case today.

She and her friend were given half an hour and they headed for the NAAFI. This was always heaving with both men and women and sometimes the queue was so long there wasn't time to actually buy anything. They were lucky today and took their egg and chips to a table with two vacant places.

The other seats were occupied by two WAAFs and two pilots. These were always easy to identify, not just because of the gold wings on the uniform but by their air of confidence and superiority. They were the elite of the service and didn't they know it.

Oscar and Roy weren't like that. They were really nice and didn't show off at all. 'I suppose we should have written to them, but it seemed a bit forward. I'm really glad they contacted us.'

'I'd like to go somewhere more exciting than the cinema this time. Have you ever been to a nightclub?'

The question was so absurd Jane laughed. 'Of course I haven't. Until I became a WAAF last September the only place I'd ever been was to my boarding school in Surrey. I've led a very sheltered life, you know.' She regretted having spoken about her past the moment the words left her mouth. The last thing she wanted was to talk about her life before she joined up.

'Do you know, we've become good friends but I don't even know how old you are, or anything at all about your family.'

She looked down at her food and what had seemed

appetising was now the reverse. She stuffed her irons back in their bag and jumped up. 'I'm sorry, I hope you can scoff this. I need the loo more than I need to eat.' Somehow she forced herself to smile.

'I'm absolutely starving, so I can polish that off with no trouble. I'll buy you a bun if I have time.'

Jane forced herself to stroll away when what she wanted to do was run. She headed for the nearest ablutions block and had recovered her equilibrium by the time she returned to her post.

During a lull in proceedings Elizabeth handed her a bun. 'Quick, there's no one looking, eat this. You must be ravenous.'

She gobbled it down and just had time to brush the crumbs from her uniform and put her headset back on when it crackled into life. Despite the fact that the weather was horrible, aircraft were in the air because the runways had been cleared of snow and there'd been no fresh falls in the last week.

Elizabeth had managed to reserve a room for them and her friend was bubbling with excitement at the thought of spending two nights in London escorted by a handsome flying officer. Jane was no longer sure she wanted to go but could hardly back out now.

'I hope the two of them don't think we've stood them up,' Elizabeth said.

'I'm sure they'll understand. We'll go there tomorrow in the hope that they turn up. After all,' Jane said, 'they don't actually know that we're coming.'

Travelling on the underground, catching a bus and walking around London now felt familiar to her. Even the fact that it was almost dark didn't bother her. There was something they hadn't discussed and if she didn't want to find herself going to a nightclub, she'd better speak up now.

'I want to do the same things we did last time. Have a lovely meal at that restaurant and then go to the pictures and come back to the hotel for coffee. If you and Roy want to do something more glamorous then go ahead, I'm sure Oscar won't mind.'

'And I'm sure that he will. He's a red-blooded RAF officer – he'll expect to do something a bit more exciting this time. You said that you like to dance, surely that's more interesting than sitting watching a boring film.'

'I couldn't possibly go anywhere smart as I didn't bring an evening dress.' She giggled. 'Actually, even if I'd wanted to bring one that would be impossible as I don't own anything like that.'

Elizabeth looked at her as if she was insane. 'None of us has got any civilian clothes. We had to send them back in a parcel. All service personnel will be in uniform like us.'

She stopped so abruptly a businessman in a bowler hat and pinstriped suit was obliged to step into the road to avoid bumping into her. His immaculate black shoes and spats were spoiled by the dirty slush he was forced into. They had arrived in London as businesses were closing down for the night and the pavements were busy with similar gentlemen in a hurry to get home.

He scowled at her and muttered something rude and for a moment she thought he was going to poke her in the stomach with his umbrella. The incident cleared the air.

'What an unpleasant individual he was. Come on, Jane, let's show them we won't be pushed aside.'

They linked arms and continued to walk down the centre of the pavement ignoring the muttered curses from those who had to step aside. When they reached the hotel they were giggling as they walked through the doors and sidled around the blackout curtains.

15

By the time Oscar and Roy got a lift to the station in a police car they were dishevelled and filthy. They found a decent café and after three mugs of tea and a couple of dubious sandwiches Oscar felt a lot better. On entering the premises they had received several raised eyebrows and disapproving looks from the other occupants but, by the time they'd finished, the atmosphere had changed. Word had obviously spread about the accident.

When he asked for his bill the proprietor shook her head. 'On the house. You saved a lot of lives today and some of them are my regulars.'

There was a spontaneous round of applause and he exchanged an embarrassed grin with his friend. 'Thank you, I just wish we could have done more. Do you happen to know when the next train goes to London?'

'I do indeed, you've got ten minutes so you'll have to leave pronto if you want to catch it. Mind you, it's usually late nowadays.'

They left the pleasant warmth of the café and slithered their way to the station.

'We're not going to get to London in time to meet the girls. Thank God we've reserved a room at the same hotel so we can make a grovelling apology,' Oscar said as the train steamed into the station.

'We don't even know if they're going to be there – it'll be a magnificent coincidence if they can get leave at the same time as us. I'm knackered, I'm going to catch a kip if we can get a seat,' his friend replied.

They were fortunate and found an empty compartment. It was icy, but they didn't care. Oscar slumped into the window seat opposite Roy, stretched his legs out and promptly fell asleep.

'Feet off the seats, you two, and show me your tickets.' A bad-tempered ticket collector jerked him from his slumbers.

He swung his legs to the floor and looked across at Roy who was apparently still asleep, or maybe just ignoring the interruption and leaving him to deal with it.

'We were involved in a bus accident, three fatalities, many injured. No doubt it will be in the papers tomorrow.' He couldn't prevent a yawn. 'I'm sorry, but we didn't have time to buy tickets.'

'I should have realised you two were the blokes they're talking about. You've got your feet on your bags – you relax and get a well-deserved sleep. Don't bother about the tickets.'

The door to the compartment was closed a lot more quietly than it had opened a few minutes ago. Roy opened one eye, grinned, and went back to sleep.

It was mid-afternoon, already getting dark, when they eventually emerged from Liverpool Street station. They caught the District and Metropolitan underground to Charing

Cross and then decided to walk along the embankment to Westminster Bridge and then to the hotel.

Despite approaching it from the opposite direction he had no difficulty leading them to the hotel. If the concierge recognised them from their previous visit, he showed no hostility.

'Welcome, Flight Lieutenant Stanton and Flying Officer Cross.' He pushed across the book and they filled in their details. The key was handed over and they were told their room was on the first floor adjacent to the bathroom and WC.

'Let's get spruced up, then come down and have a beer.' He was disappointed that Jane's name wasn't in the book.

Roy slapped him rather too hard on the back, making him stumble forward. It also made him laugh.

'Don't worry, they might turn up tomorrow. Shall we book a table for dinner? I don't fancy wandering about tonight.'

'Okay, pity it's not for four.'

The room they'd been allocated was adequate, but not as luxurious as one might have expected in a hotel in such a prestigious area of the city.

'I'll take the one on the left – not that there's any difference.' There was a neat pile of towels stacked on the end of his bed. He grabbed the largest. 'I'm going to have a bath. If I leave the water in you can legitimately add another five inches.'

'Fair enough. Aren't you going to take your boots and things off first?'

'Not thinking straight. What happened this morning

has really shaken me up. You do realise that it was us who killed that poor woman?'

'Jesus Christ! Don't start blaming yourself or me for that. We both saw the dent in her forehead. That's what killed her, not us landing on top of her.'

Roy's vehemence did the trick.

'You're right. Sorry. Three more unnecessary deaths so soon after Johnny's – I suppose we'd better get used to it.'

'You're not like Riley, it'll always knock you sideways. That's what makes you a good bloke. You just need to deal with it better.'

'Yes, sir.' He straightened and did a mock salute before going in search of the bathroom and a much-needed soak.

An hour later he was refreshed and ravenous but dinner wouldn't be served until six o'clock. He would have to ignore the rumblings until then.

Roy had taken charge of the key and after locking the door he dropped it into his jacket pocket. Luckily the worst of the grime had been on their greatcoats and flying boots. Their uniforms underneath were relatively unscathed – if a bit creased.

There was no need to hand the key in as they weren't leaving the premises. 'Bar or coffee lounge?'

Roy didn't hesitate. 'Definitely bar. I booked a table for six thirty – that means we've got an hour and a half's drinking time...' He stopped as the blackout curtains billowed outwards as the front doors were opened.

Oscar was moving before he realised it. He'd recognised Jane's laughter immediately. She and Elizabeth emerged from behind the material still giggling helplessly.

'Good evening, ladies, what a delightful surprise. We thought you weren't coming.' He desperately wanted to snatch her up and kiss her breathless. She was quite enchanting when she was happy.

To his delight she dropped her bag and held out her hands. 'We thought we'd missed you. I'm so pleased to see you, Oscar. We've had such fun making grumpy businessmen step into the snow.'

He grasped them but made no attempt to draw her closer. 'We've had a dismal day until now. Everything's better now you're here. We've a table booked for six thirty, which gives you plenty of time to sort yourselves out and come down and join us. Shall I get you a shandy?'

Even through her thick gloves the sensation of her hands being held by Oscar was thrilling. Then the memory of *that man* grabbing her, dragging her into his study so he could thrash her, made her snatch them away.

'A shandy would be lovely. Sorry, urgent need for the bathroom. It's been a very long journey.' She was talking nonsense and they both knew it.

His smile was a trifle forced as he moved aside to let her rush past. Elizabeth was being soundly kissed by Roy and this just made her run faster. She'd no idea which room they were in this time so headed for the closest bathroom, which was on the first floor. When her friend extricated herself from her embrace no doubt she would sign them both in and collect the key.

She bolted in and locked the door behind her. The mirror was steamed up and condensation trickled down the tiles

– someone had just had a bath. The thought that a naked person had been in here moments before made her uneasy and she was out again in seconds.

The loo was next door and she hid in there instead. She leaned against the door until her heart stopped thudding in her ears and her hands were no longer shaking. After rinsing her face with cold water she was ready to emerge.

Elizabeth was just coming up the stairs. 'We've got the same room; they must think we liked it so much we wanted to stay in it again. I say, are you all right? Did you have words with Oscar?'

'I'm absolutely splendid, thank you. Just needed a pee. All that laughing is bad for the bladder.'

This time they hung up their coats instead of dumping them on the bed. They were about to make their way back to the foyer when she recalled something Oscar had said. 'I wonder what happened to them for him to have said he'd had a dismal day. Did Roy tell you?'

'No, there wasn't time for conversation. He's a really good kisser – I bet Oscar is too when you get that far.'

'I'm not that sort of girl. I don't want to do that with anyone until we're engaged.' This was entirely the wrong thing to say as Elizabeth took it personally.

'Are you saying that I'm *that sort of girl*?' Instead of being angry her friend looked hurt.

'I'm sorry, there's something I want to tell you that will explain everything. It's a secret and I don't want you to tell anyone else.'

Elizabeth's expression changed to one of sympathy. 'Golly, how awful. You don't have to tell me what happened if you don't want to.'

They sat down side-by-side on a bed and she told Elizabeth what *that man* had done to her, how this had made her nervous around any man – even one as lovely as Oscar.

'That's dreadful, you poor thing. No wonder you're as jumpy as a kitten.'

'Do you think I should tell Oscar? He must think I'm deranged the way I've been blowing hot and cold with him.' She shuddered at the thought.

'No, he doesn't need to know until he's actually your real boyfriend. I promise I won't say anything to anyone.'

'Thank you. I wish I could be as mature as you about things but... but you can understand why I'm not.'

When that horrible officer at the dance had molested her, it had made her feel sick. She intended to avoid being touched like that, even by Oscar who was a respectful and charming young man who treated her wonderfully.

Elizabeth touched her arm as they reached the lower landing and brought her back to the present. 'Have you thought any more about suggesting that we go to a nightclub or something tomorrow night?'

'I don't want to go anywhere in this weather. We're having dinner with them tonight. I'd rather wait and see how things go before committing myself to another date tomorrow.' Whilst Elizabeth was locking the door she decided to tell her about her nasty experience after the dance.

'Oscar knocked the man down for you. If I was you I'd be thrilled to have someone as gorgeous as him falling for me.'

'I am sort of thrilled, but just when everything is going so well, I panic. I hated being touched by that other man and don't want to be in that position again.'

'I'm afraid that beautiful girls like us are bound to be noticed and inevitably some of us are unlucky and do get mauled through no fault of their own.' Elizabeth's expression was pensive before she continued. 'I wish I was more like you; sometimes I let my impulses overtake my common sense. We'd better not hang about. They'll think we've changed our minds.'

'Thank you for the compliment, but it paints a rather grim picture, doesn't it? I think I'd rather be a plain Jane if that's what I have to look forward to. Don't forget, we're surrounded by airmen of all ranks where we work and there are bound to be a handful of bounders amongst them.'

'I've had a couple of near misses myself. The only advice I can give you is not to put yourself in unnecessary danger by being alone where there are a lot of strange men.'

'I think all men are rather strange.'

She pinned on what she hoped was a happy smile and ran down the last flight of steps. Oscar was talking to Roy and they were looking at a poster on the wall and didn't see her coming. She paused on the bottom step to look at him more closely.

'He really is a very handsome man. I don't understand why he's interested in me.'

'Have you looked in the mirror lately? Come on, let's see what they're finding so interesting.'

He sensed her approach and turned. His smile made her feel warm all over and she wasn't sure if that was a good thing or not.

'At last, we thought you'd abandoned us.'

'What are you two reading?'

'There's something on at the Ritz – an afternoon tea dance. I rather thought that would be perfect for us. It's in the Palm Court and is being broadcast on the wireless. What do you think?'

'It sounds wonderful but won't all the other guests be dripping with diamonds and mink coats – not to mention grand afternoon tea dresses?'

Elizabeth overheard her query. 'There will be loads of people in uniform, I expect. Anyway, even if there isn't, I don't care. My only reservation is that it might be too expensive.'

Roy was still studying the poster. 'Not for us it won't. It says here that anyone in uniform pays only half the cost. I think Oscar and I can manage the three and six a head. No, don't argue, girls, this is our treat.'

'Then that would be absolutely spiffing, but if you're paying tomorrow then at least let us split the bill for dinner tonight,' Jane said and Elizabeth nodded.

'I know you get far more than us each week but unlike you RAF chaps, we don't have massive bar bills to pay.'

This remark was greeted by laughter but Jane noticed neither of them denied it. She rather thought that if she was a fighter pilot – in fact, any sort of pilot – with a very short life expectancy once battle commenced, she would drink herself silly every night too.

Oscar put his arm lightly around Jane's shoulders and was relieved when she didn't shrug him off. 'Why don't you two go into the coffee lounge and bag a table whilst Roy and I get some drinks in?'

'That's good as I'd much prefer to have my shandy there; that is, if we're allowed to take alcoholic beverages in.'

'I'm sure we are. I assume Elizabeth's gone with Roy.'

For some reason this information upset her. 'I'm not sure I even want a drink now. Maybe I'll go upstairs and leave you three together. I'll come down later.'

There was something going on here. He hated to see her so distressed and was determined to discover what it was. 'No, let's find a quiet corner and you can tell me what's wrong.'

He saw panic in her eyes and knew she was about to bolt. He put his arm firmly around her waist so she couldn't escape and bundled her into the lounge, which fortunately was empty. She was trembling; he hoped to God it wasn't his actions that had caused this.

Her arms were tense when he gently pushed her into a chair. He swung another one round so that when he sat his knees were so close to hers that she couldn't escape.

'I need to know what's wrong, sweetheart. You're like a startled kitten. It can't go on like this.'

Her knuckles were white where she was gripping the arms of the chair. She refused to raise her head and look at him. Was she upset or angry? He tried again.

'Jane, you need to share your secret with me if this is going to go anywhere.'

She mumbled something but he couldn't quite catch what she said. He leaned forward. As he did so she shot up and the crown of her head caught him square in the mouth. The pain was horrendous. His lower teeth had gone through his lip. Even worse, they appeared to have caused a gash on her scalp from which blood was flowing freely. His chair had toppled backwards.

'Bloody hell – I'm sorry,' he spluttered. Then snatching his handkerchief from his pocket, he pressed it on her injury.

She looked up, eyes wide and tear-filled. 'There's blood dripping down your face. Quickly, take the handkerchief from my pocket and press it on your mouth.'

Roy and Elizabeth walked into this carnage. 'Sod me – there's blood everywhere. Elizabeth, press this on top of the one Jane's already holding on her head. Oscar, let me look. I hope to God you haven't broken your teeth. You wouldn't want to spoil your pretty face.'

His mouth was full of blood and he didn't think it would be appreciated by the management if he spat it on their pristine carpet. The concierge rushed in, having heard the racket. Took one look at the pair of them bleeding profusely and took charge.

Moments later he was given a handful of napkins and was able to spit the contents of his mouth into a couple and then hold the others over his injury. He was more concerned about Jane.

Roy pushed him into a chair. 'Sit here, you silly bugger, someone's sent for a medic. You're both going to need stitches. Don't try and speak – I can see it's bloody painful.'

The initial shaft of pure hell had now settled to an unpleasant throbbing. He was more concerned about the blood coming from both inside and outside, which was filling his mouth and causing him to spit repeatedly into the napkins. He had his tongue pressed firmly on the back of the injury in the vain hope this would at least stop it coming out from that side.

Someone had told him a human had eight pints of blood. From the mess he thought he was probably down to seven by now. One was supposed to hold an injured limb above one's heart to slow the bleeding but neither of them could do this.

Moving his head just sprayed gore in every direction so he couldn't even look across and see how Jane was doing.

16

Jane was watching Oscar with horror. There was so much blood. As fast as he mopped it up more came. This was her fault. If she hadn't tried to run away the accident wouldn't have happened.

Elizabeth was kneeling beside her and looked as stricken as she felt. 'What a disaster! Shall I hold the pad on your cut for you so you can give your arm a rest?'

'Thank you. My head's throbbing and I've not got a clean shirt and this one's ruined.'

'They've sent for a doctor so hopefully he'll come and sew you both up. I hope neither of you has to go to hospital.'

'So do I. What a waste of a thirty-six-hour pass that would be. I think this might be the doctor coming in.'

Her friend looked round and nodded. 'The black bag's a bit of a clue.'

'Tell him to go to Oscar first.'

'There's no need – he's already doing that. Here, why don't you drink your shandy. I seem to remember from my St John's Ambulance course that one has to replace any blood lost with fluids.'

'I daren't move my head as I think I might faint or, even worse, be sick all over the floor.'

Elizabeth hastily scrambled to her feet, letting go of the pad. Jane put her hand back just in time. A few moments later a china basin was dropped into her lap. 'Just in case. How ever did this happen?'

'I was looking down and then I think he must have been leaning over to talk to me when I decided to get up.'

'Good gracious! I can't believe doing something so ordinary could have caused so much damage.' Elizabeth flopped down on the chair beside her. 'I suppose we're going to miss our dinner tonight after all this.'

'How can you think of food when Oscar and I are mortally wounded?' Her comment had the desired effect and her companion smiled.

'I'll go and speak to the head waiter and see if they'll save us something.'

'I think you and Roy should eat – the table's booked and it would be a pity to waste the reservation. We can get a sandwich if we want one when the doctor's patched us up. I couldn't possibly go into the dining room looking like I do and Oscar's uniform is in a worse state than mine.'

'If you're sure you don't mind me leaving you, I'll suggest it to Roy.'

Jane was disappointed even though she'd suggested her friend leave. She wouldn't have gone if their positions had been reversed. Maybe Elizabeth was a bit squeamish and the sight of all the blood was making her unwell.

She risked a glance in Oscar's direction and was disconcerted to see that he was looking straight at her whilst the doctor completed stitching his injury. 'I'm so sorry; I can't believe how much damage I've caused by my stupidity.'

Obviously, he couldn't speak, couldn't even move his head, but he raised a bloodstained hand and from his gesture she thought he was disagreeing with her.

Unwanted tears trickled down her cheeks mingling with the blood already there. If only things were different – if only *she* was different – she really thought he could become someone special in her life.

She didn't have another handkerchief, or even a free hand to reach for a clean napkin, so closed her eyes and tried to pretend she wasn't sitting in a public room, covered in blood, waiting to have her head stitched together for the second time.

Then Oscar was beside her and gently wiping her face with a damp, warm cloth. 'Don't cry, Jane, none of this is your fault.'

His voice sounded odd, as if he was talking with cotton wool in his mouth, but his concern was still apparent from the way he spoke and from his actions. No one had ever shown her so much kindness and this made the tears flow more freely. He put his arm around her shoulder and she leaned against him feeling protected, feeling safe for the first time in her life. Her free hand was held firmly in his.

'Miss Hadley, I apologise for having to keep you waiting so long.' The doctor spoke from beside her but she didn't open her eyes and was incapable of a verbal response. 'I'm going to take your hand away now and look at the injury.'

An extremely unpleasant, but mercifully short, time later the stitches were in and the gash covered with a clean dressing.

'There, all done. You will both need to see a medic at your base and, Miss Hadley, you'll need to get the dressing changed in two days. I'll leave a couple for you just in case. The stitches must come out in six or seven days.'

Oscar mumbled an answer for both of them. 'Thank you. Your prompt assistance is much appreciated. Please leave your bill with the concierge and I'll deal with it before we leave tomorrow.'

'No charge, Flight Lieutenant Stanton. Least I can do for two patients in uniform.' The doctor rummaged around and handed Oscar something, then collected up his medical items, put them back in his bag and vanished.

'He didn't even introduce himself,' she said. 'I must go upstairs and clean up.' She pointed to his uniform, which made him look as if he'd been in a major accident, not something as trivial as a few stitches in his mouth.

'The medic has left us some painkillers as well. I think we should both retire, get ourselves sorted and then take a couple of pills and go to bed.' His words were muffled and he winced every time he spoke. His lower lip was horribly swollen and she was to blame.

'I've ruined your furlough with my clumsiness. Don't try and answer me – I can see how painful it is for you. I don't suppose eating or drinking is going to be easy either.' Then she had a brainwave. 'Wait there a minute, I'm going to get you a straw; then at least you can drink your beer before you go. You need to rehydrate after losing so much blood.'

He waved a hand to indicate he agreed and she rushed off to find a waiter. He was only too happy to help and she came back with half a dozen paper straws. Oscar was leaning back, his eyes closed, his face much paler than usual. She felt strangely light-headed and thought it had been unwise to run so soon after being stitched up.

She put out a steadying hand and took several deep breaths. 'Here you are. They offered to bring some soup but I think that would be too hard to suck that up through a straw – and anyway the paper would probably disintegrate.'

Although his face was pale his eyes were alert and he held out his hand for his beer, smiling his thanks. He took three long sucks on the straw and then raised his thumb to show it was working. Happy she'd been able to help for once she collected her own shandy and drained it in half a dozen swallows.

'I think it was rather mean of Roy and Elizabeth to abandon us in order to have a delicious dinner. They haven't even checked back to see how we're doing. I know you and Roy have been friends for years, but I only met Elizabeth a few weeks ago and don't really know her very well.'

The revolting noise coming from the bottom of his glass indicated he'd also finished his pint. 'You told them to go. Can't blame them.'

'Well, I didn't think they'd take me up on my suggestion. Would you like me to get you another beer?'

He shook his head and stood up smoothly. It was just her that was light-headed as obviously he was perfectly fine apart from his stitches and associated discomfort. This was a huge relief as she'd never forgive herself if she'd done him any serious harm.

Oscar was conscious that both he and Jane would put off the paying customers if they entered the restaurant in their blood-soaked clothes. Apart from finding speaking difficult, he was perfectly well. She, on the other hand, looked fragile and frighteningly pale. The sooner she was tucked up in bed with a hot water bottle the better. He held out his hand and she took it.

'I'll have a look and see if the coast's clear. I'm sure the management don't want us to be seen by anyone else if possible. If I look half as bad as you do then I'm certain we'd put them off their dinner.'

She didn't release her hold, but peered around the open door whilst still attached to him.

'No one there. Have you got your key? Elizabeth has mine. I've asked a waiter to collect it for me.'

He shook his head. 'I'm sure Roy will hand it over at the same time. I asked them to put a jug of water in our rooms as well as a hot water bottle in our beds.' He pulled gently on her hand and she moved closer.

They lurked out of sight waiting for the keys to be fetched. A waiter arrived and handed them over. 'Is there anything else you require? Miss, sir?'

'No, thank you,' she replied and took them, checked the numbers and handed his over. 'It's safe to go. The foyer's empty now.' She stepped forward but swayed and put her hand on the wall to steady herself.

'Shock. Making you wobbly.'

She nodded and allowed him to place his arm firmly around her waist without comment. 'I was trying to ignore it, but I do feel very shaky. The doctor did some tests and was certain I'm not concussed.'

He already knew the girls had the same room they'd had last time. If she stumbled again, he would carry her. The pint of beer had sorted him out and he now felt fully fit, apart from his face.

They reached the second floor without mishap but when she attempted to unlock the door her hands were trembling. He put his over hers and guided the key into the aperture and then turned it.

'I don't know why I'm in such a state. I've already had an extreme response to my inoculations, was knocked senseless when that dog attacked our column and I didn't feel like this. Why have I reacted this time in such a soppy way?' He was about to answer when she twisted in his arms. 'No, that was a rhetorical question. We can talk tomorrow when your face has gone down a bit. Good night, Oscar, hopefully I'll see you at breakfast.'

He cupped her face with his hand but obviously didn't attempt to kiss her. Her eyes glittered. She turned away abruptly and closed the door firmly behind her. He was convinced someone had hurt her badly when she was young. A wave of fury surged through him. No one would ever hurt her again if he had anything to do with it. He rarely lost his temper and never swore, but then he'd never been in love before.

Despite the circumstances, and his throbbing face, he made his way to his own room feeling happier than he'd ever been in his life. Whatever was coming – and he knew it was going to be bad – as long as he had Jane in his life he would be content.

She'd tucked the spare straws into his top pocket and he carefully removed them before taking off his jacket. He stared gloomily at the stains. Tea at the Ritz tomorrow was impossible on both counts now. He stripped off his soiled shirt and wondered if soaking it in the washbasin might remove the blood.

There was a tentative knock on the door. He strode across and opened it half-hoping it might be her returning to see if he was okay. There was a chambermaid smiling nervously outside the door.

'Excuse me for disturbing you, sir, but I'm to take your jacket, shirt and tie to housekeeping and they'll be returned to you by morning.'

'Miss Hadley?'

'Yes, sir, her uniform has been collected too. It'll be tickety-boo tomorrow.'

He handed over his garments along with half a crown. She beamed, thanked him profusely and all but skipped away. He'd been overgenerous with his tip, but tonight was different. He was praying that even if it took a year or more, eventually, he could persuade Jane to marry him.

He drank two glasses of water through a straw and was about to remove his shoes and trousers but decided he'd use the WC first. He shrugged on his leather flying jacket and hoped if he met any other guests they wouldn't notice he was improperly dressed.

When Roy came in hours later he was pleasantly drowsy but not quite asleep. He pushed himself up on one elbow. The strong painkillers were working wonderfully.

'Do you need anything, Oscar? I'll nip down and get it if you do.'

'No, thanks. Did you have an enjoyable evening?'

'Good, thank you. I'll not bore you with the details. You look a lot better and the swelling's already gone down a bit. Good night. Tomorrow's going to be interesting.'

As Oscar was drifting off, he wondered what his friend had meant about tomorrow being interesting. A tea dance at the Ritz could hardly be called interesting, so what was he missing?

Jane woke when the early-morning tea tray arrived. The stitches in her head pulled at her scalp when she moved but apart from that she felt no ill effects from the accident. She sincerely hoped Oscar was also feeling better. She'd no idea when her friend had returned but she was obviously back. Jane waited for Elizabeth to get up but there was no movement from the shape in the bed on the other side of the room.

The chambermaid knocked again slightly louder. 'I'm coming, sorry.'

She opened the door and took the tray from the waiting girl and put it on the bureau. Her freshly washed and ironed shirt and her sponged and pressed jacket had been hanging on the doorknob. She collected these before attending to the tea. Only then did her friend stir.

'Wonderful, a hot cup of tea is exactly what I want. I don't suppose you've got any aspirin?'

'I haven't, but you can have one of my painkillers if you want, as I don't need any more.'

Elizabeth sat up, her hair mussed, her eyes a bit bloodshot and groaned. 'I've got a stinking hangover. I really shouldn't have had a G&T, three glasses of wine and a large brandy last night.'

'No, you really shouldn't. Shall I bring you a pill?'

'Yes. Be an angel and fetch my tea. I don't want a biscuit.'

Fussing about with the teapot, tea strainer and sugar tongs meant Jane didn't have to reply. If she had, she might have told bossy boots she wasn't there to wait on her. Although they spent a lot of time together she didn't really know Elizabeth that well.

She thought longingly of Charlotte and Nancy who were genuine friends. There was writing paper, pen, ink and envelopes stacked neatly in the stationery tray. She would write to both her friends after breakfast and tell them what had happened. She would write to her mother and put it in a quick note to Mrs Jackson, the vicar's wife.

There was no kind enquiry about her head injury from her companion. It was as if nothing untoward had happened last night. She drank her tea quickly and then pulled the lacquered screen, provided for privacy, around the washbasin.

There was still no movement from the other bed and she peeked round to see that Elizabeth had drunk the tea and had apparently fallen asleep again. This would give her time to write her letters before she went down for breakfast.

After sponging the blood from her head she was ready to attempt to put her hair up in such a way that the stitches wouldn't show. She'd removed the dressing to wash her hair and decided not to put the compress and white dressing back as there was nothing oozing from the wound.

She deftly twisted her hair into a French pleat and pushed in the pins to hold it in place, relieved that this hadn't hurt her one jot and now nobody could see anything unpleasant.

A plaintive voice came from the body in the bed. 'Can you pour me another cup of tea?'

'I should think it's cold by now. I'm going down for breakfast. I'll leave the key on the inside of the door so you can lock it after me if you want.' Her letters could wait.

She was out of the door before Elizabeth could answer and closed it firmly behind her. She glanced at her watch. Eight o'clock – perfect time to have breakfast. It would be an unnerving experience going into the dining room on her own but she was certain she could manage it.

She wasn't exactly sure which room Oscar and Roy occupied, but she could hardly knock on their door and ask if they were coming down. If Elizabeth had a rotten hangover then it was quite possible Roy was similarly afflicted. Was Oscar sufficiently recovered to eat or would he have to stick to drinking through a straw?

The concierge greeted her with a friendly smile. 'Good morning, Miss Hadley, I'm glad to see you looking well.'

'Thank you, it was so kind of you to have my uniform cleaned and pressed. Is it all right for me to go into the dining room on my own?'

Oscar spoke from behind her – he was remarkably soft-footed and she hadn't heard him approaching. 'Good morning, Jane, I'm glad to see you down here. How's the head?' His voice sounded normal and she turned to look at him.

'I can't believe that the swelling has gone down so quickly. Apart from the stitches one wouldn't know you'd had such a horrible accident.'

'What's happened to your dressing? I'm certain you shouldn't have taken it off so soon. The doctor gave me some spare; I really think you need to let me reapply one.'

'I had to take it off to clean my head and hair. I couldn't put my hair up with the dressing on.'

He frowned. 'You could leave it loose – we don't have

to go anywhere today – we can stay in the hotel and play dominoes or cards. It's raining outside...'

'Well, it's hardly going to be raining inside, is it?'

His smile made him look even more attractive. 'Very true. I'm ravenous – shall we go in to eat before I collapse at your feet from starvation?'

They were escorted to a table in the centre of the dining room, which meant they had no privacy and a constant to-ing and fro-ing of waiters on either side. Not ideal – but hopefully after breakfast they could retreat to the coffee lounge again.

He ordered porridge, which she loathed, having been forced to eat it when at boarding school. She pulled a face when it was put in front of him as even the look and smell of it turned her stomach. Her choice was poached eggs on toast.

He grinned between mouthfuls. 'I take it from your expression you're not keen on this. To be honest, it wouldn't be my first choice but I thought it the only thing I could eat safely.'

'You could have had scrambled eggs. I'm sorry, but it reminds me of school, something I'd rather forget.' She quickly changed the subject. 'Is Roy in bed with a hangover too? I'd have thought a hard-drinking RAF officer would have a stronger constitution.'

'I take it that Elizabeth isn't feeling well this morning?'

There was something about the way he said this that rang warning bells. 'She said she'd had too much to drink but now I come to think of it I couldn't smell alcohol on her breath. Mind you, her eyes were bloodshot and she looked very pale. I gave her one of the strong painkillers I was given last night.'

'I'd better tell you what Roy told me when he got up this morning.'

'Got up? If he's up, why isn't he having breakfast with us?'

17

Oscar shook his head. 'Maybe it would be better for this to wait until after breakfast.'

Most girls would have insisted on knowing but she nodded and returned to her poached eggs. A silver rack of hot toast was brought to them but she hesitated to take any.

'Have some, please. I can't eat it but there's no reason why you shouldn't.'

'It doesn't seem fair to gobble down delicious, hot toast dripping with butter and marmalade...' Her eyes were dancing as she reached for the first slice. The more time he spent with her the more certain he was that he'd met the girl he would eventually marry.

A young waitress approached with a plate of freshly scrambled eggs and put it down in front of him with a smile. This hadn't been ordered but was very welcome as the porridge had hardly touched the sides.

'The head waiter overheard my comment about scrambled eggs and raised an eyebrow. All I had to do was nod and hey presto – they've appeared.'

The coffee jug was empty, the toast on both plates clean and he couldn't postpone taking her to the coffee lounge and giving her the unpalatable news.

The lounge was empty and he led her to the deep-seated, leather Chesterfield in front of the cheery fire. He was dreading having to explain to her why Roy had gone and her friend was hiding upstairs.

'Come on, I'm all agog. What can be so bad that you're so reluctant to tell me?'

'Roy's gone back to base. I think it very likely you'll find that Elizabeth has taken off as well.'

Her eyes widened. 'What? Did they have a dreadful row?'

He paused, hoping she might pick up on his body language and understand why they'd been abandoned so abruptly.

'No, not a row exactly. I hate to tell you this, sweetheart, but your companion behaved badly and put Roy in a difficult position.'

She still looked puzzled but then he saw dawning comprehension. Her cheeks flushed and she looked away unable to meet his eyes. 'Oh dear! I didn't think she was like that – it must have been the alcohol. Excuse me, Oscar, I'm going up at once to see if she's all right.'

He reached out and grabbed her hand as she stood. 'She's gone, Jane. I saw her leave as we came out of the dining room.'

She looked pointedly at his hand and instantly he released her. 'Nevertheless, I need to collect the key from behind the desk and check if she left me a letter or note or something.'

'Please don't feel you've got to go. As I said before, we can stay here and get to know each other better.'

'I'm not sure. I won't leave without telling you first. I need to think about this.'

He was on his feet and moved swiftly in front of her to

block her exit. 'Jane, Roy and I talked about this and he decided he didn't want to embarrass you, which is why he left. Don't waste your pass. We can footle around together when it stops raining. We don't have to go to the Ritz for the tea dance if you don't want to.'

Mentioning the Ritz did the trick. She smiled and nodded. 'Actually, I'd absolutely love to go to a tea dance. We had such fun dancing together last time. I do want to go upstairs though; I've got three letters to write. Might as well use the free stationery whilst I can.'

'Righto. I'll nip out and see if I can find a newspaper somewhere. Shall we meet back here in an hour?'

She dashed off to get her key and he waited by the stairs so he could walk up with her. Belatedly he remembered the dressings the doctor had given him and his suggestion that she allow him to reapply one.

After collecting his outdoor garments he bounded back to the foyer but didn't hand in his key. As he was only going to be a few minutes it didn't seem worth the inconvenience.

There was a steady freezing drizzle and no break in the clouds. He would order a taxi to take them out this afternoon – that's if there was one available. It wasn't that far to Piccadilly but he didn't want her to get wet walking there.

On his return he spoke to the concierge. He was reassured that a taxi would be waiting for them at two thirty and would return to collect them at six o'clock. Two places would also be reserved for the dance.

'I doubt that we'll want a full dinner tonight, but could you arrange for coffee and sandwiches to be served in the coffee lounge at eight o'clock?'

He hoped he had enough money to pay for everything as he had no intention of letting Jane contribute. She might be in the same uniform as him but that didn't mean it wasn't his responsibility to pick up the bills and expenses.

Exactly an hour later she strolled in looking more composed. 'Did you know that I didn't have to pay for the stamps?'

'I'm sorry to tell you that the cost will appear on your bill – probably inflated by a considerable amount.'

'Goodness! I'll know better next time. Was there anything interesting in the *News Chronicle*?'

'Not much. The BEF lads are having a miserable time of it in France. Not from the Jerries, but the weather is even worse there.'

'Are we actually going this afternoon?'

'We are indeed. Tickets and taxi all booked and paid for.'

She didn't carry a handbag – no WAAF did – but she immediately reached into the inside pocket of her jacket. 'I think it likely you will run out of cash before this weekend's over. I've got more than I need to pay my bill.'

He was about to protest but she stopped him.

'I'm not suggesting I give it to you. Allow me to lend you what I've got so you won't be in the embarrassing position of not having enough.'

A loan was perfect as it meant they would have to meet again so he could repay it. Any future dates would be just the two of them as obviously Roy wouldn't be seeing Elizabeth again.

'Okay, thanks a lot.'

She counted the money into his hand. 'Exactly three

pounds. I don't suppose we can offer to do the washing-up if we can't pay the bill at the Ritz.'

He chuckled. 'A pound will be more than enough for that excursion, but I'll take it all just in case. Are you quite certain you've left yourself sufficient?'

'I have. I know because I just asked what my bill will be.' Her expression changed to one of alarm. 'I do hope Elizabeth paid her share before she left. If she didn't then I certainly won't have enough.'

'You don't have to pay her bill, Jane, they've already got her name and address. It won't go down too well with the powers that be if she has bailed out without paying.'

'I wouldn't feel comfortable not settling the account for both of us. You're right; I don't have to pay it but I'd rather do so and then ask Elizabeth to reimburse me.'

He handed her back the three pounds. 'You'd better check. We'll have to cancel the Ritz excursion if she hasn't paid.'

She walked gracefully to the reception desk. After a brief conversation she passed over some money. He was disappointed the tea dance was no longer possible. Hopefully, between them they still had enough for a decent meal in the restaurant tonight.

He quickly buried his nose in the newspaper so she wouldn't know he'd been watching the transaction.

'I had to pay for her. I'm really sorry, Oscar, I was so looking forward to going to the Ritz with you.'

'If we pool our resources we could still eat here in style.' He pulled out his battered leather wallet from his jacket and put it on the table, then dipped into his trousers and removed the handful of change he carried there. She did the same.

'Obviously my bill will be higher than hers as I'm staying an extra night and having two extra breakfasts.' She pushed aside two one-pound notes and a ten-shilling note. 'That will cover it.'

He pushed three notes aside – fortunately Roy had paid his bill before he left, including the dinner he'd shared with Elizabeth. 'I need to keep this ten-bob note and the change. I didn't have a travel warrant and might well have to pay for my train ticket on the way back.'

She stacked the coins and put them beside the remaining paper money. 'We've got the grand sum of two pounds, five shillings and sixpence halfpenny. I'm not counting the farthings.'

'Going out this afternoon is going to cost about thirty bob. That leaves ample over for sandwiches and coffee tonight and a little for emergencies.'

Her smile took his breath away. 'Then we can go after all?'

'Hang on, have you put anything aside for your travel tomorrow?'

'I bought a return ticket and only have to pay for the underground. I won't need more than a shilling or two to get back safely.'

'Then I'll let the arrangement stand.'

'You never told me why yesterday was a dismal day and that was before I injured you and... well you know what happened.' She didn't even want to talk about her erstwhile friend's behaviour.

She listened in horror as he regaled her with the story of the dreadful bus crash. 'I'm so sorry. That was an absolutely awful thing to happen to those poor women. I know innocent civilians might be killed by bombs at some point, but for that woman to die like that on the way to do her shopping is just so sad.'

'Let's change the subject. Do you prefer to play cards or dominoes?'

'Actually, I've never played either. Any sort of frivolity was banned at my boarding school.' Her stomach clenched in case he questioned her about her home, but he just smiled.

'In which case I shall begin your education. There will be times when you're hanging about waiting for things to happen and you'll need to know how to play both.'

'I can read; I can also do exquisite embroidery.'

He raised an eyebrow which made her giggle. 'What, no knitting skills?'

'Absolutely not. My school assumed that every girl would marry well. Therefore, nothing useful was taught at all. I've no idea how to do anything practical like make a frock. I can't see being able to embroider is going to be of any use to anyone.'

'You can always embroider initials on handkerchiefs and give them as presents at Christmas.'

For a moment she thought he was serious and then saw his lips twitch. 'Even better, I could embroider you a beautiful cushion cover to keep you comfortable in your Hurricane.'

'I'd be the envy of the squadron if you did. Now – shall we start with dominoes or cards?'

The remainder of the morning flew past and when it was time to go upstairs and freshen up before the taxi arrived she considered herself an expert in Cribbage, Whist, Brag and dominoes.

The taxi rumbled up. Oscar opened the passenger door and handed her in as if she was royalty. She rather liked being treated like a lady and not a schoolgirl. The weather was still miserable, the pavements full of hurrying businessmen who couldn't be seen beneath their black umbrellas.

'I suppose rain is better than snow – even if it is freezing rain.'

'It's going to snow again tomorrow. I can see the signs. I just hope I can get back to base. The roads were lethal around Debden and if it's raining there, they'll be even worse if fresh snow falls on the overnight ice.'

'I don't want to think about it. Let's pretend we're two good friends going to a dance at a grand hotel.'

'I'd rather hoped we didn't have to pretend that we're good friends, Jane.'

She glanced sideways and was shocked to see her casual comment had obviously hurt him. Impulsively she grabbed his gloved hand. 'Of course we are – that came out all wrong. I'll rephrase it. Let's pretend there's no war on and this is just a normal date.'

His fingers closed over hers. 'I'm game for that.' His eyes crinkled at the sides when he smiled. She hadn't noticed that before. 'Mind you, it's going to be hard as we're both in uniform.'

'Oh, sir, there you are quite wrong. I am dressed in the most beautiful silk afternoon gown, I'm wearing an abundance of diamonds and my mink stole is quite magnificent.'

'I do beg your pardon, Miss Hadley. You look quite exquisite.' He ran his fingers down his uniform and nodded. 'I do hope my dinner jacket, dress shirt, bow tie and matching cummerbund are acceptable.'

'A cummerbund? I refuse to be escorted by any gentleman wearing one of those. Remove it immediately if you wish to accompany me into the dance.'

What the taxi driver thought of their nonsense she'd no idea, but when it drew up outside the elegant hotel she and Oscar were both laughing gaily. They exchanged knowing smiles as they passed clusters of elegant ladies in fur coats and expensive jewellery.

'We're getting quite a few disapproving looks but I'm not sure if that's because we're smiling or because we're in uniform and not dressed to the nines like everyone else,' she whispered as they approached the enormous polished reception desk behind which stood not one, but three uniformed men all with supercilious smiles.

Her smile faded and she began to feel uncomfortable. Oscar kept her hand firmly in his and strode up to the counter. 'I'm Flight Lieutenant Stanton. I have two tickets for the tea dance booked and paid for.'

His authoritative tone and crystal-cut diction did the trick. 'Of course, Flight Lieutenant, I have them here. I hope you enjoy the afternoon.'

'A taxi will call for us at six o'clock.'

She wasn't sure why he'd told them this but the snooty young man wrote this information down in his book.

'Why aren't there any other service people here? We can't be the only ones with an afternoon off.'

'I think we're a tad early. I can't hear the orchestra so it hasn't started yet. I expect there will be others along once it gets underway.'

She followed him through the mirrored hall, which made everything look enormous, and into Palm Court itself. Despite her sheltered upbringing even she had heard of this place. It lived up to all her expectations.

'Goodness me – how incredibly grand. I'm glad there are already a few tables occupied as I'd hate to be the only ones in here.' Her voice echoed a little and she was certain everyone had heard her naïve comment.

'Sir, madam, could I have your names, please?' The waiter addressing them was so old and bent she was surprised he was allowed to continue working. He looked as if he might drop dead at any moment.

'Flight lieutenant Stanton and Miss Hadley.'

'Why don't you call me ACW2 Hadley?'

'Sorry, they can see that you're a WAAF and also that you're not an officer. So better to call you by your name, don't you think?'

The decrepit waiter returned. 'If you would care to come this way, I'll conduct you to your table. Is this the first time you've attended a tea dance here?'

'It is,' Oscar said succinctly.

The old man smiled, showing a set of hideous false teeth. 'In which case, I'll explain how things work.'

*

Three glorious hours later they ran through the hotel, dodged the blackout curtain and were out into the street where the same taxi was waiting for them.

'I had such a wonderful time, Oscar. Can we do it again?'

He opened the door and assisted her into the freezing dark interior of the ancient vehicle before he replied. 'I'd love to take you again. It really didn't matter that we weren't in our glad rags as there were at least a dozen other bods in uniform.'

'I was the only girl not in a frock but I really didn't care. I'm so glad that I paid attention in dance classes – although I rather think it went so smoothly because you're such an excellent dancer, not because I'm any good. Nobody commented on your stitches – I think maybe they thought you'd been injured in action of some sort.'

'It's a good thing they didn't have a Charleston. I don't think that would have done either of us any good.'

'I would love to have pulled my skirt up over my knees and shocked all the old biddies.'

They hadn't worn their thick overcoats and now she regretted it. She couldn't repress her shiver.

'Here, take my jacket.'

He had taken it off before she could stop him and she was enveloped in the warm, heavy weight as he draped it over her shoulders. He would freeze with only his shirt but he was a man and no doubt a lot tougher than she was when it came to adverse weather conditions.

'Thank you, how gallant of you. If I snuggle up to you maybe we can share it.' She slid across the seat and his arm encircled her waist underneath his coat, bringing her even closer than she'd intended. This time her shivers couldn't have been caused by cold as she was lovely and warm.

His thigh was hard against hers. She wasn't sure if she liked it or not. His arm was too firm. Why was he holding her so tight? She couldn't even see his face. She had no idea of his intentions.

His free hand gripped her chin and tilted her face. Then his mouth was pressed against hers and everything changed between them.

18

Oscar felt Jane stiffen and knew he'd made a catastrophic error by kissing her. The taxi lurched as it hit a pothole forcing him to loosen his hold. She flung herself across the seat. Then his jacket arrived in his lap.

'I'm so sorry, Jane. I shouldn't have done that.'

Still she didn't speak and the silence was more worrying than her reaction. She wasn't crying. He would have been able to hear that. Had his action triggered some terrible memory? Once his jacket was on and securely buttoned, he tried again.

'Speak to me. Please say something.' His sympathy was turning slowly to annoyance.

What with the blackout and the dirt on the cab windows he couldn't even see her on the far side of the seat. He stretched out a tentative hand but she was pressed against the window and beyond arm's reach.

This was ridiculous. She'd been in his arms for the past three hours without complaining. This reaction was that of a frightened child, not a grown woman. A knot formed in his stomach. Had she been abused as a child by someone she trusted – that might be the explanation for this extraordinary behaviour. He recalled his father telling him about someone in the parish this had happened to.

'Jane, don't be frightened. I'm not going to hurt you. I'll never let anyone hurt you again.' This provoked a small whimper. Encouraged by this he continued. 'You don't have to tell me what happened when you were little. I understand why you didn't want to be kissed.' She didn't deny his suggestion, which was a start.

'It wasn't that. You held me too tight. I panicked.' Her voice was so quiet he could barely hear her.

'I won't do that again. From now on, you take the lead. I'll not touch you without your permission.'

There was movement and then she was back beside him and leaning into his shoulder. Then she shuddered and gulped.

'May I put my arm around you?'

'Please, I'm so sorry. You must think me really stupid.'

She cried almost silently – he wouldn't have known for sure if she hadn't been so close to him. A few minutes later the taxi jolted to a standstill.

'We're here. Take this handkerchief and dry your eyes whilst I pay for the taxi.'

He had the coins ready, the fare plus a tip, and dropped it into the outstretched hand of the driver. He leaned across and opened the door and gently encouraged her to stand up and exit the vehicle. It trundled off into the darkness. He felt flakes of snow settling on his face. That's all they needed – more snow.

'I'm ready now. I'm going to go straight up, so would you get my key for me please?'

They opened the heavy double doors, shuffled into

the space behind the blackout curtain, and then carefully sidled round it. There were no German bombers overhead looking out for stray lights to drop their deadly cargo so it all seemed a bit pointless at the moment. Still, good practice for when it kicked off.

He'd expected her to bolt across the foyer but she walked with her usual poise, shoulders back, head erect, proud to be a member of the armed services. He was impressed and decided in that moment that whoever had hurt her in the past he would find them and make sure they suffered as much as she had.

There was no point in rushing to her room as she couldn't get in until Oscar gave her the key. Jane just wanted to be alone to process what had happened. She wasn't normal. She couldn't allow herself to fall in love with him as it just wouldn't be fair.

She leaned against the wall, waiting for him to come with the key whilst she ran through the events in the taxi. She'd loved dancing with him, liked the feel of his hands on her shoulders, around her waist, so why had she behaved like a lunatic when he'd kissed her?

It was the darkness. Memories she'd tried to push to the back of her mind surged forward. After being beaten *that man* had often locked her in his study in the dark. She'd known she might be there for hours and if she wet herself that would mean another spanking.

Her knees gave way and she slid down the wall. Oscar arrived and scooped her up, but instead of taking her to her room he took her to his own. She was too distraught to struggle, to argue. She believed him when he said he'd never hurt her and trusted him to take care of her.

Somehow, he unlocked the door without putting her down and then closed it behind them. This breach of etiquette was enough to stop her shivering.

'I can't be in here. The door's closed. You know what they'll think.'

'I don't give a damn what they think. We know what's happening and that's all that matters. Promise me you'll wait? I'm going to get us a stiff drink.'

'I can't go anywhere as you haven't given me my key.'

His smile was tender as he rubbed a tear away with his thumb. 'Here it is. I'll also get a pot of coffee. I'll understand if you're not here when I get back.'

He strode away, every inch an officer in command of the situation. He left the door ajar and she could easily have gone but was incapable of movement. Inertia had gripped her. Her limbs refused to do what she wanted and she was better sitting in the armchair than sprawling on the floor in an undignified heap.

She really wanted to love him back but doubted she'd ever be able to truly reciprocate his feelings. She smiled sadly. Why had such a wonderful man fallen in love with someone so damaged? It didn't make any sense when he could have anyone he wanted.

He deserved better than her. She could think of only one way to crush his feelings and that was to tell him the unvarnished truth. Her heart skittered, her stomach churned and her hands were clammy. Did she have the courage to reveal her secret to save this man from inevitable unhappiness?

As the minutes ticked past she had time to mull over her decision. She glanced at her watch. If he wasn't back in five minutes she would leave; somehow find the words to break off their friendship tomorrow.

When Oscar walked into his bedroom he fully expected to find it empty. But she was still there. This time he left the door half-open though he didn't give a hoot what anyone else thought about him entertaining a girl in his room – but he did care about Jane's reputation.

'Coffee and cognac.' He put the tray down on the bureau, concerned that she made no response. She looked older somehow, immeasurably sad, and he dreaded what she was going to say to him, though thought he probably knew. She was going to sever the connection and there was nothing he could do about it.

In peacetime he would have been able to give her a few weeks to think about things and then go around and see her until she changed her mind. Now, with them both serving and action likely as soon as the weather improved, if she didn't want to see him then that was it.

He poured them both a large measure of brandy in the balloon glasses provided, added several lumps of sugar to her coffee and then took hers over.

'Thank you. I need Dutch courage in order to tell you why I behave as I do.' She sipped the brandy and pulled a face.

'Tip it into your coffee – you might find it more palatable like that.'

He watched her do that and then removed the empty glass

from her hand and put it back on the tray. He downed his in one swallow and thought he was probably going to need several more. He drank the coffee as quickly and couldn't help wondering how many more times he would be able to enjoy this dark, bitter brew before it became unobtainable.

'Oscar, please sit down over there. Give me your word that you won't interrupt. It's going to be very hard for me to tell you this and I need to do it in one go if I'm to do it at all.'

She didn't look at him but kept her head lowered. Her hands were clenched in her lap. He listened with growing incredulity as she revealed the nightmare that was her life until she'd escaped a few months ago.

'My God, the bastard. I can't tell you how sorry I am that you had to endure that for so long. None of it was your fault. Anyone who treats a child the way that monster treated you should be... should be...'

Words failed him. He could hardly say out loud what he'd like to do to him. She'd suffered enough violence in her life and threatening to disembowel her father wouldn't be helpful.

Finally, she raised her head and stared at him. 'I'm damaged beyond repair. I really, really like you and know that you feel the same. But, I'm no good for you or anyone. You deserve someone whole, someone you can have a normal relationship with.'

'No, you're wrong. Sweetheart, Jane, don't do this. I think you've already guessed that I've got feelings for you. We can work this out together, however long it takes.'

She pushed herself up like an old woman. 'No, I'm right and once you've had time to think about it, you'll agree with me. I'd be like the proverbial millstone around your neck. I want you to be happy and that won't happen if we continue this.'

His instinct was to leap to his feet, hold her tight and tell her how much he loved her, that they could get married and then she would be safe from harm, but he did none of it. He had to let her go, for her sake, not his, whatever he might think about the matter.

When she was at the door he stood up, but remained where he was. 'Jane, as far as I'm concerned you're perfect. Not damaged, not stupid, but brave, brilliant and beautiful. If ever you change your mind just write to me. I expect I'll be posted elsewhere but with my name, rank and number any letters will always catch up with me.'

She brushed a hand across her eyes, shook her head, and walked out of his life. He wanted to go after her but knew it would be no use. She'd gone and his only consolation was that maybe in a year or two when she was a bit older and her past wasn't so raw, she might reconsider.

One thing he was quite certain of – neither of them would be starting a new relationship. He wondered if he would ever meet anyone else or would he remain a bachelor forever in love with someone unobtainable?

Despite his misery his lips curved at his nonsense. He sounded like something from a cheap romance novel. *Get a grip, man – there's a war on.* From now on he would avoid female company and concentrate on his duty. King and Country came first. Being disappointed in love was trivial compared with what was about to happen.

He didn't want to bump into her tomorrow morning so hastily packed his overnight bag, slung his gas mask over his shoulder, and headed for the reception desk. He'd thought he would have to pay for the room as he'd left it so late to check out but the hotel was busy and there were two couples waiting hopefully to see if a room became vacant.

It was too late to get back to base tonight so he would find himself a cheap guesthouse near the station and catch the first train in the morning. He was lucky and found a bed for the night somewhere respectable. He then went in search of the nearest pub to drown his sorrows.

Jane knew that if she gave in she would spend the night crying into her pillow. She would remember Oscar's heartbroken expression for the rest of her life. She wished he hadn't fallen in love with her so easily. She wasn't a lovable person – didn't deserve someone as wonderful as him.

After washing her face in cold water, she took several deep breaths and was ready to face the world. She'd thought she would never, ever tell a living soul everything that had happened to her and now Oscar knew. Even though they were no longer together, she was glad that she'd trusted him with her secret.

Walking to the underground in the dark, with only a pinpoint of light on her torch to guide her, wasn't as terrifying as she'd imagined. She knew the route, had a good sense of direction and was able to get back to Bentley Priory as if she'd been travelling around London on her own for years.

After signing in she looked down the page for Elizabeth's name. It wasn't there. Why hadn't she returned this morning? For a second or two Jane was worried but then remembered that her erstwhile friend was far more sophisticated than her and probably had half a dozen people in Town she could stay with. Having something else to think about took her mind off her own unhappiness and she was able to put on a brave face for the others and was confident no one would know anything was amiss.

There was still no sign of Elizabeth at breakfast the next day. There was only half an hour before the bus came to take them to the filter room. She was cutting it a bit fine. Only as they trooped out to get on the bus did the missing girl eventually arrive.

'I'm so sorry, I only realised I hadn't paid my bill later on. I rang the hotel yesterday and they said you'd settled it. That was so kind of you. I'll tell you everything later when we get a minute to ourselves.'

'I'm so glad you got back in time.' She couldn't think of anything else to say that she didn't want to be heard by those sitting behind them in the bus. 'Have you noticed there're always so many pretty faces around the table?'

One of the girls sitting behind her leaned forward. 'Didn't you know, quite a lot of them have been recruited from the Cochran girls?'

Jane was none the wiser but her friend understood the reference immediately. 'Do you mean the girls who do high kicks on the stage in London?'

'I do. It surprised me that so many of them had the high level of education required for this job.'

'There won't be much flying today as it's snowing heavily,' Jane said and wished it wasn't so. She really needed to be busy and keep her mind off things.

'I expect they'll have dummy runs – those reporting the plots need practice as much as we do,' Elizabeth said.

'When do you think the real war will start? Things are happening at sea but nothing in the air so far. It must be dreadful having a family member in the Royal or Merchant Navy as the U-boats are sinking our ships. Just imagine being on board, never knowing when one of them is going to send a torpedo and sink the vessel.'

'I don't want to imagine it; I don't even want to think about it, thank you very much. What's the point in agonising about things we can't change? I'm just going to concentrate on my present, my dangers and my job.'

The ancient bus rattled to a stop and they piled out into the freezing, snow-filled darkness. As expected, there was nothing going on in the sky. However, a little light relief was provided when one of the officers on a specialised course at Fareham, where she was plugged into, came online and began chatting her up. At first she was tongue-tied but then relaxed as a little harmless flirting over the wireless couldn't possibly do her any harm.

She hastily disconnected when an officer on the balcony turned his beady eye in her direction. There was nothing doing and soon those in charge decided it would be safe for the majority of the girls to take a break.

The officer that announced this followed up with the reminder that they couldn't expect to have breaks when the phoney war ended.

'I'm going to the loo before I head for the canteen. Elizabeth, could you please get me a tea and any sort of sandwich or cake that's available?' Jane handed over her mug and a handful of coins.

'I'll bag us the table as well and then you can hold the

fort whilst I go. It was absolute agony last shift because I was so desperate – I'm not going to do that again.'

When Jane returned her friend was waving frantically amongst the sea of blue uniforms. Although everyone was dressed the same, they were all shapes and sizes, ages and complexions and there'd been no need for the wild gesticulating as she'd immediately spotted Elizabeth without all the fuss.

'I managed to get us both an actual cheese and pickle sandwich and an iced finger, which we can share.'

'Thank you, do you want to go now or are you going to eat first?'

'I want to explain why I rushed off – or did Roy tell you?'

'Roy left too but Oscar said something about you getting a bit drunk and doing something you regretted.'

'Well, that's a polite way of putting it I suppose. I threw myself at him, tried to seduce him, but all I did was make myself look cheap. He's a gentleman and didn't take advantage of what was offered. I know I disgusted him, which is a shame as I thought we might have got to like each other.'

'But where did you go afterwards?'

'I went home. My family live in St Albans.'

'Golly, did you tell them what you'd done?'

'Are you doolally? I might get on well with them but that's just not the sort of thing you tell your parents. I just said I'd had a row with my boyfriend and needed to lick my wounds in the comfort of home.' She delved into her inside pocket and pulled out her purse. 'How much do I owe you?'

The cash was handed over and Jane was pleased Elizabeth had been open about what had happened. 'I'm not seeing Oscar any more either. He was getting too involved and I just don't want that sort of commitment at the moment.'

'I'd have thought that was exactly what you want – something to take your mind off what's going to happen.'

'If ever I do get serious it won't be with someone who is likely to die.'

'In which case you'll have to wait until this lot is over or settle for a middle-aged widower with a brace of screaming children.'

Jane smiled, but couldn't push the image of Oscar from her head.

19

The temperature throughout January remained below freezing, which meant flying was dangerous. Oscar stayed on the base and avoided talking about his disastrous weekend, with Roy or anyone else. Even if he wanted to, going to London was impossible at the moment. He was obliged to kip down wherever he could find a space as getting to the village and his comfortable billet was impossible.

Towards the end of the month the weather deteriorated further and he was staring morosely out of one of the windows in the Officers' Mess when Roy joined him, a beer in one hand and a cigarette in the other.

'Crikey – what the hell's happening out there today? Is that rain or hail?'

Oscar shrugged. 'Not the foggiest. Freezing rain is a new one to me – I wouldn't want to be out in that. Absolutely lethal.'

'If this continues there are going to be telephone and power lines down. Don't envy the poor bastards having to work outside in this lot.' Roy finished his beer. 'Shall I get you one?'

'It's not even afternoon – I'd lay off the booze if I were you. I'm speaking as your flight leader, not your friend.'

Roy laughed. 'You're no fun – but you're right. I'll get us both a coffee if there's any going. Fancy a game of arrows?'

'Why not? There's nothing I like better than being humiliated at the dartboard.'

The unprecedented weather conditions continued for several days. Every surface was like a skating rink and the narrow lanes impassable. Getting up a hill in any vehicle was impossible. Eventually the temperature rose a little but was then followed by more snow, keeping everyone inside. Tempers were fraying and twice Oscar had to intervene when disagreements between members of his flight became physical.

By the time the thaw arrived at the end of the month they were going stir-crazy. Within two days the snow had gone and things were back to normal. They were able to fly the occasional sortie and practise dogfights but no actual action anywhere apart from at sea. Nothing much going on at Debden, that was for sure.

Roy now had his own battered bicycle and could finally pedal back to Debden. Their landlady was unimpressed by their prolonged absence.

'I cannot abide waste. I was obliged to throw away good food because of your dereliction, Flight Lieutenant.'

'As you were paid for our board and lodging I can't see you have anything to complain about, ma'am.' Hardly conciliatory but he wasn't in the mood for her unpleasantness. The cottage was warm and welcoming – pity about the owner.

'We want a hot lunch served in an hour when we've had

time to bath and change.' He didn't wait for her to argue but strolled off smiling to himself. About time the old bag toed the line.

After lunch he suggested they go for a walk. 'It's Saturday – maybe we can find out if there's something going on at the pub tonight. The shop should be open and I need a few things.'

The temperature had risen but it was still hovering around freezing point so his flight boots were called into action again as was his sheepskin flying jacket. After a long, enjoyable, but cold walk, Roy pointed hopefully at the Plough, one of the local hostelries. The White Hart had been the pub they'd frequented most but that was a bit further away.

'Did you know someone fell in the pond outside the village hall last year after drinking too much at the White Hart opposite? Too bloody cold to take a dip tonight,' Roy told him with a smile.

'The Plough's open – might be time to grab a quick drink before afternoon closing. Better than going back to the frosty reception at the cottage.'

'Fair enough – we've only been in there a couple of times so far. Time we got to know the blokes who drink in this one.'

Oscar was forced to duck through the door and narrowly avoided cracking his head on the beams of the low ceilings in both the saloon and public bars. The place was smoky, not just with cigarettes but from the massive log fire. The chimney needed sweeping.

He found an empty table by the window in the hope that the air might be more breathable there. The place was full, only men, and most of them propping up the bar. None of them seemed bothered by the fug. There were also several from the base but he didn't recognise any of them.

From the window he could see the village and from the steady trickle of villagers going by he thought there might be something going on in the hall further down the road. Maybe a jumble sale?

Roy returned with two brimming pints and put them down without spilling a drop. 'Good news, there's some sort of shindig at the village hall tonight. Just what the doctor ordered.'

'You're right – nothing like a bit of a party to cheer a fellow up. What sort of event is it, have you any idea?'

'It's something called a social, not a dance, which is a shame. According to Bertie, the barman, it's for all the family, children as well. No alcohol – just tea and biscuits.'

'Good grief – I'm not sure I'm up for an evening of family fun. Think I'll give it a miss.'

'Don't be a killjoy, Oscar, old chum. There's going to be dancing for the adults, party games for the children and Whist for the old folk. Although there's no drink allowed at the do, according to Bertie, people come over here or to the White Hart to have a beverage when the need takes them.'

One of the locals overheard their conversation. 'It ain't a social, not really, it's a beetle drive, silly games and then a few dances.'

'What the dickens is a beetle drive?' He was intrigued but wasn't convinced it would be worth the effort of going out in the dark. The old man explained and his interest waned. He sipped his beer and spoke quietly to his friend. 'I'm too old for children's games, Roy. I quite liked the idea of the social but I'm not going to attend this event. Don't let it stop you, if you want to go.'

'Not sure that I do. Let's compromise. We'll have a few beers in the White Hart and then go across for the dancing. It starts at five and finishes around eight o'clock so plenty of time to enjoy ourselves afterwards. There are bound to be girls to talk to and I'm starved of female company after being snowed in on the base for so long.'

'I'm told the accommodation for the WAAFs will be completed by the summer and then there'll be women on the base and we can hold our own dances like we did at Catterick.'

But there was only one girl he wanted to spend time with and she was lost to him.

Jane was eager to complete her last shift as she had a forty-eight-hour pass and was meeting up with Nancy and Charlotte at the Sanctuary Hotel in Westminster. They had been exchanging regular letters but seeing them in person would be so much better. It had taken weeks for them to have coinciding leave. Both girls were being posted elsewhere and had three days' leave first.

Although she still shared a duty roster with Elizabeth, they were no longer close – more the other girl's decision than hers. After the initial shock of learning about what had happened between her friend and Roy she had been prepared to put the matter aside but Elizabeth, possibly embarrassed by the fact that someone else knew about her bad behaviour, had withdrawn. This was a shame as Jane had hoped Elizabeth might have become a good friend like Nancy and Charlotte.

They had very little free time even though their shifts were usually tedious. With the bad weather, the skies were empty of aircraft of any description.

This time she would be sharing a room with her friends. She'd been surprised, but delighted, that Nancy hadn't preferred to go home and see her family. Jane rather envied the lively, close-knit community in Poplar from which her friend came.

There'd been no further communication with Mr or Mrs Jackson as they no longer had her whereabouts and she'd never given them her service number. That part of her life was over and she would never go back there under any circumstances.

The last letter she'd received from her mother, several weeks ago, had said that *that man* had people looking for her and it would be better if she stopped writing altogether. Jane believed that she would be safe from discovery if she remained on her base, but refused to let him ruin the rest of her life.

There was no evidence of the snow anywhere in London. In fact, the temperature had risen and had a spring-like feel to it. There seemed to be fewer civilians and more in uniform this time and she preferred it like that as she was now invisible. Exactly the way she wanted it to be. One girl in a WAAF uniform looked very much like another, especially with her cap pulled down and the collar of her greatcoat turned up. She straightened her shoulders, raised her head and strode forward, confident that no one would recognise her.

As she approached the hotel her pulse quickened. What would she do if Oscar happened to be staying there as he had last time she'd been in town? The odds of this occurring were minimal and, even if he was there, he was a gentleman and wouldn't approach her as she'd made it very clear their brief relationship was over.

A well-remembered voice yelled her name. She spun, beaming, as Nancy hurtled towards her, almost unrecognisable. The uniform suited her and her friend had somehow grown into it.

'Jane, you look ever so smart and so much older. I ain't half pleased to see you.'

'And I, you.' They hugged and immediately the world looked brighter. 'How long has it been since we were together? It must be months now.'

'October – bin far too long. I've got so much to tell you.' Nancy linked her arm through hers and they hurried towards the hotel, ignoring the glares and frowns of disapproval from pedestrians who had to step around them.

The concierge recognised her, which was gratifying. 'Miss Hadley, there was a telephone call for you earlier. I took a message.' He handed over a slip of paper.

'Oh no, Charlotte can't make it. Her leave has been cancelled for some reason.'

'Never mind, I'm still here. I ain't one for writing letters so better that we meet. I reckon she can write you anything important.'

The concierge had listened to this exchange. 'Miss Hadley, I thought you and Miss Evans might like the room that you and Miss Fenimore stayed in before you joined up.'

'Thank you, that will be perfect.'

They signed the register, collected their key and dashed up to dump their overnight bags. They were downstairs minutes later and ready to explore the sounds and sights of London.

'Let's go to that caf where we was the first time we met. We can have a cuppa and I can tell you everything what's happened to me.'

After a few false turns they found the café and the same lady in her wraparound apron was serving. They draped their coats over the back of the chairs along with their gas masks and Nancy waited until the toasted teacake and mugs of tea were delivered before starting her story.

'I was an equipment assistant, just like what I wanted to be, but then was offered promotion if I went into catering. I'm moving to Hornchurch with Nora and another girl when I get back. I liked being in the stores, ever so interesting, and I've learnt the names of all sorts since I started. I'm ACW2 like what you are, Jane – I was promoted last week and ain't sewed on me extra stripe yet.'

'That's really good. I'm afraid I can't tell you what I do as it's top-secret. But, it's very enjoyable and I think I was given the right trade.'

'Charlotte's doing something ever so hush-hush too. But then, you two are cleverer than me so only to be expected.'

'We have a better education, but that doesn't mean we're more intelligent. We get paid the same – two shillings and sixpence a day – so our jobs are equally important to the war effort.'

'It ain't that I wanted to tell you. I've met ever such a nice man, Tommy Smith, and we're engaged.'

'Congratulations, I'm so happy for you. It must be recent as you don't have a ring.'

'You're wrong, it's around me neck on a gold chain.' She delved beneath her collar and tie and pulled out the chain. 'It belonged to his nan; it's ever so old.'

'I think it's quite beautiful. If ever I get engaged I hope I'm given one just as lovely.'

'It's a real diamond, not glass, and me dad wanted to have it off me and take it down the pawnshop. Mum gave him a wallop with the frying pan and he didn't say nothing else about it.'

'Good heavens! Good for your mother.' Jane now understood why Nancy hadn't wanted to go home.

'Tell me all about Tommy. I want to hear everything.'

'He ain't much older than me, twenty last birthday, and as he ain't got good hearing in his left ear he couldn't be aircrew, which is what he wanted. He's a mechanic – one what looks after them bleedin' great bomber things.' Nancy smiled, her eyes moist. 'He were a car mechanic before, all trained and everything, so they was prepared to overlook his ear.'

'How did you meet him?'

'They had a New Year's Eve dance in the NAAFI and I met him then.'

'Is he handsome? Taller than you? Dark or fair?'

With a shy smile Nancy produced a slightly dog-eared photograph from an inside pocket. The picture was of a dark-haired young man with a devil-may-care sort of smile. 'He's gorgeous. If he's half as kind as he's handsome then you're very lucky.'

'He treats me like a princess. No hanky-panky, he's happy to wait until we're married. We've set the date for September. I'm not one for rushing into things.'

'I hope Charlotte and I can get leave. Will it be in Poplar?'

'I'm not sure. Things ain't the same there with half the little 'uns evacuated. Folk are saying them Germans will be bombing the docks and it ain't going to be safe in the East End, not for no one.'

'There weren't any children when I went to see your mum. Have some come back?'

'I ain't sure how many but I know some of the little devils wasn't happy in the country. It were nice of you to go and I got your letters.' They sipped their mugs of tea for a few moments then Nancy continued. 'I'm sorry things ain't worked out as well with you and that Oscar. He sounds a lovely bloke. Will you be able to come to me wedding, do you think?'

'If I'm still posted where I am then I might be able to. Shall we have another cup of tea or go for a stroll?' She'd been dreading being asked about her own love life as she really didn't want to talk about Oscar, but equally, was reluctant to lie to Nancy.

'It's going to be hard to be moved from Tommy, isn't it?'

'I ain't going to be. That's why I agreed to change trades. Tommy's already gorn to Hornchurch. He's transferred to fighters now.'

Oscar wasn't as eager as Roy to venture out to the White Hart that evening. With no streetlights, no moon, and an absolute blackout imposed, finding their way down the uneven village pavement with only a pinprick of light allowed from their torches wasn't going to be fun.

Even the thought of a couple of pints wasn't enough to make this venture enjoyable. He delayed their departure as long as he could. Finally, in exasperation, his friend threw his outdoor garments in his lap. 'Cheer up, you miserable bastard, you were moaning about being unable to leave the base and now you're complaining again.'

'Okay, I'm coming, but under protest. I refuse to enjoy myself and maintain my right to be as miserable as I want all evening.'

Roy slapped him on the back and good relations were restored. As soon as they stepped out of the cottage, they could hear voices and see half a dozen wavering beams of light. The excited chatter of children, the laughter and happy banter coming from the adults, was enough to lift his mood.

'Sorry, let's get a pint and then go straight across. Being amongst families is exactly what we both need – it'll remind us why we signed up.' It would also remind him of what might have been if Jane had not ended things between them.

'We don't have to join in the beetle drive. There are bound to be chaps willing to play a game of darts with us – that's if they've got a dartboard over there.'

The White Hart was packed and so noisy a normal conversation wouldn't be possible. Just like the Officers' Mess most nights. He shouldered his way to the bar, found himself sandwiched between a local and someone he recognised from the base. Hardly surprising as Debden was the nearest town and had two decent pubs in it.

He shouted his order and was pleasantly surprised at how

quickly the barmaid pulled the pints. He dropped the coins on the counter, nodded to the officer he recognised, and wriggled backwards, relieved to be away from the crush.

'Here you are, Roy, let's get this down and then get over to the village hall. I know smoking is supposed to be good for the lungs and calming for the nerves but I just don't like the smell.'

They retreated until they were in a space by the front door left empty because of the howling draft that came from behind the blackout curtain every time someone came in.

'As I told you before, you're a miserable old sod. Only half a dozen females in here and all of them too old or spoken for. I know you're still pining for Jane, but it's time you forgot about her. We could all be dead in six months.'

Oscar laughed out loud, making several heads turn. 'Thanks for reminding me, but hardly something either of us want to dwell on if we're going to enjoy ourselves tonight.'

Roy wasn't to be deterred. 'Hitler's fuming at the delay caused by the appalling weather all over Europe. It's a godsend, don't you think, as it's given us time to build more kites and train more pilots and aircrew.'

'The British Expeditionary Force are having a rotten time in France. The merchant navy's getting hammered by the U-boats. It hasn't started for the RAF but it has for the Army and Navy. Now that you've got that off your chest, can we change the subject and pretend everything's tickety-boo?'

After the third time someone entered bringing the cold air with them Oscar decided he'd had enough. He drained his glass and put it on the nearest table. 'Let's go over to the village hall and see if it's more convivial than here.'

With coats buttoned up, scarves firmly tied, they braved the elements. He was amused to see three children skipping about as if it was midsummer, unbothered by the darkness or the uneven surface of the pavement.

They followed the family into the hall. As soon as the door closed behind them all seven of them stepped from behind the blackout curtains into a lobby. A jolly lady in a floral frock better suited to summer temperatures beckoned them over to her table.

'Threepence each, officers, for the cloakroom, and sixpence entrance fee. This includes refreshments.'

There were double swinging doors just ahead and someone was playing the piano with more enthusiasm than skill and people were singing. He rather enjoyed a singsong, had been in the choir at his father's church as a boy, and his foot began to tap.

'This sounds rather good, Roy, let's get our coats disposed of and join in the fun.'

There were about thirty or so gathered around the piano. A spirited rendering of Vera Lynn's 'We'll Meet Again' was just beginning. This was a song he knew all the words to and he exchanged a happy smile with his friend and they both began to sing.

He was a tenor and Roy a baritone, and soon the others became aware they had two men with excellent voices singing along with gusto. By the end of the session everyone in the hall had stopped to listen. As the final notes faded there was a spontaneous round of applause. They joined in not realising it was for them and not the pianist.

'My word, I've never heard anything quite like that,' an elderly man in a dog collar said as he offered his hand. 'John

Culley – delighted to meet you. I don't suppose you'd be prepared to join my choir whilst you're stationed here?'

Oscar introduced himself and Roy, which gave him a few moments to consider the offer. He'd been going to refuse but said the opposite. 'My father's a country vicar like you. I'd be happy to sing with your choir but I've no idea how often that will be. I'm familiar with all the popular hymns so think I could drop in and out without causing your choir master problems.'

Roy shook his head. 'Sorry, Padre, unlike my friend I'm not a churchgoer.'

The children's games didn't appeal but he liked watching them enjoying themselves. After that the pianist was persuaded to start playing something suitable to dance to. There was a flutter of excitement on the far side of the hall where a bevy of young ladies were grouped.

'I'm going to dance. That's why we came, isn't it?'

Roy was right – for some reason Oscar was reluctant to join the other men who were heading for the overexcited girls. He looked around and saw there were several older women tapping their feet. He made his way towards one of them.

'Good evening, I'm Oscar Stanton. Would you care to dance with me?'

'I'd love to. I'm Joyce Cunningham. It's my hubby's the one torturing the piano.'

He enjoyed dancing with Mrs Cunningham and after the waltz he then accompanied her a second time in a lively polka.

'I won't monopolise you, Flight Lieutenant; there are

others eager for your company. Thank you, you're an excellent dancer.'

Whilst his friend danced with most of the single girls, he made a point of sticking with the more mature women. He had no wish to indulge in pointless flirting. The only girl he wanted to kiss was unobtainable.

The remainder of the evening was noisy, and got more so as the majority of the attendees made frequent visits to the White Hart. Roy was one of them. He was decidedly unsteady on his feet at the end of the event but refused to return to the cottage.

'Bloody hell, it's not even nine o'clock. I'm going to enjoy the rest of the evening downing a few more pints.'

There were about a dozen other chaps from the base and they were in that happy state somewhere between legless and a bit merry. He was completely sober and had no intention of joining them. As one of the few men who hadn't been drinking, he decided to remain behind and help clear up.

The sound of the airmen larking about with the village girls – the boys in blue had been in high demand for the dancing that had finished the event – made him smile like an indulgent uncle. Then someone yelled. There was the sound of breaking wood, an almighty splash, and then the screaming started.

20

Nancy wanted to go to Trafalgar Square and feed the pigeons. 'They'll be half-starved in this weather, and I don't reckon anyone's selling stuff for them neither.' The teacake had been slathered with margarine, which Jane hated, so she'd left hers.

'It's against the law to feed birds. Hope we don't get arrested.'

'Don't reckon anyone will notice.'

'We can take this,' Jane said. 'The square isn't far from here. Only a short walk along Whitehall and we'll be there.' She surreptitiously wrapped the teacake in her handkerchief and pushed the soggy parcel into her pocket. From the glare they got from the proprietor as they left she thought she hadn't been surreptitious enough.

They chatted of this and that, made comments on the attractiveness of any man in uniform, and spent most of the walk arm in arm and giggling at each other's nonsense. If Nancy was upset about her father's behaviour, she certainly wasn't showing it.

Nelson's Column was as impressive as she'd hoped and the lions even better. The fountains weren't working and there was no water in the surrounding ponds. There was a war on so everyone was saving water.

'Good heavens, there are loads of people here. I expected it to be deserted in the middle of the day especially as it's a Thursday.' She carefully removed the teacake from the hanky and handed half to her friend.

There'd been only a few pigeons hopping about but within moments of just taking the food out, without even sprinkling it on the ground, they were surrounded by hundreds of birds.

Hastily she gave her offering to Nancy and backed away from the flock, her heart pounding, uncomfortable with being so close to so many birds. Until that moment she hadn't known she was afraid of them. From the safety of the empty fountain she was happy to watch the crumbs being scattered in order that as many pigeons as possible got a bit.

They weren't all grey. There were white ones, brown ones – in fact every conceivable mixture of colours. Some of them even had fantails so must have come from someone's dovecote. She enjoyed viewing from a distance and was smiling at their antics and her friend's attempt to distribute the cake fairly.

Something made her look round, made her uneasy. An unpleasant-looking individual in a shiny, cheap suit was staring at her. Her stomach lurched. Was this the private detective her father had employed to find her?

Then Nancy was at her side. 'Don't take any notice of that bloke. He's a flasher if ever I saw one.'

The watcher merged into the swirling crowd and the band gripping her chest loosened. 'What's a flasher?'

'A bloke what shows you his bits and pieces.'

For a moment Jane didn't understand and then her eyes widened as the penny dropped. 'Golly, I've never heard of someone like that. I'm glad you came along when you did. He's gone now. The Portrait Gallery's just over there. Shall we go in and have a look round?'

'Wouldn't be much to see. Them grand pictures was taken away last year so when them Germans start dropping bombs on us they won't be destroyed.'

'That's a shame. I suppose the National Gallery and the Tate will be closed as well. They can't move the Tower of London, so shall we go there? I've never seen it and even if we can't go in and look at the Crown Jewels it will be a treat to wander about outside.'

They went to the pictures after seeing the Tower and it was a relief to sit down after all the tramping about. The film was a musical called *Swing Time* and starred dancers called Fred Astaire and Ginger Rogers. She was spellbound and quite prepared to sit through the entire program again if Nancy had only agreed.

'That was absolutely spiffing, Nancy, so much better than the film I saw last time.'

'I love a good romance, me. It were ever so good. I ain't usually much for dancing and such but them two certainly know how to cut the mustard.'

'I'd never heard that phrase until today when it was used in the film. I think I might adopt it.'

'I'm a bit peckish. Let's find a caf and get somethink to eat. All them business blokes will be milling about soon so we better find somewhere soon.'

At dusk as they were returning to the hotel she was

convinced she saw the man from Trafalgar Square on the other side of the street. She grabbed Nancy's arm. 'Quickly, look over there. Isn't it the man you called a flasher?'

Nancy shook her head. 'No, you're seeing things. It weren't him, he were younger and fatter than that bloke over there.'

'Are you quite sure?' She hesitated but then decided to take Nancy into her confidence. After all Charlotte knew some of it so it only seemed right to share it with Nancy. When she'd finished explaining why she was so concerned about being followed, her friend was horrified.

'Bloody Nora, Jane, I ain't surprised you're twitchy. If I ever see that bastard what did that to you, I'll cut his balls off.'

She was so shocked by such a graphic response that she forgot her fear and laughed. 'Shush, you mustn't say things like that. Do you think I'm worrying unnecessarily?'

'I do. Even if that were a detective, *that man* can't do nothing to you. You signed up for the duration like what I have and there's sod all he can do about it. He ain't going to snatch you off the streets, now is he?'

'Please, Nancy, don't swear so much. It brings back terrible memories of the one time I was stupid enough to repeat something I'd heard a workman say.'

'I'll do me best. My lot ain't too great neither. Me brothers are a bit simple like and can be right nasty sometimes. Me dad's more interested in the boozer than he is his family and me ma rarely has enough housekeeping. That's why he wanted me ring and why I ain't going back there anytime soon.'

'But he's not violent towards any of you, is he?'

'Me ma would soon sort him out if he tried anythink like that. Let's get inside. We can keep a lookout through the bedroom window as it's got a smashing view of the street.'

When they collected their key, the concierge – who had been in the back office – hurried out to speak to them. 'Miss Hadley, an undesirable gentleman was making enquiries about you. I sent him packing.'

Her recently eaten meal threatened to return. 'Did he ask for me by name?'

'He did but I told him no one of that name was a guest here. Do you wish me to telephone the constabulary?'

'No, nothing like that. However, I'm going to cut my visit short and only stay one night. Can you prepare my bill now so I can leave at first light?'

'Would you like me to send you up some coffee and sandwiches later on?'

The thought of food revolted her but Nancy would want to eat. 'Yes, thank you, that would be very kind. Make sure that they're included on the bill. I'll come down and pay before I retire.'

Nancy had remained silent up until this point and looked as worried as she did at this unexpected interruption to their leave.

'You ain't going nowhere without me. I'll take me bill too; we'll leave together.'

Jane didn't feel safe until she was inside the room with the door closed and the key turned in the lock. 'I don't understand how that detective found his way to this hotel?'

'Hang on a minute, I need to ask that bloke behind the desk a couple of questions.'

Jane hardly dared approach the window in case there

was someone watching from outside. Once the blackouts were drawn, she couldn't look out anyway. There was a knock on the door and she ran over. It was Nancy and she let her in and then relocked the door.

'It was what I thought. It weren't the same effing bloke, Jane. There's two of the bleeders looking for you. God knows how they discovered you was staying here. It don't make no sense to me.'

She collapsed on the bed. 'Oh God – *that man* must know I'm in here. I'm under age – I forged his permission when I signed up – that could mean he might be able to legally remove me from here. He could turn up here at any moment accompanied by policemen. What am I going to do?'

'Ain't nothing you can do at the moment, but I reckon that bloke downstairs is on your side and will let us leave by a back entrance tomorrow.'

'That's all very well, but what if *that man* barges in tonight?'

Nancy patted her arm. 'I ain't one for gossiping but I told him downstairs what's what. He'll not let anyone come up here.'

'I wish you hadn't. I hate the thought of strangers knowing my business. You shouldn't have done that.'

'Far worse if that bastard gets hold of you.'

She managed a weak smile. 'You're right. I'm sorry. If I give you my share of the bill, will you take it down now and make the arrangements for first thing?'

Jane didn't sleep much that night. Every time she heard a voice outside in the street, a noise in the corridor, her heart lurched and she sat up in bed. She slept in her underwear just in case.

At six o'clock they were both dressed when there was a soft tap on the door. Someone had come to escort them through the sleeping hotel and out through the staff entrance that led into a narrow, cobbled street.

'Good luck, miss. Take care of yourself.' She heard the uniformed porter bolting the gate behind them. It was dark and frosty. Nancy had been given clear instructions on how to find their way to the underground station without being seen in the main streets.

They were going in different directions and she expected to part company with her friend at the turnstile.

'I ain't leaving you until you're safely back on your base. No point in arguing. I've made up me mind.'

'That's so kind of you. I was rather dreading travelling on my own as every stranger who looks at me fills me with terror.'

They eventually parted company in front of the entrance to Bentley Priory.

'Blimey, it's bloomin' huge. You'll be safe in here. TTFN. We'll be closer when I transfer, even if we're not at the same base.'

Sadly, Jane waved goodbye knowing she wouldn't be venturing outside whatever base she was on until she reached her majority. It was possible he'd already traced her here so she would put in for a transfer immediately and hope that this would be enough to keep her safe.

The pandemonium outside the hall after the sound of someone falling in the pond continued. Oscar's greatcoat was the only one left. He snatched it up, raced out of the door, skidded around the end of the building and ran towards the crowd of shouting, drunken men and women.

He was quite prepared to jump in and pull whoever it was out of the water. He was a strong swimmer and even the cold would be no deterrent.

His mad dash to the rescue proved unnecessary. Two miserable-looking airmen were already clambering out of the pond, dripping with icy water, teeth chattering. Then he realised the watching crowd were actually laughing and cheering the unfortunate men, that the racket wasn't caused by panic.

Roy appeared at his side, his teeth flashing white in the torchlit darkness. 'Bloody hell, that was fun. Not for those poor sods, of course, but I've not laughed so much in months.'

Someone from the pub had appeared with blankets and sympathy and the unfortunate duo were escorted away accompanied by hoots of laughter and hearty slaps on the back.

'I'm going back in the hall as I'm not needed here. I'm helping them tidy up.'

'I'll give you a hand. The cold air has sobered me up. But it was a damn good evening. Who would have thought a beetle drive could be such fun?'

By the time they'd finished stacking chairs and sweeping floors there was no one outside. They shook hands with the three ladies who'd been in charge of the event and headed for their billet.

The front door was kept permanently locked but they

had their own key so this was no obstacle to them getting in. To his surprise Mrs Branston appeared from her sitting room and was actually almost smiling.

'I heard there was some excitement at the village hall earlier. Mildred, she's on the committee you know, popped in to tell me that the two of you had remained behind to clear up. She also said that you, Flight Lieutenant, have agreed to sing in our choir when you can. It would appear that you have a beautiful tenor voice.'

He exchanged an amused glance with Roy. The village grapevine was certainly efficient. 'Fortunately, ma'am, the two idiots who fell in the pond are little the worse for their experience. I always avoided any similar functions when living at home, but wish now that I hadn't. We both thoroughly enjoyed ourselves.'

'There's something arranged on the last Saturday of every month. I'm too decrepit to attend myself, but Mildred always calls in on the way home to tell me what happened. Now, young men, I've put a jug of coffee and some freshly made sandwiches in your sitting room. After all the excitement I expect you're in need of nourishment.'

'Thank you, that's exactly what we do need. But, please don't feel you have to give us coffee every day. We can get some occasionally at the base, but once yours is gone I doubt you'll be able to replace it.'

'Fiddlesticks to that! I'm in the fortunate position of being able to send to Harrods or Fortnum & Mason's for anything I require. Run along and put your coats away, boys; your supper will be waiting for you.'

He said nothing until they were in their bedroom with the door shut. 'I think things here are going to be a little less frosty in future. I wonder which of the ladies we met tonight was Mildred – no doubt we'll discover that next time we go to a social.'

The following morning, despite every encouragement, Roy refused to get out of bed and accompany him to matins. Therefore, he ate his substantial breakfast on his own. Mrs Branston, elegant in a moss green tweed coat and matching pillbox hat, was waiting impatiently in the entrance hall.

'There you are at last, young man. I haven't been to church myself for weeks because of the inclement weather. I'm expecting there to be a large congregation today and I've no wish to be stuck behind a pillar.'

He escorted her into the church and then made his way to the vestry. He was welcomed enthusiastically and one of the flustered female choristers attempted to find a gown of the appropriate length.

'This one will be fine. I really don't mind if my ankles are visible. The rest of me is suitably covered.'

He glanced at the list of hymns displayed next to the choir stalls and knew all of them. He was so familiar with the order of service he scarcely had to look in the book to follow the responses. The choir consisted of four elderly men, six assorted women and three choirboys. He was a welcome addition and, when the service ended, he was glad he'd made the effort.

He had always made a point of attending the short services put on by the padre at whatever base he was stationed at but rarely went in search of an actual church. In future he wouldn't be so delinquent in his thanks to the Almighty. He was going to need all the help he could get once things kicked off. On the way out the vicar took his hand and pumped it vigorously.

'Excellent, thank you so much for making an appearance this morning, Flight Lieutenant. Are you coming to Evensong?'

'I certainly am. If you'll excuse me, sir, Mrs Branston is waiting for me to accompany her home.'

By the end of March, he, like everyone else on the base, was aware that the phoney war would soon be over. His flight, and the entire squadron, was as well prepared as they could be. The powers that be decided wasting valuable fuel and ammunition on dummy runs and practice dogfights wasn't cost-effective. Therefore, each flight was stood down in turn and given a travel warrant to go anywhere in the country.

'Roy, we've got seven days' leave. What shall we do with it?'

'What about Norwich? Might be worth a visit.'

'Sounds good to me. Hang on, Riley's heading this way.'

'Good show, glad I caught you blighters before you departed. Leave's cancelled, I'm afraid. Just heard the squadron's being relocated to Kenley.' Riley frowned and tweaked his moustache. 'We'll be the first kites there. I gather the place isn't operationally ready. Probably be utter chaos.'

'They'll have it ready when it's needed. We'll be closer to the action. When do we leave?'

'As soon as the other chaps return. They will all have reported by midnight tonight. The bigwigs want us in situ before lunch tomorrow. We're staying in Fighter Group 11, just in a different sector. Prefer to be in the thick of it when it starts.'

'Okay. I take it my chaps know or do I need to find them myself?'

'I'm detailed to tell flight leaders. Up to you, old boy, to inform your bods.'

There were two married men in his command and they were the only ones fed up about the cancellation of their home leave.

'I'm sure it'll be reinstated once we're settled at our new base,' he told them hoping this would, in fact, be true. A move to an airfield only half-constructed after being at Debden would probably mean their accommodation might well be in a Nissen hut rather than a comfortable billet.

On the plus side they would be closer to London and he and his men would be able to visit the capital more often. He wouldn't go back to the same hotel in case he bumped into Jane. That would be hard for both of them. In fact, they were probably close enough to spend the evening in Town and still get back before curfew.

He was sorry to say goodbye to his landlady and doubted that he'd ever have such a comfortable billet again. 'Please pass on my apologies to the vicar. I enjoyed singing in his choir these past few weeks.'

'I didn't intend to take in any further officers, but to my surprise I found I've rather enjoyed having you living under my roof. Good luck to you both.'

21

Jane's request for a transfer was refused. She could hardly explain why it was crucial for her to move somewhere else as that would reveal that she'd signed up without parental permission. Disappointed that she now had no option but to spend any free time on the base, she threw herself into being the best she could be as a plotter.

A week after her return she wrote to Charlotte telling her what had happened and asking her advice. She also passed on the good news about their mutual friend's engagement. The reply arrived the following week.

Dear Jane,

How absolutely dreadful for you. I think you're right to keep silent about your reason for remaining on base. Your father must have influential friends to have discovered you so easily. I think that your mother must have told him you were in the WAAF. There's no other explanation for him being able to track you down.

The Sanctuary Hotel was recommended to us when we arrived in London so I think it quite possible that's why he made his enquiries there. Somehow one of those creepy detectives must have got a look at the book and seen your name there.

Keep asking for a transfer. Eventually, something will come up and they'll be prepared to let you go.

I'm sorry I couldn't meet you last week. I doubt that we'll get the opportunity again as everyone here is convinced Hitler will start attacking the low countries now the weather's better.

Thank you for giving me the news about Nancy. The first of us to fall in love – neither of us are likely to do so given our circumstances. Let's hope they can get married as planned in the autumn and that we can get the time off to attend.

Take care of yourself and don't despair – I rather feel that even if your father appeared at the gates they wouldn't release you. You're far too valuable to them now.

Jane was somewhat comforted by this letter and prayed that her friend was right. She volunteered for any extra duties, offered to stand in for others when they wanted a day off for something special, and she now had experience in most of the sectors on the table.

As the days passed without any further scares she began to believe she was safe. The weeks passed and although a little lonely without any special friends, she was on good terms with a dozen or more girls as she became known as someone who would always step in and take an extra shift, if she could, when asked.

The first week in April was busier than any preceding

it from an operational viewpoint. She was so proficient at calculating distances, locations and altitude and then moving the counters around the map on the table, that her name began to be mentioned by those relaying the information. She'd heard that Fighter Group HQ at Uxbridge needed more experienced plotters and filterers to work there.

Immediately she went to the adjutant's office and asked if she might be transferred there. This time she wasn't sent away with a flea in her ear.

'We were already intending to move you, Aircraft Woman Second Class 374,' her commanding officer said with a smile. 'Your work is exemplary and we shall be sorry to lose you. You will be taking a more senior position and have been promoted to ACW1.'

Jane saluted smartly. 'Thank you, ma'am. When do I transfer?'

'Two others will be going with you. Details will be posted on the board later today.'

'Will there be transport or do we make our own way?' The thought of lugging her heavy kitbag on and off trains wasn't a happy one.

'You can travel with the airmen. There are a dozen transferring at the same time as you three. Not officers – not pilots or aircrew.'

There was no need for anything further to be said. The lower orders, those of similar rank to herself, could well make the journey embarrassing. It was all very well flying off the slippery benches and showing one's knickers to other girls but quite different when it was men watching.

Her name was already removed from the duty roster and somebody else's written in its place. Horrid to be leaving somewhere she'd spent quite a long time and not have anyone to say goodbye to.

They'd had a full inspection quite recently when everything had to be laid out on the bed in a certain order and anything missing had to be replaced at one's own expense and then that unfortunate WAAF would be written up.

This meant that her gear was already neatly folded, which made it much easier to pack. Her stationery folder, documents and personal items went into a canvas shoulder bag. Everything else had to be crammed into the tubular kitbag. She left the top unlaced so she could put in her toiletries, nightwear and so on when she got up tomorrow.

Last time she'd transferred she'd had to drag the wretched thing behind her. She picked it up and to her surprise it seemed much lighter. A wave of panic flooded through her as for a moment she thought she must have omitted to put half her kit inside. She checked the locker and it was empty, as were the pegs by her bed.

For the first time in several weeks her smile was genuine. By some miracle she'd become stronger and fitter – it wasn't the bag that was lighter at all.

The two girls accompanying her to Uxbridge were named Angela Westley and Emily Defoe. They were the same rank as her, but apart from that Jane had no idea who they were. She couldn't remember speaking to either of them. The lorry taking them to Uxbridge would be leaving Bentley Priory at eight o'clock the following morning.

She was about to head for the recreation room when a tall, slim, fair-haired girl rushed up to her. 'I say, Ange and I have been hanging about here for ages waiting to see who was coming with us. I'm Em. Ange has gone to bag us a table in the rec room so we can get to know each other.'

'I'm pleased to meet you. You already know that my name's Jane. Uxbridge is only about twelve miles from here so it won't take long to get there tomorrow.'

The girl about her own height and of similar colouring who was waving from the far side of the room must be the missing Ange.

'It's going to be strange working underground and not on an actual base,' Jane said as she sat down. 'I'm looking forward to being somewhere smaller, somewhere easier to get around and where it's easier to get to know the other people working there. I suppose having the ops room sixty feet below the surface is sensible but it's an awful lot of stairs to go up and down, isn't it?'

'It's a good thing we girls are so fit. Are you claustrophobic?' Em asked. 'I don't like heights, but am absolutely fine travelling on the underground and so on.'

'No, not as far as I know.' Her hands clenched under the table as she lied. Having been locked into a variety of enclosed spaces during her childhood, including the broom cupboard and coal cellar, had made her fearful of being shut in anywhere.

'It's a real feather in our caps to be selected for this posting. We're the best of the best and I intend to be an officer before the end of the war,' Ange said.

They spent a pleasant afternoon getting to know each other but Jane was relieved when the other two joined their friends for a farewell drink at a local pub. She'd been invited but had politely refused saying that she didn't drink alcohol.

*

The journey to Hillingdon House, Uxbridge, in the back of the lorry wasn't nearly as unnerving as Jane had feared. The airmen were accompanied by a fearsome NCO and behaved impeccably. No ribald comments, no suggestive remarks – they were all perfect gentlemen.

Their accommodation was excellent, no huge dormitory with dozens of iron bedsteads but a real bedroom shared only with Angela and Emily. They were very chummy, had known each other since basic training, had attended similar expensive boarding schools, and obviously found her dull and ignorant as, after the first day, they didn't include her in their conversations or invite her to socialise with them.

The underground bunker had been built close to Hillingdon House where all the other admin offices were housed. After a few days she was resigned to her less than ideal circumstances, with only the thought that it was unlikely *that man* and his detectives would trace her to her new posting.

Two weeks after her arrival she had a forty-eight-hour pass on the same days that Charlotte was going to be free. Her friend had leave as she was being relocated too.

In a short telephone conversation, they'd managed to organise their break.

'I'm still not entirely confident about leaving the security of Hillingdon House, Charlotte. I've become quite chummy with one of the guards and he promised to keep a lookout for any strangers hanging about.'

'I take it there haven't been any.'

'Nothing out of the ordinary at all. I'm so looking forward

to seeing you, especially if you're going to be unable to get to London very easily in future.'

'I arrive at Charing Cross. Shall we meet under the clock?'

'As we don't know exactly what time we'll be there, that might be problematic. I don't know if there's a café, but if there is, shall we meet there?'

'If there isn't, then whoever gets there first can stand under the clock.'

Oscar's arrival at Kenley was as expected. The two new concrete runways were still under construction and they were the first, and only, squadron on the base since it had been recommissioned last year.

The brown jobs were busy setting up their ack-ack guns around the perimeter. It seemed rather pointless bringing them here when nothing was ready.

Win Co Riley was equally browned off. 'You'd have been better staying at Debden. Even if all hell breaks loose, there's bugger all we can do about it until we can refuel and rearm.'

'They've got hangars but no mechanics to work in them,' he replied.

'The only positive to this almighty cock-up is that you can all take your leave. I was informed that it's going to be another couple of weeks before things are battle-ready.'

The atmosphere changed from fed up to that of a crowd of boys being released from school for the holidays. A couple of hours after their arrival he and Roy were on their way to London.

On arriving at Charing Cross his eyes were drawn to a WAAF pacing up and down under the station clock. His pulse accelerated. Without thinking he was across the station and beside Jane.

'I can't believe it's you. What are the odds of us both being here at the same time?'

'Oscar, how lovely to see you. I'm waiting for my friend and am becoming concerned that she's not going to come after all.'

Roy joined them. 'Jane, you're the last person I expected to bump into. How are you?'

'Tip-top, thank you. Look, could I ask you both an enormous favour? I desperately need to visit the ladies' room and don't want to miss Charlotte. Could you possibly wait here until I get back?'

'Happy to help a damsel in distress. What does your friend look like?'

'She's a WAAF – slightly shorter than me and with dark brown hair.'

Jane took off like a scalded cat and he exchanged a happy grin with his friend. 'I can't believe my luck. If we'd caught a later train I would have missed her.'

'She seemed pleased to see you. I think the Big Man upstairs is looking out for you – no other explanation.'

They'd not been standing there more than a few minutes when the missing WAAF arrived. She was very attractive, and he saw Roy's eyes widen in appreciation.

'Excuse me, are you by any chance Charlotte waiting for Jane? I'm Oscar Stanton…'

The girl raised an eyebrow and laughed. 'Are you indeed? I can see why Jane was so interested in you. I'm horribly late. I was worried she wouldn't be here.'

Roy stepped forward and offered his hand. 'Roy Cross

– delighted to meet you. Jane asked us to look out for you. She won't be long.'

'I didn't know she was still in touch with you, Flight Lieutenant. And she certainly didn't tell me we were going to spend our leave with you both.'

Jane arrived at a run and the two girls embraced fondly. 'Sorry, I didn't know Oscar and Roy would be here. It's just a mad coincidence. I thought they were both in Debden.'

'We've just been posted to Kenley but nothing's ready for us so we've been given a week's leave. Would you care to join us for lunch somewhere?'

He thought Jane was about to refuse but her friend got in first. 'Good idea. We haven't got anywhere to stay so need to find a cheap hotel or guesthouse first.'

'We've booked at the Sanctuary. There must be plenty of places around here. Why don't you both find somewhere and then we could meet up at that restaurant in Piccadilly?' He checked his watch. 'Let's say at one thirty? That should give us all time to check in.'

'Yes, that's sensible,' Charlotte said, but Jane remained silent and he rather thought neither of the girls would meet them again.

They parted company and he was quiet on the walk to Westminster. He should have asked where she was based, waited and seen what hotel she booked into – but too late to dwell on that now.

'Don't worry, Oscar, Charlotte will make sure she comes. There was a bit of a spark between us and I think she'll want to get to know me better.'

'For sheer arrogance you take the biscuit. I'd like to think that you're right and she will persuade Jane to come. I've been given a second chance and I don't want to waste it. I'm absolutely besotted – a hopeless case – and if I can't have Jane then I'm just not interested in anyone else.'

They checked in and then he headed for the Abbey. 'You don't have to come in with me, Roy, but I want a few minutes in there if you don't mind.'

'I'll come and wander about whilst you commune with whoever. We've got half an hour before we need to head to the restaurant.'

When he left the church he was calmer. Whatever happened today he now believed that one day, if he survived the war, he and Jane would be together.

They arrived at the restaurant a few minutes before the appointed time and he glanced up and down the street but could see no sign of the girls. He looked in but they weren't there either. 'Could you go in and book the table, please, Roy? I'll hang about out here.'

'Doesn't do to look too keen, old boy; don't want to put her off again.'

He was about to reply when he saw Charlotte racing towards him, dodging through the pedestrians, her face white. She was alone. He ran to her and she threw herself into his arms. For a few moments she was incoherent; then she pulled herself together.

'Her father's taken Jane. He appeared at the guesthouse accompanied by two really nasty individuals and they just grabbed her and pushed her into a car.'

For a second he couldn't think straight. His eyes blurred. His fists clenched. He had murder on his mind.

Then his head cleared and he was left with a grim determination to bring this bastard to account. He took several deep breaths and spoke quietly to the shaking girl. 'How do you know it was Hadley? Did you see who was driving?'

'Of course it was her father – why would anyone else want to grab her off the street? A woman was driving but I didn't get a good look at her.'

'Let's go inside. We don't have to eat but we can get a stiff drink and you can tell me exactly what happened.'

'There's no time. You have to go after her now. He's already got half an hour's start on you.'

'I don't know where he lives and can't do anything until I have that basic information. Don't worry, I'll get Jane back and can assure you nothing like this will ever happen again.'

Roy appeared at the door and took one look at the two of them and his expression changed. He didn't know Jane's history but the fact that she wasn't there and her friend was in tears was enough to tell him something was seriously wrong.

'Not in here – too busy. Let's find a pub. There are several in the back streets.'

Roy led the way and he followed with his arm around Charlotte's waist. She was still so shocked he thought she might not be able to stay on her feet without his assistance.

The interior of the pub was dark and smoky but for once he didn't comment. 'The saloon bar will be best.'

Roy went to the hatch that opened into the public bar and ordered drinks.

'Tell me exactly what happened, every detail, every word spoken by anyone. Take your time. There's no rush.' The longer Jane was in the hands of that brute the more likely it was he would harm her. Every second counted but until he knew more there was nothing he could do.

'We found a little guesthouse and checked in. We were just coming out when a man suddenly appeared in front of us. He grabbed her arm. The two men with him got behind them and she was inside a big black car before I could even scream. I saw there was a woman behind the wheel.'

'Did they say anything?'

'That's what was so terrifying. None of them said a word. Jane was so shocked she didn't have time to struggle. It was over in seconds.' She looked up, fresh tears trickling down her face. 'I don't understand how they knew where we were. We didn't even know where we were going to stay tonight.'

'They must have been following you…'

'I knew her father had employed private detectives and they turned up at the Sanctuary Hotel last time she was in London. That's why she wanted to move. She hadn't been off the base for weeks just in case. She should never have come to meet me. We both thought she was safe now.'

Roy had been listening. 'How the bloody hell did they know she would be arriving at Charing Cross today?' He sat down and pushed a double whisky in front of each of them. 'Surely he couldn't have been paying someone to watch the exit all this time?'

'That's the only explanation that makes sense. He must have friends in high places and was able to get Jane's service number. Once he had that it wouldn't be too hard to track her down. He brutalised her for her entire life. She signed up to escape.'

'I guessed it was something like that. Charlotte, do you have her home address?'

'No, but I know the name of the vicar and the village as I once posted a letter for her.' She sat up so abruptly her drink slopped onto the table. 'The car was an Austin – one of the big ones. Petrol's rationed so I don't understand how he could even be driving now.'

'That's exactly what I needed to know. You're right, there are so few private cars around now; he should be fairly easy to trace. What's the vicar's name?'

'Jackson, the village is called Lattimore – or something like that.'

'We need the telephone number of the vicarage. Stay here with Roy – I need to make some calls.'

Roy got his drift immediately. His role was to take care of Charlotte whilst he took care of Jane. There was no point in both of them getting cashiered or possibly arrested for murder. His first point of call was Victory House in Westminster where someone in authority would take very seriously indeed the kidnapping of a WAAF involved in something hush-hush.

22

Jane had been paralysed by fear. Just seeing *that man* had returned her to a place she'd never thought to be. Before she was able to utter a word of protest she was bundled into his car. He was gripping her arm so painfully it was hard to think straight.

Instinctively she closed her eyes – as she had always done – hoping if she couldn't see what was coming, it wouldn't be so bad. Then slowly sanity returned and with it came a remnant of the courage and confidence she'd achieved over the past few months.

'Let go of my arm. You're hurting me.' She was pleased her voice sounded firm – no sign of the terror she was feeling. This was the first time she'd had the temerity to speak back to him and he was so shocked that his fingers loosened and she was able to tear her arm away.

She pushed herself straighter on the seat, wishing she could make herself thinner, create a gap between herself, *that man*, and the obnoxious person who had been following her around these past few weeks. Despite the thickness of her uniform she was aware of the heat coming from the thighs pressed so hard against hers. Her stomach was churning. She had to remain calm if she was going to survive this.

She kept her eyes firmly to the front. The other so-called detective was in the front passenger seat. Then despair overwhelmed her. The driver of the car was her mother. Why was she involved in this abduction? Although her mother had known about the beatings, Jane had never thought she would actually be complicit in something as dreadful as this.

There was blood in her mouth. She'd bitten her lip. The metallic taste was horribly familiar. Why had he wanted her back? If they hated her so much they should have been pleased when she'd left them.

The sound of the engine roaring, as the accelerator was pressed down, filled the car. No one spoke. Their silence was unnerving. Then she remembered that Charlotte had been there when she'd been abducted. She wasn't entirely alone. Her friend would go to Oscar and Roy and between them they would rescue her.

Her heart was thudding in her ears. It was impossible to think straight. Were they going back to Lattimore? Slowly she regained a modicum of control and the hammering subsided. Without turning her head she began to take note of what was zooming past the car windows. She hadn't known her mother could drive. There was so much she didn't know.

Having never travelled by car anywhere but around the village, the jumble of streets and houses that flashed by were meaningless to her. Her eyes blurred. She blinked to clear them. It didn't help that they were travelling too fast to make anything recognisable.

It would take more than an hour to reach the village. No point in worrying now. She would pretend to sleep and hope that one of them might say something that would help her later. It took all her resolve to slump sideways so her head was resting against the shoulder of the detective. He might be malodorous but still preferable to being closer to *that man.*

Having something concrete to do helped. They didn't know she was a different person – stronger and braver – they would think her the same pathetic, cowering girl she'd been until last September.

Breathing in and out slowly was, for some reason, wonderfully calming. Whatever happened to her in the next few hours she would endure as somehow Oscar would come for her.

She continued the pretence. The car continued to roar; occasionally they slowed to turn a corner and the gears crunched. Her mother wasn't a good driver. Eventually her patience was rewarded.

'What if that girl reports what she saw, Sydney? What will you do if the police come?'

'Keep your eyes on the road, woman. Don't ask stupid questions. Do as you're told.'

Nothing else was said for another few miles; then her mother spoke again. 'She's a WAAF, Sydney. She will be considered absent without leave and the military police might come to arrest her.'

Jane almost gave herself away. Why hadn't she thought of this? Being AWOL, especially when one was doing something so secret and important, would be taken very seriously. Her lips curved slightly. These people didn't know she wasn't an ordinary WAAF, but a highly trained and skilled plotter who was going to be essential to the war effort once things got started.

The shoulder she was leaning against smelled of tobacco, alcohol and body odour. She hoped she didn't gag and give herself away. The car continued to lurch. The brakes were suddenly applied violently and she was flying forwards unable to prevent herself from crashing against the back of the driver's seat and into the floor well.

The car skidded, spun and then shuddered to a halt. She was firmly wedged behind the seats. Breathing was difficult. Everywhere was painful. Her head was fuzzy. The man she'd been leaning against was slumped across her, moaning softly. *That man* recovered first.

'For Christ's sake, you stupid bitch, you could have killed us. Get this bloody car back on the road and moving before some interfering bastards get involved.'

Hearing him use such profanities should have shocked her but she already knew his pleasant urbane exterior was a lie.

'Get yourself back, Brown, and stop whingeing. My wife can't drive with you sprawled across the back of her seat like that.'

That man must have grabbed the semiconscious detective as he certainly didn't make any effort to remove himself. As soon as the weight was lifted she sucked in a mouthful of air and immediately her head cleared.

She was about to wriggle free when her shoulders were gripped in a vicious hold and she was heaved onto the seat. If she'd broken anything this could have been catastrophic – but *that man* wouldn't care how much he hurt her.

'Don't say a word. Don't move. I'm going to deal with you when we're home. You're going to regret having run away and putting me to this trouble.' His whispered words sent her spiralling back to the days when she'd been in terror of offending him.

She was about to start apologising, begging for his forgiveness, promising she'd be a good girl and not upset him again when the car reversed noisily and returned to the road.

She closed her eyes and bit her lip until she regained control. She wasn't the same person. She was braver. She was a WAAF and whatever he did to her she'd never grovel to him again. Oscar would find her. All she had to do was survive until rescue came.

As the journey proceeded she became increasingly concerned about the man beside her. Did she dare to suggest to her abductors that they should stop at a hospital? Things couldn't be any worse and she feared the man might be seriously injured – could even die if he didn't have immediate medical attention.

'The detective is dying. You'll be murderers if you don't take him to a hospital.'

'Shut up.' She didn't see the blow coming. A shaft of agony exploded in her head and everything went black.

Oscar hurtled through the streets dodging around pedestrians when necessary and arrived at Victory House scarcely out of breath. Pilots carried a revolver in case they were shot down in enemy territory. He wished he had it with him now.

No one challenged him as he took the steps at the double. He must stay focused – not think about what might be happening to the woman he loved. He skidded to a halt beside the most senior officer he could see. The man had the insignia of a wing commander.

'Sir, a WAAF has just been abducted. She's on special duties, working at Bentley Priory.'

'Good God – come with me, Flight Lieutenant, we need to get something organised immediately.'

Oscar had deliberately not said it was Jane's father who'd done the abducting. If the bigwigs thought she'd been kidnapped by German spies they would be desperate to get her back. He doubted they would have reacted so swiftly if they'd known the truth. He gave them the description of the car and told them that Jane had seen someone following her the last time she was in London.

'Excellent. We'll get somebody looking for the vehicle straightaway. Are you a close friend of Miss Hadley?'

'Miss Hadley and I went out a couple of times but I've not seen her for several weeks. Flying Officer Cross and I bumped into Miss Hadley and her friend by chance at Charing Cross station.'

'We have no home address for her. Do you know why she put a hotel down as her residence?'

He had to come clean. Jane would hate her personal business being discussed but he had no choice. 'She was brutalised by her father all her life. With the help of the local vicar, the Reverend Jackson and his wife, she was able to escape and sign up when war was declared.'

The three officers looked suitably shocked. 'Her home address – do you know it?'

'I know that bastard's a bank manager in St Albans and the village she lived in is called Lattimore.'

The direct question was coming and he couldn't lie to

his superiors. 'Do you think it could have been Hadley who snatched her?' The Win Co stared right through him.

'I think it could be, but the man would have to be insane. Why would he go to so much trouble? He can hardly keep her prisoner and she won't remain with him willingly.'

'Nasty business. Can't abide physical abuse. However, like you, I think it unlikely the man is so deranged he would do such a thing. I suggest that you investigate in Lattimore and leave us to explore other avenues.'

An NCO came in and handed the Win Co a piece of paper. He scowled and his expression changed from mildly concerned to grim. 'ACW1 374 is a highly trained and skilled plotter. We need her back.'

'Am I still going to Lattimore solo, sir?'

'Absolutely not. Take a motorbike and depart immediately. A car will follow you.'

Oscar set off at the double. Jane had been taken about an hour ago. If that bastard was taking her to Lattimore she would be arriving about now unless there was some sort of hold-up. He hesitated in the entrance hall, not sure in which direction to go to find his transport.

An NCO beckoned from the front door. 'Good luck, sir. You'll need these.' The young man handed him a pair of goggles and some flying gloves.

'Thank you. Much appreciated.'

A motorbike was waiting on the kerb. It was a powerful beast and he thought he'd be able to travel the thirty miles far quicker than in a car. He kicked it into life, opened the throttle and took off with a roar. He was out of the city and halfway to St Albans in less than half an hour.

His mind was blank. His full attention was on the road

and getting to Lattimore in the shortest possible time. What he was going to do when he arrived could be dealt with later.

Lattimore was a compact, well laid out little village and the spire was visible as he raced in. He braked furiously when he saw the church. The vicarage was usually fairly adjacent. Two middle-aged matrons emerged through the lych gate. He shouted over the wall.

'Excuse me, ladies, can you direct me to the home of Mr and Mrs Hadley?'

'Go to the end of this street and it's the large Georgian house on your left. It has a green front door.'

'Thank you, ma'am.'

He accelerated the remaining half a mile and saw the building he wanted just ahead. He braked, turned off the engine and kicked down the stand. No point in giving them warning of his arrival.

He moved stealthily beside the neatly clipped hedge, keeping his head low in case it could be seen from the house. There was a drive of sorts just ahead and it appeared to lead around to the rear of the place. He needed to see if the car was back.

The track led to a series of outbuildings. None of them contained a large black Austin. His stomach clenched. He'd pinned his hopes on the fact that she would be brought here. If she'd been taken somewhere else he might never find her.

He reversed his steps, grabbed the motorbike and headed for the vicarage. He rode up the drive and saw a curtain move as he dismounted. He'd been seen and hopefully one of the Jacksons would be able to throw some light on this disaster.

The front door opened as he walked up to it. 'Good afternoon, young man, how can I be of assistance to you?' The man with the dog collar reminded him of his own father and this gave him the confidence to be open about his reasons for being there.

'Reverend Jackson, I'm Flight Lieutenant Stanton. I'm a close friend of Jane Hadley's. Her father abducted her earlier today and I've come to get her back.'

'That's very bad news indeed, young man? I take it you know what that poor girl's situation was until she managed to escape last year.'

'I do, sir, which is why it's imperative that I find her as soon as possible. I checked the house and the car's not there. I'm hoping you might be able to tell me where he might have taken her.'

'I do know but I'm afraid it's some considerable distance from here. A great-aunt of his left him a substantial property in a small village called Churt. It's about fifteen miles the other side of Guildford.'

'That's about forty miles from here. Can you give me directions or an address?'

'Whilst you turn your bike round, I'll fetch it. I have it written down in my study.'

Unfortunately, the vicar had the address but no idea of the exact whereabouts of Sumiton Manor. Oscar did know how to get to Guildford and just prayed he would be there in time. He'd been travelling flat out, weaving in and out of the army lorries and occasional civilian vehicle, for some time when he remembered that he had neglected to tell Jackson to ring Victory House with this new information.

Whoever was following him would now be even further

behind so it would be up to him to effect the rescue. How hard could it be to take Jane from the clutches of a middle-aged bank manager and a couple of private detectives?

Jane slowly opened her eyes. Why was it so dark? Where was she? What had happened to her? Who had dumped her on the floor of a freezing cold cellar?

She attempted to move her hands but they were tied together. Her feet were free, which was a good thing. Her head hurt most dreadfully. She was finding it hard to think coherently. The cold seeped through her clothes and this helped her to concentrate. If she stood up she would be less uncomfortable.

Using her feet as levers she scuffled and wriggled and managed to roll onto her back. A wave of nausea almost overwhelmed her and she tasted bile. Maybe it would be better to keep still.

She closed her eyes again and let her mind drift in the hope she would recall the events that had led up to her incarceration. What did she know? One – she was a prisoner. Two – she was hurt. She shivered.

Had the Germans captured her? That couldn't be true as there were no Germans wandering about London. No point in dwelling on this. Her priority was, first, to get herself off the floor and second, find something to sit on.

This time she was more cautious. Keeping her head as still as possible she carefully pushed herself up on her elbows. Painful, but so far so good. If she straightened her arms she would be sitting up, which would be an improvement, but with her hands tied this was impossible.

On her knees – that would be easier. She took several deep breaths before gingerly rolling over. It was several minutes before she was in control again and able to put her bound hands to the floor and push.

Eventually she was semi-upright, on her knees, but wasn't sure if, without her hands to balance, she would be able to get to her feet. Whoever had taken her would expect her to be in a miserable heap on the floor. She was determined to be upright so she could face them.

Her eyes had slowly adjusted to the darkness and there was a faint glimmer of light coming from what was possibly a boarded-up window. She wasn't in a cellar. This knowledge galvanised her into action. Ignoring the nausea, the pain in her head, the cold and stiffness of her limbs, she rocked backwards and then leaned forward whilst pressing her toes into the ground.

It worked. She was standing. She wasn't sure how long she could remain like this as her legs were trembling, her head swimming and she thought she was about to be sick. Breathing slowly through her nose and out through her mouth did the trick.

Turning her head was impossible so she slowly moved her feet in a circle to examine her surroundings. She was in a shed or outbuilding of some sort. The walls were brick, the floor mud, and the window had been blocked from the inside. Holding her hands out in front she paced first the length and then the breadth – probably about eight feet by ten.

There were heaps of debris, crates and boxes, piled against the wall at the window end. With any luck she would find something to use to prise off the rope around her wrists. She remembered reading in a murder mystery that a captive had used a broken bottle but she wasn't sure she was brave enough to do this even if she found one.

She was a bit warmer after moving about and her brain was functioning better. She still couldn't remember how she'd come to be here but she wasn't going to worry about that at the moment. She moved towards the window. Even with her hands bound she thought she could move some of the things blocking the light.

As long as she moved slowly, she could manage. Her instinct was to tear at the things, let the light in before her captors came back. There was something she couldn't quite grasp – fleeting images and thoughts that made no sense.

With some difficulty she removed several boxes and then welcome light flooded in through the gap she'd made. She stared at her arms. She was in some sort of uniform. Air Force blue – she was a WAAF. Why couldn't she remember any of this?

She reviewed again what she did know. Someone had taken her prisoner. Had the Germans captured her? Did she work in some secret place, have vital information, and they were going to interrogate and torture her?

The stream of sunlight was enough for her to see to drag a couple of packing cases over to the window and sit on them. Tears trickled down her cheeks. How could she ever escape if she didn't even know her own name or where she came from?

She must have dozed off, as she woke later with a jolt. Someone was coming.

23

Oscar drove like a maniac. He flashed through villages and towns narrowly avoiding unwary pedestrians and other road users. He paused in Guildford for directions to Churt, but that was his only stop.

His face was numb. Thank God for the goggles and gloves. Several times he'd had to use his feet to prevent disaster and, from the feel of it, one of them was now missing the leather sole. Not wishing to draw attention to himself as he arrived at his destination, he slowed to a more sensible speed.

He found the house easily enough. It was isolated, set in extensive grounds, a mile or so from the village itself. He chugged along until he found a track – no doubt the tradesmen's entrance years ago – and turned into it. The hedges on either side were high enough to conceal his progress and he was pretty sure that travelling at this speed no one would hear him either.

Halfway along the engine spluttered and died. He'd run out of petrol. The Almighty had done his best, had got him here; now it was up to him. His first task was to find Jane, make sure she was safe. After that he would deal with the bastards who'd taken her.

He dumped the motorbike in the ditch, removed his greatcoat, goggles and gloves and dropped them on top of it. His arms needed to be free. He wished again that he had his revolver with him.

He jogged along the lane until he saw the red-tiled roofs of the brick-built stables, stores and barns just ahead. The house was several hundred yards away. The first thing he saw when he emerged from the end of the track was a large black Austin. A surge of excitement shot through him. He'd come to the right place.

Keeping low, he crept to the car and put his hand on the bonnet. It was cold. Not good – it meant it had arrived some time ago. As he moved away he glanced into the rear of the vehicle. What was that on the seat against the right-hand passenger door?

Ignoring caution, he threw it open. He'd not been mistaken. It was blood. In fact, now he looked closely, there was also blood in the footwell and smeared across the back of the seat. He wanted to smash his fist through the window. Jane had been injured – possibly, no probably, seriously.

It would be better if he didn't meet that bastard as Hadley was unlikely to survive the encounter. He decided to do a cursory search of the outbuildings first. It was unlikely Jane would be locked in one of those but it made sense to look before he headed for the house.

He checked he couldn't be seen before heading for the first barn. This was a coach house, open-fronted, so this didn't require more than a glance. There was a row of stables – also empty. That left a series of sheds and storerooms to investigate. That shouldn't take long.

All these were windowless and all were locked. He rattled

on the doors and called her name quietly. As expected, there was no response. He bitterly regretted not having contacted Victory House and given them the new directions.

He would have to be more cautious approaching the house. He wanted to get Jane to safety before he dealt with her captors. It would be better if reinforcements arrived before he came face-to-face with that bastard as the way he was feeling right now he wouldn't be able to control his fury. He wasn't a violent man – but this was different.

There was sufficient shrubbery for him to dodge behind. He was facing the rear of the building and the shutters were closed. He would break in from this side – there was bound to be a loose catch on one of the shutters. If he'd been wearing his flying boots he could have used the knife he kept pushed into the top. This was an essential piece of kit for a flyer. It was to cut the strings of his chute when he landed if he was obliged to bail out.

There was a wide flagstone terrace, which was broken halfway along by steps leading into a formal garden. Maybe he would be better breaking in through the French doors that faced the lawns. Better to have a recce where he was first and then decide.

The windowsills were shoulder height, which was going to make climbing in problematic. Another reason to use the doors to enter. The shutters opened when he pulled. He needed to find something to stand on if he was going to be able to push up this window and clamber in.

There might be something in one of the storerooms he could use or he could just creep along the terrace and go in from there. He grabbed the edge of the sill and heaved himself up so his elbows were jammed on it and he could see into the room beyond.

What little furniture there was in there was draped with dust sheets. From the look of it nobody had been in there for years. He dropped to the ground and was about to try his luck further along when he heard someone coming through the shrubbery behind him.

He rolled under the nearest overhanging rhododendron bush not a moment too soon. He heard voices. Bloody hell – there were two people coming. Should he stay where he was or make a dash for it?

'I tell you, Jimmy, the owners are here. My Molly swears she saw a big black car go up the drive a while ago.'

'I reckon if you're right, Dave, we can ask to be paid what we're owed for keeping the grounds tidy.'

Gardeners – not looking for him. He could hardly pop out and speak to them so it would be better to lie doggo and avoid awkward questions.

As soon as the men had vanished around the corner, no doubt heading for the back door, he scrambled out of his hiding place and brushed himself down. He was about to continue when he paused to think.

There being unwanted and unexpected callers was to his advantage. The longer they stayed to argue their cause the better it would be for him and for Jane. The gardeners would hardly be invited into the drawing room so it would be the perfect time to prise open those doors and slip in to search the house.

He put his shoulder to the frame, the wood splintered, and they sprung open. He froze. Had anyone heard the racket? He was across the room before he understood the significance of the furniture in here also being under covers. The house was basically unoccupied. Jane had been brought here because Hadley thought he would be undisturbed.

Cautiously he opened the double doors at the far end a fraction and put his ear to the crack. Yes – there were voices, but they weren't close. He slipped through into a substantial entrance hall. Where would Jane be imprisoned? Upstairs was the most likely place.

He looked in all the rooms on the first floor and found nothing. The staircase to the upper floor was at the end of the passageway. There was a window overlooking the outbuildings. He glanced sideways. He clutched the wall. That bastard was hurrying towards the locked sheds that he'd dismissed as being empty. He was swinging a folded leather belt in one hand.

Jane no longer cared who was coming. What really frightened her was the fact that she'd lost her memory. Nothing anyone could do to her could be as bad as not knowing who she was. She wasn't even going to bother to stand up and face her captor. She was comfortable leaning against the wall on a packing case with the sun playing across her face.

Someone was unlocking the door. She shifted slightly so she could see the person. If he was a German he'd hardly be wearing SS uniform but she was curious to know who had gone to so much trouble and what they wanted from her.

The door opened and a middle-aged man, smartly dressed, with dark hair flecked with grey, stood framed there. He didn't look like a kidnapper. He looked like – well – an ordinary person, but a very angry, tight-lipped ordinary person.

He remained in the doorway glaring at her. She smiled. This enraged him more and suddenly she was terrified. She didn't know why, but this man meant her harm.

'You dare to smile at me? I was too lenient with you in the past. That's changed. Things will be different now. I'm going to show you the error of your ways.' He was holding a belt in his hand.

She was unable to move. Why did this stranger talk to her as if he knew her? Why did he hate her and want to hurt her? She needed to get up but her limbs refused to obey her instructions and she remained frozen, hunched on the packing cases, pressing herself against the wall.

'On your feet. Get over here. Do it now.'

She shook her head. That was a mistake. Her eyes blurred and reality began to slip away.

Oscar was hurtling down the stairs, through the drawing room and out of the broken French doors seconds after he saw the figure approaching the sheds. He entered the shed at full speed, shoulder first, and Hadley didn't stand a chance. He went down as if poleaxed. The belt flew from his hand and skittered across the floor.

A white-hot rage engulfed him. The bastard was pushing himself upright. He let him stand and then floored him a second time with a right hook that lifted Hadley from his feet. This time he remained down. Unconscious.

Jane was staring at him, eyes wide, no sign of recognition.

One side of her hair was matted with blood and her uniform collar was red. A blow to her head must have caused the confusion. He moved to her side.

'Jane, I'm Oscar Stanton. I was sent to rescue you. Do I have your permission to pick you up?'

'Yes, I don't know who that horrible man was. I'm glad you knocked him down.'

Even her voice sounded different. It took all his self-control not to hold her tight, reassure her that he loved her and no one would ever hurt her again. Time enough to worry about her memory loss when she was safe in hospital.

He carried her out and then, holding her steady with one hand, he pulled the door closed and relocked it. Then he retraced his steps. The two gardeners saw him approaching.

'Miss Hadley has met with an accident. I'm going to take her inside and do what I can but she needs urgent medical attention. Is there a telephone box where one of you could make the necessary phone call?'

'There's one in the village. I've got my bike – I can get there in a jiffy. Dave, you help the gentleman – you know a bit about injuries and such.'

The speaker dashed off at a creditable speed, leaving him with his companion. 'I'm Flight Lieutenant Stanton. I was sent to reclaim Miss Hadley. Reinforcements will be arriving to arrest the Hadleys.'

'I'm Jimmy Roberts. Me and Dave have worked here this past five years taking care of the grounds for Mrs DeVere. I've never met the new owner.'

Jimmy removed the dust sheet from a sofa. 'This is clean enough. I know where there's a first-aid box. I'll fetch it and then find some blankets.'

Oscar was surprised no further questions were asked. Jane had drifted off again. He placed her down carefully and was horrified when he removed his hand to find it bloodstained. He needed to stem the flow immediately.

His handkerchief would serve but only as a temporary solution. She was too still, too cold, and he feared for her life. He sent up a fervent prayer asking that the Man upstairs would spare her. Jimmy came back with a well-stocked box. With his able assistance Oscar bandaged the gash and was satisfied there would be no further bleeding.

'That cut isn't deep enough to have done much damage. There must be something else causing her to remain unconscious,' he said as he examined her head for further injury.

'Sod me, that's a nasty bruise,' Jimmy said quietly. 'I'm going to get some blankets from upstairs.'

'This is a serious injury. I pray to God that there's no permanent damage been done.'

'So do I, sir, so do I.' The gardener clattered off, his outdoor boots loud on the wooden floor in the hall.

Someone came into the room and he spoke without looking round. 'Good, that was quick…'

'My poor girl – I never meant this to happen.'

He shot to his feet and turned to face the speaker. This must be Mrs Hadley. As far as he was concerned, she was as guilty as her husband. Her very presence here made her culpable.

'Too late for regret, madam – you will both answer to the authorities for what's happened today.'

Belatedly he remembered there had been four people involved in the abduction. Where were the two detectives?

'Where are Hadley's henchmen?'

The wretched woman sniffed and dabbed her eyes. 'One of them was hurt when I inadvertently ran the car into a ditch. Sydney abandoned them on the side of the road. Where is my husband?'

'I dealt with him and he's unconscious in the shed your daughter was locked in.'

'I hope you killed him. I don't care what happens to me as long as he can never harm Jane again.'

Maybe this woman wasn't quite as evil as her husband after all. Jimmy returned before he could comment and Oscar forgot about her. When they had finished tucking Jane up in a cocoon of warm blankets Mrs Hadley had vanished.

Had she gone to let her husband out? Then the welcome rattle of crockery on a tray told him his fears were baseless. It didn't seem right to be drinking tea whilst Jane remained in a stupor. Her mother returned with a basin of hot water and clean cloths.

She wanted to minister to Jane herself but he didn't want that woman anywhere near his precious girl. Dave had just returned when the two cars eventually arrived.

By the time he'd explained to the senior chap, the ambulance had turned up. The drivers were accompanied by a medic. The doctor checked Jane's vitals and straightened without speaking. Oscar clenched his fists at the man's grim expression.

'Miss Hadley has a serious head injury. Her pulse is weak. This could go either way.'

'She didn't recognise Hadley or me.'

'Retrograde amnesia is a common side effect of such an

injury. It can be temporary or permanent. Only time will tell.'

Oscar stood aside as the ambulance drivers transferred her to a stretcher and then, accompanied by the doctor, they carried her out to the waiting vehicle. She was being taken to the hospital in Guildford and as soon as he had petrol for his motorbike, he would follow her there.

'This is a bad business, Flight Lieutenant; even if the poor girl makes it, she'll be of no further use to us without her memory,' the Wing Commander said.

For a moment Oscar was at a loss for words. How could a senior officer say something so crass? He had to be careful what he said next or he would be no use to them either as he would be in the glasshouse for striking an officer.

'What about Hadley and his wife and the two so-called detectives he employed?'

'Another ambulance is on its way to collect Hadley. The local constabulary will take the wife into custody. God knows where exactly the other two were dumped. I've got men looking for them now.'

'I don't suppose either of the cars have a spare can of petrol in the boot, do they, sir?'

'My driver has taken care of that, Stanton. You'll be required to make a statement in due course. Don't worry if Hadley dies – there'll be no charges.'

'I have a week's furlough and will remain with Miss Hadley at the hospital. Would you be kind enough to let my CO, Squadron Leader Riley at Kenley, know my whereabouts in case I'm needed back before then?'

'Will do, happy to oblige. Means a lot to you, this young lady?'

'Yes, she does. If she's forgotten me, I'll just have to start again. I won't give up on her.'

'Good man. Mind you, could be tricky if her father dies. If she doesn't recall the circumstances, she might not take too kindly to the man who killed him.'

Oscar turned his back on the idiot and marched out. The motorbike was now on its stand outside the front of the house. He pulled on his greatcoat, gloves and goggles, kicked the bike into life and roared off.

He refused to even contemplate the idea that Jane might die. She would recover – she had been concussed before and got over it. The bike swerved and he almost pitched headfirst over the handlebars. They didn't know she'd had a previous head injury a few months ago. This knowledge might well be crucial.

He increased his speed and was at the hospital not long after the ambulance. He made his way to the emergency department and found a man in a white coat. He told him about Jane's previous accident and the medic nodded gravely.

'Thank you, that would explain why a relatively mild blow to the head has put her into a coma. I'm afraid there's nothing we can do apart from wait and pray.'

Oscar had to hang about for an hour or more before he was allowed into the side room where she'd been put. She was breathing without assistance, but remained deeply unconscious. She was receiving a blood transfusion, which hopefully would replace what she'd lost.

He'd only been allowed to sit with her when he'd lied and said that he was her fiancé. She was on the critical list and only family members were allowed to visit. She had no family. He would take care of her in future, if she would allow him to. If he told her they were really engaged would she believe him? He couldn't be so underhand – he'd never lie to her.

Time dragged. He'd never prayed so much and so enthusiastically in his life. He would ring his father and ask him to get the congregation to add her to the prayer list for Sunday. The more the Almighty heard her name the better.

Nurses came and went and checked her vitals and then the consultant arrived and he was turfed out. He visited the bog and then went in search of the public telephone. His mother answered and when he explained she assured him Jane would have their prayers.

'My dear, how are you? It must be so hard for you.'

'It is, but despite the odds being against her I somehow know that she'll recover.'

He replaced the receiver, stacked up another pile of coins and rang the Sanctuary, the hotel where he and Roy had booked. With any luck his friend would have returned there and be waiting for news.

The concierge had been expecting his call and moments later Roy was on the line.

'Thank God. Charlotte's here as well waiting for news.'

When he'd finished explaining what had happened Roy was shocked and sympathetic. 'She won't have anywhere to go as the WAAF don't want her if she can't remember who she is or what her duties were.'

'I can't believe they'd abandon her like that. She's one of us now; they have to take care of her until she's well enough to either be demobbed or go back to work.'

'More to the point, Oscar, old mate, how are you going to play this?'

'It's possible she'll never recover her early memories but equally possible that things will gradually come back to her over the next few weeks.' He hadn't told Roy that Jane's life hung in the balance. Just saying it out loud made it seem horribly real.

24

Jane came round slowly but didn't open her eyes immediately. She was in hospital. Just the smell was enough to tell her that much. She remembered being tied up in a shed. A terrifying man had come in and threatened to hurt her then she woke up again and a young man in RAF uniform took care of her.

A slight sound beside her made her open her eyes. The same man was sitting beside her. He looked unkempt, as if he'd slept in his clothes and not shaved for several days. Why was he here?

'Jane, I can't tell you how pleased I am to see you awake. How do you feel? Do you know who I am?'

'I've got a bit of a headache, feel very tired, but apart from that I'm fine. I'm sorry, I don't know your name but I think you're the person who rescued me.' She frowned. 'I take it my name is Jane – I'm afraid I don't remember anything about myself or how I came to be here.'

'I'm Oscar Stanton. I had to tell the hospital that we're engaged or they wouldn't have allowed me to stay.'

Now she was even more confused. 'Why would you want to stay if we're not engaged or anything? I take it we do know each other quite well.'

He ran his hand over his bristly chin and smiled sadly. 'We've been out together a few times. You broke it off but I always hoped we'd make a go of it one day.'

'I seem to remember I was wearing a uniform like yours. Am I a WAAF?' This was all very strange as she seemed to know quite a lot of things but absolutely nothing about herself.

'Yes, you're a highly trained and skilled member of a secret team. The powers that be are hoping that your amnesia will soon pass so they can have you back at your post.'

'How long have I been here? And where exactly is, here?'

'You're in Guildford Hospital and you've been here four days – which is why I look so dishevelled. I'm going to ring the bell and let the nurses know you've come round. Whilst they take care of you, I'm going to see if I can find somewhere to tidy up. I won't be long.' He was at the door when he turned back. 'There are things I've got to tell you but they can wait until you're feeling better.'

She was prodded and poked by several doctors, asked interminable questions, and then allowed to get up to use the commode. None of these physicians could give her a definitive answer when she asked how long it would be before her memory came back.

'Miss Hadley, would you like a bed bath or can you manage to wash yourself?' The student nurse looked overeager to wield the flappy flannel in her direction.

'I prefer to do it myself. I don't suppose anyone thought to bring me in a clean nightie, toothbrush and so on?'

The girl smiled. 'That bag arrived two days ago. From the label I think it was forwarded from a London hotel. Would you like me to see if there's anything useful in it?'

Whoever had taken the trouble to post the bag would hardly have brought unnecessary items all this way. Half an hour later she was sitting up in bed, in a clean nightgown, drinking tea and eating toast and marmalade.

There were several important questions she needed to ask her pretending fiancé. The first was why her parents hadn't come to sit with her but left it to Mr Stanton – no, from his insignia he was a flight lieutenant. She smiled to herself, pleased her brain had retained some information, even if it wasn't anything about her past and what had happened to her.

The door had been left open and a clean-shaven and happier looking Flight Lieutenant Stanton strolled in. 'Excellent – apart from the stitches in your head you look almost back to normal. Thinner and paler of course – but can't expect anything else after what you've been through.'

He resumed his seat beside her. 'I'm sure you have questions but I think it might be quicker and easier if I just tell you everything that happened. It's going to upset you, but you need to know.'

She listened, hardly able to comprehend what he was telling her. The tea and toast got cold on her lap. When he'd finished he looked so worried on her behalf that some impulse made her reach out and take his hand.

'Oscar, none of this is your fault. In fact, my having lost my memory is a good thing in some ways. If I can't remember the horrible things that happened to me then I can't worry about them, can I?'

'Only you could put a positive spin on this. I expect someone from the WAAF will come and see you now you're awake. I was told they're going to keep you under observation for another week but then you will be discharged and you need to have somewhere to go to recuperate.'

'I can see why I went out with you. Why did I break it off?' For some reason this seemed the most important question she'd asked so far. He was so handsome, charming, intelligent and kind that she couldn't imagine any reason why she'd want to end the relationship. Had he been unfaithful?

'You told me you were damaged beyond redemption and could never trust a man…'

'Is that all? I don't believe that now. I know I've only known you a short time as far as my brain's concerned but you seem so familiar somehow. I trust you absolutely. Don't give up on me whilst I get better, will you?'

His smile was spectacular. He took her hands and she loved the roughness of his skin against hers. 'I'm in love with you. I'm not sure you ever felt quite as much for me as I did for you. I'm hoping I can persuade you to fall in love with me if you give me a chance.'

His eyes darkened, his fingers closed more firmly over her own. She wanted him to kiss her so why was he hesitating? She leaned towards him and this was all the encouragement he needed. When his mouth touched hers it was as if electric shocks travelled from her toes to her head. She didn't want it to end.

'Miss Hadley, Flight Lieutenant Stanton, you might be engaged but this kind of behaviour is not approved of on my ward,' the ward sister spoke sharply from behind them.

He stroked her cheek before sitting back looking quite unrepentant. 'Sister, I don't give a damn whether you approve of my kissing my fiancée or not. I've sat beside her thinking she might die and by some miracle she is not only awake, but almost better. I intend to kiss her as often as I can.'

Jane hardly dared to look up but risked a glance and to her surprise saw that the nurse was smiling at them. Not so disapproving after all.

'I think it might be wise to move Miss Hadley into the main ward where I can keep an eye on you both.'

The thought of being placed among strangers, of not being able to have Oscar beside her all the time, was making her head spin. 'Please, let me stay here until Oscar has to go back to his base.' She flopped back on the pillows unable to continue.

Instantly the nurse was at her side. 'Take a deep breath, my dear. Too much excitement is bad for you. You need to keep calm. You might feel better, but you're still seriously ill as far as your consultant is concerned.'

Oscar smoothed her hair back and kissed her gently on the forehead. 'I'm not going anywhere, darling, until I absolutely have to. Rest, go to sleep; everything's going to be fine.'

Obediently Jane closed her eyes and was immediately asleep. Oscar looked up at the ward sister. 'She is just sleeping, isn't she?'

'She is. I came to tell you that there's been a phone call from an officer in the WAAF. They spoke to Miss Hadley's consultant and Mr Lansley said that your fiancée would receive a letter in the next day or two.'

She bustled off, her crisply starched apron crackling as she went. He didn't like the sound of a formal letter being sent instead of someone coming to visit in person. Whilst Jane was asleep he was going in search of this Mr Lansley to find out for himself exactly what had transpired.

Eventually he tracked the consultant down. He wasn't condescending or dismissive, but remarkably helpful and pleasant – which made a welcome change.

'I'm going to be blunt, Flight Lieutenant, I can't see Miss Hadley being fit for duty for weeks, possibly months. Severe head trauma can cause problems for the patient for the rest of their lives.'

'Can, but not for every patient.'

'Of course, Miss Hadley might be one of the lucky ones and make a full and speedy recovery. Her memory might return completely or she might regain some of it. We do not fully understand the brain. However, the fact that she has suffered two traumas in less than six months is a negative indication to recovery.'

This was hard to assimilate. His hands were clammy. He hardly dared to ask the question. 'Are you saying that her life remains at risk?'

Lansley looked at him as if he was an imbecile. 'I'm saying no such thing. Miss Hadley will be physically fit after a few days' rest. I cannot be as sanguine about her mental health. I'm sorry this wasn't the information you were hoping for. To make matters worse I must warn you that Miss Hadley is about to be dismissed from service as unfit for duty.'

The man nodded and strode away to deal with more pressing problems. This was the worst possible news. He'd thought Jane would be kept on until she was able to resume active duty. There was obviously no room in this war for invalids – she was going to be left high and dry.

There was a decent café a short distance from the hospital and he headed there needing to get away from the all-pervading smell of disinfectant and boiled cabbage. He stopped to look at the sunshine, tulips and daffodils everywhere, but none of it gladdened his soul.

A taxi pulled up and to his delight he saw Roy jump out. He bounded down the steps and shook hands vigorously with his friend. 'Just the man I want to see. Jane's out of the woods, health wise, but up to her neck in it as far as everything else goes.'

'I've got news for you as well, which might help Jane's situation. Were you on your way to that café? We can talk there.'

They managed to persuade the proprietor to bend her rules and not only did they have a decent meat sandwich, they also got a piece of Victoria sandwich to go with their pot of tea.

'I didn't know it was now an either or, situation,' Roy said as he tucked into his sandwich.

'I'm not sure there's an actual edict that a customer can't have two items from a menu. We're not regulars and I expect she's keeping things back for those. What's the news you've got for me?'

'Riley has proved invaluable as far as keeping me up-to-date. It appears that one of the blokes dumped on the side of the road was dead before the ambulance arrived. It took several hours to find them. The poor bugger would have survived if he'd been taken straight to hospital, so both Hadleys now face a possible murder charge as well as one of kidnapping.'

'Even if it's not considered murder, it's definitely

manslaughter. I'm not sure that Mrs Hadley was a willing participant. I'm prepared to speak up for her in court. She was bullied into participating. I take it that Hadley has recovered.'

'Unfortunately, he has. He's got a broken jaw and concussion. He's not going to be allowed out on bail but his wife might well be.'

'You said that your news would help with Jane's situation. Are you suggesting that she might go back to her family home and be taken care of by her mother?'

'I was thinking along those lines, yes. If she can't remember what happened there then I can't see why she couldn't live there until she's well enough to re-enlist.'

The more he thought about it the less Oscar liked the idea. 'Absolutely not. It's quite possible her memory will return suddenly. Imagine how traumatic it would be for her to wake up in the one place she'd vowed never to set foot in again?'

He spoke more vehemently than he'd intended and his friend threw his hands up as if in surrender. 'Don't shoot the messenger, mate. Just making a suggestion. Do you have a better one?'

Oscar spoke without thinking. 'I could marry her and then find her digs near the base. Or, even better, she could stay with my parents in Suffolk.'

'A bit extreme, don't you think? What if she wakes up one morning and remembers that she'd decided she didn't want anything more to do with you?'

He ignored this comment, although it was a valid one. 'Things have changed between us. When I explain the alternative, I think she'll agree my solution is the best one for her. Don't look so disapproving, Roy, I'll not sleep with her. Then we can get the marriage annulled if that's what she wants.'

'Bloody hell, that's altruistic of you. You're a good bloke and I hope it works out for you.'

'Another thing: if I go for a Burton, which is more than likely, my family will take care of her. She won't be alone.'

They finished every last crumb and ordered a second pot of tea. There was a constant coming and going of nurses and doctors from the hospital and he admired their dedication. How many of them would transfer and become army medics when this phoney war was over?

'I think I need Riley's permission to get married. I'd like my father to marry us. Hopefully you and some of my flight will be able to get the time off and attend. I'm going to speak to Jane now – come with me as I'm sure she'll be delighted to see you. By the way, what happened with you and Charlotte?'

'Nothing exciting. I like her but turned out there's no spark after all. She's a bit abrasive for me.'

Oscar smiled at the description. 'Abrasive? I think you mean independent and assertive. You like your women to be overawed by your personality and charm. Charlotte's not that sort of girl.'

'She certainly isn't. Anyway, she's a good egg and dashed back to the guesthouse and then paid for Jane's bag to be sent here.'

They had to pass the public telephone, which was in the foyer of the hospital. 'I'm going to ring my father before I go up. I've a nasty suspicion no one will be getting leave of absence by the end of the month. Hitler's getting ready to move and we're going to be needed to support the BEF.'

'They've already got several squadrons out there. I don't envy them – but at least things have improved now the winter's over. Kenley will be fully operational soon and our job will be to stop the Luftwaffe from bombing London.'

Oscar returned from his call happy with the response he'd had from his father. He slapped Roy on the back. 'It appears there's no need to call the banns for three weeks nowadays. We can just turn up and get married. All I have to do is convince Jane this is her best option.'

Roy was an entertaining visitor but didn't outstay his welcome. The ward sister had told him as Jane was no longer critically ill normal visiting hours were going to be imposed in future. This meant after today he couldn't visit in the morning and would have to leave by eight o'clock each night.

'I've booked us into a B&B.' His friend smiled. 'I've got your overnight bag with me. You could do with a change of shirt.'

'Thank you, much appreciated. If you hang around, I'll be down in half an hour.'

Now had come the tricky part of his plan – convincing the woman he loved that marrying him, in name only, was her best option. When he'd thought about this moment he'd imagined it would be in a romantic setting, that he'd go down on one knee and then ask her to marry him.

He didn't want to frighten her so explained quietly why he thought this was her best option. Her smile was blinding.

'I'd love to marry you, as long as it's… it's not a physical thing. Even though I don't remember the abuse I suffered you're right to say going back to Lattimore would be a mistake. I was dubious about being kept on by the WAAF and was panicking about what would happen to me.

'I'm overwhelmed by your kindness. I know you won't take advantage of me. I do think you're very attractive and I'm hoping that even if my memory doesn't return I'll fall in love with you eventually.'

'I'm going to do my damnedest to make that happen. Hopefully, you'll be discharged at the weekend and I'll just have time to take you to Suffolk. They know the circumstances and are delighted to welcome you into the family – even if at some later date you decide you want to annul the arrangement.'

'Don't look so despondent, Oscar, I think it far more likely I'll want to make the arrangement permanent. Just give it time.'

A student nurse appeared in the open door and rang the bell loudly. Time to go. He hesitated, not sure if she was ready to be kissed a second time. She solved that problem for him by taking his hands and pulling him closer.

A very satisfactory few minutes later he reluctantly left her to the ministrations of the nurses. Roy was standing on the steps admiring the spring flowers and this time Oscar was in the mood to appreciate what he saw.

'She's agreed to marry me. Let's find the nearest hostelry and have a drink to celebrate.'

25

Over the next few days Jane was interviewed by the police, received a formal letter from the WAAF saying she was demobbed, and the consultant agreed she could be discharged on Saturday after her stitches had been removed.

She no longer remained in bed in her nightclothes but got up every morning, had a quick bath and then got dressed. She only possessed her uniform and from the end of the month she would have no right to wear that.

Oscar had been reading the letter and nodded as he handed it back. 'You've got another two weeks on full pay and then you're getting a generous severance payment of £25. From this it would appear that you've got more than six weeks back pay owing, so you'll have enough to buy what you need when you become a civilian.'

'It says there that I've got to return my uniform and everything else I was issued with or the cost will be deducted from my salary. That means I'll have to go to Uxbridge to collect it and then formally hand it over. Before I can do that I've somehow got to get to the shops and buy something to wear. I don't think I've got enough to cover my expenses, especially for our wedding. I expect your family will want to see me in the traditional white gown.'

'My sister will lend you hers. I've given her your measurements and she's letting down the hem and taking it in at the waist. Once we're married, I'll take care of everything.'

'It's not a real marriage, so I don't see why you should have to pay my bills. I have money in my post office account. I've been saving for years.'

He was staring at her, his eyes wide, his mouth opening and shutting like a stranded fish. Whatever was wrong with him?

'You've just remembered something about your past.'

She couldn't keep back the squeal of excitement and without thinking threw herself into his waiting arms. He held her tight whilst they laughed and cried together. Eventually she sat back and he handed her a handkerchief to mop her face.

'Your memory's coming back. I can't believe it's happening so soon.'

'More to the point, my post office book is in my bag. I've no idea how much I've got – shall we have a look and see if you're marrying an eligible heiress?'

He rummaged around in the zipped pockets at the front and brought the cardboard-covered book over to her. When he offered it she shook her head.

'No, you have a look. It's really strange that I don't recognise it at all even though I just told you I had it.'

He flicked it open. 'You've got thirty pounds in here. A wealthy woman indeed!'

'Good gracious – that's quite a lot. With my back pay and so on I can manage for a while.'

'There's something we haven't discussed and I suppose

now's as good a time as any. My pay goes up when I marry, enough for both of us to live comfortably but not in the lap of luxury. I don't have any savings but I do have a small annuity courtesy of my now deceased grandfather.'

'I seem to recall that you said you were a career serviceman, not a volunteer. Do you intend to stay in the RAF after the war?'

'I don't think I told you that I went to Oxford University and did a degree in theology. My parents both thought I would take orders and were disappointed when I changed course so drastically and became a pilot.'

'Why did you?' The more she learned about this man the better she liked him. She hardly liked to tell him that she didn't believe in God when he was so obviously a devout Christian. Would he still marry her if he knew she was an atheist? More to the point, would his father, a vicar, be so happy to take her in if he knew he was welcoming a heathen into his home?

'I saw what was happening in Germany and after they bombed the Republicans during the Spanish Civil War it was obvious what was coming. Despite the fact that my father's a pacifist I knew I had to join the RAF and be ready to protect my country from invasion.'

'He must find it very hard to have a son who's a fighter pilot.'

'It would be a lot harder if I was a bomber pilot – which thank God I'm not. I realise I haven't actually answered your question about my plans after the war. I always thought I would be ordained, but now I'm not so sure. I think I might become a commercial pilot. Air travel is going to be important in the future.' He handed her back her post office book. 'I was about to ask you what you'd intended to do but of course you can't tell me.'

'I can't think that far ahead. I've a nasty feeling this beastly war is going to go on as long as the last one. People were saying it would be all over by Christmas when it started in September – which Christmas? We might still be saying that in four years' time.'

On Saturday morning she looked around the room she'd been in for the past week – it had become familiar to her and she didn't know anywhere else. Most of the time since she'd woken up it hadn't bothered her that she'd lost her memory; now, faced with leaving hospital with a man she barely knew, her pulse was racing and her hands clammy.

Then she was in his arms, he was stroking her back and murmuring words of encouragement, and her world righted again. He had both their bags over his shoulder leaving him free to hold her hand.

'It will be all right, sweetheart, just let things happen naturally. Here, put my gas mask around your neck. Apparently yours has vanished.'

'Thank you. I lost my first one but managed to get another one from the stores so this will be the third one I've got to get.' Her hand tightened in his. 'That's the second thing I've remembered. I really think my memory is going to come back completely over the next few days.'

He kissed the top of her head and a bubble of happiness settled in her chest. The world wasn't such a scary place if she had him beside her.

They were squashed together in the compartment on the

London train with a naval officer on the other side of Oscar. Opposite were three elegant women obviously on their way to shop at Fortnum & Mason's or Harrods. They ignored the disapproving looks when he put his arm around her.

She'd never been so happy and she relaxed against him. Suddenly memories were returning in quick succession. She had two good friends that she'd met when she was training: one called Nancy and the other Charlotte. In the space of half an hour the fog in her head was all but gone. She remembered everything her father had done to her but it no longer held the same terror. She was a plotter at Uxbridge.

'I remember everything. I can return to my job and you don't have to marry me in such a rush after all.'

He tried to hide his devastation but the glitter in his eyes gave him away. 'That's the most wonderful news, Jane. We can go to Victory House instead of shopping and you can give them the good news. I'll let my parents know.'

She swivelled on the seat – the armrests were already up to allow them to sit closer together – and she touched his face. 'I love you, I think I always have. I do want to be engaged to you and will definitely marry you but I want to do it properly.'

He ignored her tears and kissed her passionately. When he lifted his head there was a spontaneous round of applause from the other four in the compartment. She'd completely forgotten they weren't alone and that their conversation had been clearly audible to the others.

She hid her scarlet cheeks against his shoulder whilst he gave them a brief, edited version of what had taken place.

'How absolutely splendid. Instead of buying clothes, young lady, you must go with your young man and select an engagement ring and make your betrothal official.' The speaker, the lady in the central seat, was smiling at them both despite previously judging their behaviour as reprehensible.

The train steamed into the station and Oscar whisked her away before the curious trio could ask any difficult questions. He'd not given their names and she was glad about that.

'Victory House first – hopefully we can find you another gas mask there, then I have to telephone my family and update them on the situation. Then we'll find you an engagement ring and go for a celebration meal.'

There was a great deal of hanging about before she eventually was able to speak to someone who could help with her unusual situation. The two officers read her letter of dismissal and then listened carefully to her story.

'This is the best possible news. However, you will have to be formally assessed by a medic and cleared for duty. Then, to be certain, you will have to demonstrate that you still have the necessary skills.' With a flourish the RAF officer, with a magnificent bristling moustache, tore up her letter.

'Report for duty at Uxbridge immediately. Dismissed – and welcome back, ACW1 374.'

She jumped to her feet and saluted smartly then marched out fizzing with excitement.

Jane travelled back to Uxbridge a different person. Her abduction and rescue had changed everything. Her father would never bother her again. She leaned against her fiancé's shoulder and he kissed the top of her head.

'Darling, are you sure you don't want to ask for

compassionate leave? You only came out of hospital this morning and were critically ill a week ago.'

'No, I'm eager to prove I can go back on duty. You didn't have to come with me although I'm really glad that you did.'

'I don't know when we'll get the opportunity to be together so I'm making the most of every minute.'

She sighed. 'Charlotte's a brick, isn't she? If she hadn't found you goodness knows what might have happened.'

'I thank God every minute that she did. Both your parents are incarcerated. It's going to be difficult for you when it comes to court, but I'll be there if I possibly can.'

'The inspector said it might be a while before that happens. Anyway, we'll be too busy to bother about that. I'm going to forget about what happened, if I can. They have other witnesses and our statements. That will have to do.'

She relaxed and tilted her head for his kiss. 'Did I tell you that Nancy is getting married in September. Maybe we could have a double wedding?'

He smiled. 'Double, triple, I don't give a damn how many people share the ceremony as long as we can get married at the earliest possible opportunity.'

Oscar arrived at Kenley to be greeted by Riley like the prodigal son. 'Bloody good show – there's a frightful flap going on. The squadron's going to France. Still got three bods missing.'

All thoughts of romance vanished and immediately he was fully focused on the matter in hand. 'Whose flight are they from?'

'Not yours. Two from mine and one from Cross's. You've got to leave immediately. I'm moving someone across and the three missing chaps will join me.'

'Righto. I take it everybody knows?' Riley nodded. 'Excellent. I need to collect my gear and then I'm ready.'

He wasn't surprised they were transferring. Things were going badly over there and Hitler was on the move. British troops were pulling out of Norway. It looked as if the war was finally starting. May was going to be a busy month. He'd got an acquaintance at the Admiralty who'd told him the Navy had sunk all but a handful of Germany's destroyers. This should mean that whatever Hitler wanted it was going to be hard for him to get across the channel as the Royal Navy, with five times the ships, could sink any of the barges.

The buzz across the water was uneventful and the two flights landed safely on the temporary airstrip in France. He was waved to a space on the perimeter and taxied into place. The bowsers trundled over and immediately refuelled all the kites. He noticed there were armourers waiting – he wasn't looking forward to firing his guns in anger.

They were told they were billeted in tents – not ideal but at least the weather was decent for a change. After dropping his gear, he went in search of the commanding officer. He needed the recent gen because, as far as he could see, there was nothing much happening. No sounds of guns, no Luftwaffe roaring overhead dropping bombs.

The Win Co, his handlebar moustache bristling with indignation, was waiting and gestured that he accompany him to the headquarters, which was a hastily thrown-up Nissen hut. Must've been evil living here during the winter.

'I know what you're thinking, Stanton, where's the action?' Oscar was about to answer but his unidentified commanding officer continued. 'The Huns have begun the offensive. Reconnaissance kites have reported the tanks are moving fast and will be in Luxembourg today. It's going to be dammed busy. Would have preferred a squadron of Spits, but you will have to do. Hurricanes aren't fast enough.'

Not an encouraging start to their posting. 'We'll do our best, sir, let's hope the Maginot Line holds them back.'

'It had better or our boys are going to be trapped on the beaches.' He twiddled with his moustache and then, grim-faced, told him what orders he'd been given. 'We have to provide cover as long as we can but if the Panzers break down the line then we've got to abandon the brown jobs and scuttle back to England. We're woefully short of fighters and can't afford to lose what we've got here.'

Oscar saluted to avoid having to reply to such a devastating order. Britain was facing defeat and the next step would be invasion. It made sense to have as many kites as possible available to protect the country.

Riley and the others turned up later that day and he passed on what he'd been told. 'Just heard that Chamberlain has resigned and Churchill has been asked to form a coalition government. He has to be better than Chamberlain.'

'It doesn't look good. Nine months of phoney war and now it might well be over in a matter of weeks with us on the losing side.'

'None of that defeatist talk, Stanton. We are British – we will fight to protect our families. The alternative doesn't bear thinking of.' Riley strode off muttering to himself.

He explained the situation to the other bods and they

were equally gloomy. They weren't being defeatist, merely realistic.

'Pity the bloody army – been stuck out here since last September doing bugger all and now it looks as if they could be wiped out. Do you agree with our orders?' Roy asked.

'We follow them regardless. There are squadrons out here that have got Fairey Battles and have no chance. We're the lucky ones. Our Hurries are relatively modern, not outdated like their bombers. The government should have been pouring money into the RAF, not cost-cutting.'

'The Germans have been equipping the Luftwaffe since the last war and their pilots got practice in the Spanish lot. None of us have battle experience. God help us.' Roy was usually the most upbeat of them all. If he was pessimistic then things were really bleak.

'I think a stiff drink is called for. Any idea where the mess tent is?' This question from one of the bods was echoed by the others.

Nobody bothered to square away their kit – there was hardly likely to be an inspection on the battlefront.

This was the last opportunity they had to socialise as it kicked off the following day. Over the next ten days they scrambled continuously in a vain attempt to prevent the German bombers and fighters attacking the retreating army. The BEF were being driven relentlessly back towards the beach as Hitler tore through Luxembourg, Belgium and the Netherlands. France was being overrun. The Panzers came around the end of the Maginot line as if it wasn't there.

He flew sortie after sortie, narrowly escaped being shot down twice, and had three successful kills to his name. So far he'd lost nobody from his flight but Riley had lost three of his men – all dead – none of them able to bail out successfully.

They were exhausted and fighting what was obviously a losing battle. Riley told him they'd received the order to return to England. Their base was no longer safe and the bigwigs didn't want to lose any aircraft unnecessarily.

'Kenley is fully operational and we'll be based there again. We'll continue to support the troops as best we can but have to fly from there.'

'Won't give us as much fuel to play with, sir, and we'll be spending as long getting there as we can in dogfights.'

'Don't state the bloody obvious, man, but at least there's less chance of our kites being bombed when they're on the ground.'

The sound of battle was clearly audible and on the last sortie he'd flown he could see columns of soldiers and refugees already fleeing towards the coast. God knows what would happen when they got there – hopefully Churchill was arranging for destroyers and other naval vessels to come to their rescue.

This time they landed on the new runway and were directed to their designated place on the perimeter. They'd been flying non-stop for two weeks and were to be back on duty the following morning. Not allowed to leave the base but sufficient time to write to Jane, and call his parents. The squadron had departed so suddenly there'd been no time to contact anyone. Neither his fiancée – how he loved being able to use that word – nor his family knew he'd even left the country.

26

Jane having been given the all clear by the doctor, and having passed all the necessary procedures to allow her to return to work, was eager to know with whom she would be working. She'd expected to be the centre of attention after her exploits but if anyone knew they were certainly not pestering her with questions.

Her bed had been as she'd left it, the biscuits neatly stacked, and she slotted back into her routine as if she'd never been away. The three girls she was working with now were equally experienced and she was delighted to find herself on the Kent section of the table, which was the busiest.

She scarcely had a moment to catch her breath and the days of being allowed out to get a cup of tea and a bun were long gone. The atmosphere in the bunker was positively crackling with anticipation. RAF bombers, accompanied by the fighters, had made successful raids on targets to help Norway, Sweden and Finland who were being invaded. Hitler was beginning to force his way through the Netherlands and she had to concentrate to keep up with the information flowing through her headset.

Plotting actual raids in and out became routine and she

was satisfied she was pulling her weight. There were now an equal number of WAAF in the underground bunker as there were RAF and there was no shortage of requests for her to go out with one of them. She always refused with a smile and said that she was engaged to a fighter pilot. This always did the trick because they didn't want to steal a girl from a fellow officer.

She had written twice to Oscar and was concerned she had received no reply. She had the telephone number of the vicarage and rang them from the call box. Mrs Stanton answered.

'How lovely to hear from you, Jane. Like you we are becoming concerned at the lack of contact with our son. However, if anything had happened we would have been notified.'

'With this awful business in Dunkirk I expect he's got no time to write. At least I'm not worried now.'

Was Mrs Stanton right in thinking she would be the first to hear if anything happened to her son? Surely, as his fiancée, it was to her the news should be sent? She would write to Nancy and Charlotte. None of them got more than a few hours off in between shifts so meeting up was just impossible.

At the moment she was plotting RAF aircraft in and out – so far no marauding German planes flying in to bomb London. It was heartrending that they always seem to be far fewer inward plots than there were outgoing. The days passed so quickly there was scarcely time to worry about the continuing silence from her beloved Oscar.

She was amazed that a lot of the girls preferred to do without sleep when they were off duty and went gallivanting into London at every opportunity. No doubt she would have joined them with enthusiasm if she wasn't already spoken for.

Things were looking grim for the troops who were streaming towards the beaches near Dunkirk. If the British army was destroyed did that mean the war was lost? The thought of the jackbooted Germans marching into London filled her with horror.

She was on her way to the recreation room when someone called her name. 'There is an urgent telephone call for you, ACW1 374. Come with me at once.' The NCO beckoned her from across the hallway and Jane ran across, her stomach churning.

She picked up the handset lying on the desk. 'Hello, who is this please?'

'Thank God, I didn't think they'd fetch you. I told them it was a family emergency.'

She had the sense to turn away from the curious eyes before speaking quietly into the receiver. 'Oscar, I can't tell you how glad I am to hear your voice. Are you well?'

'I am now I've spoken to you. I've just got back from France. We're based at Kenley again. I got your letters but I don't have time to reply. Keep writing, darling, even if I don't write back.'

'I spoke to your mother last week and she said if anything happened to you then they would be the first to hear. Could you make sure that I'm on your list of family members?'

'Already done it. Have you had any problems with your memory, headaches and so on?'

'Absolutely splendid my end. There's no point in my telling you to take care. I know what you have to do as

I spend all day plotting our boys in and out. I love you and I want to marry you as soon as we can get time off together.'

'I love you too, sweetheart, and can't wait to make you my wife. I'll let my father know.' The pips went. 'Sorry, no more change. Bye, darling.'

The line went dead before she could answer. She blinked furiously, pinned on a smile and turned to face the two WAAFs who'd been listening to the conversation. 'Thank you for allowing me to take the call. That might be the last time I ever speak to him.'

'Brenda, she's sitting over there, lost her fiancé last week. Dreadful business this war is and especially for our boys.'

This was hardly encouraging but the girl meant well. 'Thank you again. I have to get back as I'm on duty in half an hour.'

This wasn't strictly true as she intended to return to her room and write some letters before she was needed again. Both her friends were up-to-date with the situation with Oscar and her parents so there wasn't a lot to tell them apart from the fact that she was hoping to be married as soon as possible.

There was just time to hand in the letters before going on duty. There was idle chatter. The plots came thick and fast, and she had no time to worry about what danger Oscar might be in at that very moment.

When she finished her shift she headed for the mess along with the three girls she'd been working with. There was something different about tonight. All had been gloom and doom this morning, but now people were smiling and acting as if there'd been a great victory of some sort.

'What's happened? Why are people looking more cheerful than they did first thing?'

The NCO waiting in line in front of her overheard her question and smiled. 'You wouldn't believe what's happening right now over near Dunkirk. Hundreds of little boats belonging to civilians are collecting our boys from the beach. It's a blooming miracle, that's what it is.'

'What about the Navy? Why aren't they doing it?'

'Dunkirk Harbour has been bombed to bits so the big ships can't get in. These little boats are ferrying people backwards and forwards as well as bringing them home to Blighty.'

'That's amazing. Even the weather's on their side at the moment. No wonder we were so busy last shift.'

It wasn't exactly a victory but when everyone had thought the entire British army would be captured or killed it was certainly good news. There would be exhausted soldiers arriving at the coast right now, even as she was drinking her tea in comfort. Their families would have been so worried these past few weeks and so relieved to have their men back in England.

The sorties were relentless. Oscar and his squadron did what they could to protect the hundreds of little boats from aerial attack but there weren't enough of them. He'd flown non-stop for hours; only on the ground long enough to be refuelled and rearmed and grab a mug of tea and a pee behind the kite. He'd lost one man – he'd gone down in flames on the beach.

His radio chattered, warning him there were bandits

approaching rapidly. Then a Spit flashed past and engaged the Messerschmitt about to fire on him. His task was to shoot down the bombers before they could drop their lethal load on the helpless soldiers cowering on the beach below.

When the bombs dropped, a geyser of sand shot into the air leaving behind death and destruction. The radio burst into crackling life again. 'Skip, big bastard heading our way. Tally-ho.'

Oscar should have led the attack but things were more fluid up here. Flying in rigid formation was impossible – in fact, downright dangerous. The three of them dived in unison at the German bomber. He fired three continuous bursts into the fuselage, exhausting his ammunition, and then flew upside down to see if he'd been successful.

The other two bods did the same and saw that smoke poured from the bomber. A hit – a kill. 'Yellow leader to yellow two and three. Return to base. Fuel is too low to continue safely.'

He didn't see the Messerschmitt but he felt the impact of the bullets as they ripped through the kite. He immediately lost power. He was too low to bail out safely. He would have to ditch and hope someone picked him up before he drowned.

It was strangely peaceful with no engine sound filling the cockpit. His radio was kaput so he couldn't send a Mayday with his position. He watched with a sense of unreality as Yellow two and three went in pursuit of the kite that had shot him down.

Thank God it was calm and sunny today. Ditching in the sea when it was rough was usually fatal as there was little hope of rescue finding a pilot in large waves. All flyers were trained to land without an engine but none of them had actual experience of doing it in water.

He was in God's hands now. There was nothing he could do apart from release his harness and pray that his kite stayed afloat long enough for him to scramble out.

The channel was approaching faster than he'd like. He'd opened his cockpit but hastily slammed it shut. There could be a tidal wave of water when he hit and then it would pour into the cockpit and the plane would go down instantly.

He braced himself. The nose hit first. Then the wings – and the kite bounced but remained on the surface. All he had to do was open the cockpit and wriggle out. He must take his chute as the dinghy was attached to it. The cockpit refused to move. The water reached his knees. He hammered frantically on the Perspex and it slid back.

He was up to his neck in cold water. The weight of his sheepskin jacket would drag him down. With a despairing heave he was free. The suction from the sinking plane took him down with it. He remembered to keep his mouth shut whilst kicking his boots off.

His Mae West served its purpose and he slowly bobbed to the surface. His chute was floating next to him with the inflatable hopefully still underneath. He was alone – no boats anywhere and no sign of his mates in the sky. It would be dark in a couple of hours and zero chance of being picked up after that. If he knew in which direction to go, he could paddle to France. First, he must get the dinghy to inflate and scramble in.

He managed to release his chute but the little boat was damaged and hadn't inflated, as it should have done, on impact. There were things he needed somewhere in a side pocket. He must try and find them before the dinghy sunk, taking him with it. He found an oilskin package and wriggled it out. He stuffed it inside his life jacket just as the chute and boat vanished beneath the waves.

What seemed like a millpond from above was in fact the reverse – the swell of the waves meant he couldn't see in any direction. It was June the first. Was this going to be the day he died?

Jane was coming off an all-night shift, weary to the bone, and eager to get some breakfast before she fell into bed for much-needed sleep. She was too tired to chat. Although she insisted to anyone who cared to ask that she was tickety-boo, she really wasn't. It might have been better to have taken the base doctor's advice and had a further week on sick leave.

She had a persistent dull ache behind her eyes, which even aspirin didn't alleviate. She poured tea into her tin mug but ignored the cooked breakfast on offer and just took toast. She found a space on the long table, nodded to the others who nodded back. They'd all been on nights and just wanted to eat and go to bed.

She tipped her irons onto the table and was about to butter the toast when someone tapped her on the shoulder.

'ACW1 374, the adjutant wishes to speak to you.'

Blearily she dropped her cutlery, took a swig from her tea and followed the NCO out. She knew her food would be waiting for her when she got back – she might not be especially friendly with her co-workers but they wouldn't let anyone steal her toast.

Only as she approached the open office door did she stop to think why she should be summoned so formally. Her stomach plummeted. Waves of nausea almost overwhelmed her. She swallowed furiously, pressed her nails into the palms of her hands, hoping the pain would steady her.

She wanted to turn and run – not go in and be given the worst possible news. She remained for a second frozen in the doorway staring at the WAAF officer sitting behind the desk. Her knees almost crumpled when she saw the sympathetic expression on her face.

'Come in, my dear girl; sit down. I think you realise the news is not good.'

Her heart was hammering so loud she thought the officer must be able to hear it. She collapsed on the chair and gripped her hands in her lap, hoping she would be able to remain in control when they told her that her beloved Oscar had been shot down.

'I'm very sorry to be the bearer of such dreadful news...'

'Is he dead?'

'I'm afraid so, my dear.'

She didn't wait to hear the rest. She was on her feet and running from the room just wanting to get away – to be on her own – to grieve in private. Oscar wouldn't want her to fall apart. She had to be brave for him – carry on regardless and do her job the way he'd done his.

Where should she go? Outside there might be a corner she could weep in without being seen. She stood in the early morning sunshine, scarcely able to comprehend that the man she loved was no longer in this world.

She found a corner to hide in and slid down the wall until she was huddled on the ground with her head buried in her knees, her shoulders shaking as she tried to control her sobs. Eventually she was done and scrabbled for a handkerchief so she could blow her nose and wipe her eyes.

Somehow she pushed herself upright, straightened her skirt, and keeping her head lowered hurried through the building and up to her dormitory floor. She dashed into the bathroom to sluice her face with cold water and then made her way to the room she shared with three others.

The room was quiet, the blackouts kept drawn to keep the sunlight out whilst those back from night duty got some sleep. She undressed silently and despite her misery folded and hung her clothes in the approved manner.

All the beds were occupied and she scrambled into hers hoping fatigue would help her sleep. Things wouldn't be better when she woke up but she hoped she would be more able to cope. As she was drifting off her head was filled with images of Oscar. She cried herself asleep.

When she awoke the room was empty – the others must have got dressed really quietly allowing her to remain. The girl called Brenda had lost her fiancé last week and she was carrying on with her duties and she must do the same.

Her head was heavy. Somehow it seemed too big for her neck to support. Her eyes were gritty, her throat raw from crying so much. Every breath was an effort, as if there was a physical weight on her chest. She needed to pull herself together. She was a strong young woman and had dealt with far more than most in her life. She wouldn't give in to her grief – wouldn't ask for compassionate leave – but just grit her teeth and get on with it.

Everything seemed so much more difficult today. Even washing and dressing was a major effort. She glanced at her watch and saw she had two hours before her duty started. She'd been asleep for almost eight hours and yet was so fatigued she could scarcely keep her eyes open.

However difficult it was she must ring Oscar's parents and offer her commiserations. She should have stayed to hear how he had died, if his body had been recovered, if there could be a funeral or just a memorial service.

Lying tidily on the top of her locker was the cloth bag containing her irons. Someone had collected her mug and cutlery and returned it to her. This small act of kindness proved too much for her fragile self-control.

She collapsed on her unmade bed and rocked back and forth with her arms around her middle as if somehow doing this would hold her together when she was falling apart.

'My dear girl, I'd no idea you were so attached to your father. I thought the reverse was true and can't understand why his death has devastated you.' The adjutant was standing by her bed.

For a moment the words didn't make sense. Then her addled brain picked out the salient point. 'My father is dead? Not Oscar – I thought it was my fiancé who died.'

'Oh dear, how absolutely dreadful. I should have made myself clear from the start. Come with me; what you need is a hot drink and something to eat whilst you recover from the shock. Small wonder you were overcome.'

The band around her chest vanished, the weight lifted and she surged to her feet and flung her arms around the unfortunate officer who'd come to her rescue. 'I'm glad that man is dead. I don't want to know the details. I should have stayed and heard the rest, so it's my fault I got the wrong end of the stick.'

'I'll arrange for you to speak to your young man. You will need to hear his voice before you can believe he's well.'

'That would be splendid, thank you, ma'am.'

'First you will eat and drink, then the telephone call.'

Jane was ushered into the office from which she'd fled a few hours ago. Tea and toast were fetched and whilst she tucked in Captain Bevan rang Kenley.

27

Oscar was a strong swimmer, confident and competent in the water, and knew his best chance of survival was to conserve his energy and remain in one place. He kept his legs moving in the hope that it would keep his body temperature up but after an hour of doggy paddling in circles he could no longer feel his feet.

The sun was setting, casting orange light across the sea. He smiled wryly. If this was the last thing he was going to see on this earth it wasn't such a bad view. He'd had plenty of time to think about what might have been.

He might have been married to the woman he loved. He might have had children with her. He might have survived the war and become a vicar like his father. He wasn't afraid of dying – his faith protected him.

What almost unmanned him was the thought of how devastated his beloved Jane would be when she heard that he'd died. She'd had more than enough misery in her life and didn't deserve to lose the one person who loved her.

Hypothermia was beginning to kick in – he recognised the symptoms – lethargy and wanting to fall asleep. His teeth no longer chattered. He was quite relaxed and ready to move on to the next place.

Bloody hell! His eyes opened in shock when he remembered the package he'd rescued. Was the distress flare inside it? His fingers refused to obey his command but suddenly there was a glimmer of hope. It was difficult unwrapping the small bundle and several times he went under, swallowing water and emerging spluttering and even colder.

When his fingers gripped a hard cylinder, his spirits soared. He had a flare. If he let the rocket off now it was dusk it might be seen – if he'd done it earlier when the sun was out, he doubted it would have been. Maybe the Almighty had plans for him on earth and it wasn't his time to go after all.

The flare had been submerged in the sea for hours but the oilskin cover should have kept it dry. Would it still fire when he pulled the string? He held it above his head and prayed. There was a faint hiss and a wonderful, beautiful, red fountain sprayed into the darkness.

It continued to burn for several minutes and he held it aloft twisting his head from side to side and listening for any sound of a ship approaching. Then there was a faint chugging of a small motor and the flickering beam of a handheld torch began to quarter the water.

He would have shouted if he had the energy but holding the dying flare was all he could do. Then something splashed into the water by his head.

'Grab hold of it; we'll pull you in.'

From somewhere he found the strength to hook his arm through the cork ring and hang on. Minutes later he was being pulled out of the sea. He was barely conscious but was aware the little boat was packed with soldiers. 'Bloody miracle, that's what it is, that we happened to be passing just when his flare went off.'

'No point in putting a blanket round him. He's bloody soaked. Let's get his clobber off.' The speaker grabbed his arm. 'Come on, mate, help us get them bleeding wet things off of you.'

He raised and lowered his arms and legs on command but had little control over his movements or theirs. 'Thanks,' he managed to mumble. 'Stan…' He was trying to tell them he was Oscar Stanton but the words wouldn't come.

'Stan, it's dead man's clothes, mate, but poor Jimmy won't mind. He can have the blanket.'

He was warmly dressed in the dead soldier's uniform and plied with hot sweet tea. This was accomplished in the confines of the small boat and reminded him of a parlour game he'd played as a child.

'There you are, all right and tight. Jammed in next to me and Bob you'll be warm enough. Get some kip, old son; it's a bloody long run to Dorset.'

At dawn the boat docked along with dozens of others. He stumbled ashore, still half asleep, and was bundled onto a waiting train. He slept on and off, only waking when the train pulled into a station and well-wishers passed beer and food through the window.

Everyone thought him a soldier rescued from the beaches of Dunkirk and for some reason this amused him. The bods who'd saved his life weren't with him or they could have explained but he was too damn tired to bother.

When the train rattled and clanked to a halt everyone piled off but he remined where he was. His legs refused to function, his head hurt and he was finding it hard to swallow. Better to sleep until he felt better. He was roused by a guard.

'What we have here, then? Your mates forgot to wake you. Up you come.'

Oscar wanted to tell him he was ill, knew there was something else he had to say but instead he closed his eyes again. He was vaguely aware of being manhandled onto a stretcher, being wrapped in a blanket and then woke up in what he thought might be an emergency department of a hospital.

Two nurses were deftly removing his clothes. There was something about his uniform that he should tell them but he felt too awful to bother. He wasn't dead and that was all that mattered – the rest could wait.

Jane listened to the one-sided conversation and gathered Oscar wasn't available. Captain Bevan put down the receiver and shrugged. 'Flight Lieutenant Stanton is safe and well and at this very moment his Hurricane is being rearmed and refuelled. The officer I spoke to has promised to get him to telephone here when he is free to do so.'

'Thank you very much for trying. I don't expect him to have time to ring. He's going to be concentrating on helping with the rescue of thousands of soldiers from the beaches. I apologise for being silly this morning. I'm fully recovered now and I suppose I must hear the details about my father's demise.'

'If you're quite sure. He took his own life. He hanged himself in his cell.'

'That's a relief.' The look of shock on the captain's face made her hurriedly continue. 'Oscar knocked him out and if he'd died from those injuries that would have been so

329

much worse. I suppose he couldn't stand the shame and humiliation of a trial.'

'Do you wish to apply for compassionate leave?'

She was about to refuse but then reconsidered. 'My mother's being held on remand as well. I must go and see her. I suppose that I'll have to arrange the funeral and so on.'

'How long do you think you'll need?'

'No more than a day. If I am able to get a visitors' pass then I'm certain I can get to Holloway prison and back before blackout tomorrow. I'll do my shift tonight and then leave immediately afterwards. I will be back on duty the following day.'

'I'll issue you with a twenty-four-hour pass and a travel warrant. I'll arrange for you to visit your mother late morning. That should give you ample time to make the necessary arrangements for Mr Hadley.'

Jane arrived at the prison in good time for her visit, which was scheduled for eleven o'clock. The building looked more like a castle than a place where women were incarcerated. The guards were impersonal when they searched her and she was ushered through various checkpoints and into a bleak room and told to sit on one side of a table. There was a chair on the other, presumably for her mother.

A few minutes later a woman she scarcely recognised was brought in. No longer smart, her grey hair lank around her face and dressed in prison clothes. All her animosity vanished. Whatever her mother had done, she didn't deserve this. Her life had been miserable too and she had probably been bullied and coerced into cooperation and was as much a victim as Jane had been.

Ignoring the female guard, she jumped to her feet and rushed over to hug the emaciated woman. 'Mum, I'm going to get you out of here. That horrible man is dead and we're free of him forever. He can never hurt either of us again.'

She was waiting to be told sternly to sit down but to her surprise when she looked round, they were alone. 'I couldn't believe it when they said my daughter had come to see me. I thought I'd never see you again. How can you forgive me for what happened?'

'It's in the past, Mum, we must both forget about it. Sit down and I'll bring my chair around next to you as we've got so much to talk about.'

If she'd been surprised to be left alone, she was astonished when the guard returned with a metal tray, two mugs of tea and a plate of biscuits. The woman put them down with a smile and then left them to continue their conversation in private.

'I don't know what you want me to do about a funeral…'

'Nothing at all. I believe we could have him cremated and no sort of service at all.'

Her mother had obviously been thinking about this as it hadn't occurred to her this could be arranged. 'Right, I'll get in touch with the authorities and set that in motion. I can't believe that you're still being held here. Why hasn't your solicitor got you released on bail at least?'

'I refused to see one. I thought I deserved to be here as my cowardice almost killed you. I knew what he was going to do but thought if I was there then I could help you get away.'

'We can talk about it when you're away from here. I'm going to speak to someone now. I'm sure I can find a solicitor to represent you.'

'I don't know where I'm going to go if they do let me out. I don't want to go back to that house.'

'That house must belong to you now. Sell it and then you can buy something smaller. Do you want to live in Lattimore or somewhere else?'

Her mother had become more animated as she drank the tea and ate the biscuits. 'I've got friends there even though I couldn't see as much of them as I'd have liked to. I like Mrs Jackson. Do you think they would let me stay at the vicarage whilst I found myself somewhere else?'

'I'm sure that they would. I can hear someone coming so I think I'm going to be asked to leave. I'll do my best to get you released today but it might take a bit longer. I'll get in touch with Mrs Jackson and ask her to meet you. She could go to the house and bring you something to wear as well.'

The door opened and a tall, thin middle-aged man, with sharp eyes and a nose like a beak, stepped in. He was accompanied by a younger man with a pronounced limp and a smart suit. 'Good morning, I'm Mr Thorogood, governor here. This is Mr Denny, a solicitor.'

They shook hands and the two guards rushed in with extra chairs. 'My mother wishes to be represented now and I hope Mr Denny has come here to do that. I don't want to press any charges. I want her released immediately if possible.'

'Excellent. The police have no wish to pursue the matter now that Hadley is dead. Mr Denny has some papers for you to sign, Mrs Hadley, and then you can leave with your daughter immediately.'

Two hours later Jane and her mother were in a taxi heading for the station. The clothes that her mum had been wearing had been found. With her hair up in its usual French pleat and a modest amount of make-up, Jane was satisfied no one would know she'd just been released from prison.

The governor couldn't have been more helpful – apologetic almost – and had allowed her to use his telephone to call the vicarage. Mrs Jackson would be waiting at the station to collect them. In the rush to leave there'd been no time to ring the prison where *that man* had died. This would have to wait until this afternoon.

The vicar offered to make the arrangements for the cremation. He also made an appointment for her mother to see a solicitor in order to get all the financial matters settled.

'I'll go to the post office right away and withdraw sufficient for Mum to have something in her purse. I'll reimburse you for her board and lodging, obviously. She might be with you for a few weeks as she can't buy herself another house until everything's done.'

'You'll do no such thing, Jane. Your mother is welcome to stay as long as necessary. In fact, there's a cottage available in the village as the tenant moved away to live with his daughter somewhere in the North of England. It would be ideal and the rent isn't extortionate.'

'That sounds perfect. Thank you. I really need to go. I was given until tomorrow morning but I would like to get back as soon as possible.'

'We can take your mother to see the cottage tomorrow

morning. I think my wife is taking her to collect some clothing and toiletries from the house before it gets dark. Goodbye, Jane, please bring your young man to meet us if you get time.'

He patted her on the shoulder and she smiled her thanks. She gave her mother a quick hug, refused a lift to the station, and set off briskly to walk the two miles. She was fortunate as a train to London steamed in half an hour after her arrival. She crossed the city on the underground and had time to find herself something to eat before catching the train to Uxbridge.

After only walking half a mile a car, driven by a WAAF, pulled up and the driver offered her a lift to the base. It was becoming increasingly difficult to keep her eyes open as she'd now gone twenty-four hours without sleep.

On her arrival she checked in and then headed straight for bed. It seemed as if she'd only just closed her eyes when someone was shaking her shoulder. 'Jane, Jane, you're wanted immediately downstairs.' As the blackouts were drawn she had no idea if it was night or day but the fact that the other three beds were unoccupied must mean that the girls were on duty – so on balance it had to be night-time.

'Golly, I'll be as quick as I can. Thank you for coming to fetch me.'

The WAAF who'd been sent with the message left Jane to get up and in record time she was correctly dressed and flying down the stairs. She'd left her bed unstacked and could be put on a charge if she was unlucky enough to have an NCO make a spot inspection of her dorm.

Normally at this time she was on duty and everyone else was in bed. The place was eerily empty. She had only been told to report to the office and assumed one of her team had been taken ill and she was needed to replace them.

There were no officers around in the night and minimum staff on duty. A bored-looking girl was reading a magazine and gestured towards the telephone, which was off the hook. Jane stared at it unable to move for a moment. There was only one reason she would be summoned to take a call at this time and she didn't want to pick it up. If she didn't know then it wouldn't be true.

She forced her legs to move but her hands were shaking so much it was hard to grasp the receiver. 'ACW1 374 speaking – that is to say – Jane Hadley.'

'Wing Commander Brotherton, Kenley. I'm sorry to have to tell you that Flight Lieutenant Stanton was shot down yesterday and is missing.' He cleared his throat noisily. 'He landed in the drink and was seen alive and well afterwards. His position was noted and we are still searching the area. It's bloody chaos out there, hundreds of boats of every description plying back and forth rescuing stranded soldiers from the beach. It's possible he was picked up by one of them so don't give up hope that he will be found, Miss Hadley.'

'I see. Thank you for taking the trouble to inform me. Have you told his parents as well?'

'You're his fiancée – his letter is addressed to you, but I won't send it to you yet. It might be several days until we know anything for certain.'

She replaced the receiver without responding or saying goodbye. Oscar couldn't be dead. She wasn't going to fall apart this time but would keep believing he was alive and well somewhere. The girl with the magazine was now on her feet.

'I say, I am most awfully sorry. I should have realised you wouldn't be called to the telephone for anything but the worst possible news.'

The other girl pulled out a chair. 'Sit down and I'll rustle up some tea. You look a bit peaky, love.'

'He's missing but they think he might have been picked up by one of the little boats. I really wish they didn't feel obligated to inform people until they know for certain. Now I'm just going to worry myself silly until I get...' She couldn't continue and swallowed the lump in her throat.

'My brother is a captain in the army and we don't know if he's alive or dead. Ma said it could be days before things are sorted out and those who have been rescued can contact their families.'

'I was told that Oscar had written me a letter but I wouldn't get it yet. He writes me letters all the time so why would he have given it to his commanding officer?'

'I haven't the foggiest. Elsie might know. We can ask her when she brings the tea.'

Despite the circumstances Jane couldn't help noticing that one of the girls was incredibly posh and the other sounded more like Nancy. The WAAF didn't discriminate, but just trained up the girls and put them in the positions they would be the most use.

Elsie returned with the tea and had managed to find some biscuits to go with it. When asked about the reference to a letter she nodded. 'All servicemen have to write something to be sent to their nearest and dearest if they go for a Burton.'

'Then I must hope I don't get any mail for the next few days. Now I'm up, I'd rather be busy than go back to bed and fret. Is there any admin I can do for you?'

She was handed a pile of filing and asked to answer the telephone if it rang and the two of them dashed off to smoke a cigarette in the recreation room. Smoking was disapproved of in this office.

Not knowing one way or the other was going to be difficult and she decided it wouldn't be fair to worry his parents. Better to wait until things were clearer.

28

Oscar opened his eyes and looked around. He was in a ward, in a bed adjacent to the door. The overhead lights were off, only a glimmer from the one on the nurses' table. It must be night-time. He'd no idea how long he'd been out but had no intention of malingering here a moment longer. The other beds were occupied by sleeping patients.

He needed to get to a telephone. More importantly, he needed to find the bog urgently. He ran his fingers over his chin. Good God! He must have been here several days. He looked inside the locker and found the borrowed uniform neatly folded inside.

He drew the curtains and got dressed. He smiled as he pushed his feet into the boots of the dead soldier. Literally waking in a dead man's shoes. They were a bit loose, but better than the other way. He picked up the notes hanging from the end of the bed.

He wasn't listed as Flight Lieutenant Stanton. As far as they were concerned he was a nameless soldier waiting to be identified. For God's sake why didn't they look at his tags? He put his hand to his neck and realised they were missing – they must have come off when the soldiers had dragged him into the boat.

The adjutant would have informed Jane he'd been shot down. She would be frantic waiting for news. He prayed they hadn't declared him missing, presumed dead and posted his farewell letter. Footsteps were approaching and the curtains were drawn back briskly, the rattle loud in the quiet room.

'You shouldn't be out of bed, and you certainly shouldn't be dressed,' the young nurse said flapping her hands and gesturing that he return from whence he came.

'I'm Flight Lieutenant Stanton. I was fished out of the sea and put in these clothes. My fiancée and my CO will think that I'm dead.' Instantly her expression changed.

'Come with me, Flight Lieutenant, you can use the telephone in matron's office. You were brought in unconscious three days ago.'

'The WC first.'

'It's the first on the left. The office is at the end of the corridor – it's clearly marked.'

His watch, despite having been immersed in water for hours, was still functioning. It was just after nine o'clock at night. Hopefully someone who knew who he was would be on the base when he rang. After several whirrs, clicks and long pauses he was connected to Kenley.

'Flight Lieutenant Stanton, I need to speak to the officer who is in command tonight.'

The WAAF who'd answered dropped the phone. He clearly heard her running footsteps fading into the distance and then the clatter of male boots approaching equally fast.

'Riley here. Is that really you Stanton?' Oscar wasn't given the opportunity to answer as Riley continued. 'Where the bloody hell have you been these past four days? We've sent the bloody letter to your fiancée and told her that you perished at sea. I expect she's told your parents.'

'I feared as much.' He quickly explained how the misunderstanding had occurred. They were both laughing when he'd finished.

'Damn good show, old bean. You can't trundle about the place dressed as a brown job. Where exactly are you?'

'I haven't the faintest idea. Just a minute, I'll see if I can find something in here that will give me a clue.' He put the receiver down and then flicked through a pile of letters. 'I'm in St Thomas's in London.'

'Right. I'll send a driver with what you need. I'm pretty sure your young lady is with your parents in Suffolk. Operation Dynamo is over and things have calmed down a bit. Somehow we turned a crushing defeat into a sort of victory.'

'How many were saved, do you know?'

'I heard that Churchill hoped to get back around forty thousand but in fact it was nearer three hundred. They also got off over a hundred thousand French and Belgian troops.'

'How many men did we lose?' He didn't like to ask after Roy by name.

'We were bloody lucky. Only the two chaps in my flight.'

'That's terrific news. Don't contact my parents. I'll do that myself.'

'I can't tell you how pleased I am to have you back. Take a few days' leave. It's Tuesday, June the fourth, today in case you were wondering. Report for duty next Monday.'

He put the phone down, overwhelmed by what he'd heard. His stomach rumbled loudly. He was desperate for a drink of some sort. He couldn't remember the last time he'd had anything to eat.

The nurse was waiting by an open door adjacent to the ward. She beckoned him and he shuffled up to her, his feet slipping about in the overlarge boots. There was a student nurse in this little room and the wonderful smell of hot toast drifted out.

'Nurse Kelly will take care of you, Flight Lieutenant. I'm sorry I can't find you anything more substantial than toast and tea. You must be absolutely starving.'

'Anything will be gratefully received. Thank you. They're sending a driver with my uniform and once it arrives, I can get out of your hair. My fiancée and family think I'm dead so I've got to see them pronto.'

Nothing had ever tasted quite as delicious as the six slices of toast and four mugs of hot sweet tea that the young nurse provided. He was allowed to remain in the tiny ward kitchen until word came that his driver had arrived.

'I'll go down and get your bag, Flight Lieutenant. Why don't you nip into the bathroom and have a shave and a bath? I'll bring your clean clothes in to you.'

He wasn't comfortable with the idea of a young lady seeing him naked but he supposed he was being unduly modest as she'd probably already seen everything there was to see when he'd arrived.

'I'll do that, thank you. Unfortunately, until my kit arrives, I don't have a razor.'

She beamed. 'Just a minute, I've got what you need here. We don't expect serving soldiers and so on to arrive from the battlefront with the necessaries.'

Equipped with razor, soap, brush and a large white towel he headed for the bathroom. He drew the regulation five inches and stepped in, relieved to be able to remove the remainder of the ingrained dirt and salt from his long immersion in the English Channel.

He was out, towel wrapped around his waist, shaving when the nurse knocked on the door. 'Come in, I'm decent.'

'Here you are. Your driver's waiting out front but can't stay where she is for long as it's the area where the ambulances pull in.'

In double quick time he was dressed and on his way downstairs with his kitbag over his shoulder. He'd abandoned the army uniform and supposed that it would be recycled somehow. He felt better in his own clothes and certainly his feet were more comfortable in shoes that fitted.

He regretted the loss of his flying boots and sheepskin jacket as well as the rest of his uniform. They didn't fly with any personal items so he now had his wallet, identity papers and ration book in his pocket and brand-new dog tags around his neck.

He tossed his bag onto the rear seat and climbed in beside the WAAF. It was going to be strange driving in the blackout with only the small lowered beam that was allowed on each headlight of the staff car. 'Thank you for coming – you made good time. I hope you've got ample petrol as it's fifty miles to my family home.'

'Yes, sir, I filled up and I have a spare can in the back. I know the way to Ipswich but you'll have to give me directions after that.'

'We don't go to Ipswich – we turn off at Chelmsford and

head to Braintree. Chalfont Major. Not nearly as far as you thought.'

'Then I won't need directions for a while so why don't you get some rest? It will be light when we get there but still very early.'

She was an excellent driver and after the first few miles he stopped worrying about her competence and did as she suggested.

It had been two days since she'd received the dreadful news, along with the heart-breaking letter from Oscar. She read it so many times it was crumpled and tear-stained but was the most precious thing she owned. She knew every word off by heart.

My darling Jane,

If you're reading this then you will be devastated. You mustn't be sad for me – know that I'm in a better place but that I'd much rather be with you.

I love you and I always will. Keep my memory in your heart but don't grieve for long. You have a job to do and must put your feelings aside and carry on.

I wish we had had longer together but things didn't work out as we'd hoped. One day you will meet somebody else and fall in love with them. Do so with my blessing. Be happy, my love, but sometimes think of me.

Yours for eternity

She still couldn't believe Oscar was dead. The thought that she would never see him again was unbearable. Somehow she'd held herself together, said all the right things, collected her kit and headed for his family home. She could have gone to Lattimore but she wanted to be the one to tell his parents and then they could share their grief.

Her journey to this small town, Chalfont Major, had passed in a blur. She arrived at the vicarage on a rattling local bus. She had to stand outside for several minutes gathering herself before trudging up the path and knocking on the front door.

She didn't know how she was going to break the news but trusted the words would come to her. There was no need for her to say anything apart from her name. The woman who'd opened the door took one look at her and held out her arms.

'My poor dear, come in, come in. There's no need to give us the details – that can come later when you're feeling better. A nice cup of tea is what you need.'

Jane leaned into her embrace, comforted by the fact that this was Oscar's mother. The one person who would understand exactly how she felt. If she started to cry again she wouldn't be able to stop. She had to be strong for Oscar's sake. He would want her to be a comfort to his parents not a burden.

She couldn't remember the last time she'd eaten or drunk anything but still thought she wouldn't be able to swallow whatever was offered. Her throat was raw. She felt as if she'd swallowed a large stone and it had settled somewhere in the centre of her chest.

A tall man, an older version of Oscar, with the same ash blond curls, but his were sprinkled with grey, appeared from somewhere and took in the situation at a glance. 'Jane, thank you for coming in person to tell us that our son is dead. It took the most amazing courage and we appreciate what you've done for us.'

If he'd started to tell her that his son was in a better place, suggest that they pray together, she couldn't have borne it. If there was a God then he wouldn't have taken away the man she loved. He wouldn't have stood by and allowed someone as monstrous as Hitler to be taking over the world. She had gone to church because it was the one place she'd felt safe but she'd stopped believing in the existence of a higher power by the time she was eleven or twelve years old.

Her prayers that the brutality and abuse would stop went unanswered. The loving God that Mr Jackson had spoken about with such conviction would never have allowed a child to suffer the way she had. She envied those who still believed, but she wasn't one of them.

She managed to swallow the tea but ignored the slice of cake placed beside it. She sat with her head lowered unable to say anything but then rallied. They'd just heard that their son had died and she couldn't sit here wallowing in her own misery when they must be suffering unbearably too.

'I'm so sorry for your loss. Oscar was shot down somewhere in the English Channel and... and his body wasn't recovered. This happened four days ago but they didn't declare him dead until this morning. They checked every boat that docked but no one reported having an RAF pilot on board.' She managed to raise her head and look at them. 'I didn't believe it until I got the letter. They only send that out when they're certain.'

'My poor child, after all you've been through. When I spoke to him last he was so happy – he was looking forward to spending his life with you. You might not have been married but as far as I'm concerned you will always be part of this family. That's what he would have wanted.' Mr Stanton cleared his throat and wiped his eyes. He was holding his wife's hand and she seemed incapable of speech.

'I'll stay for the memorial service, but then I must go back and get on with my job. I've already had far too much time away from my station.'

Mentioning a service that wouldn't include a coffin was too much for Mrs Stanton. She broke down and her husband offered what comfort he could.

Jane had slipped away, leaving them to grieve together.

That had been yesterday. By the afternoon the house was full of relatives offering sympathy and she wished she hadn't come. She was a stranger to them, an unnecessary and unwanted guest.

She checked her watch – it was a little after four a.m. and would be light enough to leave. She had already written a letter to the Stantons thanking them for their hospitality and apologising for leaving so abruptly.

Her bag was packed and she was ready to depart. The ancient family dog, a smelly black Labrador, thumped his tail as she walked past his bed but was too lazy to get up and investigate. She put her letter on the kitchen table and then exited by the back door, which was never locked.

When she was outside in the road she realised she had no idea in which direction to walk. She'd been so distressed when she'd arrived that she'd scarcely taken any notice of her surroundings, or the direction in which she'd come.

She'd caught the local bus at Braintree and it had stopped outside the vicarage – that much she remembered. Had she had to cross the road? No, she hadn't, so she needed to be on the other side. She didn't want to hang about outside so would walk until she found a bus stop a mile or two away and then wait.

There was unlikely to be a bus of any sort for hours so she just had to keep walking until one came. She had been trudging along for a few minutes when she heard the sound of a car approaching. It was going in the wrong direction or she would ask for a lift.

It roared past but then screeched to a halt. The noise jolted her from her misery and she turned round to see why it had stopped so suddenly.

The front passenger door flew open and a man leapt out and was running towards her. She dropped her bag and threw herself into Oscar's arms. She clung to him, ablaze with happiness, unable to form a coherent sentence and he was in no better shape.

'Darling, I'm so sorry. Don't cry, please don't cry. I'm here now and everything's all right.'

Oscar's cheeks were wet. Jane was shaking, laughing and crying simultaneously. What the hell was she doing creeping about at dawn? Eventually she wiped her running nose on his shoulder, sniffed loudly and looked up at him. He'd never seen anything so beautiful, so perfect, despite her blotchy cheeks and snotty nose.

He lifted her from her feet and kissed her. The touch of her lips on his rocked him on his heels. To think that he'd almost lost her – or to be more accurate she'd almost lost him.

The driver cleared her throat noisily behind them and reluctantly he raised his head but kept his arms firmly around his darling girl.

'Excuse me, sir, I'd like to get off now. Hopefully, I'll be back before the end of my shift. Good luck, it's made my week to see you two so happy. Precious little joy around at the moment.' The girl dropped his kitbag by the gate leading into his family home, saluted smartly, and hopped back in the car.

She reversed into the drive and then took off back towards London, leaving the two of them alone.

'Jane, when do you have to be back on duty?'

'I've got a week. What about you?'

'The same. As of yesterday my squadron thought I'd gone for a Burton. I think I could have asked for twice as much and the CO would have agreed.' He dug a handkerchief from his pocket and wiped her face as if she were a small child. She didn't object. She was just staring at him as if she couldn't believe her eyes and hanging on to him as if her life depended on it.

'I expect you're wondering why I'm out here so early. Your house is full of your relatives and I felt I was intruding.'

This made his decision even easier. 'Let's get married tomorrow. Might as well make the most of the family being here. They came for my funeral but can celebrate our wedding instead.'

'That's absolutely perfect. There's so much you don't know. There's a seat in the back garden. Can we sit there and talk before we go in and you get smothered by your family?'

He kept his arm around her waist as they walked to the bench. He lifted her onto his lap and she snuggled into him whilst she told him about the suicide and her mother's release. 'I'm surprised you're still on your feet after having to deal with all this over the past few days.'

She tilted her face and he obliged with a tender kiss. 'I was all right until I got your letter.' Her smile slipped and she pulled away from him. There was more bad news to come. 'There's something I need to tell you and you might very well change your mind about marrying me when you hear it.'

'I don't care what you tell me, sweetheart, I'm going to marry you tomorrow and there's nothing you can do about it. Come on, what's this dreadful secret?'

'I'm very sorry but I'm an atheist.'

For a moment he couldn't believe what he'd heard. Then he started to laugh and couldn't stop. She poked him in the ribs but he just shook his head. Eventually, he recovered enough to explain.

'I'll tell you something Dad said to me many years ago. "It doesn't matter if you don't believe in Him, he believes in you and will always be there if you want him." I don't give a damn about your religious beliefs, my love. It makes absolutely no difference to how I feel about you or how my family will feel when they know.'

'I've been so worried about telling you, knowing how Christian you all are. It's such a relief to know it doesn't matter. I'd like Mum to come. Maybe Mr and Mrs Jackson will bring her as he still seems to have petrol for his car when nobody else does. I can't see that a vicar should be exempt from petrol rationing.'

'Dad certainly isn't. He visits his parishioners on his bicycle and his car's on wooden blocks in the garage for the duration.'

'I'll see if I can get in touch with Charlotte and Nancy – it would be wonderful if they could be here too. They don't know that you were declared dead – there hasn't been time to write to them.'

'It's after five, sweetheart, and I'm absolutely ravenous. Shall we go in and give the good news to my family?'

Jane could still hardly believe that Oscar had been declared dead when he was sleeping quite comfortably in a hospital bed in London unaware that he was officially missing. Yesterday had passed in a blur of happiness.

Today was her wedding day. The beautiful white silk dress that had been altered for her was hanging on the back of the wardrobe door. She even had a pair of pretty white court shoes as well as an antique lace veil. The family and the village had been bracing themselves for a funeral and it would appear that everyone was now invited to the wedding and the wedding breakfast afterwards to be held in the church hall.

That on its own was exciting enough but not only was her mother coming with the Reverend Jackson and his wife, but also Nancy had been given special dispensation to attend. It would seem that she and Oscar had become something of a talking point throughout the RAF. News of the suicide and then the erroneous announcement of Oscar's death had made them famous.

There appeared to be a lull in the fighting and Roy and several others from his squadron were also coming. They had commandeered some sort of transport and were going to collect Nancy and her young man from her base and return her that night. Jane couldn't wait to meet Nancy's fiancé, Tommy Smith.

Normal rules regarding wedding etiquette had been dispensed with because of the unusual circumstances. She and Oscar were not supposed to see each other on their wedding day until they met in church, but as they were living under the same roof this was going to be almost impossible. She'd been helping with the flowers for the hall and the church whilst he had been busy erecting trestles in the garden and bringing out folding wooden chairs. The weather was set fair and as the village hall backed onto the vicarage garden, they were going to make it a garden party as well.

He'd also been helping prepare two rooms upstairs in the attics for them to use tonight. The thought of what would happen between them in the large double bed made her tingle all over. When Mrs Stanton had said they could spend their honeymoon in the attic where they wouldn't be disturbed she'd turned pink all over.

Although not exactly sure what marital intimacy involved, she did know that doing it often produced a baby. She was not even nineteen years old, and had a role to play in the war effort; she would love to have his babies one day but hoped it wouldn't be right now.

There was a knock on the door and she sat up in bed. Olivia, Oscar's older sister, came in with a tray. 'Good morning, Jane. I come bearing gifts. Boiled eggs and soldiers, toast and marmalade, and a jug of real coffee.'

'How absolutely spiffing. I hope Oscar got his breakfast in bed as well.'

'He certainly did. Now, we've got the old and borrowed

covered. I thought these would do for the blue and the new.'
She put down the tray and pointed to the two items that lay
alongside the food.

'A pair of blue garters – how terribly risqué. Wherever
did you get them?'

'Mum and I made them for you.' There was an extra cup
on the tray and Olivia poured herself some coffee and sat
down on the end of the bed. 'You're painfully young – I
don't suppose you know very much about making love. Is
there anything you'd like to ask me?'

'Actually, there is something. I really don't want to have
a baby until after the war's over if possible.' She hesitated,
not sure if what she was going to say would upset her future
sister-in-law. 'We've been so lucky; both of us could be dead.
Oscar survived this time but he might very well not do so
if he gets shot down again. I don't want to bring up a child
on my own and I have a very responsible job, which I'm
not allowed to talk about. I expect you think I'm heartless.'

'I think you're nothing of the kind. Forget what I said just
now about being young. You might be short of years but
not of maturity. There are two things a couple can do. First
– if you avoid having marital relations in the middle of your
cycle and second – there's something called a prophylactic
that Oscar can use.'

Jane understood the reference to her cycle but had no
idea what a prophylactic was and didn't like to show
her ignorance by asking. 'Thank you. I only finished my
monthlies yesterday so that's absolutely perfect.'

Olivia left her to eat her breakfast in peace. Jane could
hear voices and footsteps on the stairs and outside in the
garden. The ceremony was taking place at midday. No one

in his family had been the slightest bit bothered about the fact they were harbouring a heathen in their midst. None of them had found it quite as funny as he had, but it clearly wasn't a problem to them.

One might almost believe a supreme power was watching over them – but that was nonsense.

She'd washed her hair and had a bath last night. All she had to do was get dressed nearer the time. She wished she had something less utilitarian for her wedding night – WAAF-issue underwear was hardly glamorous and the nightdress was even worse. It seemed such a shame not to have something silky and attractive to wear under her beautiful gown.

She drifted over to the open window, her hair around her shoulders and down her back, and looked out.

'Darling girl, are you well? You look quite enchanting with your hair loose.' Oscar, his glorious, sun-streaked hair tousled, was in rolled-up sleeves, shirt open revealing the strong, tanned column of his neck. She'd not seen his naked arms before. A surge of something settled in a most peculiar place.

'I'm wonderful. I love you but we shouldn't be talking together – it's supposed to be bad luck.' Hastily she stepped away and she could hear him laughing as he strode off. She loved him so much it hurt.

At exactly a quarter to twelve she stood back to admire herself in the long mirror propped against the wall. Olivia had arranged Jane's hair in an elaborate style, which suited the elegance of the antique lace veil. Her silk stockings were held up by the garters and her bosoms and bottom were suitably encased in silk camiknickers, which had mysteriously arrived whilst she was getting ready.

There was nobody to give her away and she was rather dreading walking to the church, and then down the aisle, on her own. The house was quiet. Everyone would be in the congregation awaiting her arrival.

At the top of the stairs she paused to pick up her skirts and Oscar stepped into view. He was wearing his best blues. They exactly matched his eyes, and he'd never looked more handsome or desirable.

'We're going to walk together, darling, the way we'll walk through life in future, arm in arm and hopelessly in love.'

He was right. They were meant to be together. 'I love you, darling, and from now on I just know I'm going to be happy.'

Acknowledgements

I want to thank all those men and women who gave their lives, literally, in thousands of cases, to protect this country. Bibliography for Girls in Blue series.

Hornchurch Scramble, Richard C Smith

Chronicle of the Second World War, J & L

One Woman's War, Eileen Younghusband

The Stepney Doorstep Society, Kate Thompson

We All Wore Blue, Muriel Gane Pushman

Secret Listeners, Sinclair Mackay

Sand in My Shoes, Joan Rice

Christmas On the Home Front, Miles Brown

A to Z Atlas and Guide to London, (1939 edition)

Oxford Dictionary of Slang, John Ayto

Wartime Britain, Juliet Gardiner

How We Lived Then, Norman Longmate

The Wartime Scrapbook, Robert Opie

RAF Airfields Of World War II, Jonathan Falconer

The Day of the Typhoon, John Golley

About the Author

FENELLA J. MILLER was born in the Isle of Man. Her father was a Yorkshireman and her mother the daughter of a Rajah. She has worked as a nanny, cleaner, field worker, hotelier, chef, secondary and primary schoolteacher and is now a full-time writer.

She has over fifty Regency romantic adventures published plus four Jane Austen variations, four Victorian sagas and eight WW2 family sagas. She lives in a small village in Essex with her British Shorthair cat. She has two adult children and three grandchildren.

Hello from Aria

We hope you enjoyed this book! If you did let us know, we'd love to hear from you.

We are Aria, a dynamic digital-first fiction imprint from award-winning independent publishers Head of Zeus. At heart, we're committed to publishing fantastic commercial fiction – from romance and sagas to crime, thrillers and historical fiction. Visit us online and discover a community of like-minded fiction fans!

We're also on the look out for tomorrow's superstar authors. So, if you're a budding writer looking for a publisher, we'd love to hear from you.
You can submit your book online at ariafiction.com/we-want-read-your-book

You can find us at:
Email: aria@headofzeus.com
Website: www.ariafiction.com
Submissions: www.ariafiction.com/we-want-read-your-book

◼ @ariafiction
🐦 @Aria_Fiction
📷 @ariafiction